THE GOD SLAYERS

MANIFESTATION MAGICIAN SERIES

MANIFESTATION MAGICIAN SERIES

In reading order:

The God Slayers

The Psychic Architects

(Coming: November 2026)

THE GOD SLAYERS

MANIFESTATION MAGICIAN SERIES

PATRICK BRYCE WRIGHT

WICKED INK

PUBLISHING

Copyright © 2025 by Patrick Bryce Wright

Published by Wicked Ink Publishing Ltd.
www.wickedinkpublishing.com

Cover and book design © 2025 by Wicked Ink Publishing Ltd.
Editors: Raymond Griffiths & Adam Bamford

First Edition: July 2025
Printed in Canada

Library and Archives Canada Cataloguing in Publication

Title: The god slayers / Patrick Bryce Wright.
Names: Wright, Patrick Bryce, author.
Identifiers: Canadiana (print) 20250221217
Canadiana (ebook) 2025022674X
ISBN 9781998278152 (softcover)
ISBN 9781998278169 (EPUB)
Subjects: LCGFT: Dystopian fiction. | LCGFT: Fantasy fiction. | LCGFT: Queer fiction. | LCGFT: Novels.
Classification: LCC PS3623.R54 G63 2025 | DDC 813/.6—dc23

To Keith J. Miller, who has seen me through every draft of The God Slayers from 2018 to its publication.

THE
GOD
SLAYERS

MANIFESTATION MAGICIAN SERIES

When gods fall... humanity rises.

ONE

AT FIRST, KENZIE OKUDA'S SUMMER JOB AT THE SOUTHERN Blessings clothing store had taken his mind off of waiting to enter the magic university of his dreams.

However, after two months, it was torture. What he really wanted to do was hide in his house and wear his late father's old clothes, coveted treasures that helped him stay sane long enough to escape from the United Republic of America. He didn't stand a chance as a transman unless he could get over the border into the United States. His skill with magic was his ticket out. That certainty burned in his veins.

Even with an acceptance letter from Jefferson-Crowley University and a student visa, Kenzie faced the problem of being barred entry. Kenzie and his friend Moriah Goldstein both feared rejection from the U.S. customs agents, who stood between this hellhole and freedom.

Tomorrow was it: August 21, 2095, the day he would either succeed or fail to flee the URA.

By noon, Kenzie felt like he would die if one more customer called him "miss." So, of course, the antique bell on the door jingled, and a mother and daughter came into the store with an air of anxious expectancy.

By the time they looked his way, Kenzie had pasted on a toothpaste commercial smile. "Good afternoon! God be with you." His Georgia accent gave the words a drawl. "Can I help you, Mother?" This job required his best manners. The store manager's lecturing voice ran through his mind: *All married women are "Mother," not "Ma'am." Assume a woman is married until she tells you she's not. Don't start with "Ma'am" and switch to "Mother."*

"God be with ya." The woman had an even thicker Georgia accent than he did. She was standard-issue URA: brown hair tucked into a bun and a gray dress down to her ankles. No makeup, no jewelry, no bright colors. "My daughter's lookin' for a Dedication Sunday dress. She's turnin' twelve at the end of this week."

The girl was a miniature replica of her mother, all the way down to the gray dress, except with acne. She stared at the floor, frowning.

"Oh, how exciting," Kenzie said with as much warmth as he could muster. Dressed as he was, he looked no different: black hair down to his knees and a brown dress that almost dragged the floor. It made his gender dysphoria crawl all over his skin like a million fire ants. "Yes, you have to wear something special for your Dedication Ceremony."

What followed was roughly equivalent to wandering for forty years in the desert. All the Dedication gowns were either "so last year" or too tight on her daughter's body, and this year's in-vogue color, hunter green, made her daughter look sallow. Finally, Kenzie hit on the mad notion of showing the woman the shop's bridal gowns, and it *worked*. The mother latched onto a Victorian-style lace gown.

"Praise Jesus!" The woman clasped her hands in front of her chest in prayer posture. "This is just what my daughter's been lookin' for. We've been to three stores, and none of them had this exact cut. I don't know why the designers are makin' girls' clothes *tighter.* It's ungodly. And this dress is even in her size!"

"Praise the Lord." Kenzie longed to trade conversations like these for lectures in courses like Magic Science I, Mind Magic I, and Strategic Magic I. *I want to learn how to perfect my telekinesis, not talk about dresses being too form-fitting.*

"Ya look just like an angel," the mother told her still-frowning daughter. Tears welled up in her eyes. She pulled a handkerchief out of her purse and wiped her eyes.

"I am so proud of ya." She looked to Kenzie. "My, they grow up so fast. Already twelve years old. And think, in two years' time, my daughter will receive her first marriage proposal. It gives me chills."

"Me, too," Kenzie said. *But not for the same reason as you.*

Their most dominant religion, The Apostles' Way, had petitioned for the legal marrying age to be lowered to fourteen and won. He rang them up as quickly as possible to get them out of his air. He didn't want to breathe the crazy.

"Ya'll have a blessed day," Kenzie chirped through his fake smile.

"Have a blessed day, too, young lady."

Kenzie ground his teeth at the misgendering. The bell on the door jingled as the customers exited, announcing his deliverance from them.

He slumped over the counter. *I absolutely have to get out of here.*

THE NEXT DAY, KENZIE SAT IN HIS MOTHER'S CAR, 40 FEET AND two vehicles away from freedom. Now that he was here, he doubted everything. Horror stories about border crossings scrolled through his head: strip searches, rejected passports, detainments, property seizures, confiscated paperwork ...

The Tennessee-Kentucky border between the United

Republic of America and the United States towered high above Kenzie, his mother, and their car. Hundreds of feet of concrete topped with barbed wire kept the URA citizens trapped in hell and the U.S. citizens free of the sight of their suffering. The eight lanes of Interstate 65 North paused at this customs checkpoint beside Elizabethtown, which had become the southern-most U.S. city in Kentucky after the Second Civil War.

Kenzie's fear snatched him and internally dumped him off a bridge with no bungee cord. He gasped as his lungs seized.

"What if I don't make it? They won't care about you. You're White. And you have a PhD and scholarly books published and tenure as a professor. And no one knows you can do magic. You're everything they would want to accept, anyway. And you're not even the one staying! But I look like Dad."

He pointed at his "forbidden" almond-shaped eyes and his lack of a double eyelid.

"They'll reject me. They'll never take me. I'm only half White!" He ran his fingers into his long, black hair. *Why am I even trying this? I'm crazy! Supposedly, the U.S. is less racist than the URA, but not by much.*

He still felt traumatized by the pastor of his church praying over him the previous Sunday. There had been a shooting at an Asian market in Louisville, Kentucky three weeks ago, and two victims were Japanese. The gunman had said he wanted to kill all the Chinese immigrants in Louisville, but he'd opened fire on the entire market. Hearing in detail what his pastor supposedly *hadn't* wanted to happen to him left him wracked with terror, neck muscles so tight he'd had a nonstop headache.

Turning back would be better than being stuck at the border in a detainment cell for three days because we broke a rule we didn't even know existed—or one they make up because they see my face and pitch a racist fit. His mind raced over the list of contraband items again from the Homeland Security Administration website: *no guns, no fruit, no cigars, no alcohol, no drugs…*

The truck in front passed through the gate, and the SUV ahead of them rolled forward. Kenzie's mom eased forward as well, her knuckles white from gripping the steering wheel. Her blonde hair was bound in a tight French braid, and she wore a black dress down to her ankles with a black blazer. At least for the URA, it was pristine professional attire.

"Moriah made it." Alexandria Okuda's voice was tight but calm. "She texted you that she didn't have any problems. And everyone says they make exceptions for college students. It has to be true or Jefferson-Crowley University wouldn't have accepted you."

"I'm *not White*." Kenzie inhaled until his lungs expanded fully, pressing the seatbelt out. *Of course, Moriah is part Jewish,* he tried to reason with himself. *But then again, she looks White. Okay, fine. Goldstein is an obvious Jewish name, but most people don't keep track of that stuff anymore. And people claim the U.S. isn't as bigoted against magicians. The customs agents probably didn't even blink when Moriah came through.*

Logic was not comforting.

The SUV pulled away, and the quick exit did not surprise Kenzie. It had New York plates. That lucky person was a U.S. citizen returning home. *Who would come to the URA, even to visit family? Maybe it's a journalist. But if the U.S. cares about what's going on, why haven't they done anything?* He couldn't understand the line of cars in the opposite, in-bound lane. *You're all crazy.*

Alexandria pulled forward. The sign said to roll open all windows, so she did, admitting a blast of August heat, the stench of exhaust, and the furious yelling of the customs agent one stall over. Kenzie tensed. *Is someone being arrested? Am I next?*

A White man with a long, bored face and black hair stepped up to the driver's door. On Kenzie's side, a petite blonde woman with blue eyes stepped up, a vision of Aryan perfection. They wore identical uniforms: black button up shirts and pants, a belt with a digital walkie-talkie, a baton, and a gun. On their shoulders were the embroidered insignias of the U.S. Customs and Border Protection. Already this was a taste of the gender equality in the U.S.: women could wear pants and work in security jobs.

"State the nature of your business," the man drawled, his voice flat. "What is your purpose in visiting the U.S.?"

"My daughter is a student at Jefferson-Crowley University." Alexandria handed her passport to the man. "I'm taking her to get settled into the dorm."

The woman held out her hand to Kenzie. "Passport, please."

Kenzie handed over his green passport book with its computer chip, heart racing. *Please don't reject me.* His passport said he was female, so there was no way around this part, not to mention the fact he wore a floor-length navy dress.

"Acceptance letter." The woman motioned with her hand.

Kenzie handed over the paperwork the university had sent. Few paper products still existed in first world countries, but paperwork for customs was an exception. Both e-copies and paper copies were required.

"Show me your e-copy," the man said.

Alexandria handed over her phone.

The agents stepped back into their booths and scanned both copies' official seals and codes at their stations, and the woman returned, clenching the paper copy. She scrutinized Kenzie, her blue eyes inspecting his brown ones, his black hair, and his East Asian appearance.

"So. You're a magician." Her tone was curt. Her lips pressed into a thin line.

"I am." Kenzie's voice wavered. *And here it is: You're too brown, and you're a nasty little magician. Entry denied.* He squeezed his seatbelt with his hands.

Her eyes narrowed. "What's your specialty?"

"Telekinesis." *Why do you care? Or will my answer make a difference in whether you let me in?* Kenzie's breaths quickened until he panted. A sweat broke out on his upper lip.

"Oh." The woman's expression relaxed. "We'll need more of you when the Reunified Soviet Union invades both our countries." She held out the paperwork. "I hope you can graduate before it happens."

"God, me, too." Kenzie accepted the paper with a shaking hand.

The man handed Alexandria's cellphone back. "Take good care of that one, lady. We don't have enough telekinetic soldiers."

"I absolutely will." Alexandria's tone was emphatic.

So my specific ability won the day? Kenzie's heart pounded in his ears until he felt half-deaf. *If they'll let me in, I can have a real life.*

"How long will your visit be?" The man's voice remained flat and bored.

"For me, just one day, sir," Alexandria said. "Kenzie has a scholarship for the entire school year."

The man typed into his tablet and then held it out. "So noted. Thumb print here."

Alexandria pressed her thumb to the screen.

The blonde woman held out her tablet. "I recorded your student visa as lasting a standard college academic year, as per your paperwork. Your legal permission to reside in the U.S. will expire on May 31, 2096. Record your thumb print here." She pointed at a box on her screen.

Kenzie stuck his hand out the window, glanced over the screen to make sure it really said May 31, and then pressed down his thumb, electronically recorded and tracked for the U.S. government.

"Proceed," the man drawled.

"Good luck with college," the woman said.

"Thank you." Kenzie trembled in his seat. *What? They're going to let me through because of my telekinesis? Really?*

The gate bar lifted, and Alexandria rolled the car forward, hitting the gas once she was clear. In front of them were eight lanes of U.S. highway, and now they were only 45 minutes from Jefferson-Crowley University in Louisville, Kentucky.

Alexandria closed the windows as the wind shear picked up. "Okay, we're in. Now we have options. We can stop here in Elizabethtown and pick out men's clothes for you, and you can get a haircut, too. Or we can wait until Louisville to do those things."

"Now." Kenzie's shock at being admitted to the U.S. was offset by his burning need to get out of his dress and have his hair cut for the first time in his life. "And I want chest binders, too."

"You got it." Alexandria took the first off ramp, where both she and Kenzie discovered the stunning fashions of the U.S.

⚡

A RAINBOW HAD BARFED ALL OVER THE CLOTHING STORE: impudent neon reds, greens, and oranges, bold purples and blues competing for which color was richer, and splashes of yellow here and there. Not only that, but also the sizing charts assumed everyone wanted their clothes to be form-fitting.

Kenzie shot past the women's clothing and buried himself in the men's department, snatching up not only jeans but also shorts and t-shirts, preparing to bare his arms and legs.

After that shopping spree, they located the nearest hair salon, and Kenzie had his hair bobbed up to his jaw and fixed in a sleek style the hairstylist called "boy band chic."

And so Kenzie Okuda arrived at Jefferson-Crowley

University in men's jean shorts, a black t-shirt, and short hair. Even though he was required to live in the women's dorm because he was pre-gender affirming surgery, he was so thrilled with his haircut and shorts that he didn't care. He'd been around girls and women his entire life. He knew how to get along with them. Having female dorm suitemates would be fine.

Alexandria parked by the row of dorms, and Kenzie climbed out and glanced around. Red brick buildings surrounded him, all of them at least three stories high. The leaves of towering maple and oak trees rustled in the wind. Sidewalks crossed green, manicured lawns, and the sweet scent of freshly cut grass filled the air. *So this is my new home. At least for the next four years. God, I hope I can get a job in the U.S. when I graduate.*

His mom climbed out and walked around the chair, pulling him into a hug.

"You're free. I'm so happy for you! No matter what, you're fighting to stay here, regardless of what it takes. You hear me? Don't worry about me. Fight. Fight with everything you have. Because your true self is always worth fighting for."

Tears burned Kenzie's eyes, and he embraced her tightly. "Okay. I will."

Before he ended up sobbing, Kenzie released her and fished his two rolling suitcases out of the trunk. He extended the handles and pulled them behind him as he walked away.

For all he knew, he had just ridden in his mom's car for the last time. She might have become, with this life decision, a face on a laptop screen or a voice on a phone. His mom might remain trapped in the URA until her death, and never seeing her again might prove to be the price of his freedom from lifelong oppression.

As crushing as that was, Kenzie cemented her words in his heart: *I will fight with everything I have.*

And I cannot afford to fail.

TWO

Kenzie tugged his suitcases down the sidewalk, passing by a row of identical red brick dorm buildings. Like some apartment houses, two suites occupied each level with an outdoor stairwell centered between the suites.

Spying suite 243-C, he turned down the walkway, the towering maple trees in the yard shading him from the summer sun, and then entered the stairwell, hauling his suitcases upstairs to the landing. Using the student ID bracelet that had arrived in the mail as part of his welcome pack, he presented his ID to the door scanner, and it unlocked and opened.

Rolling the suitcases inside with him, Kenzie entered a short hallway and spied the living room at the end. As he exited the hallway, a second hallway led to four tiny bedrooms, and a bathroom stretched to the left. He bypassed it and walked into the living room, which extended into a full kitchen on the left.

Kenzie scanned the suite that would be his home for the next four years, since he intended to stay enrolled year-round. It was a basic apartment with white walls, brown burlap carpet, and white Venetian blinds on the windows. Two brown chairs and a brown couch, which bore more resemblance to office furniture, filled the seating area, along with an oak end table and coffee table. The kitchen held an oak table, oak cabinets, and a stainless steel stove, microwave, and refrigerator.

This setup looked no different in the U.S. than in the URA. Kenzie faced no real technological surprises, either. Everyone said the U.S. was more advanced than the URA, but the speed of technological advancements in both countries had slowed to a crawl thanks to the financial devastation of World War III and the Second Civil War.

With the exception of magic science, their technological innovations lagged compared to countries like Japan, Australia, and Germany.

Releasing the suitcase handles, Kenzie sighed. *My first apartment. Sort of.*

Moriah Goldstein, his good friend from high school, rounded the corner from the bedroom hallway. She wore traditional URA clothing: a floor-length white prairie dress with a blue daisy print. It hugged her waist, revealing how tiny she was.

"Kenzie!" Her brown eyes widened comically. "*What* did you do to your *hair*?"

Kenzie gawked in return. Moriah had bleached her long black curls blonde and tied them into two pigtails on either side of her head. "You dyed your hair!"

"You cut yours off!"

They stared at each other.

Kenzie laughed. "Well, I guess we both had the same reaction to getting our freedom. We changed our hair." *No way am I telling her I'm trans. I don't know how she'll react. I've never heard her even say the word "trans."*

"Do you think it's too sinful?" Moriah rubbed one hand over her bangs.

Kenzie shot her a look. "People all over the world dye their hair. It's no big deal."

"But our pastor would still say I'm sinning." Moriah's gaze traveled down Kenzie's body, taking in the t-shirt and shorts. "You went all the way."

"Absolutely." Kenzie vibrated inside, expecting Moriah to lecture him about morals and the Bible. *I have to stand my ground.*

An East Asian woman swept out of the bedroom hallway and grinned at Kenzie. Like Moriah, she had bleached blonde hair and pigtails, but her hair only reached her jaw. She sported a summer tan and wore a hot pink, spaghetti strap tank top with a short white skirt covered in hot pink polka dots.

"Hey! An Asie like me!"

"Asie?" Kenzie echoed, lost. *Wow! So much bare skin!*

"Oh, I mean someone of East Asian descent." She held out her hand, revealing her electric blue fingernail polish. "I'm Zoe Wang. Nice to meet 'cha!"

Kenzie shook her hand, preoccupied with the fingernail polish for a moment. He only saw polish in old movies; in the URA, women weren't allowed to wear it. "Kenzie Okuda."

"Nice to see an Asie face on this campus." Zoe released his hand and bopped into the kitchen, all sunshine and energy.

"It's so *Aryan* around here. I haven't even seen *one* Black student. That's creepy." She yanked open the refrigerator, pulled out a Coke can, and popped it open. "We POCs have gotta stick together!"

Kenzie smiled and relaxed. *At least I'm not stuck with three White students who think I'm ruining their White party.*

"Zoe bleached my hair for me." Moriah padded over to the worn brown couch and sat, arranging the folds of her prairie dress and staring at her lap, head bowed. "I just wanted to look different. You know, have a fresh start here at college."

"Well, sure." Kenzie winced at the sheer level of fear in Moriah's wobbling voice. "Everyone should want to break out of their box when they reach college. We're adults now."

Moriah smiled at her lap.

"I did great, right?" Zoe bounced over to one chair and plopped down sideways, her legs dangling over the arm. "I should have a side gig as a cosmetologist."

Kenzie smiled. *I like your spirit.*

The door opened, and Kenzie turned to meet his final suitemate. A young woman with straight black hair down past her waist entered, carrying a red and blue Jefferson-Crowley University shopping bag. She wore a black Victorian gown with bell sleeves—the height of fashion in the URA. Her dark brown eyes were dull, and she had a straight, strong nose with no dip.

"This is Kenzie Okuda," Moriah said from the couch.

"Rachel Abrams." She held out her hand. Like Kenzie and Moriah, she wore no fingernail polish and no makeup.

Kenzie shook her hand. "I'm from Georgia. You?"

"Georgia. Atlanta, specifically."

"I'm from Seattle." Zoe swung her legs back and forth, and her white patent flip-flops nearly fell off her feet. "Looks like I'm the only U.S. native in this suite."

"You're in for quite the education, then," Kenzie said.

Zoe grinned. "I enjoy learning about other cultures."

Rachel held up the bag, which had JCU's crest pictured in the middle. It featured a shield crossed by a sword and a wand. In the shield's corners were sections, each displaying the symbol of an element: fire, water, earth, and air. A golden chalice sat in the center between the four quarters.

"You might want to go buy your uniforms. The line at the store is short right now."

Kenzie tried to comprehend that a store could be open on Sundays.

"You didn't just order them through the internet?" Zoe asked.

Kenzie shook his head. "The shipping cost to the URA is really high." He grabbed his suitcase handles. "So which bedroom is mine?"

"You got left with the first one," Moriah said. "We kind of picked ours out already. I'm surprised you didn't arrive sooner."

"I worked until the last possible moment," Kenzie said. "And the first one is fine."

He rolled his suitcases around the corner and entered the first bedroom, which was on the left. A tiny room with an oak twin bed, nightstand, desk, and chest of drawers presented itself. It had an equally tiny window and closet. He shrugged and left his suitcases by the closet. *It'll do. Anything's better than being trapped in the URA.*

Before heading to the store, Kenzie returned to the kitchen and fished a Coke out of the refrigerator. *I'm not going back out into the 100-degree weather without a Coke.* He popped open the can and swigged half of it down; the carbonation burned his throat.

Rachel stood at the kitchen window, which made an L-shape with the long bank of windows filling the living room wall. She narrowed her eyes at whatever she stared at.

"What's up?" Kenzie crossed the white tile, his new men's sneakers silencing his footsteps.

He glanced out the window. At first, all he saw was the leafy canopy of an oak tree and the red brick side of their neighboring dorm.

Then, below on the sidewalk, a tall man wearing a black top hat sauntered into view and stopped by a lamppost fashioned like an antique oil lamppost. He appeared perhaps seven feet tall, given how he measured against the post, and he wore a black suit with coattails. He swayed on his feet.

"A top hat?" Kenzie took another sip of Coke, noting that

it tasted only half as sweet as a Coke in the URA. *Why such a huge difference?* "No one in the U.S. wears top hats. Bowler hats have been in style for at least five years now."

"Then he's not from the U.S.," Rachel murmured. She turned and marched out of the kitchen. "Maybe it's some kind of welcome week event."

The man blinked out of sight, and Kenzie jerked backward. "He just vanished!"

"It was probably illusionary magic, then," Zoe said from her chair. "Maybe someone's having a contest to see who can cast an illusion the longest. There's a big contest tonight to see who can summon fire the best. You have to light as many candles as possible in ten seconds. The winner gets a free JCU t-shirt."

Kenzie's stomach tightened. He experienced the same dark feeling he had right before learning his dad's cancer returned. *You're wrong. That was something else. Something not good.*

"Really? I'll pull up the JCU webpage and see what else is on for tonight." He strove to sound casual.

"Pick something you're great at," Zoe said. "Otherwise, the seniors will just call you naff."

Naff? Oh, God. I've got to learn U.S. slang—and fast.

"I believe you." Kenzie gulped the rest of his Coke and dropped the can into the recycling machine, using the opening tagged *aluminum.* Then he pulled out his phone and left, using the campus map app to navigate to the supply store, which sold school uniforms and other items like JCU flags, scarves, mugs, and tumblers.

When he returned to his room, Kenzie unpacked and then settled on his bed with his phone. He studied U.S. culture by streaming U.S. television programs. Now that he had unlimited, unrestricted access to U.S. media, he needed to find out what he was dealing with. Just hearing newscasters, game show hosts, and characters on sitcoms made him worry.

He took notes on his phone: *Don't call anyone "bro" or "sis;" don't say "God be with you" with every greeting; don't pray over meals; don't greet elders with "Mother" or "Father."* And there was a huge list of slang words people his age were using.

Good words were "smoky," "snazz," "lish," "mythical," and "deranged," but "bot," "murk," "feeder," "woob," and "naff" were bad. After a while, his brain went numb, and he felt overwhelmed. He pocketed his phone and headed to the Idoni Student Building for supper, hoping he educated himself well enough to survive his first day of classes.

However, something worried him more than not knowing the local slang. He was plagued the rest of the night by the memory of the man wearing the top hat, and by the time he climbed into bed, he knew what he sensed:

Twisted magic.

THREE

IN THE MORNING, KENZIE AWAKENED AT 8:28 AM, TWO MINUTES before his phone alarm went off, a stunning feat from such a dedicated night owl.

Adrenaline crashed into his blood, shooting him into clear-headedness without coffee. *My first day of college, my first course in magic. No more behind-the-scenes personal trainers. This is the real deal.*

He shot out of bed, galvanized, and pulled on the black university uniform, relishing in its pants. *Men's clothes!* He barely registered the rest of his morning routine between his nervousness over his new classes and his joy over his gender-appropriate outfit.

At 8:52, Kenzie zipped out of his dorm and down the stairs to the concrete sidewalk. With the morning heat and sun intensifying, his skin faced the threat of blistering.

According to the forecast, it seemed like a typical August day in Kentucky, with a high of 102 degrees. The aggressive cheerfulness of the bright sun, chirping robins, and green grass glowing in the morning light only tightened Kenzie's nerves. The entire world seemed to yell "Yay!" while he faced the rude awakening to whatever the U.S. called magical education.

Passing by red brick buildings and towering oak trees, Kenzie reached Griffen Hall and sprinted up the porch steps. The automatic doors snapped open, admitting him into the air-conditioned lobby with its wooden floor and crystal chandeliers. Moriah awaited him, looking odd in the university's elite uniform of a knee-length white skirt with a white women's blazer.

"I was afraid you'd be late," Moriah said as they ran down the hallway to room 105.

"You know me," Kenzie drawled. "College won't cure me of sleeping in."

As they entered, several students glanced up from their computer terminals, and their gazes landed on Moriah. Kenzie wasn't surprised. Not only was Moriah beautiful with her long blonde hair curled into ringlets and bound into two pigtails, but she also was a Goldstein, the newest magician family to achieve the rank of magician nobility.

Whispers erupted through the classroom. Kenzie caught snippets such as "Goldstein," "healing magic," "ranked second," and "the United Republic of America."

Moriah blushed, averted her eyes, and peered around at the empty desks. Since all the terminals were full, except a few in the front row, Moriah pulled Kenzie to the side of the room and took the first desk by the wall. Kenzie dropped into the next desk over, feeling self-conscious.

However, the feeling had nothing to do with his near lateness and everything to do with wearing pants. No matter how wild it was, he couldn't help envisioning everyone realizing he didn't have the right to wear pants, holding him down, and stripping them off. Seeing a few other female students in the pants uniform didn't help. They were from the U.S. They'd been born with the right. He hadn't.

Once Moriah and he got settled, the whispers died. Then a

male Asian student with light brown skin and black hair muttered to the man next to him, "Ten other people saw the guy in the top hat last night."

The man, a redhead with pale skin, shifted in his chair. "Disappearing spells, though?"

The first man sighed. "I know. I need more data."

"It won't happen again," a third man said. He was tall and broad-shouldered, but not good-looking. "Seniors run experiments all the time around here. It was just a prank or someone's pre-semester homework."

Kenzie cringed. *They saw that man, too. And it wasn't a welcome week event or a contest. I knew it! It's twisted magic of some kind. But why?*

Unlike high school, no bell rang. Instead, the professor strolled into the room. She was a short, tiny, East Asian woman with long, wavy, black hair. She wore a deep purple pantsuit.

"I'm Dr. Kitamori." Her Japanese accent was noticeable, but not too thick.

Kenzie sat up straighter at hearing the accent. His dad was the only Japanese person he ever knew. He never even met his paternal grandparents.

"Welcome to Magic Application II," Dr. Kitamori continued. "Take a good look at the students around you. You are the top 20 freshman we accepted this year."

Kenzie glanced around. Some students smiled, one looked bored, and the rest appeared nervous, their eyes wide and their lips pinched. Kenzie identified with the latter set. His heart raced.

He still couldn't believe his test scores qualified him for Magic Application II. *What if I tested out of Magic Application I just to fall on my face? I don't know what the first course covered. All I know is a computer put me here.*

"As evidenced by the fact you tested out of Mag App I, you represent the magicians we expect to become the leading edge in magic, not just in magical prowess, but also in magic research." Dr. Kitamori walked toward the back of the room as she spoke.

Just hearing those expectations crushed Kenzie. *I did well to get here at all! Now I have to be the best of the best or else?* He couldn't imagine himself as a leader in anything.

"Gone are the days of bearded hags with warts bent over cauldrons chanting 'Double, double, toil, and trouble.'"

Half the class chuckled. Kenzie smiled half-heartedly. *Oh, that's not what people in the URA think of you. They think you're demon worshippers drinking baby blood and having orgies under the full moon.*

"This is science. This is engineering." Dr. Kitamori stopped by the opaque doors set into the back wall. "And this is the future of warfare."

Whispers and scrapes filled the room as the students shifted, and Kenzie bounced his knee. *Another war is the last thing I want. If World War IV breaks out, we'll all be drafted, male and female, because we're magicians.*

He thought of the customs agent and her comment about the Reunified Soviet Union. He imagined being ordered to use his telekinesis to rip someone to shreds and felt cold. *Oh, yeah. I totally came here to learn how to be a murderer. What is the cost of escaping the URA?*

"This class is about building your skills in casting spells." Dr. Kitamori punched a code into a numerical pad by the doors and then held her thumb against the fingerprint scanner. "We'll focus on your casting speed, casting power, and casting accuracy, besides challenging you to expand your spell repertoire."

The doors slid open and revealed a second classroom, this one without desk terminals. It was three times the size of the current classroom and filled with spell casting stations. Each one had a platform with a computer. Four-foot-tall steel walls partitioned the stations. The white floor, ceiling, and walls mixed with the steel gave the room an institutional feel.

Kenzie stared at the gleaming stations with their state-of-the-art computers. Jefferson-Crowley University held true to its reputation as an ivy league magic university: nothing but the best.

Dr. Kitamori gestured at the room. "As you may know, each station is set up to make you practice a different skill or spell. The stations average your score. Then the main computer averages all your scores for the class period. You get a daily rating, but the weekly rating matters more. The rankings are posted on the wall. This is a hands-on class with few lectures. Go ahead and begin. Your goal is to familiarize yourself with each machine today. Your syllabus is in the class portal. You can read it online."

Kenzie sat still, silent and unsure of himself, and so did Moriah. Everyone else stood, leaving their backpacks or purses by their desks. Kenzie traded looks with Moriah, and they stood as well, following the other students into the lab.

As the students fanned out, Moriah pointed at the farthest station. A White guy with spiky, brown hair walked up to its computer. To Kenzie's surprise, one of his ears was pierced. He looked like a punk crammed into a stuffy black uniform. Seeing him helped Kenzie relax. *So not all the students here are preppy.*

"This one?" Moriah asked.

Kenzie nodded, and they joined the guy, clustering around the station and reading the instruction screen. The sign over the station read "Elemental Magic."

"This is pretty basic," the guy said. "You just use whatever element you want to practice. You get up to three tries."

"That's not bad." Kenzie gazed up at him. He was kind of cute in an unconventional way, with brown eyes and a few pale freckles.

"What's your name?"

He smiled. "Logan Steensen."

Kenzie suppressed a flinch, trying to avoid any outward reaction. The Steensen clan was one of the Noble Seven, the top magician clans of the United States.

"I'm Kenzie Okuda, and this is Moriah Goldstein." He gestured to his suitemate.

"Hi." Moriah tugged on her skirt hem, her shyness clearly taking over.

Since the women's skirt uniform was knee-length, she was uncomfortable. The only skin women in the URA were allowed to show was their face.

"Goldstein," Logan echoed. "So you're the one who took second place on the entrance exam. I heard about your family getting into the Noble Three in the URA. Congrats. That's stonking."

Moriah blushed, her tan skin turning a shade of dull rose. She stared at her feet. "Ah, well, yes. Thank you."

"The Goldsteins are amazing," Kenzie said. "They deserved the 'promotion' to nobility."

He smothered a sigh. *'Stonking.' Yet another word to keep track of. At least it's a compliment.*

"Second place is totally smoky," Logan said. "You should be proud."

Moriah tugged at the hem of her uniform skirt again. All the ivy league universities switched to required uniforms, with Jefferson-Crowley offering both black and white versions. Moriah purchased only the white.

"Is…is it normal to do everything on a computer?"

"It's just like my high school," Logan said. "So, yeah. Is it different where you came from?"

"We had personal trainers," Moriah said. "It's weird to be evaluated by a machine."

"People think the computers are more fair," Logan said in a reassuring tone.

Moriah's brow furrowed. "Fairness is a godly concept. How can a machine understand fairness?"

"Well, computers can be programmed to be unfair, but that's unethical," Logan said. "A person still has to design the programs on the computers, and those people are held to standards of impartiality. Unlike a human, computers can be programmed to be as fair as possible and never deviate. They're never tempted or swayed by biases."

Moriah raised her head and smiled timidly at that. "So the computers are more like angels."

"I guess. Yeah."

Kenzie's face burned with embarrassment. *You must think we're freaks. Everything goes back to religion for us.*

His skin prickled at standing so close to Moriah. It didn't take a genius to see that hanging out with her was going to get him in trouble.

Funny. In high school, Moriah was always the one protecting me from the popular kids by letting me into her circle. As long as I was in her study groups, no one would pick on me for having a Japanese dad.

"You can go first." Logan gestured at the terminal. "I don't care if I have to wait in line."

Kenzie stepped up and let the computer scan the school ID bracelet. As soon as the computer displayed his name, he concentrated on the reservoir of his magic. He was past the point in his life when he needed to close his eyes. That was an amateur thing little kids did. Instead, he touched on the deep well inside his chest and relaxed. Tingling, vibrating pressure rose through his body.

When the pressure wave reached his hands, he grabbed the air around him as if it were made of clear, thin ribbons of gossamer fabric. Pulling and gathering, he fought the air as it pushed back. Gathering air felt like trying to push enormous magnets together at the matching poles. The air struggled to escape his hold as it ionized.

When he couldn't hold on any longer, he aimed his hands at the station and unleashed a torrent of wind. Sensors all around the station flashed blue, and the metal walls contained the blast. As the wind gust hit, a loud *whomp* announced Kenzie's level of force. The air pressure around him changed so drastically that his ears popped. He winced.

I hate elemental magic. The sensors triggered vacuum pumps behind vents in the walls to suck up the air instead of blowing it back in Kenzie's face.

The monitor on the podium registered his score: 82%. Elemental magic was not Kenzie's strong suit, so after two more blasts, he averaged an 83%. *With a B that low, I don't look like a top 20 student. Ugh.*

Since Moriah was next, Kenzie paused to watch her. Moriah braced her feet and spread her hands, then brought her hands together and bowed her head. She stayed in that repose of silent prayer for a few seconds. Then she flung out her hands and summoned a single blast of muddy water, perhaps from the nearby Ohio River. The sensors glowed, and a drain on the station's floor siphoned away the water. Her score registered as a 99%.

Kenzie smiled. "I see you didn't lose any ground over the summer."

"I couldn't afford to." Moriah ducked her head. "Once my family became one of the Noble Three, my parents made me practice every day, even on Sunday, although working on Sunday is a sin." She tugged on the end of one pigtail.

"Our pastor prayed to God about it, and he said that this is my calling. But our pastor didn't say anything about working Sundays."

Logan stepped up next, and five more students lined up behind him. "Hey, if your pastor said it's your calling, you're Gucci, right?"

"I guess we better move on," Kenzie said, uncomfortable with the implied question.

He didn't believe people went to hell just for working on Sundays. Or at all. Also, he didn't know what "Gucci" meant, and he was sure Moriah didn't either.

Glancing around, he picked a station with a short line. Moriah and he ended up behind three White women with platinum blonde hair, all of whom wore the white women's pants uniform. The tallest woman struck Kenzie as a natural blonde, but he could tell by their roots that the other two had bleached their hair.

The tallest woman scanned her ID and held out her hand. There were five rubber blocks on the station floor, and when the woman's hands glowed green, the blocks floated upward four feet into the air. Several sensors flashed blue around the station walls. Then the cubes slammed back onto the floor, and the sensors in the floor flashed blue as well. The computer scored the woman at 99%.

With a sinking sensation, Kenzie realized the station measured gravity spells. Gravity magic was his worst weakness.

Where's the station for what I'm good at? This is a nightmare. All I need now is to have forgotten John 3:16 in front of a group of angry church deacons, and it'll be complete.

"Mythical, Iona!" said the woman with a pixie haircut. Her hair was cropped so short Kenzie thought she looked boyish.

"You're so mythical I'm dying," said the last woman, whose hair hung straight to her jaw.

Iona turned away from the station.

"What can I say? I'm the snazz." She had a thick accent that Kenzie thought was a New Jersey one, at least based on historical movies from the 1950s he saw.

Now facing their way, Iona halted and stared at Moriah with wide eyes.

Kenzie wanted to bolt, but he thought of the day three girls had surrounded him in a school bathroom and made supposedly "Chinese" noises at him, a kind of "ning, ying, wan" of faked Mandarin words. Moriah stormed in and called them out for un-Christian behavior.

Iona scanned Moriah from head to foot. She grimaced and tilted her head, her blonde ponytail falling sideways.

"Wow. I heard we accepted four people from the URA this year, but I didn't believe it until now." She pointed at Moriah's hair, which reached her thighs. "Oh, honey. This is the *United States*. Cut that stuff off. You have three feet of dead ends."

The other two women snorted with laughter.

Moriah pressed her hands to her hair and stared at her feet.

Kenzie flushed. A chemical burn scorched him at witnessing Moriah get bullied for the first time. Since Moriah was Christian, none of the kids at school had cared about her Jewish heritage, no doubt because her skin wasn't "too dark" for URA sensibilities.

In his peripheral vision, Kenzie saw other students glance their way and then move on to other stations, choosing not to get involved. *Typical.*

"It's the least you can do," said the woman with the pixie cut. "But more importantly, you two need to keep in mind this is magic *science*. Don't be one of those people walking around saying you're borrowing Jesus' holy powers or whatever."

At that, Moriah raised her head and stared at the woman. "John 14:12 tells us how humans gained access to divine workings. I'm not borrowing anything. Divine power is the reward of faith."

Iona and the two other women burst into laughter.

"What?" Iona asked through gasping breaths. Her friends giggled too hard to speak. "I expected you to be a woob, but you're a murk. Oh my God."

"Taking the Lord's name in vain is a sin!" Moriah snapped.

"Right, right…but is that as bad as a fashion sin?" Iona asked.

Her friends had regained their breath, but now they doubled over with breathless laughter.

Tears welled up in Moriah's brown eyes, and her chin trembled.

Kenzie glared at the bullies. *So meanness is the name of the game, huh? Then this isn't so different from home after all.* "Hey, Nazi Girl, you and your two hyenas *are* the fashion crime."

Moriah gasped.

Iona and the two other women fell silent. Then Iona reddened, her fair skin showing her anger. "What did you call me?"

"A Nazi or fashion crime? Because you're both," Kenzie said, deadpan and dropping into stone-cold stoicism. He'd chased off bullies when Moriah wasn't around by being even ruder than they were.

Iona crossed her arms. "Who are you, and why are you fanning this murk?"

Kenzie was glad he'd watched TV last night so he could track the slang.

"I'm not fanning her. I'm defending her from you, you girlbot. What makes you so mythical? You're attacking Moriah because you're threatened by her test scores."

"What? No!" Iona shrieked.

Kenzie ran a hand through his short hair, lifting his chin and staring down his nose at her. "I don't believe you."

"The way you're white knighting so hard, you must be one of those Jesus freaks yourself," Iona said.

"Please. Not everyone from the URA believes in Jesus." Kenzie already prepared for U.S. students to heap shame on him. He wasn't going to accept being buried in hot coals. "I stopped being Christian when I was sixteen. I'm atheist."

"Sure you are," Iona said. "I bet you think that's the snazz thing to say."

"And you apparently think that the snazz thing to say when you're afraid of someone beating you on the class scoreboard is that you don't like their hair," Kenzie said.

"I'm not afraid of Moriah Goldstein, and I'm not afraid of you!" Iona dropped her arms and propped a hand on her hip.

"Yeah," the woman with the boyish haircut said. "She's an Anderson."

Although he fought to keep a straight face, Kenzie wondered if he cringed.

The Andersons were another of the Noble Seven clans, although there was no way for Kenzie to know if Iona was from the main family or a branch family. All he knew was that Iona looked the part of an Anderson clan princess: pale skin, slim figure, platinum blonde hair, baby blue eyes, a pert nose, and full and shapely lips. If Iona had been wearing modest clothes, she would've looked like a model in a URA women's aspirational magazine. A "fashion" magazine was too shallow for the URA.

Instead, they had colorful online magazines with videos of gorgeous women in fashionable head-to-toe outfits talking about their faith. Kenzie could only guess that Iona was attractive by U.S. standards.

"And what's your name? What's your flex?" the woman with the hair down to her jaw asked Kenzie.

Flex? He cursed that his knowledge of slang only went so far. "Kenzie Okuda."

Iona sneered. "Never heard of you *or* your clan."

Kenzie smirked. "Didn't you hear Dr. Kitamori? This class comprises the top 20 incoming freshmen. Obviously, I'm one of them."

Iona's brow furrowed, and she stared off at the corner of the room.

"Oh, yeah. I remember seeing your name. You took 17th place. So you made it into our class. Barely." She locked gazes with Kenzie and leaned in. "You know, at JCU, anything less than a *B* in a magic course is the same as failing."

"Of course I know," Kenzie bit out. He was all too aware. His scholarship and therefore his visa were riding on his grades. "I also know talking doesn't make scores on machines and we're halfway through our lab period."

Iona looked at the clock on the wall, blanched, and ran across the room. Her two friends followed her.

"Oh, I am *not* coming back here later to finish! I have a nail appointment."

"Ivy league, magic nobility, and rich," Kenzie drawled. "Worst combination ever."

"Definitely." Moriah sighed.

At the end of class, everyone bunched around the computer display on the wall. Kenzie waited with Moriah until the crowd cleared, and then he stepped up to read the screen. The top 10 rankings were listed in bold, followed by the bottom 10 in regular font.

Kenzie found himself in 19th place and wilted, his shoulders slouching.

Moriah patted his arm. "You'll get better as you go."

"But look at you." Kenzie pointed to third place, trying to hide his horror at his own score. "You kicked ass today."

"*Kenzie*," Moriah hissed. "Language!"

Kenzie shrugged.

"It's just 'ass.' We're in college now. Aren't you going to enjoy some freedom?" He turned away from the computer. "The actual big deal is losing our student visas and, in my case, my scholarship."

"Right. You can't afford this." Moriah bit her lip.

Kenzie stared at the leader board.

Second to last place is not gonna cut it for me. This is my big chance to experience freedom, and if I don't stay on the honor roll, I'm going to lose my scholarship, my visa, and my freedom. Then it'll be back to living in hell.

FOUR

By lunchtime, Kenzie had been through his Freshman Composition I class and emerged exhausted and hungry. He exited the Steensen Humanities Building and stumbled down the sidewalk toward the Idoni Student Building, which held the cafeteria and six restaurant chains.

At this point, Kenzie didn't care what he ate. He just wanted food and a nap. Moriah waited for him by the Anderson Science Building. She left the shade of the front porch and fell into step with Kenzie, but their half-hearted small talk about their classes was cut short by chanting and yelling near the red brick cafeteria.

Kenzie and Moriah stopped and stared at the far side of the parking lot. Other students dodged them, streaming in and out of the Idoni Student Building, which suggested that this was a common disturbance.

A mass of adults dressed in t-shirts and shorts lined the public sidewalk and street at the campus' edge, holding signs that said STONE THE WITCHES or SUMMONING SATAN WILL SEND YOU TO HELL or JESUS HATES MAGICIANS.

The closest two adults, a White woman and a Latino man,

turned toward Kenzie and Moriah. They both waved their signs.

"Stop using magic!" the blonde woman shouted. "Pray to Jesus for forgiveness!"

The dark-skinned Latino man pointed at them. "You'll go to hell if you don't, witches!"

"I'm so done." Kenzie turned and marched toward the glass double doors of the ISB. "I'm tired. I don't need The Apostle's Way bullshit."

Moriah scrambled after Kenzie. "You know Jesus wouldn't approve of what these people are doing."

Panicked shrieks erupted behind them. Kenzie whirled around, scanning the ocean of asphalt, shiny cars, and protesters for the problem.

Then Kenzie spotted the man from the day before. The seven-foot-tall man wearing a black top hat wove drunkenly through the crowd. His face was painted white, and he wore a black suit with coattails and black and white spats. A smile drawn in red clown makeup stretched from ear to ear. A black and white swirl painted around each eye mimicked the look of an old cartoon character. His height and his disproportionately long legs made him look like a stilt-walker.

Kenzie understood why the crowd had screamed. A menacing air vibrated around the man. His looming presence and blood red smile made the Kenzie's skin tingle with fear. The bad vibes of a twisted or malfunctioning spell slammed into Kenzie's face, like the stench of a rotting animal.

Moriah grabbed Kenzie's arm and tugged. "Let's go."

The man burst into gibberish: "Goline adamia? Corporous noctunous!" Then a red pitchfork materialized in his hand. He ran the pitchfork through the nearest woman, picking her up with a single jab and holding her body high in the air as a macabre canapé, a bite of food on an enormous fork. She screamed and twitched, dropping her sign and kicking one of her shoes off.

"Corporous noctunous!" The man hurled her to the ground. She bounced once against the pavement, blood flying from her wounds, and lay still.

The crowd burst into more shrieks. People stampeded in all directions, squeezing between cars or fleeing across the street without looking. Some of them threw their signs down while others clung to them.

Moriah bolted toward the Anderson Science Building.

However, Kenzie couldn't move his legs. His body seemed to turn to granite, having decided that staying perfectly still was his best chance of survival.

Meanwhile, on the inside, his mind was screaming, *Move! Do something!*

The man spun to face the street, revealing that he wore a long, red, pointed devil's tail, curved as though a wire on the inside gave it structure.

"Goline adamia?" he shouted at the crowd.

"Goline adamia?" He gave chase, stabbing at a Black man.

That broke Kenzie's paralysis. He flipped over into fight mode, teeth baring in a snarl.

"Stop it!" With both hands, he grabbed at the UV rays beating down from the sun. He packed them all into a dense ball of light that shifted from red all the way into green as he wove his spell. Then he threw it, and it slammed like a laser blast into the man's back at the speed of light.

The man squealed and snapped around. His huge, fake smile was grotesque, and his actual lips were turned upward in a smile as well.

As Kenzie lowered his hands in shock, his body tensed at the violence the smile promised. *How is he unharmed? That should have burnt his entire back.*

Then he jerked his hands back up, terrified the attacker

would rush him. All around him, the deafening screams and yells of both students and protesters pierced the air.

The man pointed his pitchfork at Kenzie.

"Corporous noctunous!" Red lightning gathered on the tongs of the pitchfork. The smell of ozone filled Kenzie's nose.

Kenzie jumped sideways, tucking himself into a forward roll. A blinding flash of light erupted as the lightning hit nearby. The rush of electricity turned Kenzie's hair into a puff on top of his head.

Static electricity crackled in his uniform and delivered miniature shocks. Kenzie used his momentum to push back onto his feet, and he whirled toward the attacker. The man turned away from Kenzie and raced after the Latino man, raising his pitchfork.

Finally, Kenzie's magical practice kicked in and body memory took over. He held out his hand, engaged his telekinesis, and imagined he yanked the pitchfork out of the man's hand. The pitchfork flew from the man's grasp. When it hit the pavement, it vanished as if it had been illusion magic. The pitchfork hadn't even made a sound upon impact.

But illusions can't stab people. This is breaking all the laws of magic!

The man whirled toward Kenzie again.

"Kotak hoc!" He pointed a finger. A cone of flames roared from his fingertip, aimed directly at Kenzie rather than spreading in all directions.

A tsunami of water splashed in front of Kenzie and blocked the flames. The water burst into steam, and Kenzie yelped as it scalded his face and hands. A chlorinated smell stung his nose.

That was summoned from someone's swimming pool.

Then an invisible force slammed the clownish man into the sidewalk as if a 10-ton boulder dropped on him. He howled and flailed his arms and legs, but he seemed pinned. Even with the force of the impact, his top hat stayed on.

Gravity magic. Kenzie scanned the area. An East Asian man and a redheaded man raced toward him. He recognized them from Magic Application II as two of the highest ranking people in class: Shinrou Kitamori and Makari Idoni.

Makari stopped at Kenzie's side.

"I'm sorry! I tried to intervene fast enough that you wouldn't get hit by the steam, but it didn't work." He was a stunningly handsome redhead and struck a fine figure in the white men's uniform, which had black piping on its pockets and cuffs.

As the eldest son of the Idoni family, another of the Noble Seven clans, Makari was already famous as a magical genius. He won the United States' National Magical Tournament in the high school battle division, and he was rumored to have tied for first place on the university's entrance exam.

Kenzie glanced at his burnt hands.

"I don't think it's more than a first-degree burn, and it's better than what would have happened if the flames had hit me."

By now he had the adrenaline shakes, his fingers trembling. *How can I sound so calm?*

Shinrou stared at the pinned man as he continued to hold him down with the gravity spell.

"Look. He's wearing a top hat." He had a faint Japanese accent.

Kenzie looked from the top hat man to Shinrou. Compared to Makari, who was tall and had an athletic build, Shinrou was short and slender. He had shiny black hair that hung down to his cheekbones and brown eyes. He wore the black uniform, which had white piping on the pockets and cuffs. Despite the grim situation, Kenzie felt a surge of joy at meeting a second Japanese citizen in one day.

"You were talking about this before class this morning."

"That's right. A shadowy figure dressed like this was seen yesterday."

Kenzie took a deep breath and tried to compose himself. Between the heat, the shock, the pain of the burns, the hunger, and the dehydration, he felt unsteady.

"Who are you?" Makari demanded, glaring down at the man. "Why did you attack the demonstrators?"

The man squirmed and growled. "Kotak hoc!" Then he vanished.

Kenzie stared, speechless. He could barely comprehend that the man wasn't there anymore.

"*What?*" Shinrou took several steps forward, paused, and then turned to face Kenzie and Makari. "He can't have teleported. He just can't have! We haven't even figured out how to teleport a fly, much less a person."

With that, Kenzie's understanding of the world, and especially of magic science, flipped upside down.

I escaped to the U.S., and now the entire universe has changed.

FOR SEVERAL MINUTES, NO ONE SPOKE AS MAKARI CALLED 911 and asked for an ambulance. The injured female protester was in danger of dying from her wounds, and others could be injured.

Kenzie sank onto the grass and sat, given how hot the sidewalk was to the touch. Already the sun's heat leeched through his uniform. Meanwhile, a man was administering first aid to the unconscious woman lying on the sidewalk. Considering the man wore a t-shirt and jeans and not a university uniform, Kenzie thought he was a fellow protester who might have grabbed a first aid kit from his car, but he wasn't sure.

When Makari hung up, he said, "The dispatcher told me we need to wait here and give statements to an officer."

He glanced around at the crowd of students clustered around nearby buildings, staring at the scene from afar.

"This is just like yesterday. He showed up. He disappeared. At least ten witnesses saw it."

Kenzie looked in all directions. Besides the students, a few protesters had clumped together at the end of the street. He didn't see the man with the top hat, though.

"Maybe he used a speed spell. A really, really fast one."

"No," Shinrou said. "A speed spell that fast would cause a sonic boom. Also, a human can't survive going that fast. I don't care if they're trained as an astronaut or a fighter jet pilot. The g-forces would tear them apart."

"He could have used more than one spell at once," Makari said. "An air spell to manage the displacement. Motion spells to tolerate the g-forces."

"He'd have to. But I still think it's not a speed spell. Speed spells produce blurred effects. You can see a smeared color streak."

"How do we know the top hat man is truly gone?" Kenzie asked.

"I can sense the energy people naturally give off," Shinrou said. "Our bodies generate electricity. Some people call it an aura, but I mean it *scientifically*, not supernaturally."

He sighed. "What I am saying is that I felt this man's energy, and I can't feel it now. This means he's at least 500 feet away. Instantly. Without a speed spell. Somehow. Without it being teleportation."

A grumpy look crossed his face, lining his brow.

Kenzie pulled his phone out of his back pocket, wincing at how sore his hand was.

"Okay. Well, I'm texting Moriah. She can make sure the woman who got impaled is stable enough to survive until the ambulance arrives. That is, if anyone lets her use healing magic on the woman. Considering they hate magicians, they might not." *Either way, she can heal me.*

He unlocked his phone screen, tapped the message bubble icon, pressed the button for Moriah, and used smart-fill to press the phone as few times as possible with his burnt fingertip. With all the racket, speech-to-text was a bad idea.

A white van with a miniature satellite on its roof turned the corner. Kenzie caught half the logo: VE 3 News.

"Great response time," Makari muttered. "They must have been on their way already."

Kenzie groaned as he pushed his phone back into his pocket.

"That man who got away seems like he's trying to get people to hate magicians. Think about it: There's violence at a magic science university, and people were holding a protest against magic. Even worse, there's a protester who was harmed by magic. But that man is a magician himself. Why would he want his own kind to be hated? I don't get it."

"Me, neither. But if the police don't find this guy, we're all in trouble," Makari said. "Non-magicians will think we're protecting him."

Kenzie crossed his arms and curled his hands against his chest, protecting them. The backs of his hands suffered fewer burns compared to his palms and fingers.

"But the police will get him, right?" Admittedly, he knew only a little about how police worked in the U.S. "The magic he used is incredibly flashy. Someone like that can't hide from the police."

"I hope not," Makari said.

"I wish I had held him." Shinrou held up his hands and stared at them. "I can't understand it. And I need to. I need to know what went wrong."

Makari's brow furrowed.

"It's not your fault, Mori. Campus security should've been keeping an eye on this rally. It's their job to make sure things like this don't get out of hand."

Shinrou lowered his hands and looked to Makari.

"The magic I felt the instant before he disappeared wasn't normal."

"When the police find him, we'll discover what kind of magic he used," Kenzie said with more confidence than he felt. *Shinrou sensed the twisted spell, too.*

Moriah came running, long pigtails flying behind her. She turned ghastly pale at the sight of the fallen female protester. Then she approached and knelt by the man, who applied first aid to his compatriot.

"Let me pray with you. Lord, please help your wayward sheep. She is still of your flock, no matter how far she has wandered. In Jesus' name, I ask that…"

Kenzie tuned out the rest of the prayer. All that mattered was that the golden glow now suffusing both Moriah and the woman meant Moriah was stabilizing the woman's condition. Better yet, the man wasn't screaming at Moriah to get away.

The man watched Moriah as she worked.

"That's God's power flowing through you. Why does a good Christian woman like you attend an ungodly place like this?"

"To minister in the wilderness." Moriah's voice was sweet and soft.

The ambulance arrived, wailing like a grieving widow wearing sackcloth and covered in ashes. EMTs jumped out, and as they moved the woman onto a stretcher, Moriah joined Kenzie, Makari, and Shinrou.

Without speaking, Moriah took Kenzie's hands in hers and healed them. The golden glow lapped at Kenzie's burns, more cooling and soothing than aloe vera with lidocaine.

Kenzie relaxed as his hands faded to their normal color, and Moriah worked on his tight, sore face. "Thanks."

"I ran to the nearest campus security emergency summons button, but I clearly didn't reach it in time," Moriah said. "Why did this happen? I don't understand. No matter how hateful the demonstrators were, they weren't armed. It didn't have to escalate."

A campus security car pulled up on the opposite side of

the street from the ambulance. Kenzie's stomach clenched as a uniformed officer stepped out: White, buff, buzz-cut, frowning, and armed. Every cell in Kenzie's body said: not safe.

Then he reminded himself, *I look like a man now. I'm in the U.S. Maybe, just maybe, that's enough to balance out also looking Asian.*

Shocked, he watched as the security officer walked right past him and addressed Makari.

"Mr. Idoni. Glad to see a Noble Seven scion here." They shook hands.

Makari explained everything so smoothly that all Shinrou, Kenzie, and Moriah had to do was nod. Kenzie was dazed. *The power of being from one of these clans.*

Makari had as much clout here as Moriah did in the URA and then some. He was a man, and a handsome one at that. Plus he seemed to know how to interact with people in a charming but commanding way.

This is my new world, Kenzie thought. *If I'm lucky enough to get to stay here.*

FIVE

After statements to both campus security and the police, Kenzie and Moriah ate a quick lunch and then headed to Strategic Magic I. Kenzie was rattled and angry. His stomach clenched, and his mind replayed the image of the woman being impaled by a pitchfork.

However, since he was trained as a child to never let his feelings show, he pinned a smile on his face. He also didn't know Moriah well enough to confide any of his frustrations or fears. While they were friends in high school, they hadn't been best friends. He felt like her charity case. Anxiety punched his sternum, radiating tendrils of ice through his lungs.

I'm finally here, I finally made it, and the first thing that happens is a psycho with a pitchfork attacks people! He hoped his mother wouldn't see the news and worry.

Their classroom, Griffen Hall 101, looked like a small gym except with beige tile flooring. Metal bleachers covered the left-hand wall, and glass doors stood at both ends of the room. All it lacked were locker rooms and basketball goals.

A sign reading "Students Sit Here" marked one section of

bleachers. Kenzie and Moriah climbed to the fifth row and sat by Makari and Shinrou.

Less than a minute later, the three women who bullied Kenzie and Moriah in Magic Application II entered and ascended the bleachers toward them. They all looked classy in their white women's uniforms with the black piping on the pockets, cuffs, and hems. He swallowed a groan.

Although Kenzie dreaded more bullying, his attention was waylaid by the realization women surrounded Makari and Shinrou on all sides. *Yikes. Are all these women after Makari because he's handsome and powerful?*

Kenzie couldn't help having a flesh-crawl reaction. Men and women were not allowed to sit that close to each other in the URA. Worse, he could almost smell the pheromones wafting off of Iona, Natalie, and Heather, or more likely, their floral perfume. Yet another thing women weren't allowed to do in the URA. Perfume had been declared sinful.

Iona settled beside Makari and gave him a winning smile, showing off her professionally whitened teeth.

"Hi. I'm Iona Anderson. You didn't recognize me in class earlier. But then again, the last time we saw each other was that naff cocktail party our parents had when we were, like, six years old." She gestured to one of her friends. "This is Natalie Jefferies. The Jefferies were already practicing magic in Virginia in the 1700s."

The woman with the blonde pixie haircut waved to Makari.

"And that's Heather White," Iona continued. "The Whites' magical lineage can be traced all the way back to the 1200s in Britain."

The woman with chin-length blonde hair grinned at Makari. "Hi!"

"Hi." Makari returned their smiles, although not in a flirtatious way. "There wasn't time to talk before. It's a lab class."

"Oh, true," Iona said. "I was concentrating, too."

Kenzie glared at her. "No, you weren't. You were harassing Moriah and me."

Iona leaned forward and peered around Makari and Shinrou to Kenzie, who sat by Shinrou. Iona's pristine blonde ponytail swung outward as she did, and Kenzie reflexively touched his short hair. *I never want long hair ever again.*

"Oh, yeah." Iona's brow furrowed. "I remember you. You took last place in practice this morning. Kenzie O'Gouda, right?"

"*Okuda,*" Moriah corrected.

Iona snorted. "That's what I said."

"I was 19th," Kenzie said through gritted teeth.

Iona's dig at his score hurt worse than hearing his name mispronounced. Teachers had been mispronouncing his name all his life.

Iona straightened and faced Makari with a fresh smile. "So I heard you caught the man people saw yesterday. I can't believe he attacked a crowd of students!"

"The man attacked anti-magician demonstrators," Shinrou said.

"That's even worse." Iona frowned. "That's terrible press for the university."

Makari leaned forward and rested his hands on his knees, head bowed. "Actually, he got away, and we don't know how."

"'We?'" Iona echoed.

"Shinrou, Kenzie, and I," Makari said.

Iona shot a narrow-eyed look at Kenzie as if he were intruding or eavesdropping, then returned to studying Makari. "I'm sure you'll catch him."

Makari frowned at his feet. "I turned the matter over to the police and campus security."

"But it's a matter of *honor,*" Iona said. "We're the Noble Seven."

"My dad told me to concentrate on my studies."

Iona gave him a pouty yet hopeful look, her full lips shining with pink, glossy lipstick. "Think of how impressive it would be if you *did* catch him."

The door opened one last time, and the tiniest woman Kenzie had ever seen walked in. She stood perhaps four foot eight and weighed less than 100 pounds. With her heavy wrinkles, she looked around 80 years old, and her gray hair was curly and hung down to her shoulders. Most striking of all, she wore a black karate gi with a black belt tied around her waist.

"That's our professor?" Iona whispered to Heather.

"Welcome to Strategic Magic I," the woman said. "I'm Dr. Grayson. This is a course about using magic to fight: to fight in self-defense, to fight in modified martial arts styles, and most importantly, to fight on a battlefield. You need to think tactically and cast spells strategically amid chaos."

She clasped her hands behind her back.

"You can read the syllabus in our class portal. I'm not going to read it to you. Instead, you're going to get off your tushes and spar."

Iona wrinkled her nose. "She can't have ever been married."

"Or she's blown through three husbands," Heather whispered.

Kenzie glared at them. He liked Dr. Grayson's tough attitude and wished he could learn to emulate it. He got over being respectful to elders on principle, but Dr. Grayson emanated power from her tiny body like an aura. Her posture was military-straight. That was a skill and demeanor Kenzie wished to master.

"No lethal spells," Dr. Grayson said. "This isn't a real battlefield, so don't get carried away. Bruises are allowed. No broken bones. Again, control yourselves. If you accidentally land a major injury on your sparring partner at any point during this semester, you'll automatically fail. If you land a major injury on purpose, you'll be expelled from the university."

"Never been married," Natalie murmured. "You can tell she's never been laid."

Shinrou cringed, his eyebrows scrunching as a look of horror passed over his face. He seemed offended by his fellow students' comments, and Kenzie wondered if it resulted from a cultural difference between Japan and the U.S. His father had only spoken a little about his home country.

With relief, Kenzie noted Makari ignored Natalie and Heather. *I'm glad Makari doesn't think they're funny.*

"All sparring rounds will be two minutes long," Dr. Grayson said. "I'm aiming for you to pair up with as many people as possible in each class session."

She pointed to Iona, Natalie, and Heather. "We'll start with the three whispering girls."

Most of the class chuckled.

"Fine." Iona stood and stomped down the stairs.

Kenzie could hardly believe Iona's attitude. *It's like you're in third grade. Seriously, you're mad that you got caught whispering? Oh, wait. I forgot. You're a magical princess, and you've never been called out for anything in your entire life. Someone pass me a barf bag.*

Dr. Grayson marched to the teacher's desk and typed on the keyboard there. Clear walls that appeared to be plexiglass rose from slots in the floor, sectioning off two large rooms that took up most of the gym's floor. Kenzie noticed drains in the floor, just like in the training stations earlier that day.

"You two are in room B," Dr. Grayson said, gesturing at Natalie and Heather. "What're your names?"

When they supplied them, Dr. Grayson typed them into the computer. Two giant screens filled the far wall, which was painted beige to match the floor, and the screen behind room B lit up with Natalie's and Heather's names.

Dr. Grayson gestured to Iona. "What's your name?"

Iona told her and then entered room A.

Dr. Grayson entered Iona's name, which popped up on screen A. She hit a few more buttons, and then the class roster scrolled alongside Iona's name too rapidly for anyone to see the letters. Kenzie's name popped up as the final selection.

"Who is Kenzie Okuda?"

Kenzie stood. *Dammit, of course I'd get Iona. If there is a God, he wants me to get pasted on my first day of college. That only proves there can't be one. I did nothing to deserve getting punished. If he really hates magicians, he'd be punishing everyone equally.*

"You can do it," Shinrou murmured, giving Kenzie a discrete thumbs up.

Kenzie gave him a small smile. "I don't believe that for a second. But thanks."

"Normally sparring matches are random via computer generation," Dr. Grayson told the class. "You'll have lectures on battle tactics and strategies later. For now, just remember the three banned spells: no telepathy, which is cheating for the purpose of this course, and no metal or earth spells. The walls and floor take too much damage if you summon metal, and earth takes too much time to clean up."

Kenzie headed down the bleachers, entered room A, and slid the clear door shut behind him. It felt like a high-grade polymer of some kind, likely fire resistant.

Iona gave him a wicked grin. "So, it looks like I get to out you as a last-place feeder in this class, too."

Molten lava ate all Kenzie's veins as his rage flared. His face locked into a stoic mask.

"It's weird how you're so threatened by a 'last-place feeder' that you're determined to make me drop out before I would apparently disgrace myself by falling off the scoreboard without any help from you."

"What can I say? I like efficiency." Iona struck a stance that bespoke martial arts training, lifting her arms and flattening her hands. "Besides, if you leave tonight, you can get your money back for the dorm, and I'm sure they'll let you back across the border where you belong. I'm doing you a favor. Admit it. You're a homesick little woob who misses mommy."

"You don't know anything about me or the URA. People don't live there because they want to. Not unless they're White, straight, and have a dick. My mom's been trying to get out for years, and if you paid attention to the news, you'd know…"

"No one gives a damn about the URA," Iona said. "Here in the U.S., you're a punch line."

Kenzie smirked. "I'll show you a punch line."

Iona narrowed her eyes and smirked in return.

"Feeling aggressive? You'll have to vent your feelings in this little box. That is, if you can hit me. No attack spells on campus outside of class. Break the rules, and you'll get expelled."

A buzzer sounded, and Kenzie saw a counter running backwards from two minutes on the screen behind Iona. He froze for a second. *If the university sees a video of me on social media or on security footage using attack magic this morning, they'll expel me? The university can't expel me for using magic to protect non-magicians from someone else's magic! I'll appeal.*

Iona snapped her hands downward. Kenzie slammed into the floor from a gravity spell. The air was knocked from his lungs, and pain shot through his chest. After a horrible, airless moment, he inhaled and flung his arm out, telekinetically grabbing Iona's hands midair and stopping her from casting a second spell.

Although hand movements weren't necessary, most people used them as a concentration aid. Kenzie banked on that as he hopped to his feet. Furious with Iona's attitude, he yanked light from the glaring fluorescent bulbs in the gymnasium and compacted a marble-sized ball of crackling, red light so tight it almost turned orange before he fired it.

Iona stared at her captured wrists and pulled against the spell. She yelped when she saw the laser ball and curled in on her hands. The ball grazed her shoulder, and if Kenzie hadn't held her wrists telekinetically, the impact would have flung Iona into the far wall. Iona's white uniform showed a scorch mark.

"Foul!" Iona yelled. "Too much force! I'm injured."

No buzzer or alarm sounded.

"Dr. Grayson doesn't think so." Kenzie siphoned off light energy from the bulbs again.

His hands buzzed with heat, unpleasantly reminding him of being burned earlier.

Iona glared at her wrists, her eyes narrowing and brow furrowing with concentration. She jerked free, compacted a pale red marble of light energy herself, and flung it at Kenzie's chest.

In the time it took her to do it, Kenzie dodged. *Really? Using my attack strategy against me? Why would anyone do that?*

However, the fact Iona defeated his telekinesis worried him. Telekinesis wasn't easily countered. *She's pigheaded enough, I guess.*

Before Iona's laser ball could even hit the wall, Kenzie aimed his control over particles at the air around him, shoving them out of the way. Near-simultaneously, he back-built kinetic energy and exploded it, whipping around behind Iona and unleashing a wind gust pointblank. Her blonde hair flew into her face. Since Kenzie lacked power in his elemental spells, he compensated with a close-range attack.

Iona whirled around and dropped to the floor on her hands and knees. Then she snapped out her hand. Kenzie collided with a wall and became trapped against it.

Iona can use telekinesis! Kenzie was stunned. *I thought the Andersons were famous for telepathy, not telekinesis.*

"No," he hissed, outraged at the idea of losing to Iona in his own specialty.

He hurled the entire force of his willpower against the spell, using as much desperation as anger.

The spell shattered, releasing Kenzie to stumble forward.

"What?" Iona shrieked.

The buzzer sounded, signaling the end of the match.

Kenzie turned to Iona and smiled. Between his relief and his lingering anger, his lips trembled with the facial tension. "So you're a telekinetic mage, too? Interesting."

Iona gaped at him. "Andersons are *the* mind mages! What do you mean, 'too?' You had to have been using gravity magic instead. Everyone who placed in telekinesis at Nationals last year is an Anderson, including me. And the URA doesn't even have mind mages. I would *know!*"

"You would?" Kenzie drawled, strolling toward the door. *Great. So they do have telekinesis, also.* "You said nobody knows anything about the URA and no one cares."

Iona stepped between him and the door. "Uh-uh. You can't leave yet. How did you get telekinesis? You're a nobody. I have a right to know. It's my clan's responsibility to monitor all mind magic in the U.S."

"My dad was a mind mage from Japan. You may have never heard of him, but that doesn't mean he was nobody."

Iona reddened. "Japanese noble clans don't count! This is the U.S.! Go back to Japan if you want to be famous."

Kenzie realized Iona had taken his words the wrong way and assumed his dad, Daihachi Okuda, had been noble, but he refused to stop and correct the impression.

"I can't go *back* to a place I've never been. I was born in the URA. And I'm not going back there. So sorry I added a plus one to your country's population." He pushed her out of the way, slid the door open, and exited, headed back toward his seat on the bleachers.

People can be somebodies without being literal nobility.

He felt so disgusted his stomach churned up the grease from his lunch of a hamburger and fries.

Moriah pointed at the computer monitor on the far wall with an urgent expression. Kenzie turned and read the scoreboard screen: Iona Anderson vs. Kenzie Okuda—tie.

Kenzie grinned. "Awesome." His stomach didn't feel any better, though.

"It is not a tie! We are not the same!" Iona shrieked. She whirled to Dr. Grayson. "I demand a rematch!"

"This isn't World Wrestling Entertainment," Dr. Grayson said in a dry tone.

Some students laughed at that, but Iona fell silent, her shoulders stiffening. Her gaze snapped to Kenzie.

As thrilled as Kenzie was not to have lost to Iona, he also figured he just made an enemy for the entire length of his college career.

SIX

After supper, as Kenzie and Moriah left the cafeteria, Kenzie studied the crowd collecting by the campus. Four vans from various news stations packed the street by the Idoni Student Building, and portable lights shone in strategic locations.

Police and campus security kept the crowd from spilling onto the campus proper by holding them on a lot across the street where the remains of a burnt-down dorm sat. Kenzie wondered if magician-haters had set fire to the dorm. *Or worse, that psycho in the top hat.*

"This is a nasty show," Moriah said.

"Yeah. And look at all the new signs," Kenzie sighed.

The typical JESUS HATES MAGICIANS signs peppered the crowd, but now people wielded new ones like BURN IN HELL and even TAKE YOUR WITCHCRAFT BACK TO ENGLAND.

Moriah shook her head. "They don't understand the first thing about magic."

"And yet they feel qualified to critique it." Kenzie wondered why some people seemed to have the strongest opinions about things they knew little or nothing about. His mom called it the Stupid Paradox: "The stupider the person, the more sure they are that they're smart." It had a fancier name, too. She'd told him the real name of it once, but he'd forgotten. *Someone's name. Italian, I think. Or was it German?*

A group of five blond men approached on the sidewalk, all of them tall and broad-shouldered. Instead of their university uniforms, they wore jean shorts and t-shirts advertising their favorite sports teams. They talked and laughed, but as Kenzie and Moriah grew closer, they stared at Kenzie. When the men drew parallel to them, one sneered at Kenzie.

"Go home, Chini-dog. Chinese communists are the last thing we need."

Kenzie's entire body stung from the force of the racial slur, and a mixture of fear and rage erupted in his chest. The heat of shame and anger burned his face.

"She's not from China," Moriah snapped.

The men laughed and kept walking.

"I'm so sorry," Moriah said.

Kenzie shook his head, forcing away his emotions as best he could. "At least they didn't include you in the abuse. Who knows how they feel about Jewish people?"

Moriah flinched. "That's why I bleached my hair as soon as I got here. I hoped it would protect me, and…well, I have gotten compliments on it."

"That's because it looks really good on you," Kenzie said.

"Thank you." Moriah gave him a smile, but it died quickly. "Have you noticed just how many blondes are at this university? And I mean natural ones."

"Plus all the blue eyes," Kenzie said. "Yeah. It's been getting more and more obvious all day. And like Zoe said, I haven't seen even one Black student. Or is the term here is BIPOC? Or People of Color? I'm not clear on that yet."

Moriah rubbed her arm and looked away. "Let's get back to the dorm."

She didn't have to say she felt unsafe. Kenzie didn't feel safe either. People were apparently keeping the U.S.'s Reformative Eugenics Program going strong by marrying the "right" people, even though the program had ended over fifty years ago because it was finally ruled unconstitutional.

I've seen more Aryan people today than I have in my life. Anyone who claims the URA conquered the market on racism doesn't know what they're talking about. He wondered if the Anderson family was like that. If they were, that explained why Iona was messed up. *Ironic. She's from a family of mind mages, and she's the one who needs therapy more between the two of us.*

Once Kenzie and Moriah reached their dorm, they retreated into the welcoming A/C. The white walls, brown burlap carpet, and white Venetian blinds on the windows still struck Kenzie as institutional, but at least it was apartment-like. Kenzie enjoyed the idea of buying his own groceries and stocking the kitchen with food he selected for himself, with no one to bug him about the healthiness of his choices.

Kenzie and Moriah changed out of their uniforms and then dropped onto the couch and discussed their English classes. They only had to wait 15 minutes for Zoe Wang to rush through the door. Zoe changed out of her uniform and into a pair of jean shorts and a hot pink tank top. Her bleached blonde hair was pulled up into a high ponytail.

"Did you hear?" she asked as she flounced into the living room, a shopping bag in hand. "They can't find that weird man in the top hat anywhere. The police and campus security have done a sweep of the whole campus plus the surrounding area. Hours of security footage have been reviewed. But there's nothing. Just nothing."

"What?" Kenzie's arms prickled.

He peered out the window, but no one was walking on the sidewalk between the dorms.

"No, I hadn't heard." *Great. Just great. That crazy guy just vanished altogether.* "Did you find the hair dye I asked for?" He'd decided to follow suit after Moriah and dye his hair for the first time in his life.

Zoe opened the bag and pulled out a pack of four hair clips and a box of magenta hair dye. "Yep, here are your supplies. Since the campus is crawling with reporters, we might as well get to work. We have nothing better to do unless we want to go gawk at the camera crews."

"No thanks." Kenzie transferred to a kitchen chair.

He stared down at his bare legs. Although he loved having men's clothes, he felt half naked wearing nothing but shorts and a t-shirt.

"And, yes, save me. I've spent my entire life looking like a woman from the 1800s."

"I bet." Zoe got a towel and a comb, draping the towel over Kenzie's shoulders. Then she combed his hair. "I get why you don't want to wait one second more."

Moriah stood and crossed to the windows, hovering as if waiting for the man in the top hat to appear. She changed into an ankle-length khaki skirt, covering her legs. She wore a white button-up shirt with it.

"Are you sure about this, Kenzie? I mean, what about when you go home over Christmas Break? I can dye my hair black again, no problem. Blonde is easy to cover up. But magenta?"

"That's Winter Break here," Zoe said. "The U.S. has freedom of religion, so not everything automatically refers to Jesus."

"So does the URA," Moriah retorted. "We freely became a godly nation."

Zoe made an 'are you for real' face, raising her eyebrows, and let that one pass.

Kenzie was relieved that didn't turn into an instant fight.

"I'll tell anyone who asks I'm a college student from the U.S. visiting family. They can just suck it up." He crossed his arms. "They can't police what I do while I'm living in a different country."

Zoe set down the comb and picked up the box.

"All right. We'll bring you up to 2095 in an hour or less." She opened the box, pulled out plastic gloves, and slipped them on.

Moriah fell silent for a moment. Unfortunately, for only a moment. "I understand why you want to fit in here, but this isn't our home. Winterville is."

Winterville was just outside of Athens, Georgia, and near the University of Georgia, where Kenzie's mom worked.

"Winterville isn't the home of anyone female, BIPOC, LGBTQIA+, or disabled." Kenzie couldn't help spitting out what his mom had been saying all his life.

He had ample evidence for it from the news, his mom's contraband history books, rumors, and his own experiences.

Moriah folded her arms over her stomach. "Home is a complicated concept. But I feel like you know what I'm saying. If there's one thing I'm sure of after being here on the first day of classes, it's that we don't belong here."

Zoe gave Moriah the side-eye. "What do you mean, you dang murk! You took second place in the entire freshman class." She combed Kenzie's hair into sections and clipped them out of the way.

"There's more to life than test scores." Moriah's eyes filled with tears. "This is the real world. And I can't make it."

"Whoa, hey, girl, you can't crack up and ask for a white jacket on the first day of school," Zoe said. "Everyone's first day is rough."

Moriah wiped her eyes and watched Zoe pour one bottle of liquid into another bottle with a cone-shaped top.

"You'll get the hang of this," Kenzie said.

"I hope you're right," Moriah said. "In fact, I *have* to. My parents say I have to stay and represent the URA. My family finally earned a place in the Noble Three, and I have to prove we're worth our title. Besides, I have to show people that not all Christians are like the people who were protesting on campus today."

"Well, I'm staying even after I finish my degree," Kenzie said. "I'm never going back to a place that can't respect the most basic facts about who I am. You should consider doing that, too, instead of living your entire life being oppressed for being both a magician and a woman."

Moriah's lips stiffened. "I understand our differences. Your mom is telling you to do one thing, and my parents are telling me to do a different thing. The Bible says we both have to honor our parents. I still respect you."

Yikes, Christian throw-down boundary moment. Kenzie winced. "I still respect you."

Moriah sighed. "Thank you."

"I side with Kenzie," Zoe said, "but I get where you're coming from, Moriah. I wouldn't want to throw away all that hard work to become a Noble clan. Personally, I think both of you have it tough."

She shook the squeeze bottle and picked up a lock of Kenzie's short hair.

"My only goal now that I've finally made it to college is to have fun. Don't hate me if I throw crazy parties around here sometimes, okay? It's my dorm suite, too."

"Must be nice," Kenzie groused. *I'll be studying, not partying.*

Moriah shuddered. "Aren't you scared? My pastor talked about how dangerous college parties are."

She crossed her arms tighter over her stomach and hunched forward. "You could get drunk. Or worse, violated."

"Lucky for me, I don't have any pastors to scare me," Zoe said. "I've been a Buddhist since my mom remarried, but it's not like I'm super into it. Not like my stepdad is."

Moriah frowned. "Our job as magicians is to learn how to be Christ-like. Would Jesus spend his time at Jefferson-

Crowley University throwing wild parties? No matter what anyone tells you, what we do as magicians isn't any different from what Jesus did when he was alive, so we should follow his example."

Zoe wetted another lock of Kenzie's short hair and then secured it out of the way with one hair clip.

"How's it not any different? I thought Christians believed Jesus used God's power or whatever. Healing magic is science. You know, cell regeneration and stuff."

"But Jesus would have understood cell regeneration while he was doing his healings. God created us, and God knows everything."

"No theology talk." Kenzie's stomach twisted. "This day's been stressful enough already."

Moriah grabbed one of her blonde curls and worried it, wrapping it around her finger over and over. "God still loves you, you know, even though you don't believe in him right now."

"Then tell him not to send me to hell for cutting my hair, dyeing my hair, wearing pants, and using magic."

An hour later, Kenzie stood in front of the bathroom mirror. His hair, which was five inches long and styled to look windblown, shone magenta. According to school policy, he couldn't dye his hair unnatural colors, but he hoped the magenta was close enough to red for him to get away with it.

The boyish haircut transformed his face, making it appear more oval and less full-cheeked. He stared at his reflection, taking in the red men's t-shirt and men's jean shorts he'd bought. Hundreds of miles from home, in the pseudo-safety of the U.S. and beyond the clutches of the religious tyranny of The Apostles' Way, Kenzie finally relaxed into his identity.

I'm a man. Really, truly a man. I can never go home. They'll kill me.

Kenzie shot into the hallway and raced into the kitchen.

Moriah was there, but not Zoe. *Time to come out. I'm not holding in my truth any longer.*

"See? I don't look dumpy anymore. Also, I've realized something important about myself, and I hope you'll still be my friend once I tell you."

Moriah turned away from the window, her eyes wide and face pasty-white. Without speaking, she pointed at the ground below.

Kenzie dashed forward and peered outside. From underneath the oak tree in the dorm's side yard, a pair of red eyes stared up at them from the darkness, unblinking. Kenzie's breath stuttered. "What is it?"

As if the creature heard him, it stepped out from under the tree and into the glow of a security light. It was the seven-foot-tall man who had attacked the protesters. This time, he was wearing a solid red suit and a red top hat. His eyes appeared to be cartoonish white and red swirls. He still wore the red devil tail and held a pitchfork.

"He thinks he's Satan," Kenzie whispered. *Are those specialty contacts?*

The man lifted his hat to them, revealing slicked-back, short, black hair. The painted-on smile made him look maniacal. He spun on one heel, heading back into the darkness. Then he vanished.

Moriah sank to her knees. "What if he *is* Satan?"

Kenzie's heart pounded in his chest. *I finally make a break from The Apostles' Way by cutting my hair and wearing men's clothes, and the first thing that happens is that Satan shows up? Why? To show me I've fallen off the straight and narrow path?*

He felt his pulse in his throat as the fear burned through him, and the glass windowpane appeared too far away as his vision distorted.

Then he inhaled deeply. *No. I don't believe in God or Satan anymore. I have to leave these old ways of thinking behind.* Kenzie forced himself to focus on Moriah.

"Satan is a spirit—a fallen angel. He doesn't have a physical body." He set aside the fact he no longer believed in Satan so he could comfort Moriah. "And why, out of everywhere in the entire world, would he manifest himself here?"

With a sharp inhale to match Kenzie's, Moriah pressed her hand to her chest. "Right. Of course. That man is human. A powerful magician, but a human."

"Exactly." Kenzie pulled his phone from his pocket.

A webpage had been created by JCU to record potential sightings, and he posted to it, listing his dorm and the time.

"It's probably someone pranking us because we're from the URA. You know, like Iona Anderson. She's a mind mage. I wonder if she can do illusion magic. If she can, she could cast an illusion of that guy. We have to report it, but we don't know it was really him." *I'll just keep telling myself that.*

The door opened, and their final suitemate, Rachel Abrams, whisked in. She wore the skirt version of their black school uniform. Her hair was black, wavy, and held back from her delicate face by a purple headband. A frown pressed her lips into a line.

"Welcome back, fellow refugee." Kenzie decided some comic relief might be in order.

Rachel paused in the middle of the living room.

"Refugee?" Then her shoulders relaxed. "Oh. I get it."

She walked into the kitchen and glanced at Kenzie's hair.

"That looks good on you. But if you go home like that at Christmas, people might attack and beat you. Maybe even rape and kill you."

Kenzie clenched his fists. "I know I can't go home now."

From the floor, Moriah held up her hand as though wanting a teacher to call on her. "We saw Mr. Top Hat. Just now. He was outside."

"Mr. Top Hat?" Kenzie echoed.

"That's what other people are calling him," Moriah said. "I overheard."

Rachel stepped up to the window and peered out. "People were quick to stick him with a nickname. I don't see him. "

"He disappeared somehow." Kenzie crossed his arms. "I want them to catch him just so we can find out how he's doing that."

Rachel stared into the darkness. "I've heard that Japanese magic scientists have been working hard to make teleportation a reality. Maybe they've had a breakthrough."

"Shinrou Kitamori said they hadn't even teleported a fly yet," Kenzie said.

"How does he know?" Rachel asked.

Kenzie's brow furrowed. "Well, he told me after Strategic Magic that he's majoring in magic science research. If that's his major, why wouldn't he know? Besides, he also said Dr. Kitamori is his aunt. Magic Science and Application is her field. Shinrou could hear about new findings from her."

Rachel turned away from the window. "I guess so, but it could be a secret Japanese military project."

"Why Japanese?" Moriah stood and brushed off her skirt. "Why couldn't it be a secret Chinese military project?"

"Why are you so focused on Asian blame?" Kenzie asked, irritated.

Moriah held up both hands. "I'm not! It could be German or Australian or Canadian."

Rachel headed to the refrigerator and used the touch screen to search its contents. "For all we know, Top Hat is an alien from space and the U.S. government already knows and is refusing to stop him because they want to see what he does next."

"Conspiracy theorist," Kenzie teased her.

Rachel paused. "Okay, fine. I'm a little paranoid sometimes. Aren't you?" She opened the door and fished out a can of sweet tea.

"A bunch of bitter, middle-aged and old people have been chasing us around nitpicking the way we tie our shoes or the color of our barrettes or the color of our lip balm. Don't we have a right to be paranoid?"

Kenzie groaned. "Yes."

"Exactly." Rachel grabbed the stylus and scribbled *"more sweet tea"* into the refrigerator's grocery app.

"Just for the record, I don't actually think Mr. Top Hat is Japanese. Or an alien. I think he's American—as in, from the URA. I'd bet my entire jewelry collection that The Apostles' Way is involved somehow."

Moriah shared a look with Kenzie. "You mean the jewelry collection you don't have?"

"Exactly. Betting is a sin. If I bet something I don't own, then I'm safe, right?" Rachel swooped into the hallway, heading to her bedroom.

Kenzie watched her go. "Intense."

Moriah nodded.

"But she's been nice to me so far." She tugged on one of her curls. "You don't think she's right, do you?"

"About The Apostles' Way?" Kenzie snorted. "No way. John Paul Smith, Jr. secures his own personal magician to wear a devil's tail and wave around a pitchfork? Never. Besides, Mr. Top Hat attacked the protesters, not the students. Smith would want us students dead."

Moriah deflated like a shriveling helium balloon. "Well, you're right about that."

Kenzie wished he hadn't blurted out that the most powerful religious leader in the URA would hate Moriah, but the damage was done.

Zoe bounded into the room.

"Hey, let's watch a movie." She pointed at Kenzie's hair. "Girl, that looks awesome."

"Thanks." Kenzie flinched.

That'd be "man," actually. But should I really tell my

roommates I'm trans? I just met two of them, and Moriah is a hardcore Christian. It's probably not safe. He lost his nerve. *I can't come out yet. At least Mom accepts that I'm trans. Her PhD in sociology saved my ass.*

Moriah trudged toward her room. "I should do my homework."

"What'd I say?" Zoe asked Kenzie.

"Nothing. It's what I said about Smith." Kenzie shook his head.

"How do I explain to someone from the U.S. just how important and terrifying John Paul Smith, Jr. is? The closest thing I can think of is to say that if Smith decides he hates you, it would be like having CIA operatives out to assassinate you." He cringed. "Or the CIA, as it was portrayed in movies from the 1950s, anyway."

He knew that his knowledge of the modern U.S. was spotty at best. The URA only allowed music, movies, and TV shows from 1960 or earlier.

Zoe wrinkled her nose. "Ugh. You mean that religious freak that runs your country? All of us people in the U.S. know your president is nothing but a puppet. The so-called saintly Rev. Smith is, like, a second Hitler or whatever. But what does he have to do with anything?"

"He'd want Satan to kill us for being magicians." Kenzie stared out the bank of windows spanning their dorm suite's combined living room and kitchen. His gaze fell on the green oak leaves. "He's like the pope of The Apostles' Way, so anything he says goes. In our religion—my former religion— magicians are always evil."

"But it's all science!"

"Hey, you don't have to convince me." Kenzie excused himself to his room. He had to brainstorm paper topics for his Composition I class.

"Wait, so I'm watching a movie alone?" Zoe called. "Some roommates you are."

As much as Kenzie wanted to watch modern movies, his grades mattered more. Still, when he settled at his desk with his laptop, all he could think about were the red eyes staring at him from the darkness.

⚡

IN HER TINY BEDROOM, WHICH HELD LITTLE MORE THAN A TWIN bed, a nightstand, and a desk, Rachel Abrams inched off her black uniform blazer, cringing as her back pain pierced her like knives carving up her ribs.

Her first day of college was hell already, and the injuries she fought to hide had only made it worse. She draped the blazer over the desk chair and unbuttoned her white Oxford shirt, her gaze pinned on her black laptop on the desk.

Someone knocked on her door, and Rachel flinched at the sharp rapping.

"Give me a moment." She would have to force the blazer back on now; her shirt might be bloody.

Moriah flung open the door.

"Can I talk to you about Mr. Top Hat?" She halted, her stare snapping to Rachel's back.

Terrified and humiliated, Rachel's stomach roiled until she nearly vomited. Her whole body clenched, the tension vibrating through her arms and legs. *No! Don't see me! Don't see what he did to me.*

"I said give me a moment!"

"I'm sorry." Moriah stepped in and shut the door behind her.

"I think I misunderstood you through the door." She held out one trembling hand. "Let me help. I have healing spells."

Rachel froze, lungs constricted by iron bands of fear, and curled in on herself. No doubt a dozen red-brown lines discolored her shirt, her bandages unable to absorb all the blood. Her uncle's mottled face, his nostrils flared and blue eyes bulging, flashed through her mind.

His shouts rang in her memory: *Don't disobey your heavenly father, and don't disobey me! I'm the man you must answer to now, girl.*

"You can't. My—my father did it." The lie felt cold on her lips. *I must be a dark person to malign my father's name when he was the only light in my life.* "He's furious I attended a magician's university. He—he might come to visit over Labor Day weekend, and if the lash marks are gone…"

Moriah bowed her head, her brown eyes filling with tears. "Oh. He thinks magic is a sin. It's a wonder he didn't order you to go to a Bible college back home."

At Moriah's factual acceptance and tears of empathy, Rachel's horror eased until she could breathe properly. *You understand. You won't pity me.*

"He talked like that for six months." She superimposed her uncle onto her father. A pulse of icy guilt spiked through her for lying, but if her uncle discovered she'd bad-mouthed him, he'd kill her. "Then he changed his mind. But, you know, I'm still 'going to hell' for being 'dark and evil.'"

Moriah sniffed and raised her head, fire lighting her eyes. "Well, I should at least reduce the bleeding, even if I can't completely heal your back. That's what Jesus would do! He would never let you suffer. Your father should be more like Christ instead of being a Pharisee about this."

Rachel emitted a sharp, hollow laugh, as if her chest were made of tin. *If you only knew.*

"I guess. Help me get off the shirt and bandages, and then you can do a little. My healing magic is weak. I can't shape it well enough."

"Sure!" Moriah marched over to Rachel, her jaw clenched and hands fisted, a picture of determination and resolve.

Considering how shaken Moriah had been about Mr. Top

Hat, Rachel reassessed her suitemate. *You're terrified of violence, but you're determined to help. There's some grit deep down inside of you.* She inhaled deeply and braced herself for the agonizing process of working off the shirt and removing the bandages.

Once her back was bared, Rachel pulled her long black hair over one shoulder so Moriah could see the wounds and then crossed her arms over her breasts to hide them. She couldn't wear a bra in this condition.

"Please don't tell anyone. Definitely not Kenzie or Zoe. I can't handle anyone else knowing. It's just too…"

"I understand." Moriah's voice trembled, but the tenor sounded more like rage than fear, as if Rachel's being lashed offended her personal sensibilities.

Golden light filled the tiny room as Moriah cast her spell. Rachel bit her inner lip and fought to hold in tears of relief as the pain eased. An image of her uncle's fist raised, belt in hand, flashed through her mind, and she beat it away. *I don't want to see that! I don't want to be haunted by that memory.*

"I think people like your father are wrong," Moriah murmured. "Magic isn't a sin. Jesus gave us the ability to do miracles so we could heal people and deal with the harsh elements on our planet. Before Jesus left to go back to heaven, he said, 'He that believeth on me, the works that I do shall he do also; and greater works than these shall he do; because I go unto my Father.' It's right there in John 14:12, so people like your father shouldn't be so disapproving of magicians."

Rachel rested one hand on the white cinderblocks of her dorm room wall. The coldness of the rough, bumpy block seeped into her hand.

"I'm afraid my family doesn't agree. Then again, to them, religion is an opiate. They're addicted to it, to their supposed righteousness in following it. This world is nothing but suffering, so they pin their hope on a next life that doesn't exist. It's denial. Religion apparently started out as a way of showing respect for the dead, but now it keeps humans infantile, hiding in denial and telling themselves rosy stories of a nice little afterlife where nothing hurts."

"That's a terrible way to think," Moriah said. "You don't believe in God anymore?"

"No, there's nothing." Rachel traced the indented line of mortar between two cinderblocks.

The white paint had left it smooth. *Artificial smoothness painting over ugly gray. Artificial righteousness painting over ugly, evil hearts.*

"If there was a God, the URA wouldn't exist, and there would have never been a World War I, II, or III. Humans wage war out of their own dark hearts, and there's no God to waylay it. If he existed, he would have destroyed the world to stop all our evil."

"I can see why you would worry about that." The golden light vanished. "That's all I can do, or I'll completely heal you." Moriah stepped around to Rachel's side.

"After Labor Day weekend, let me heal it the rest of the way. Okay?"

Rachel gave Moriah a sad smile. *You're too nice for this world. I'm afraid it'll kill you.*

"All right. Once I'm sure there's no danger left, I'll let you finish."

Moriah patted Rachel's upper arm. "Good. Jesus doesn't want us to suffer. He wants our lives to be filled with love and hope and peace."

She turned and slipped out the door, apparently having forgotten her question about Mr. Top Hat.

Rachel stared at the door as Moriah shut it behind her. *Love, hope, and peace? I wish. It's better than the meaningless void we actually have.*

She walked over to the closet and pulled out her bathrobe,

but her thoughts diverted to Mr. Top Hat and his violence. *More violence for a violent world. No one wants that, but there's nothing I can do about it.*

Can I?

SEVEN

The following morning, Kenzie, Moriah, and Rachel walked together to Griffen Hall since they all had Energy Work I at 9:30.

Kenzie carried his backpack today, as well as his dad's Zippo lighter, which he tucked in his pocket. When he was six years old and discovered his first talent, pyrokinesis, his dad told him to always carry a fire source for personal protection, rules against minors casting magic be damned.

After Kenzie's father died, he carried his dad's Zippo in his pocket everywhere he went for years. Once telekinesis became his strongest talent, he thought that he didn't need to carry a lighter anymore, but his telekinesis had been next to useless against Mr. Top Hat. *I've got to fight with fire now.*

They arrived at Griffen Hall with ten minutes to spare. One of Kenzie's classmates from Magic Application II was in the lobby, the punkish Logan Steensen. Kenzie had learned from Zoe that Logan was as famous as Makari Idoni, except instead of winning the battle division at Nationals, he won the most controversial division: spirit summoning.

To most people in the URA, it was like saying he'd won

first place in talking to Satan. *I'm impressed he was so nice to Moriah and me.*

"Cool. We can handle that," Logan was saying to a short woman with slicked-back, black hair that curled upwards at her neck.

They were the only two people hanging out in the otherwise cavernous foyer with its hardwood floors and crystal chandeliers. They stood under a six-foot-tall painting of the black-haired Emily Griffen, the founder of the Griffen clan, and a clear donor to the university.

A girlfriend? Kenzie wondered.

The woman wore the black women's uniform with the pants, and she had both hands stuffed into her pockets. She had a dainty diamond stud in her nose.

Logan's gaze passed over Kenzie. He looked back at the woman as she spoke, but then he swung toward Kenzie. His eyes widened. "Whoa! Are you Kenzie Okuda?"

Kenzie had to laugh. "Yeah, I'm me."

He stopped by Logan, and Moriah and Rachel continued toward the classroom.

"You dyed your hair." A grin bloomed across Logan's face. "Looks deranged."

"I don't know if you'll get away with that color or not," the woman said, "but I hope you do. It's mythical."

"Thanks." Kenzie had never received compliments like these in his life. He had to remind himself "deranged" was a good thing in the U.S., but Logan's admiring tone went a long way in boosting his confidence.

Logan jabbed his thumb at the woman.

"This is Rikki Griffen. She's the president of the Noble 10 Student Committee. That's the committee that combines the Noble Seven and the Noble Three students on campus."

"Oh! Hi." *There's a whole committee just for that? Wow, everyone is really obsessed with social class around here.* "Speaking of school policy, aren't facial piercings banned?"

Rikki shook her head. "You can have up to two, but your jewelry has to be discreet. Nothing big or flashy. Just a tiny stud or a slender ring."

"Smoky." Kenzie turned to Logan and smiled. Just because he was a transman didn't mean he was a straight transman. "That's it. Find me someone who does piercings."

In the URA, women weren't allowed to have any piercings. They claimed jewelry went against the Apostle Paul's teachings in the Bible.

"Mythical! Sure thing. I'll help you with that." Logan flicked a wave at Rikki and headed down the hall with Kenzie. "So I heard a rumor that you energy-blasted Top Hat yesterday."

"I did, but it didn't do any good. He wasn't even singed. And seriously! How is he evading the police?"

Logan narrowed his eyes. "I know, I know. My dad and I video-conferenced about it for, like, four hours last night. He says no one has a clue and all the clan leaders are talking to each other about it."

"I saw Mr. Top Hat by my dorm last night." Kenzie pushed open the fire door and headed farther down the hallway.

Logan kept pace, his jaw clenching. "He followed you? Creepster. Do you think it's because you attacked him earlier and stopped him from killing the protesters?"

Kenzie hadn't thought of that. *I want it to be Iona playing a prank, but what if it is a psycho holding a grudge?* "Thanks for the credit, but I didn't. Makari Idoni and Shinrou Kitamori did."

"I believe you, but does Top Hat see it that way? If he's a misogynist murk, then he might blame you for standing up to him because you're a woman."

Actually, I'm a man, and there's no one in the entire world I can tell other than my mom. This really sucks. "I'm officially freaked out. Please stop."

"Well, Dad video-conferenced with the university

president this morning, and Dad said Mr. and Mrs. Idoni video-conferenced with the president yesterday. Toss in a few more clan leaders, and it'll be like an official clan summit. Don't worry. It's the Noble Seven's job to track down assholes like Top Hat and keep them from hurting people. The police might not be able to find Top Hat, but the Noble Seven will."

Kenzie relaxed at Logan's conviction.

"It's almost like having American royalty." They reached the staircase and headed up side-by-side.

What are the Noble Seven really like? Logan is being nice, but Iona is bullying me.

"Should I be intimidated?"

Logan snorted. "Nah. I mean, most people are intimidated. My dad's stonking powerful—a Merlin Class magician and all. But to me, he's just my boring old dad. And I don't go around bragging that I'm famous or anything."

Struck with a wave of relief, Kenzie nodded and tried to act casual.

"Cool." *Then I guess I can flirt with you and not offend you. If I can figure out how to flirt.* He didn't exactly have practice.

"Actually, I drive some of the other Noble Seven students here murky. They call my family stoners and ghetto and stuff, but it's not true. They say we don't 'live up to our station.' You gotta love that: 'our station.' They talk like they're 80 years old or something."

Kenzie laughed. "Well, aren't you supposed to be a prince or something? With nicely groomed hair and a $100,000 suit you wear every day when you're not in uniform?"

He opened the door as they exited the staircase. Their class was the first one on the right.

"Ha!" Logan stopped by their classroom door. "I haven't worn a suit in three years, and the last time I did, I looked like a butler. If you want a prince, go for Makari Idoni."

Kenzie grinned. "But I'm not royalty."

He swept into the room and sat by Rachel, dropping his

backpack on the floor by his chair. Rachel logged into her desk terminal and started reading.

Logan followed Kenzie in, smiling as well. Kenzie's pulse raced. *I flirted with him! I actually flirted with a guy. What if I went on a date? God, I wouldn't even know what to do. Maybe I should binge-watch more secular TV and get some ideas.*

Scanning the room, Kenzie distracted himself by seeing if Iona and her minions were present. The classroom itself was standard issue for the university: white walls, white tile floor, and a few steel accents. The institutional feel was broken only by the large bank of windows running down the left-hand side of the room. And there, in the back corner, at three of the steel computer terminals, sat Iona, Natalie, and Heather. *Ugh. Just great.*

The professor entered, a tablet in hand, her blonde hair pulled into a casual, messy bun that contrasted with her dark brown skin. She wore a white lab coat over her suit. A bindi decorated her forehead between her eyebrows, but instead of being a red circle, it was aqua. Kenzie had no idea what that meant.

The professor set her tablet on the podium and gazed at the students.

"Welcome to Energy Work I." She had a mild, lovely Indian accent. "I'm Dr. Taksande. The objective of this course is to fine-tune your energy control. Those who can master this skill can do things such as become powerful healers who can spare people from painful surgeries. However, the healing isn't limited to injuries. You can adjust the energy flow in people's bodies, preventing certain diseases from occurring, and prompt cell regeneration to stop cancers from forming."

Impressive. Kenzie wasn't interested in being a mage doctor, but he could imagine a future of less invasive medical care.

Eight years ago, when his father was diagnosed with cancer, they used a cutting-edge approach that combined prayer spells to activate his father's immune system, gene therapy, and, when those failed, surgery and chemotherapy. Dr. Taksande's lecture implied the treatment for cancer today had evolved past what Kenzie had witnessed.

An aching pulse of grief shot through his chest. His dad had been his best friend. His mom was great, but all the best years of his life so far were labeled in his mind "me and my dad."

"Also pertinent to this course is mind magic, such as telekinesis and pyrokinesis," Dr. Taksande continued. "Fine-tuning your energy control is necessary to move any object, but especially small or lightweight objects."

Kenzie relaxed. *I'm in the right place. This course should help me.*

"This course includes a lab from 2:00 to 4:00 every Tuesday," Dr. Taksande said. "Your syllabus is in your class portal. Read it for more details."

She gestured to the door. "Today I'll take you to the lab in order to introduce you to the course's basic concepts in a hands-on way. We're heading across the hall."

Kenzie grabbed his backpack and stood along with the other students. They filed out the door and into the lab, which was another spacious white and steel room with a large bank of windows spanning the right-hand wall. It reminded Kenzie of the science lab in his high school: two-person steel counters with a sink, microscope, and computer terminal. There was no smell of disinfectant, though: just a slightly dusty, plastic smell most classrooms had.

"Hey, sit with me." Logan stepped up alongside Kenzie. "I'll cut open a frog with you."

Kenzie grinned, the joke calling up memories of biology class. "Okay."

He followed Logan to a counter by the windows. A faint blush heated his cheeks. The feeling was palpable to him. *He asked me to sit by him. He's flirting back! Oh my God, what do I do?*

Moriah and Rachel sat at the counter in front of them. Rachel stared out the window.

Kenzie peered out as well. The angry crowd still stood clustered by the ruined dorm. It was too far for him to read their signs, but he could guess what they said.

"Those people still?" Logan groaned. "They need to get a life."

Kenzie was distracted from the crowd by Dr. Taksande's explanation of using visualization and mental focus to narrow the area of impact for one's energy. Dr. Taksande demonstrated the concept by using telekinesis to stack a collection of kids' ABC blocks and then set the class loose to try on their own.

While Logan and Moriah grabbed boxes of blocks from the shelves at the back of the room, Kenzie found himself staring outside again. So was Rachel. A news van had arrived, and now a limousine drove up, escorted by four black sedans. Their hoods shone like beetle shells, their windows darkly tinted.

"Someone's all fancy and important," Kenzie said.

Those four cars have to be the bodyguards for whoever's in the limo. He'd seen entourages like that on TV during coverage of political rallies.

"Must be someone from the Noble Seven," Rachel said.

The driver opened the door of the limo, and a tall, broad-shouldered man stepped out. He wore a white trench coat but no hat, which was backwards for the raging heat outdoors. His pale hair shone in the sun. The crowd cheered so loudly that it penetrated the classroom even with the windows closed.

Rachel gasped and stood. She pressed one hand against the glass and leaned forward until her forehead touched the window.

Kenzie's heart jumped. "Who is it?"

"It's John Paul Smith, Jr." Rachel's voice was a harsh whisper. All the color drained from her face.

Logan and Moriah returned with boxes of blocks.

"Smith? Really?" Logan set down his box and glanced outside. "Just what we don't need: the king of all far-rightwing nut jobs visiting our campus."

Moriah flushed and dropped her box of blocks onto the table. The unnecessary force made the blocks rattle. "Rev. Smith is not a nut job. I know he doesn't always say politically correct things, but he is a great man of faith."

Kenzie ground his teeth. "Like his faith that we shouldn't exist? Yeah. Great. The university president shouldn't even allow someone like him on campus."

"Oh, here in the U.S. we believe in diverse perspectives," Logan said, his tone ironic.

Kenzie turned to face him. "So you invite people who don't have them to come talk to you about being more bigoted? Or ask them to insult you to your face?"

Logan laughed. "Pretty much."

Rachel plopped back onto her stool as though her knees gave out. She covered her lips with her fingers.

"Not good," she muttered. "Not good."

Rachel's panic attack surprised Kenzie. *Why is she so afraid of Smith? Sure, he's terrifying, but it's not like he's in the room with us.*

Moriah squeezed Rachel's shoulder. "It's okay. It's not like Rev. Smith will be lecturing us or something. We didn't do anything wrong."

"In his worldview, the fact we exist at all is wrong." Rachel dropped her hand to her lap. "According to him, we're an abomination in God's eyes."

Moriah sank onto her stool and bowed her head. "I know. But we've accepted Jesus, so even the worst of our sins is forgiven. Rev. Smith is a great man, but if he still persecutes us after we accept Jesus, then he is a misguided man, too."

Rachel snorted. "'Misguided.' I don't think that word is sufficient."

Dr. Taksande walked over to their tables. "Don't get distracted. Those people will probably be on campus for the entire next week. They do this every fall. Ignore them. This isn't why you came to college here."

Rachel turned away from the window. "Yes, ma'am."

A whole week? Kenzie internally grumbled. He unloaded ABC blocks from the box. As of yet, he hadn't figured out how he would do the assignment, which was to rearrange the blocks in alphabetical order using energy alone. *My telekinesis is not that refined.* "Do you know how to do this?"

Logan settled by him. "Yep. No problem. One of my majors is energy work. What's yours?"

"I'm undecided." Kenzie made sure the blocks were mixed up well. "They have me doing general magic studies right now."

There was a mind magic major, but Kenzie thought it wasn't a good fit. He hadn't inherited telepathy or psychic empathy.

"I'm hoping one of these introductory magic classes will help me figure out what I want."

Logan held his hands over the blocks. "I'm sure it will."

Thin strings of blue energy extended from his fingers and lengthened until they touched the tops of ten of the ABC blocks. He moved his fingers as if he were typing on a keyboard. The blocks danced around each other, pattering against the table. Within a matter of moments, he lined up them up in alphabetical order.

Kenzie watched with awe. "I've never seen anything like that before. I've never even *heard* of something like it."

"I learned it from my grandmother." Logan grabbed

another ten blocks with light strings, arranged them, and then rounded up the final six.

Kenzie supposed he should expect nothing less from one of the Noble Seven clans.

"Cool. So are you going to be a mage doctor?"

"Nah. My other major is strategic magic, although everyone calls it battle magic." Logan released his energy strings once all the blocks were lined up. "I'm not really sure what I'll do career-wise because I don't want to be in the military. But if I went into the military, I'd want to be black ops."

Kenzie didn't know what to say to that. He couldn't imagine Logan killing people. However, he was saved from replying by a burst of voices. He glanced up. Half the students stared out the window, and they slowly stood.

"Now what?" Logan stood as well.

Kenzie looked out the window. There, in the quad in front of Griffen Hall, was Top Hat. He gazed up at the second floor, right at Kenzie's classroom, and held up his hand, wiggling his fingers in a wave.

Once again, he wore a solid red suit and red top hat, and his eyes were white and red swirls. However, his face was painted red as well, and his oversized smile was painted on in black. His devil's tail whipped back and forth as though it were real.

He took off his hat, revealing a bald head this time, along with a small pair of red horns, and he bowed with a flourish. Then he popped his hat back on and summoned a black pitchfork. Just like before, instead of seeming to create the pitchfork step-by-step like a regular magician, one moment there was nothing and the next there was a fully formed pitchfork.

"Dr. Taksande, call campus security." An electric surge of adrenaline shot through Kenzie. "The fugitive from yesterday came back, and he's armed."

Dr. Taksande ran to the window.

"He did?" She grabbed her cell phone from her lab coat pocket. "Everyone, stay calm. We're up here, and he's down there. Campus security will handle this emergency. Come away from the windows. We'll erect emergency barriers until security gives us the signal that it's safe."

Top Hat whirled to face a group of students approaching him on the quad and flashed toward them like a speeding car. He ran his pitchfork through a man and hurled him 20 feet across the grass. His body flopped end over end and landed hard, like a gymnast who couldn't stick the dismount at the end of a routine. The ugly, crumpled way the man lay on the manicured lawn brought Kenzie flashbacks of horror stories about school shootings. The cloudless sky poured sunlight on the motionless, uniformed man, its cheer glaring in contrast to his suffering.

For an instant, everything stood still. Shock wreathed the world in muffling silence. Then screams erupted in the quad. The remaining students ran. Kenzie broke through his paralysis and backed away from the windows, along with the rest of the students. Glowing blue barriers of energy a foot thick snapped into place over the windows. Kenzie turned toward the professor.

Dr. Taksande's hands remained stretched out. She lowered them. "Everyone follow standard emergency procedures."

Logan dashed for the door. "I gotta get down there!" He narrowly evaded Dr. Taksande's expanding barrier spell, slipping through sideways before she finished blocking the door.

"Logan Steensen, you will return to lockdown with the rest of your fellow students!" Dr. Taksande shouted.

"Noble Seven member! Can't!" he called from the hallway.

Dr. Taksande lowered her barrier spell, shut the classroom door, and erected a glowing blue shield over it again. She faced the other students.

"If we are attacked, you barricade yourselves under the tables, understood?"

Rachel stared out the window still, motionless as a doll. She didn't even seem to breathe.

Kenzie looked around in shock. *No Mariah.* He crouched, scanning for her. Moriah was already under the table curled up on herself, knees hugged to her chest.

He sighed. "Moriah…"

She squeezed her eyes closed and hugged her knees more tightly. "No. Not again. Not again. Tell me when it's over."

Several classmates, still watching through Dr. Taksande's barriers, shrieked. The barriers were translucent, so their professor couldn't actually stop them from seeing the scene below. Kenzie straightened and jerked toward the window. Four students now lay on the ground, crimson stains blooming across their white uniforms.

He's slaughtering them! Kenzie ran for the door and smacked his hand against the blue energy barrier.

"Let me out! What good does it do to hide up here? No one's been able to stop him, anyway." *If I'm going to die, I'm going to die fighting, not trapped in a classroom!*

Dr. Taksande marched over to him. "You are a student. It is my responsibility as a member of the faculty to protect you during emergencies."

Footsteps pounded in the hall. Then Logan opened the door and stared through their professor's energy barrier.

"Dr. Taksande, my dad ordered me by text message to bring backup, and I want Kenzie. She fought Top Hat once before and lived. I need her."

Dr. Taksande's nostrils flared. "I can't stop you, but I can certainly stop Miss Okuda from endangering herself."

"I waive my legal right to protection," Kenzie snapped. "Happy?"

His classmates screamed again and bumped into each other, reacting to whatever was happening in the quad.

Dr. Taksande faltered, glancing toward them.

Jumping on the opportunity, Kenzie smashed through her energy barrier, breaking the molecular bonds between the particles and sending them scattering like safety glass. He dashed out before she could fix the hole.

Logan sprinted down the hall and caught up with Kenzie, pacing him. "Stonking moves, gladiator. Now let's stop that murk."

"What will we do differently?"

"We grab him and hold him until the police arrive."

"But Shinrou Kitamori tried that."

"There will be more than one of us this time."

By the time they exited into the quad, a dozen professors and students were bearing down on Top Hat's position. A news crew hovered by the library, filming the incident and no doubt broadcasting it live.

Logan attached five blue energy strings to Top Hat and five to the pitchfork, yanking his hands as if the strings were lassoes instead.

"Double trouble, boil and rubble," Top Hat howled, thrashing. The pitchfork disappeared as if it had never been real.

Kenzie helped pin Top Hat's arms with his telekinesis, imagining a giant pair of hands crushed against Top Hat and holding the madman still.

"How is he this strong? It's taking two of us to restrain him." *Even if the Top Hat last night outside my dorm was fake, this one is real.*

Logan's energy strings broke. Unlike physical strings, they disintegrated into flickering motes of blue light and vanished. He reeled backwards and caught his balance. "Damn it!"

"I can't hang on!" Kenzie shouted.

Top Hat's force of will slammed against his invisible hands. His telekinetic barriers flexed. He poured in as much concentration as he could into the spell, but he knew another flexing motion like the first would buck him off.

Top Hat tore free of Kenzie's spell and raised his arms, leering in Kenzie's direction.

A blue energy sphere the size of a beach ball erupted across the quad and slammed into Top Hat. He hit the ground so hard dirt and grass sprayed six feet into the air and rained down onto the lawn.

Kenzie flinched and glanced over his shoulder just long enough to see Makari running toward Logan and his position.

For a moment, Top Hat screamed and thrashed, but then he hopped to his feet. There wasn't a mark on him. Somehow, not even his clothes showed damage. At the least, his clothes should have been set on fire or incinerated where the energy ball hit.

The sharp, icy burn of panic needled Kenzie's veins. *What is he?* He jumped backwards a foot. Every fiber of his being screamed that Top Hat wasn't human.

"Grab him!" Logan yelled. He flung out more energy strings, thin as piano wire and then broadening as they encircled Top Hat.

Kenzie imagined wrapping Top Hat in duct tape, forming a telekinetic cocoon. It seemed to work, but he sensed how fragile his spell was. He was too shaken to pour in the conviction he needed.

Top Hat cut Logan's energy strings with a slashing motion of his hand that simultaneously ripped open Kenzie's telekinetic cocoon.

Logan stumbled back. "Impossible!"

"Shit," Kenzie hissed through his teeth.

Makari ran up beside Logan. "Who *is* this guy? My blast alone should have killed him."

Logan threw out more energy strings, but Top Hat materialized his pitchfork and used it to cut them again.

"More like, *what* is this guy? And where the hell is campus security?"

Top Hat hurled his pitchfork at Makari.

The pitchfork crashed to the ground under an invisible weight.

Kenzie whirled. Shinrou stood twenty feet back, holding out one hand, palm down. He lifted his other hand and made a slamming motion. Top Hat crashed to the ground as well.

Four people from campus security, two men and two women, arrived. They were distinguished by black uniforms that were a cross between the university's student uniform and police uniforms.

"Everyone, clear the area," one man said, his voice booming in a magically amplified way.

Top Hat thrashed like an insect pinned to a board. "Corporous noctunous! Sixpence for your hate!"

"Great! Now how do we keep him from getting away?" Logan called to Shinrou.

"I don't have enough information," Shinrou yelled back.

"Clearing the area includes you," the man with the campus police said.

"I don't think that's a good idea," Logan said. "Shinrou Kitamori is holding Top Hat down."

"That won't be necessary." The campus police officer doing all the talking drew his wand, and the rest surrounded Top Hat's position. "Sir, you're under arrest."

"Watch out!" Logan snapped. "This thing isn't human. I'm Logan Steensen, and my energy strings failed to control this thing."

Top Hat jerked to his feet, tearing free of Shinrou's spell.

Bystanders screamed.

"Not again!" Shinrou shouted.

The campus police all drew their wands and opened fire on Top Hat with energy pellets in a rainbow of colors. Their marble-sized balls of energy barraged him, but they didn't even seem as useful as paintballs. They splattered into tinier balls and disappeared.

Top Hat summoned a new pitchfork. "A sixpence for your hate!"

Kenzie pulled his father's lighter from his pocket, finally remembering that he had it. *We have to hurt him somehow.* He flicked the lighter and snapped out his hand.

The tiny flame erupted into a three-foot-tall blast that shot across Top Hat's lower back. He roared, the sound deep and guttural. Kenzie flicked his fingers again, and flames spread up Top Hat's back and onto his shoulders. The scorching heat billowed out in all directions. Heat mirages danced in the air.

Top Hat burst into maniacal laughter. His tail whipped around his body, and he pointed the end of his tail at Kenzie. "A sixpence for your hate! A sixpence for your hate!" He vanished as quickly as an antique movie projector turning off.

Kenzie lowered his hand. *He really looked like a cartoon Satan—solid red and surrounded by fire.*

Even worse, Top Hat seemed unstoppable.

EIGHT

In shock, everyone stood still and silent. Then the man who was likely the campus security chief snapped, "Fan out! We'll find him and take him down, whether or not he's a monster. I don't believe in fairy tales."

The security officers dispersed.

Flames glowed from the grass near Top Hat's position. Makari extended both hands, and a car-sized mass of brown water appeared above the fire. Makari lowered his hands, and the water drowned the flames. Kenzie suspected Makari had summoned the water from the Ohio River.

A few lingering professors and students raced toward the injured students and enacted healing spells.

Kenzie pocketed his Zippo and turned toward Griffen Hall. Faces filled every window. He located his classroom and discovered Moriah's and Rachel's pale faces. *Good, Moriah's watching now.* He pointed at her and then at the injured students.

"Come on! You can do it." He doubted Moriah could read lips, but he knew the message was clear. If she didn't move, he'd text her.

Moriah bowed her head and left the window. Rachel remained, staring at Kenzie.

Assuming Moriah was coming, Kenzie turned back to Logan and Makari. "Are we sure this thing can't teleport?"

Makari ran his hand back through his red hair.

"I have no idea. Nothing about this makes sense." He paused, his fingers still in his hair, auburn tufts sticking straight up. "Good job with the fire."

Kenzie gave him a small smile. "Thanks. It's not an elemental spell. It's actually pyrokinesis. The problem is that I need combustion. I can't make something burn out of nowhere."

"No one could do that," Shinrou said, joining them. "And yes, good job."

He pointed to the impact crater from Makari's energy ball.

"That should have killed Top Hat, and Kenzie's spell should have incapacitated him. And yet he just vanished. I think we need to consider the possibility that Top Hat is a spirit."

Logan frowned. "But spirits are incorporeal. Your gravity spell wouldn't have worked, and Kenzie couldn't have set him on fire."

"You're a spirit summoner," Shinrou said. "What do you think of the theory that spirits materialize if fed enough energy?"

Logan snorted. "No way. Energy's still just energy. No matter how much energy you pour into something, you can't make it solid. If you add more lightning to lightning, it's still just lightning."

Shinrou held up one finger. "Unless, of course, the summoner overlapped it with a second spell every time, perhaps a transmutation spell. If you can fuse a spirit to something material, you could graft the spirit to a body."

Logan stared at Shinrou. "No wonder you're majoring in magic science research. And that's insane! I mean, you'd probably have to use a corpse and fuse the spirit to the corpse."

"That would have the highest chance of success," Shinrou said. "It would be kind of like a spirit possession, except it would happen because of a magician's spell and not because a spirit jumped into a live person's body."

"It would be puppetry," Logan said. "And since the spirit doesn't actually live in the body, it wouldn't react if the body were damaged."

Despite feeling overwhelmed, Kenzie wanted to stay in the conversation. "But the body wasn't damaged. Neither were the clothes."

"True," Shinrou said, "but that could be a matter of a simple illusion spell. And if the caster is a master of energy work, then repairing the damaged corpse would be easy. They could even slow down the decomposition of the corpse, especially if the body had already been embalmed."

Kenzie rubbed his forehead. "That's one hell of a magician. Merlin-class, definitely."

"Or an entire group of Merlin-class magicians," Makari said.

"Whoever it is, and however many of them there are, we need to find them," Logan said.

"Why was Top Hat made?" Shinrou asked. "That is the question we must answer if we want to predict when and where he will appear next."

"We might never know that," Logan said. "Crazy people don't have motives that make sense." He faced Makari. "I say we need to focus on being wherever Top Hat is and stopping him from killing people. Campus security can't do that. I don't even think the police could do that, and the National Guard isn't for magical problems. This falls on us students from the Noble Seven. Plus we have a few heirs from the URA's Noble Three going here."

Makari paled. He turned to Shinrou.

Shinrou frowned. "The clan leaders of the Noble Seven need to handle this. We need to attend classes and work on our homework. Fighting Top Hat is not our place unless he directly attacks one of us. I only stepped in yesterday and today because Makari did. That was his decision, and I wasn't going to let him do something that dangerous by himself. But our place is to attend our classes as if nothing is happening."

Makari nodded slowly.

Kenzie bristled. "As if nothing is happening? That's easy for you to say! Top Hat didn't show up outside *your* dorm and stare at *you*." He was now convinced that it had been the real Top Hat.

The way Top Hat laughed at me before disappearing, Logan has to be right. He is a psycho with a grudge.

"This thing, or whoever made him, wanted me to know he could get me any time he wanted me. That's not exactly going to make it easy for me to study."

Shinrou's expression turned intense, his brow furrowed and his face tight.

"Well, I can't argue with that." He whipped out his cellphone and tapped the touch screen, pulling up the official website for the university. "We need to keep posting our sightings to the student chatboard for the Online Commons. The campus police probably won't release information to us, and we need to track Top Hat's movements and see if there are safe routes we can plot across the campus—places where he doesn't show up."

Makari pulled out his phone, too. "I'm texting my dad."

"We can't just let our parents work on this alone," Logan said. "We've got to pitch in and help, especially since this is our campus."

Makari's jaw tightened. "Just a second. I'm texting my dad. Okay?"

He stared at the phone screen and texted with his thumbs. His phone let out a *pling* as he sent the message. The phone emitted a series of notes in a scale downward as his father responded.

"Ugh!" Anger flashed across Makari's face, reddening his pale cheeks.

He texted a response. *Pling.* Another musical scale followed. Makari shoved his phone into his pocket.

Shinrou gazed up at Makari, concern shining in his brown eyes. "What does your father want you to do?"

"My father says this is my opportunity to show what a Noble Seven heir is made of." Makari crossed his arms and glared at Logan's shoulder. "Count me in. We're going to protect our campus."

Logan gave Makari a sharp nod. "There! That's what I'm talking about."

"If that's your decision, I can't let you do this without me." Shinrou raised his fist. "Teamwork!"

Makari reached out with one arm and bumped fists with his best friend.

"I want to be on the team," Kenzie said, finding the right moment to speak up. "For all I know, Top Hat won't leave me alone because I've attacked him and hurt the pride of the person who made him. I'm not hiding in my dorm like a frightened victim. And the magician behind Top Hat knows where I live on campus, anyway. There is no hiding. I refuse to sacrifice my scholarship and go back to the URA, so all that's left is to fight."

Logan grinned. "You go, girl!"

Kenzie flinched and wished he could tell Logan he was a transman.

"Let's all trade numbers, then." Makari pulled out his phone again. For all that he'd been afraid and angry a moment ago, now he seemed calm. For Kenzie, he was difficult to read.

While everyone did that, Kenzie looked over at the injured

students, hoping to find Moriah. To his relief, both Moriah and Dr. Taksande were present and working now.

"Once Moriah's done healing people, you can try to recruit her. She's pretty shaken up, though."

Makari took Logan's phone and entered his number into it. "That's understandable. Someone who looks vaguely like Satan is trying to kill people all over our campus. Makes me wonder what John Paul Smith, Jr. is thinking."

"Huh?" Kenzie looked around. Smith stood on the steps to the library, arms crossed over his chest. A dozen security guards and people in black suits hovered around him. "I'm sure he'll tell the world Satan attacked this campus, and it was God's will."

Logan mimicked a retching sound. "The freak. King of the Murks."

Kenzie smirked at that.

Once everyone had traded numbers, Makari turned to Shinrou. "We better get back to English class. Neither of us can cast healing spells."

"Right." Shinrou headed off with Makari. "See you all later."

"See ya," Logan sighed. "My healing spells are weak, but I'll see if I can help, anyway."

"Okay." Kenzie watched Logan jog toward the nearest injured student.

"Kenzie Okuda!" Dr. Taksande called, marching his way.

He headed over to her, closing the distance.

"Don't run out on my class again." Dr. Taksande's brow furrowed. "Technically, no students should fight Top Hat, and attack spells aren't allowed outside of a class like Strategic Magic. Safety is campus security's job, although the professors may have to help in this case. I admit the Noble Seven students are trained from birth to see these problems as their responsibility, so it's hard to stop them. But you're a regular student, and we can't afford for you to get injured, or worse, killed. Let the adults handle it."

"Yes, ma'am." Kenzie felt the flash of cold pain, followed by the burning heat of humiliation. His cheeks stung.

"Thank you." Dr. Taksande headed toward Logan and the student he was working on. "Logan, I need to talk to you."

"I kinda need to concentrate," Logan muttered. A weak blue glow suffused his hands.

"You can't ask other students to place themselves in danger. You're not the head of your clan, and you don't have the right to recruit Kenzie or anyone else on this campus to help you perform your clan duties."

At hearing this, Kenzie turned and walked toward Griffen Hall, heading back to the classroom. His heart thudded with lingering embarrassment. Dr. Taksande sounded factual rather than angry or condescending, but Kenzie wasn't any less mortified.

He'd never been a troublemaker, and yet he was lectured on his second day of college. On top of that, his actions had gotten Logan in trouble, since apparently the right thing to do would have been to tell Logan he was staying indoors to play with toddler toys. *Let the adults handle it?*

At least Dr. Taksande wasn't saying Noble Seven students were adults and all the other students were still children. Dr. Taksande saw them all as children, regardless of their legal status.

However, reality pressed on Kenzie hard. *Dr. Taksande is in denial. Campus security can't handle it. This situation is already out of control.* And he burned to be a part of the taskforce Logan and Makari were forming. *If the Noble Seven is so great and there are enough of you on campus to make a committee, then where are the rest of them? I don't see any of them running out to help. Moriah may be scared, and she may be new to the whole nobility thing, but she's out here helping now that the danger is gone. You can't tell me she's the only noble student with healing spells. Damn it. Are we the "future of warfare," or are we a bunch of babies who adults are responsible for safeguarding? Are we the top twenty students, or are we helpless?*

With every step, he was working himself into a rage, and he knew from hard experience adults couldn't handle it when children or teenagers got angry. So until he could talk to Logan and Makari again without seeming pushy, given they both still thought he was a woman, he'd have to smother his feelings with the fire retardant of stoicism.

IN THEIR DORM SUITE THAT NIGHT, KENZIE, ZOE, MORIAH, AND Rachel piled onto the drab brown couch and chairs, all sipping on calming herbal teas as they talked about Top Hat. The tea was Zoe's idea. She brought a coffee maker from home that used pods of tea, coffee, or hot chocolate, given the university did not provide expensive, high-tech machines like food regenerators.

Instead of loading raw items into a food regenerator, the students had to *cook* if they didn't want to go to the cafeteria —or, in this case, use a lesser machine to make tea.

Moriah changed into a blue prairie dress, and she had her legs tucked beside her on the couch. She opted to sit there by Kenzie.

"It's just too scary. We're being attacked by an indestructible dead body?"

"It's just a theory right now. An unproven one." Kenzie had changed into another pair of jean shorts and his only tank top.

Instead of feeling half naked today, he felt more at ease as he adjusted to wearing men's clothes. Since the URA didn't permit women to shave, he didn't even have to grow out his body hair to look more masculine. Body modification of any kind was illegal unless it was strictly medical.

"Mr. Top Hat looked more like Satan today," Moriah muttered, staring into her mug.

From her chair, Zoe extended her legs and propped her bare feet on the coffee table. Like Kenzie, she wore a tank top and shorts, except hers were yellow women's short shorts.

"Well, he's not. Satan's not real." She grinned. "Too bad Top Hat looks like Satan. It would be much cooler if he looked like someone else. Thor, maybe? Ra? Anubis? Aphrodite? Oh, I know: Adonis!"

Kenzie laughed, shocked that Zoe could joke around. "Because it would be much more fun to be murdered by one of them."

"No one's actually died yet," Rachel said, staring at her tablet, which was in her lap.

Unlike the rest of them, she still wore her black school uniform, the version with the knee-length skirt. Kenzie wondered if the short length bothered her. If so, Rachel didn't show it. She simply donned opaque black tights to hide her skin and sat primly in her chair, her ankles crossed.

Moriah leaned forward. "Really? Thank the Lord."

Kenzie was surprised. "I just assumed…"

"Nope," Zoe said. "Despite the healing spells, all of them had to go to the hospital, but Top Hat's victims are alive. I heard all of them went home instead of coming back to campus."

"I don't blame them." Moriah bowed her head. "If my parents weren't insisting that I stay, I'd go home, too."

"You called your parents asking to go home, and they won't let you?" Rachel asked.

Moriah nodded without looking up.

Kenzie felt terrible. "I'm sorry. That's not right. You could always go home for a semester and come back when all of this is over."

Although he never even consider going back to the URA, Moriah had made it clear she felt safer there, and he didn't think it was right that Moriah's parents were cutting off her avenue of escape.

"They think it looks bad," Moriah whispered.

Zoe frowned. "Sounds like my parents. Appearances are all they care about."

Moriah raised her head with a startled look, her eyes widening.

"No, my parents really love me. It's just we have so much to prove. And if I can't…" Her face crumpled. "We'll lose our spot in the Noble Three. The Noble Three is only the Noble Three because we joined. Our entire *nation* is counting on me to—to—"

Kenzie slipped an arm around her. "Breathe."

Moriah took a deep breath. Then she spoke so quickly her words nearly ran together like one long sentence: "I just have to be like Jesus. He had the world depending on him, and he was man incarnate, and he got scared sometimes, but he never gave up, and he trusted in God his father, and he did what needed to be done."

"He also had twelve apostles and many more followers helping him," Kenzie pointed out, sidestepping the issue that, in his mind, this was all mythology.

Moriah was in crisis. He couldn't imagine what he would be feeling if his mother expected him to prove that he was one of the best magicians in the world, even though he was still a college freshman.

Rachel held up her tablet. "You will probably appreciate this."

She turned the screen around, revealing a frozen video of John Paul Smith, Jr. He stood in front of their library.

"You meant that sarcastically, right?" Zoe sipped her tea.

Rachel hit play.

Smith jumped to life on the screen. "Can we really say we're surprised that Satan himself would show up on the North American continent? Regardless of whether we're talking about the U.S. or the URA, or even Canada, there's a lot of moral corruption."

Zoe snickered. "Oh, yeah. Because nowhere else in the world has any problems."

"And, more than any other place, can we say we're surprised Satan himself has shown up at a university that focuses on degrees in magic?" Smith continued. "I'm told that fully 99 percent of the students here are magicians."

"It's not a hundred percent?" Moriah's forehead creased with confusion.

Zoe stifled herself with one hand clamped over her mouth.

"God has lifted his hand of protection from Jefferson-Crowley University." Smith's voice rose in volume; he was headed into preacher mode. He lifted his fist. "Our great God has looked down upon the wanton sin displayed so openly on this here campus, and he's passed judgment! Like in the days of Job, God has permitted Satan to have free reign, except instead of testing a faithful servant of God, Satan is here to punish the wicked on God's behalf!"

Kenzie's lip curled. "God can't just do all the punishing himself? You know, that whole burn in hell forever thing? Or that world-wide flood thing?"

"And so it has begun!" Smith lifted his fist higher. His voice reached a fevered pitch. "Satan has struck out at the faithless and the unfaithful, and because Satan is so wicked, he's even injured the faithful along with them. Beware, all you obedient Christians! This campus is not safe. Louisville itself may not be safe! Satan rages among those whose souls he has won to his side. Their hubris—thinking they can play God with their witchcraft!—matches his own great pride that convinced him he could steal the throne of heaven. And so he roams among them like a lion, striking out at will."

"Ah, turn him off!" Kenzie thunked his mug down on the coffee table.

Rachel tapped the screen, pausing the video. "We all knew he'd say that." She put her tablet to sleep. "I heard he was asked to leave campus before he started a riot, but he's staying at a hotel somewhere in Louisville."

"Too bad the U.S. didn't deny him entry," Zoe said. "I wonder if the Pope will come visit next."

She held up her hands as though gesturing to a banner.

"Pope Fabian II flies to Louisville, Kentucky, in order to see Satan with his own eyes!"

Moriah groaned. "Don't even joke about that. What we need isn't a flood of religious leaders. What we need is Jesus."

"Please tell me that was a joke," Zoe said.

The room fell silent. Moriah's hurt gaze, Rachel's frown, and Kenzie's wordless hugging of Moriah was the answer Zoe got.

"Oh my God," Zoe groaned. "Look, Top Hat isn't really Satan. We don't need Jesus. We don't need religious leaders. We don't need angry Christians picketing our campus. What we need is a good detective, preferably one who's a magician. This is a magician problem, and it needs to be solved by magicians."

"Well, two of our classmates in the Noble Seven agree with you." Kenzie filled them in on Logan and Makari's plan to form a student team. "And I volunteered to be on it. I'm not allowed to skip class, but I can still help."

"Good!" Zoe stood up and padded across the room with her mug, the brown carpet silencing her footsteps. "That sounds like sanity and reason to me. I might join."

"Makari and Logan were talking about having you join," Kenzie said to Moriah.

Moriah cringed and held up both hands. "No, I couldn't!"

Kenzie sighed. "We can't make you." He was disappointed, but not surprised.

Rachel's phone rang, and she jumped. She stared at it where it lay on the coffee table, its display lit up.

"You gonna get that?" Zoe returned with a steaming cup of fresh tea.

Rachel leaned forward in slow motion and picked up the phone. She swiped the screen to answer the call, but didn't speak. A male voice emerged from the phone, but without the phone on speaker, it was just a low, commanding drone.

Finally, Rachel replied, "No."

Another burst of talking commenced.

"I understand," Rachel said.

A few words followed, and then Rachel lowered the phone without saying goodbye.

"I have to go out for a while and help someone." Her voice sounded wooden. "I'll be back late."

She stood and headed for the door, her head bowed.

"Are you okay?" Zoe asked her.

Rachel didn't answer. She simply left.

"That's weird," Zoe said.

"That worries me," Moriah added.

Kenzie frowned, disturbed as well.

"What do you know about her?" Zoe asked.

"Not much," Kenzie said.

Moriah twirled a lock of her blonde hair around her fingers and looked away. "She's...very sad. I offered to pray with her, but that didn't do much good. She no longer believes in God. She thinks life is meaningless."

"Cheerful," Zoe grumbled. "Someone get that girl antidepressants."

It might come to a mental health intervention, but I don't have a clue how to do that. Kenzie thought of all the girls he'd gone to school with who'd committed suicide. It was a high number, despite sermons claiming that suicide was a sin. Boys committed suicide, too, but the suicide rate for girls in the URA was four times higher than for boys.

Of course, the suicide rate for transgender teens in the URA was sixteen times higher than for other at-risk groups.

That was one of the many reasons his mom was desperate to evacuate him, and why no matter what kind of freakish and dangerous things happened at JCU, his mom texted him earlier and urged him to find a safe way through the situation and stay in the U.S. As a result of her plea for him to stay safe, he hadn't told her about the taskforce or his determination to be on it. If she didn't know, she couldn't worry.

RACHEL WAS STILL GONE WHEN EVERYONE WENT TO BED. KENZIE was the holdout who had stayed up studying. He stumbled his way through his night routine in the bathroom and went to bed at midnight.

Shortly after 1:00 AM, the suite door opened and then slammed shut, waking Kenzie.

He rolled over and faced the dorm's white cinderblock wall. *Rachel? It's got to be.* The image of her face when she left came back to him. *She didn't have to go help anyone. She got in trouble for something. Does she have relatives here in the U.S.? Why would they be angry with her?*

Having no answers, Kenzie slipped back into sleep.

NINE

Kenzie's goal for college was to sleep in until at least 8:00 every morning. Therefore, when shrieks and laughter erupted outside the dorm at 7:12 AM, Kenzie was furious. He sat up with a groan.

"Shut up, you idiots. The sun's barely up." He climbed out of bed and peered through the blinds.

A few students ran through the grass. More shrieking and laughing followed. He would have assumed it was Top Hat attacking again, but the laughter spoke of excitement, not fear.

Kenzie headed out of his room and into the kitchen area, looking out the bank of windows there. Someone, probably Zoe, had pulled the blinds up so the room would be sunny and bright. A row of redbrick dorms, intersecting sidewalks, and green grass met his inspection, along with a towering oak tree. A cardinal flew from the tree, knocking two leaves down in its rush. It seemed ordinary enough.

Then, ambling into view on the sidewalk between Kenzie's dorm and the backs of three others, was Jesus Christ.

"No," Kenzie whispered.

I'm hell-bound, after all. The weight of God's disapproval of and disappointment in Kenzie pressed down on him. His body flashed cold, as if he was flash frozen.

Then sanity broke in. *No, it's just a prank.* Kenzie slumped with relief. *Don't scare me like that, you assholes. You might think it's funny, but I have to live with this garbage in my brain. Oh, God. I hope Moriah doesn't see this.*

The brown-haired man with a beard walked surrounded by students in uniform and a few adults, smiling and making grand hand gestures. His hair was shoulder length, and his beard was short. He wore a flowing white robe with a maroon sash hanging diagonally across his body from one shoulder. The students held up their phones, no doubt recording footage and taking pictures.

Zoe stumbled into the kitchen wearing a red pair of men's boxers and a white men's undershirt. Her blonde hair was falling out of a messy ponytail, and her almond-shaped eyes were only halfway open and looked glazed.

"What's all that noise?"

"Jesus H. Christ," Kenzie said, deadpan. "On a pogo stick."

"What?" Zoe scrambled over to the window.

"I'm joking. It's some media stunt." *One that gave me a panic attack.*

A long, low groan escaped Zoe. "This is awful. It's going to be a raging media circus here for sure. It was bad enough already! But Jesus here to fight Satan? This is ridiculous."

"What did you say?" came a thin gasp.

Kenzie and Zoe turned. Rachel stood in the living room. She wore a lacy black nightgown that covered her entire body and included a high neck. Her black hair hung around her in tangled waves.

Kenzie felt glad that his mom had let him wear nightgowns that looked like oversized t-shirts instead of dresses from 1890. "Someone is outside dressed up like Jesus."

Rachel's lips parted, but no sound emerged. She stumbled over to the window as though her knees were failing her and stared outside. Jesus H. Christ turned the corner and headed toward the classroom buildings.

"Not good," she whispered.

"You're telling me!" Zoe sauntered over to the refrigerator and pulled out a carton of orange juice. "But maybe we can all laugh about this someday. Or maybe someone will make a video game of it: Jesus H. Christ vs. Top Hat Satan!"

Kenzie laughed. "I want to see that. The first level will be on the quad and the second level inside Griffen Hall's magic sparring gym."

Rachel staggered to the kitchen table and sank into a chair as though she feared she would shatter like fine china.

"It won't be so funny if a fight breaks out between the two spirits."

"You don't think it's just a media stunt?" Kenzie leaned against the window and crossed his arms. He wore his first men's PJs, a red t-shirt and shorts set. "Top Hat isn't really Satan, and that is definitely not Jesus."

Rachel remained grim, her eyes narrowed and lips pinched. "If they're spirits summoned by opposing magicians, they'll attack each other."

"But if it's the same magic, then doesn't the same person have to be responsible?" Kenzie asked. "It's magic no one else knows."

Rachel looked away, staring at the floor, the black curtain of her hair falling over her face.

"Maybe 'Jesus' is a man in a costume. You're right. I'm making too many assumptions."

Zoe plopped down at the table and drank straight from the juice carton.

"As long as they only attack each other, it'll be a like a demolition derby. But instead of monster trucks, we can have monster spirits. Or corpses. Or just monsters. Too bad

Moriah's missing all this. She was the one who wanted Jesus to show up."

Kenzie pushed away from the window and fished through the cabinets. Someone loved chocolate. Besides a tub of cocoa and a bag of chocolate candy bars, there were prepackaged brownies, fudge swirls, fudge cakes, chocolate-covered peanut bars, and chocolate chip cookies.

"Do we own anything that isn't junk?"

The door slammed open, and Moriah raced in. She wore a floor-length denim dress instead of her uniform. "Did you see? Did you see? Jesus came! He really came!"

Zoe and Kenzie stared.

Rachel slumped. "If Top Hat shows up…"

"Jesus will paste him!" Moriah clasped her hands in front of her chest and smiled.

"Level one," Zoe intoned. "Jesus pastes Satan out on the quad."

Kenzie needed the crazed glow to leave Moriah's eyes.

"Please remember that Jesus' Second Coming will be announced with trumpets and angels, and he'll appear in the sky. Even if we say that World War III was the Battle of Armageddon, we still don't have the other events, like the Rapture, and the Antichrist hasn't come."

"Unless he's John Paul Smith, Jr.!" Zoe piped up.

"And we don't have the one world government and the one world currency yet, either," Kenzie continued. "Or The Beast. Or—"

Moriah held up both hands. "Okay, okay. You're right. All the signs and precursors prophesied in the Bible are missing. But this guy is even speaking in Aramaic!"

"We're in the U.S.," Zoe said. "Why wouldn't he just speak English? Or, failing that, at least Spanish? It's Jesus, right? He should be able to speak any language on Earth or whatever."

Rachel took a deep breath. "It's either a media stunt or a

spirit summoning. If it's the latter, we really need to stop the caster before Top Hat shows back up."

Moriah recoiled, her brow furrowing. "But what if Jesus came to save us from Mr. Top Hat? We can't fight that creature on our own. And how could you believe God would allow some spirit to falsely use Jesus' image?"

Back in his bedroom, Kenzie's phone rang, and it was the ringtone he assigned to Logan when they traded numbers the day before.

"I'm betting that's the Noble Seven jumping into action." He raced into his bedroom, irritated at having left his phone on the nightstand.

According to the display, Logan was sending a holographic video feed. Kenzie accepted it, and the screen projected a 3D version of Logan's face. He looked similar to Zoe: half awake, his spiky hair half mashed and half tousled.

"Have you seen this bullshit?" Logan turned his phone so the camera pointed away from him.

The camera tried to focus on his windowsill, and then it refocused on the people passing on the sidewalk below his dorm window.

"Jesus H. Christ," Kenzie said, deadpan again.

Logan laughed. *"Oh, man. Good one."* He turned the camera back to himself. *"We've got to cut to the chase now. I'm going to summon a spirit myself and start asking questions. I assume you want in on that action."*

Kenzie wasn't sure whether to be scared out of his mind or excited about an adventure. "Sure do."

"Invite Moriah, if you think she can handle it. My dorm is 122-E. Co-Ed visiting hours don't start until 8:00, so you don't have to kill yourself getting here."

Kenzie checked his activity tracker. 7:31. "Gotcha." They hung up, and Kenzie returned to the kitchen.

Moriah had settled at the oak table and was eating a chocolate donut. A whole bag of them sat in front of her.

"All that chocolate is yours?" Kenzie asked.

Moriah nodded, eyes wide and childlike as though she expected to be chastised.

Kenzie glanced her over. "You can't weigh more than 100 pounds. How can you eat all that chocolate and stay so skinny?"

"A five-mile run every morning," Moriah said. She stuck one foot out from under the table, revealing a pair of well-worn blue sneakers.

"In a floor-length dress?" Zoe asked.

Kenzie walked to the refrigerator and rummaged through it, locating an apple. "That's the URA for you."

Moriah snagged another donut. "I couldn't possibly exercise while showing my legs. That would be a temptation to men."

"That shouldn't be your problem," Zoe said. "You should have a right to look cute without guys getting handsy."

"Women's bodies make men think lustful thoughts," Moriah said.

"Yeah, I know, but they should be able to keep those thoughts to themselves," Zoe said.

Kenzie intervened with a topic change. "Moriah, Logan's invited you to the first student Noble Clans meeting. It's at 8:00 in his dorm."

Moriah swallowed a mouthful of donut and stared at him. "A men's dorm? I can't."

"It's not like you'd be alone," Zoe said.

"What is the meeting about?" Rachel asked.

"Logan's going to summon a spirit and question it." Kenzie found peanut butter in one cabinet and got a knife. *No bread. Okay, peanut butter-covered apple slices, then.* He wrote "bread" on the grocery list app.

Moriah lowered the half-eaten donut. "Kenzie! Summoning spirits is a sin."

Zoe stood. "I wanna go!"

"Why?" Moriah gasped.

Zoe held up one finger. "I took third place in spirit summoning in the National High School division. I'm going."

Moriah squeaked like a toy mouse. "*You* summon spirits?"

"I intend to make a career from summoning spirits." Zoe grinned. "That's why I'm majoring in energy work. It should help me."

"I'll pray for you."

Zoe just laughed.

Moriah crumpled the top of the donut bag in one hand. "I'm going to find Jesus, and I'm going to join him. If I were you, I would consider repenting now that Jesus has arrived. The Bible warns against summoning spirits." She stood, finishing her donut, and marched toward the door.

"I guess we'll see you in class," Kenzie said. He couldn't think of anything else to say to that.

Moriah turned toward Kenzie with a strange expression. "Class? Don't any of you understand? Jesus has come."

Kenzie wanted to take Moriah by the shoulders and make her sit back down, but he wouldn't patronize Moriah that way. "I thought you agreed it's not the real Jesus."

Moriah scowled, her face reddening. "I don't know why the Bible didn't prophesize this event as happening in this way. I can't explain it. But I feel in my heart that Jesus has come, and the Holy Spirit is telling me to be with Jesus. If you change your mind, I'm sure Jesus will welcome you." She ran out the door and left it hanging open.

Rachel rubbed her temples. "Don't judge Moriah too harshly."

Zoe made a mock innocent face. "Who? Me?"

Kenzie sighed. "Moriah is...All her life, she's been trained to be this way. It's not her fault. Her world is church services, youth groups, and Bible summer camp, not to mention volunteering in soup kitchens and practicing the gifts of the spirit, like speaking in tongues and prophesy.

Rachel's right. This is what The Apostles' Way does to people."

Walking to the door to shut it, Kenzie held back from repeating verbatim one of his mother's favorite lectures on historical context, but he couldn't help dwelling on it.

Before the Second Civil War, The Apostles' Way was called ALS—Apostles of the Last Supper. ALS distinguished itself from the other branches of Christianity by bringing back Apostles and teaching people to hear prophecies and receive visions from God. During the Second Civil War, ALS split into two sects. In one of them, John Paul Smith, Sr. became a Super Apostle. Then he took over the Rebels and led them.

Once the Second Civil War was over and the Rebels had won, he cut the URA off from the United States, including going onto its own power grid for electricity and making its own currency.

Kenzie shut the door and stared at its bland white paint. *I got a history lesson in the truth thanks to my mom, but most people from the URA are like Moriah: They've never heard the truth about their own religion. Back in the old days, some Christians didn't even consider ALS Christianity, and that was back before it split into two sects.*

Now the U.S. might have to face The Apostles' Way and its influence, because John Paul Smith, Jr. is here in Louisville and will not fail to react to Jesus' apparent presence on this campus.

Kenzie couldn't think of anything he wanted less.

AT 7:58, KENZIE AND ZOE GRABBED THEIR BACKPACKS AND walked to the redbrick dorm numbered 121.

Just like the women's dorms, each unit was three stories high and had two suites per level, with a staircase between them. They climbed the concrete stairs to Suite E, which was on the third floor, and knocked on the door.

Kenzie wore the black pants uniform, which was the only style he'd agreed to purchase, while Zoe had opted for the white skirt uniform today. The skirt-based uniform looked nice, even though Kenzie didn't want to wear it. The knee-length skirt was pleated and flared outward. The blazer had wide lapels and a fitted waist, and the hems flared stylishly. For the white uniforms, black piping outlined the breast pocket and hems. Still, Kenzie's uniform was snazzy, too, with its white piping.

All the uniforms had Jefferson-Crowley's school insignia on the breast pocket of the jacket: a shield over which a sword and a wand were crossed. The shield was sectioned into corners, each containing the symbol of an element: fire, water, earth, and air. A golden chalice was in the middle of the four quarters.

Zoe patted her blonde hair, which she pulled into two pigtails. Apparently, pigtails were in style in the U.S. "What do you think? Do I look okay?"

"Mythical," Kenzie said. "Why?" He hoped Zoe didn't have a crush on Logan, and his stomach clenched at the thought.

"Makari Idoni will be here, right? He's totally hot."

Kenzie relaxed. "True. And it looks like over half the women on campus agree with you."

In the cafeteria the night before, Makari and Shinrou were once again surrounded by women.

Zoe twirled, her skirt flying up two inches, then posed with one hand on her hip. "I've got an edge. I actually share classes with him."

Logan opened the door and smiled at them. His spiky brown hair had been fought into its usual fashionable perfection, and he wore the black university uniform, the blazer unbuttoned to reveal the white Oxford shirt underneath.

"Hey, Zoe." Logan stepped back so they could enter.

Kenzie had texted Logan and secured approval for Zoe's attendance, so Zoe's presence was no surprise. "I remember you took third in spirit summoning at Nationals."

"Yep!" Zoe bounded into the living room like an excited puppy. "And I've heard *all* about you."

Logan grinned. "Only the bad parts are true."

Kenzie laughed as he followed Zoe inside. Makari and Shinrou, who both wore their white uniforms today, sat on the couch.

"Hi, I'm Zoe." Zoe waved at them.

"I remember," Makari said, smiling.

Makari's reply made Zoe glow, but Shinrou glanced down at his lap, where his hands were folded, as if Zoe's flirting bothered him. *Wait,* Kenzie thought. *Is Shinrou in love with his best friend? Or are they a couple?*

Logan grabbed the coffee table, pulling it over to the wall. "Okay, let's get to work."-Next he picked up a box from the table and then knelt on the thin brown carpet.

Kenzie watched him open the box with anticipation and a little thrill at witnessing something forbidden.

"Yes, how does this work? I don't believe the rumors about people like you summoning demons and making contracts written in blood."

Glancing up at him, Logan snorted. "Blood is a terrible idea as an ink substitute on a contract. It's biodegradable."

Makari chuckled.

"Okay, seriously, though," Logan continued, "all magic is bound by the laws of physics, but no one quite understands the science of spirit summoning yet."

"Exciting, right?" Zoe's brown eyes lit up. "How do spirits exist? What are they? Where do they live when we're not summoning them?" She spread her hands wide. "No one in the world knows the answers to any of that!"

Kenzie set his backpack on the floor, dropped onto one brown chair, and watched Logan set out a cloth bag, four brass bowls, a bag of sand, a red votive candle, and a box of incense cones.

"You don't know how it works, but the rituals you do make the spirits appear?"

"Well, the rituals help us concentrate, if nothing else." Logan opened the cloth bag and poured out little wooden tiles with marks on them. "Scientists have proven the rituals aren't necessary, but my family prefers the rituals, anyway. The ritual helps us focus and concentrate."

"What do those symbols mean?" Kenzie asked.

Logan held up one tile, which had a slanted *F* on it. "These are Nordic runes." He formed the rune tiles into a circle.

"That looks Wiccan, though." Zoe leaned against the bank of windows.

"Our family's Neo-Wiccan. We follow the Norse deities. They aren't spirits to us. They're divine."

"I love the Norse deities," Zoe said with a beaming smile.

"What does your family say about the spirits?" Shinrou asked. "What's their theory about what the spirits are?"

"We don't have a consensus. Several of us have asked the spirits themselves, but we get all different answers." Logan didn't seem bothered by this.

All of Kenzie's arm hairs bristled. But despite his initial surge of fear, he felt the longing for real divinity that had haunted him ever since he'd lost faith in Jesus and God. *What does a higher power look like? Is it possible to summon a deity? God and Jesus don't show up on command. But since they aren't real, how could they? Would a real deity care about their people?*

Then he realized Logan and the rest of the Steensen clan had merged science and religion. He was so deeply envious it burned in the pit of his stomach like he'd swallowed boiling coffee.

Logan pulled a compass out of the box, checked the cardinal points, and then set a brass bowl at each cardinal point on the circle. He poured sand into two bowls and put a brown incense cone on the sand in one. After grabbing a water bottle from the end table, he poured water into a third bowl and placed the red votive into the fourth. Finally, he lit the incense and candle.

"This all represents the elements: earth, air, water, fire."

"Got it." Kenzie glanced at Shinrou and Makari.

Shinrou leaned forward, elbows on knees. Makari reclined with his head on the back of the couch, one arm resting on the couch arm, as though he'd already seen this a million times.

Next Logan pulled a small dagger from the box.

Kenzie flinched. "A dagger?"

Logan faltered, concern knitting his brow. "Don't freak out. It's a ceremonial dagger. It doesn't cut anything. You use it to help visualize things and focus your concentration on your magic. You know, like a wand."

No bloodletting. Kenzie took a deep breath. "Sorry. There's a lot of propaganda about witchcraft and worshipping Satan back in the URA."

"It's okay. I'd rather you ask me questions so I can explain the truth." Logan sat down inside the circle by the candle. He gestured to the circle of rune tiles. "Don't disturb the sacred circle. According to the old rituals, it contains the spirit, so it doesn't, say, gallop across campus and stab people with pitchforks. Not that the spirit I'm summoning wants to do that."

Kenzie cringed. "Right."

Logan picked up the dagger and drew a clockwise circle in the air. Then he pointed the dagger at the center of the circle and closed his eyes.

For several seconds, nothing happened, but Kenzie assumed Logan was casting his spell. Then a diffuse white glow appeared in the circle. After several seconds of light, a translucent man around six feet tall popped into the circle. He brandished an enormous war hammer in his right hand. His long, blond hair hung to his waist, and he wore a helmet and a mix of leather armor and chainmail. Goat horns mounted the helmet.

Kenzie gaped. It had looked just like what he imagined teleportation would look like. *And it's similar enough to the way Top Hat appears and disappears that it means Top Hat is definitely a spirit.*

Logan crossed one arm over his chest, his hand fisted in a salute. "Great Thor, thank you for answering my petition and joining us today."

"Greetings, Great Thor!" For her position by the window, Zoe grinned and bowed.

Shinrou sat straighter and folded his arms over his chest with a small frown, examining Thor without comment.

Makari watched with a casual expression, still laidback, his legs sprawled out straight.

A skyscraper of Lego blocks seemed to topple in Kenzie's chest. He felt so jumbled up on the inside. This human-sized man in armor seemed too small and medieval to be a god.

Part of why Kenzie stopped believing in Jesus was that it made no sense for deities to deign to be incarnate. Disappointment and suspicion warred with how much he already liked Logan. *Logan believes this is a deity?*

Thor peered at the group and then inclined his head in what appeared to be a greeting.

"We've encountered a problem," Logan said. "Two other potential spirits have shown up. We're not sure what they are, but they could be spirits attached to reanimated corpses. One has attacked twice and nearly killed almost a dozen people. We're asking you for some insight and direction."

Thor cocked his head to the side, as though listening to something far away. His form wavered. Logan closed his eyes and pointed the dagger at the circle, apparently supplying more energy and concentration to the spell.

Once Thor's form stabilized, he straightened his head and began speaking. However, no sound emerged, and since

Kenzie couldn't read lips, he had no idea what was being said. Logan kept his eyes closed, so Kenzie assumed Logan didn't need to read lips to receive the message.

When Thor stopped speaking, Logan opened his eyes. "Thank you for your wisdom and assistance, Great Thor."

Thor inclined his head.

"May I ask a question?" Kenzie asked.

Logan glanced at him. Thor's form flickered like a candle flame. "Sure."

"I've never seen a spirit before. What happens if I touch Thor? Would I feel anything? Would I be struck down for my insolence?"

"You would feel something, and you won't be punished if you ask Thor's permission first," Logan said. He addressed Thor. "Kenzie knows nothing of you. May she touch you?"

Thor's lips soundlessly moved, and he extended his hand.

"You may," Logan translated. He grinned. "Awesome! It's a great honor."

"What about disturbing the circle?" Shinrou asked.

Logan shrugged. "If Thor gave his permission, then don't worry about it."

Kenzie stood, edging forward without disturbing the rune tiles, and touched his hand to Thor's. His fingers passed through. When they did, he felt something like a powerful static shock, and he recognized the magical energy as Logan's. He yelped and drew his hand back. Just in case Thor was real, he bowed.

"Sorry! Thank you for the honor." His fingers still tingled. Thor inclined his head again and vanished. Logan drew a counterclockwise circle in the air and then blew out the candle.

Logan turned to Kenzie. "So? What was it like to touch Thor?"

"Honestly, I don't know. I was only touching him for a moment before my hand went through, and then I got shocked by your circle. At least, I'm assuming that's what it was. The energy felt like yours."

"I've done that before. Yep, the circle is made out of my energy."

"I couldn't hear anything Thor said," Shinrou said.

"That's because he doesn't have a physical body," Logan replied. "You wouldn't hear him unless a high priestess or high priest invoked him—as in, let his spirit borrow their body temporarily."

Although he was afraid to hear the answer, Kenzie had to ask. "Have you done that?"

"No way," Logan said. "I'm not advanced enough yet. I've seen my dad do it, though, with Odin."

Kenzie had no idea how to feel about that, either. Christian preachers didn't invoke Jehovah to possess their bodies and speak, or at least not in The Apostles' Way. Kenzie hadn't been allowed to learn much about other Christian denominations.

Shinrou still wore a little frown and kept his arms crossed over his chest. "What did Thor say?"

Logan sighed. "It's complicated. Top Hat and Jesus H. Christ aren't what we think. They aren't humans, but they aren't spirits being controlled by a puppet master-like magician. They aren't reanimated corpses, but we're right that they have some kind of physical body."

Shinrou flopped back against the couch. "We need to get closer to one of them and touch them. Jesus H. Christ seems the safer one." His brow furrowed. "Why the *H*?"

"It's a joke based on the way some people cuss," Kenzie said. "Instead of simply yelling 'Jesus Christ!' when they're angry, some people toss in an *H* like a middle initial. I have no idea why."

"Ugh, English is difficult."

"You speak it very well," Makari reassured him.

That appeared to appease Shinrou, because his brow

smoothed out. "No, not at all. But I am determined to learn more. Well, I'm going to touch Jesus H. Christ. I need more data."

"Oh, yeah, just walk right up and touch Jesus." Zoe leaned against the window, crossing both her arms and ankles.

Kenzie rubbed his face with both hands. "She's right. The campus police are probably already involved."

"I'd like to see the campus police try to stop people from getting close to Jesus," Logan said. "People are gonna go wild. I'm sure Jesus H. Christ's presence here has already been announced all over social media."

"People will fly in from all over the world to see him," Zoe said, "either to verify whether or not he's really Jesus or because they've already made up their minds that he is the real Jesus."

Logan began rounding up the runic tiles on the floor. "But there is something weird about Jesus H. Christ. Thor said so."

Zoe uncrossed her ankles and pushed away from the window. "We all have class at 9:00. But once class is over, I'll do a summoning, too, and try to narrow down the answers. Anyone who doesn't have a 10:00 class can meet me in my dorm: 243-C." She smirked. "Thor isn't the smartest of gods. We need a second opinion."

"Like hell he isn't." Logan grabbed the bag for his runic tiles and poured them in. "You can't believe everything you read about the ancient gods. There's nothing wrong with Thor's intellect. Whose second opinion do you want, anyway?"

"You'll have to show up and find out." Zoe flounced out of the suite.

Kenzie wasn't sure whether he should be disappointed or relieved that he had a 10:00 class. He was comfortably atheist for two years, and seeing Thor shook him more than he wanted to admit. Frustration twisted his stomach.

"I'm going to talk to Moriah. She's here on a student visa,

but she wants to stick to Jesus H. Christ's side. Skipping class for however long this Jesus thing lasts will cause her to fail and get sent back to the URA. She was already panicking about disappointing her parents and our nation. Falling for a fake Jesus and failing out of college? She'll never recover."

Picking up his backpack, Kenzie slipped it on as he stalked toward the door, his shoulders tense and his mind tangled up like a logjam. *What has my life turned into?*

TEN

After grabbing their backpacks, Shinrou and Makari followed Kenzie out of Logan's dorm. They had 20 minutes before their 9:00 class. Shinrou checked his phone's social media feed. "Jesus is at the library." He sprinted down the sidewalk.

Makari and Kenzie ran to catch up, Kenzie surprised by Shinrou's speed. Makari caught up first because of his longer legs.

Given how hot it was, Kenzie broke an instant sweat. "Why are you going so fast?"

Shinrou slowed but still speed-walked. "I can't afford to be late to my aunt's class. I don't want to think about what she would do to me."

Makari's brow furrowed. "It'll be okay. We'll make it in plenty of time. What did you think of the summoning?"

"Japan's ancient magicians have a different method, but the outcome seems the same."

Fascinated, Kenzie burned with the need to ask Shinrou a million questions about Japan and Japanese ancient magic. *I wish I'd gotten more time with my dad and had asked more questions about his home culture.*

"And Thor's answers?" Makari asked.

Shinrou shrugged one shoulder. "I have no idea how a spirit could gain physical mass without being anchored or fused to a corpse."

"You're going to run your own experiment." Makari grinned. "Of course."

"Of course."

Kenzie could imagine Shinrou in a white lab coat bustling around a lab just as surely as he couldn't imagine Zoe Wang and himself doing the same thing. Contrary to the long-running stereotype about Asians and Asian Americans, Kenzie had never been a genius at science and math.

It took them five minutes to cross from the dorm to the library. As soon as they reached the quad, Shinrou halted and groaned. A mass of at least 300 people, some of them students in school uniforms and others outsiders in street clothes, had piled up in front of the library. Campus security had strung yellow police tape from lamppost to lamppost and directed pedestrian traffic to keep people moving.

Kenzie fought to catch his breath in the humid heat. "This is ridiculous. If they're what Christians call 'True Believers,' then they know he can't be Jesus."

"Well, that's what my priest would say." The sound of an approaching helicopter thrummed overhead. Makari glanced up, squinting in the sunlight. "I bet that's a news chopper."

"How am I supposed to get close to him?" Shinrou clenched his fists. "Is this something where your clan name could be useful?"

Makari peered at Shinrou, his green eyes comically wide. "Oh. Maybe. My parents don't flaunt it, but other people snap to it when they're around. Let's find out." He headed toward the stairs, walking along the edge of the crowd.

Shinrou and Kenzie followed. "What is the Idoni clan like?" Kenzie whispered. "Will this work?"

"I don't know, but I hope so," Shinrou whispered back. "I

came to live with Makari's family this past summer to prepare for entering JCU, and I've never seen Makari's parents make any power plays. I've known Makari since we were thirteen—we were internet friends first—and he's never been a snob. They all seem down-to-earth."

Makari stopped by a campus security guard, showed the man his student ID wristband, and talked with him. The guard motioned for Makari to come with him. Shinrou and Kenzie fell into step behind them. The guard led them up the side of the stairs, motioning the collected students, faculty, staff, and visitors aside.

When they emerged at the top of the stairs, they found Jesus H. Christ seated and preaching. Moriah sat at Jesus' feet and peered at him with grinning delight. Rachel Abrams had perched next to Moriah, watching her rather than Jesus. John Paul Smith, Jr. hovered behind Jesus' right shoulder, his arms crossed. Although he stood close to Moriah and Rachel, he appeared to ignore them in favor of listening to Jesus H. Christ. That was more tolerance than Kenzie expected out of him. *Of course, maybe he's hoping that Jesus will save their souls by making them repent for having used magic.*

As Kenzie's group approached Jesus, Smith glowered at Shinrou. The forbidding expression sent an unspoken but clear message: You don't belong here.

With Smith was right there, Kenzie's nerves frayed, and sweat collected under his arms. If Smith glared like that at Shinrou because Shinrou was Asian, Kenzie wasn't going to get any better treatment. *Even if he doesn't shoo me away for not being White, how do I get Moriah to come to class without angering him?*

Jesus kept speaking, quoting the King James Bible. "'Ye have heard that it was said by them of old time, Thou shalt not commit adultery: But I say unto you, that whosoever looketh on a woman to lust after her hath committed adultery with her already in his heart.'"

Kenzie risked a whisper as Jesus was silent for a moment, presumably to allow his audience to ponder his words. "Moriah."

Moriah looked Kenzie's way and smiled even wider. "You came!" she whispered back.

"Moriah, class is in—"

Jesus cut Kenzie off, continuing his sermon. "'If a man be found lying with a woman married to an husband, then they shall both of them die, *both* the man that lay with the woman, and the woman: so shalt thou put away evil from Israel. Know ye not that the unrighteous shall not inherit the kingdom of God? Be not deceived: neither fornicators, nor idolaters, nor adulterers, nor effeminate, nor abusers of themselves with mankind, nor thieves, nor covetous, nor drunkards, nor revilers, nor extortioners, shall inherit the kingdom of God.'" Jesus again fell silent for a moment.

Kenzie felt increasingly uncomfortable listening to the list of damnation, although the Bible quotes were familiar enough. He gazed at Moriah, determined to try one last time. "Moriah—"

Moriah looked blissful. "Kenzie, we don't need to attend classes anymore or anything else. Don't you see? Jesus has come. He will give us great works to do in his name." She patted her left pigtail. "Jesus even forgave me for bleaching my hair. I've sincerely repented in my heart, and he forgave me."

John Paul Smith, Jr. smirked.

Kenzie fell silent. He didn't dare say anything more to Moriah with Smith standing there, and Moriah's response told him everything he needed to know. *She's gone. She wanted a way out of college that didn't disappoint her parents, and she found it: She can't be disappointing her parents if she's serving Jesus.*

Shinrou stared at Jesus H. Christ, apparently sizing him up. Kenzie did the same. Jesus H. Christ had brown hair, brown eyes, and fair skin. Kenzie wasn't sure about the variation of skin color among ancient Jews, but he noticed Moriah, whom he knew was part Jewish, had darker skin than Jesus H. Christ. Kenzie also wondered if the real Jesus had black hair and not brown. All Kenzie could say for sure was that Jesus H. Christ looked solid.

Smith stepped forward and leaned toward Shinrou. Shinrou wasn't even five and a half feet tall, and Smith towered over him by a foot. "Why are you here, Chini-dog?"

Radiating pain lanced through Kenzie's chest, and his breath stuttered. The racial slur slammed through his gut as if Smith had spoken to him instead. Smith might as well have stabbed him.

Shinrou froze, his arms halfway to his chest in a defensive stance.

"Excuse you!" Makari shouldered his way between them and glared at Smith. "That's *sick*. How could you say that? You're supposedly serving a God who is kind and loving!"

Makari's shout caught Jesus H. Christ's attention. He peered at the trio from his seat on the stairs, halting his sermon.

"What did Rev. Smith say?" Moriah asked, clutching her fist against her sternum. "It was a bad word, wasn't it?"

Makari stared at the glowering Smith and didn't meet Moriah's gaze. "He called Shinrou a racial slur against Asians."

Moriah inhaled sharply. Rachel turned away, although Kenzie caught she was red-faced.

"'Jesus loves the little children, all the children of the world,'" Jesus said. "'Red and yellow, black and white, they are precious in his sight.'"

Moriah smiled up at him, her distress seemingly forgotten. "Oh! That was one of my favorite church songs when I was a kid."

Jesus H. Christ smiled in return and patted her head.

She gazed at him, her brown eyes shining with love.

Shinrou stepped forward. "I'm glad you don't hate me just because I'm Japanese." He extended his hand. "We're both in the U.S. right now, so we should use U.S. customs. Would you do me the honor of shaking my hand?"

Jesus H. Christ took his hand. Shinrou had to perform the shaking part; Jesus H. Christ appeared puzzled, one eyebrow raised.

A roar of clicking sounds, some of them accompanied by flashes, erupted from the crowd.

Kenzie suppressed a smirk. *A picture of Shinrou shaking Jesus H. Christ's hand will be all over the internet in seconds.*

"Thank you, sir." Shinrou released Jesus' hand and stepped back to Makari's side.

Jesus faced the crowd, returning to his Biblical quotes. "'And if thy right eye offend thee, pluck it out, and cast it from thee: for it is profitable for thee that one of thy members should perish, and not that thy whole body should be cast into hell. And if thy right hand offend thee, cut it off, and cast it from thee: for it is profitable for thee that one of thy members should perish, and not that thy whole body should be cast into hell.'"

Kenzie looked away from Jesus H. Christ, his lungs constricting until his breaths grew shallow. He'd always hated the verse about people plucking out their eyes and chopping off their hands.

Shinrou nodded at Makari.

Smith and Makari traded one last glare. Then Makari headed down the stairs along with the security guard. Shinrou and Kenzie once again followed them. Kenzie hated leaving Moriah behind, but at least Rachel stayed with her. *Please don't let this fake Jesus leave campus. If he goes on a mission to preach all over the countryside like the Biblical Jesus, Moriah will run away from campus to be with him.*

Makari didn't speak until they reached the lobby of

Griffen Hall. "That asshole! I can't believe Smith called you that. I want to kill him!"

"Thank you," Shinrou said. "I think that might have been the worst thing anyone's ever called me. Even worse than the school bullies in fourth grade."

"Smith's such a damn hypocrite." Makari radiated sheer rage, red splotches discoloring his fair face. "Okay, okay. I'll try to focus. You did a great job. What did you find?"

"Solid hand. Not actual skin," Shinrou said.

Kenzie's curiosity flared despite his stress. "Really?"

"What? He's a *robot*?" Makari ran his fingers back into his red hair and clenched them. "Okay, so can you anchor a spirit to a robot?"

Shinrou shook his head. "No. Not a robot. In Japan, we have incredibly advanced androids with equally advanced AI's. But there's one problem you can't fully escape no matter how hard you try: The Uncanny Valley."

"What's that?" Kenzie asked.

"Humans take in hundreds of cues from other humans," Shinrou said. "It's not just the way you look, it's the way you blink, the way you move, the way you smell. There are all sorts of micro gestures humans make and unconscious body language they have. Even Dr. Kenji Saito, the best android designer in Japan, can't completely reproduce all the cues that make someone appear fully human. And the weirdness of the robot can give people the creeps. They call it the Uncanny Valley."

Makari dropped his arms and stared out the glass door. "You're saying that since you saw him up close, you would have known right away if he was a robot."

"Exactly." Shinrou laid his hand on Makari's arm. "Whatever Jesus H. Christ is, it's something that lets him seem fully human. But he's definitely not a human."

Kenzie took in the familiar, affectionate gesture. Based on what little his dad had told him about Japanese culture, this gesture was unusually intimate between friends. *Is this proof that Shinrou is in love with Makari? Or that they're dating? Oh, God. It'd be nice if I weren't the only gay guy in class.*

"But he's speaking King James English in canned Bible verses and children's songs," Makari said, facing Shinrou again. "He didn't say anything new. That, at least, is like a robot."

Kenzie groaned. "Why can't people see that?"

"The fact is that they want to believe," Shinrou said. "I'm sorry. Worse, everyone gathering around Jesus H. Christ makes a tempting target for Top Hat. He seems to like crowds."

Kenzie had to accept the ugly reality of it. "If Top Hat attacks, we'll have mass hysteria. And more casualties." *It's a countdown until somebody dies.*

Kenzie and Shinrou stood at the window of the Magical Application lab, waiting for the elemental machine's line to dwindle. They'd been through all the other machines, and numerous students had been avoiding the elemental machine. Kenzie found comfort in knowing he wasn't the only one who hated the elemental machine. Most of the students had turned out to hate elemental magic and the way the machine measured their efforts. Now the line was twice as long as all the others. However, Kenzie's attention was on the quad and the progress of Jesus H. Christ. Two helicopters and one drone had flown over during the last 40 minutes. Campus security had permitted two news crews in. The police had shown up to help control the crowd and keep the campus from being overrun. Meanwhile, Shinrou had accomplished instant fame. A .gif of him shaking Jesus H. Christ's hand was all over social media.

Shinrou leaned against the side of the gravity station and

pulled out his phone, capturing video of the spectacle from afar. "Jesus H. Christ has only been on campus for roughly two and a half hours. By lunch, the campus will be drowned."

"Campus security is already stretched tight, even with the police. How can they handle Top Hat when he arrives?" As if on cue, a red figure appeared in front of Griffen Hall. Kenzie jerked. *I didn't mean to jinx us.* "Oh. Oh, no. He's here!" He pointed.

Top Hat took off his red top hat and bowed, the usual massive smile painted on his face. Today, his outfit wasn't a suit but a red leotard with a red, long-tailed coat. The devil's tail coiled around one of his arms. But now, instead of old-fashioned cartoon eye makeup, he had exaggerated "Oriental" eyes like out of an old cartoon movie.

Kenzie's hands flashed cold. *Why bow? Is he bowing to the building? Or someone inside the building?*

Shinrou clenched his fist around his phone. "The spirit summoner controlling Top Hat is commenting on the video of me with Jesus. I'm sure of it."

"What?" Logan abandoned the speed station and ran to join Kenzie and Shinrou at the window. "Oh, hell no! Racist piece of shit! Or he thinks it's funny."

Makari raced over to the window as well. "That's the last thing we need!"

By now, the crowd had split: half of them clustered around Jesus and half of them fled. Identifiable even from far away, with his platinum blonde hair and pure white suit, John Paul Smith, Jr. was among the people not budging. And at Jesus' feet sat Moriah, equally unique with her long, blonde, curly pigtails.

Makari gripped the windowsill. "Why didn't they all run? Why is the Jesus impersonator still sitting there?"

"We gotta get down there!" Logan sprinted out of the lab.

Makari and Shinrou dashed after him.

Kenzie followed, only to be physically blocked by Iona,

Natalie, and Heather. "Where do you think you're going?" Iona demanded.

"Out there." Kenzie gestured toward the window. "To fight."

Screams rang out, and the entire class mobbed the windows.

Jesus H. Christ now stood at the top of the library stairs. Only two people remained at Jesus' side: John Paul Smith, Jr. and Moriah. Top Hat stood at the bottom of the stairs, his devil's tail swishing like an angry cat.

Kenzie bolted.

"Why are you trying to interfere?" Iona called at Kenzie's back. "We'd all be better off if that naff murk killed Rev. Smith and got him off our continent."

"Shut up!" Kenzie yelled over his shoulder. "My friend's down there!"

He used a speed spell to catch up to Logan, and they zigzagged through the fleeing crowd toward Top Hat and Jesus. In front of them were Makari and Shinrou. Makari held Shinrou's hand as they ran, and he'd used the physical contact to erect a magical shield of blue energy around them.

Moriah crowded Jesus' side and yelled at Top Hat. Kenzie couldn't make out her words. Smith backed up slowly.

"Don't provoke him!" Kenzie couldn't help calling, even though he knew Moriah wouldn't hear him.

Top Hat summoned a red pitchfork into his hand and cackled. Jesus H. Christ lifted his chin, his facial expression calm. Top Hat raised the pitchfork as though to run Jesus through.

From his position in front of Kenzie, Shinrou held out his hand, apparently summoning his control of gravity. However, before he slammed both Top Hat and his weapon to the ground, Top Hat turned toward Smith instead.

"Chini-dog!" Top Hat howled. "Chini-dog Chini-dog

Chini-dog Chini-dog!" He hurled the pitchfork at Smith, who broke into a run.

Jesus H. Christ snapped out his hand and caught the pitchfork midair.

Smith leapt over a yew bush and jumped from the top stair to the ground, clearing the entire staircase. His legs momentarily buckled, but he recovered and kept running.

"Chini-dog!" Top Hat howled again. "Sixpence for your hate!" He summoned a second pitchfork into his hand and hurled it at Smith's back.

Without breaking his stride, Shinrou slammed that one into the concrete.

Jesus H. Christ stepped down and touched Top Hat's shoulder. Top Hat vanished. Then, just as suddenly, Jesus H. Christ vanished.

Smith ran toward his approaching bodyguards, which made Kenzie suspicious. *Why weren't your bodyguards with you? What were they off doing?*

Shinrou and Makari climbed the steps to Moriah, and Kenzie and Logan joined them. They all clustered around Moriah, who was crying.

"That was so scary!" She took a deep, wavering breath. "But Jesus took care of it. He protected Rev. Smith, and he made sure nothing bad happened to me."

Kenzie pulled Moriah into a hug. "But—"

"He protected me," Moriah sobbed. "And he saved Rev. Smith, even though he sinned by being hateful."

"Oh, boy," Makari muttered, releasing both Shinrou's hand and his barrier. "Let's just say that we're glad you weren't hurt."

Logan rubbed his forehead with one hand. "Moriah, there's no way that could ever be the real Jesus. This is about human magic."

"And he doesn't have real skin," Shinrou said. "When I

shook his hand earlier, it was obvious. It didn't feel right, and it wasn't warm. It felt more like touching a vinyl couch."

Moriah wiped away her tears with her fingers. "Well, of course it doesn't feel like normal skin! He has a resurrected body. A new body. It's not the same body we have."

Shinrou gawked.

Poor Shinrou. Kenzie sighed to himself. *He's never dealt with someone like Moriah before. For all I know, he may have never met a Christian before coming to the U.S.*

Shinrou recovered. "Goldstein-*san*…I mean, Moriah…you don't make the evidence fit your theory. You build a theory based on the evidence. Right now you're assuming that is the real Jesus and making the evidence support your belief. What would be far better is to collect what evidence you can and then build a theory about what that man is."

"And what I learned from my spirit summoning was that it's not a man or a deity," Logan said.

Moriah narrowed her eyes at him. "And how do you know your spirit can be trusted to tell the truth?"

"I've been talking to the same spirit for five years now," Logan said. "I've never gotten bad advice."

Moriah pulled away from Kenzie's hug. "Your spirit could be a demon, and it probably is. Other than the Holy Spirit, the only spirits out there are angels and demons. And angels won't tell you not to believe in Jesus." She marched down the stairs, head held high.

Logan's face reddened, but he didn't yell at her.

Kenzie stared after Moriah. "We lost her. She's fled deep into Christendom. She won't be coming back out. Trust me. I've spent 18 years surrounded by this."

"It's a miracle she'll practice magic at all," Makari said. "Doesn't the Bible say, 'Do not suffer a witch to live?' And since The Apostles' Way is convinced magic isn't science and all magicians are witches, shouldn't that mean Moriah can't practice magic?"

"We're allowed to do anything that we can scientifically prove in a lab," Kenzie said. "But more than anything, they don't stop us because they know they'll need us if or when World War IV breaks out."

Shinrou pinched the bridge of his nose with his thumb and forefinger. "Bizarre. It's all bizarre." He dropped his hand. "Okay, Moriah won't be helping us. We need to round up more of the students in the Noble Seven. And we have plenty to discuss: Why does Top Hat bow to Griffen Hall before attacking? Why does he look different every time? Why does he mostly speak gibberish while Jesus H. Christ quotes the Bible?"

"Why did Jesus H. Christ switch from Aramaic to King James English?" Kenzie added.

"Assuming he was actually speaking Aramaic earlier. It was Moriah who made that claim, but what if it was gibberish and she just assumed it had to be Aramaic because she couldn't understand it?"

"Good point," Logan said. "And of course there's the big one: What are these spirit-things?" He trudged toward Griffen Hall. "Class is over. We better go get our stuff."

Kenzie cringed. "I'm going to be late to my 10:00 class." He took off in a sprint, the others close behind him.

When the four of them reached the classroom, they discovered Shinrou's aunt standing in the lab's door, blocking it. "Step in."

Shinrou flinched and followed his aunt into the lab, Kenzie, Logan, and Makari filing in after him.

Dr. Kitamori stopped by the professor's computer terminal and stared them down. The lab was empty now, and their backpacks were lined up by the door. "Because you ran out of class without my permission, all four of you have been counted absent for the day."

"I accept that," Logan said. "And I'm sorry for disturbing

the class, but it was an emergency. If it hadn't been, we wouldn't have done it."

"It's an emergency," Dr. Kitamori said, "but it's not an emergency for *you*." She pointed out the window at the Torres Administration Building. "We have campus security, a president, a provost, and a half-dozen vice presidents. We have the police. A little over half of the faculty members are magicians. There are adults here to handle this problem. It's not your job."

"No offense, but at least for me and Makari, it is," Logan said. "We're part of the Noble Seven, and that makes it our responsibility to deal with magic-based crises that occur around us. That's the tradeoff. You get named modern nobility, but you have a duty to protect others with your magic."

Dr. Kitamori's lips flattened into a line, and her brow furrowed. "If Mr. Top Hat burst into our classroom, I would agree with your logic. I would welcome your assistance in an altercation. However, it's not your job to run across campus every time one of these creatures shows up. You're here to take classes and learn. Your parents can deal with this crisis."

Logan's eyes narrowed, and he crossed his arms. However, he didn't reply.

Dr. Kitamori turned to Kenzie. "The case is even clearer for you, Miss Okuda. You're not a member of the U.S.'s Noble Seven or the URA's Noble Three. You're embarking upon a task that has nothing to do with you."

Heat stung Kenzie's cheeks, but he didn't dare speak.

"Also, you're violating school policy with your hair," Dr. Kitamori said. "Your red has too much blue in it. I'll give you until Monday to fix it, and then I'll report you to the Dean of Students."

When Shinrou's aunt turned to him, he bowed to her. "*Shitsurei-itashimashita!*"

"*Yame nasai. Hara ga tatsu.* You of all students, know better than to act in such a disrespectful way. I don't know why you have done such a thing."

Shinrou remained bowed. "*Moushiwake-gozaimasen.*"

"I don't understand why you have started acting American. *Huzakenaide.* Can't you understand that your behavior will reflect on me and our family? Don't humiliate our family that way again. It would be humiliating if we were to be named the sixth noble clan of Japan and you were to behave this way in front of the world when we need you to help represent us. *Yurusenai.*"

Shinrou bowed deeper, more than bent in half. "*Makotoni moushiwake gozaimasen-deshita.*"

His aunt groaned and took a short, sharp breath. "I accept your apology, Shinrou-*kun.* I expect you to act better than this. Don't throw away the future your parents would have wanted for you."

Shinrou straightened. "Yes, ma'am."

"I'm reporting this incident to the Vice President of Academic Affairs," Dr. Kitamori said. "I'm not doing that to get the four of you in trouble. I'm doing that so she can be made aware of your dangerous behavior. We don't need students to get killed on our campus." She looked them over. "Now, all of you are dismissed."

Shinrou grabbed his backpack without looking at his aunt, and Kenzie had learned enough about Japanese culture to know why: Trying to make eye contact with her would be rude.

Kenzie snatched up his backpack and trudged off with him. Makari and Logan followed suit, and once they were halfway down the hallway, Kenzie said, "Thanks to your aunt going off on us, I can't be on time to my 10:00 class no matter what I do."

Shinrou flinched and stared at the floor, but neither Shinrou, Makari, nor Logan spoke until they reached the lobby.

"Zoe will have already begun her summoning," Logan said. "I refuse to interrupt her."

"Right," Shinrou murmured.

Kenzie slowed to a halt, and everyone stopped with him. "Shinrou, I can understand a little Japanese. My dad taught me some. I'm not trying to intrude on your family, but your aunt made you keep upping your apology until there was nothing more you could say."

Makari laid a hand on Shinrou's shoulder. "Is your aunt always this harsh?"

Shinrou glanced up, his lips parting in surprise. "Harsh? Harsh how? My aunt had every right to chastise us that way. Are U.S. teachers lax?"

Makari and Logan traded looks.

"Depends on the teacher," Logan said. "Your aunt seems pretty hardcore to me, though."

Shinrou shook his head. "In Japan, teachers are meant to be shown great respect and obedience. Apparently things had 'relaxed' before World War III, but afterwards, Japan became traditional again. My aunt's reaction was normal." He sighed. "I really shouldn't have done that, but seeing Top Hat pretending to be Asian got to me, especially after what Rev. Smith called me."

Makari clasped Shinrou's other shoulder as well and squeezed them both. "It's understandable. Don't beat yourself up."

"And I'm not sure I agree with her about leaving everything up to my dad," Logan said. "I mean, my dad lives in Phoenix, and he's the CEO of a big pharmacy chain. He can't hang out in Louisville and chase Top Hat around all day every day."

"I understand," Shinrou said. "Have you talked to him yet to see what he wants you to do?"

Logan sighed. "He told me to stay on top of the situation. But he didn't say I could skip classes."

"My parents told me something similar," Makari said. "They live in Boston, so they can't stay here, either. They expect me to go to class, but they expect me to protect people, too."

Logan nodded. "Well, we'll try not to piss off Kitamori again. But I'll tell you right now: If something serious goes down, I'm not just sitting at my desk doing nothing."

"Agreed," Makari said. "If the Vice President calls me in to talk to her, I'll argue my case."

"Well, you know I can't argue my case." Kenzie's fight gushed out of him like he was popped balloon. "And I've got to go."

As he walked away, Kenzie heard Logan as he spoke to the others. "I hope Kitamori didn't scare Kenzie off the 'case.'"

Logan's hope that Kenzie would remain involved was the only thing that kept him from dropping into depression.

ELEVEN

After lunch, Kenzie walked with Rachel and Zoe to Strategic Magic I. Like Magic Application II, this class seemed to be filled with mostly the top 20 incoming freshmen. The walls for the sparring rooms were already raised when they entered the little gym.

Dr. Grayson wasn't wasting time. Logan, Makari, and Shinrou sat on the bleachers together. Logan talked, making big gestures with his hands, and Makari laughed. Kenzie smiled and made his way toward them. Calling "hi" to them, Zoe passed Kenzie on the stairs and plopped down on the bleacher right below Makari.

After pulling off his backpack and dropping it on a bleacher, Kenzie settled below Logan and flicked him a wave. Rachel sat below Shinrou. A dozen women surrounded Makari again, which made Logan and Shinrou like bookends around Makari on a shelf otherwise filled with women.

Stationed by Logan was Iona, who was no doubt irritated to have been separated from her crush. With Logan there, Makari was too far away. She fake-smiled at Kenzie with feigned sweetness.

"Hey, mythical moves running out of class. You were right. You don't need my help to become a college dropout."

"What?" Logan glared at her. "The administration can't expel Kenzie for that. I recruited her."

Iona's princess-like features twisted into an ugly cringe. "Recruited?"

She's going to hate me even more, Kenzie thought. *If she turns out to be the one summoning Top Hat, I'm going to be in deep shit.*

"Makari and I formed a student taskforce in response to Top Hat," Logan said.

Iona scoffed. "You can't do that without bringing it up as a motion at our next Noble 10 Student Committee meeting."

"And we will," Logan ground out through clenched teeth. "But we didn't have time for that."

"Or you're doing what you always do: botting as a rebel." Iona narrowed her eyes. "Mr. Too-Mythical-for-Rules Steensen. It's no spoiler you'd recruit from outside our ranks. You did it for the hype."

A flush blotched Logan's cheeks. "I asked Kenzie because she was the first person to fight Top Hat, and unlike the dozen people who ended up in the hospital, she walked away."

Despite feeling horrified to be the topic of their argument, Kenzie lifted his chin with pride at Logan's compliment.

"Because you and Makari and Kitamori keep white knighting!" Iona gestured at Makari and Shinrou with both hands.

"No, because she's got skills outside the classroom!" Logan shouted. "Something you haven't proven to me at all."

Dr. Grayson walked over, wearing her black gi and black belt again today, and stood in front of the bleachers. "Enough chit-chat. You can gossip with each other after class. Time to get off your tushes. Be sure to scan your ID bracelets at my computer so you can be counted present today. Now let's get right to work. The first two sets of sparring partners are already up on the screen. For each set of matches, everyone will pick one pair to watch and analyze. Record your observations on their strategies into the note program in our class portal. You'll go to the link with today's date."

Kenzie glanced up, saw he was up first again, and was relieved. Now he could vent his stress right away. He'd already been angry at Dr. Kitamori, and now Iona had made him even angrier with her attack on both Logan and him. According to the screen, his sparring partner was Seth Torres.

Iona sneered at Kenzie. "Seth's a potential heir from the main branch of the Torres clan, and his brother Isidro is a genius—a prodigy 25-year-old Merlin class magician." She cupped her hands around her mouth. "Go, Seth! Show O'Gouda what a real battle magician can do!"

"Be quiet," Dr. Grayson snapped.

Kenzie grimaced and made his way toward sparring room A, his heart racing. All the other students dug out their tablets or phones so they could take notes. He felt hyperaware of his entrance exam ranking of 17th place, and today in Dr. Kitamori's class he was assigned no daily ranking because he went to fight Top Hat. Even worse, Iona was right: He hadn't made a difference.

I'm watching Moriah crash and burn, but what if that's distracting me from what's happening to me? I'm not doing much better. He squared his shoulders. *Fine. I'll show Iona and Dr. Grayson that I have skills inside the classroom.*

Seth reached the room first. He was Logan's height, perhaps five foot seven or eight, and had straight, black hair that hung down to his jaw. His Latino heritage had granted him light brown skin and eyes so dark brown they looked almost black. He wore the black uniform and had his hands shoved in his pockets.

"Okuda," he said by way of greeting.

"Torres," Kenzie replied as he joined him.

He waited for the buzzer, his heart still thudding. Seth

was a complete mystery to him. He hadn't focused on Seth's Monday sparring match. He was in Magic Application II with Kenzie, but, unlike Iona, was quiet and didn't stand out.

"A little advice." Seth's tone held little inflection, and his stare was flat. "You aren't in Idoni's or Steensen's league. You don't have to worry about failing out of our classes. You'll get yourself killed by Top Hat first. So stop."

Kenzie's eyes narrowed. Having been born Asian, non-noble, and female-looking meant he got racism, classism, and sexism in the URA. He had his fill of it and wasn't going to swallow more.

"Why killed, specifically? Because I'm physically female, Asian, or a 'peasant?'"

The buzzer sounded, beginning their match.

Seth flicked his hands outward, slamming Kenzie against the wall with gale force winds. Kenzie yelped at the force of his head hitting the wall. He grabbed at the air immediately around him and stopped the particles from moving. It turned the elemental attack into a windshield and freed him from the wall.

But before Kenzie could grab light particles and compact them into an energy ball, Seth summoned a muddy tidal wave from the Ohio River.

The water roared as it poured into the room, pinning Kenzie to the wall again. A plastic bag and an aluminum can hit Kenzie in the chest. Polluted water surged up Kenzie's nose, making it burn, but then the wave splashed to the floor. *He's weaker at water. This is my chance to break out of being on the defense.*

Kenzie grabbed light particles and redirected them at Seth's face as bright rays.

Seth cried out and stumbled back a step, blinded.

Igniting a speed spell, Kenzie whipped around behind him and used a two-handed telekinetic shove at his back.

Seth flew onto the floor, catching himself on his hands,

and used a hand spring to flip himself. He landed on his feet and faced Kenzie.

While Seth had recovered, Kenzie had time to compact light energy, but he didn't dare take the time to pack it smaller. He shot the laser ball as soon as it turned carmine. The plum-sized ball of red light knocked into Seth's shoulder. He hit the wall.

With a snarl of rage that wrinkled his nose, Seth flexed his hands. Tree branches and roots erupted around him as a living shield. "Enough," he hissed.

He's carrying acorns or seeds. Kenzie was stunned, having seen little plant magic. Seth flexed his hands again and three of the tree branches snapped toward him. Kenzie telekinetically grabbed the tree branches, but one branch arched up from the floor and coiled around him. A fourth and fifth branch followed, wrapping around him layer after layer like coiled ropes. Kenzie struggled to breathe.

Seth sauntered across the room and peered up at him. "Like I said, you're not in the Idonis' or Steensens' leagues. You're not in the Torreses' or Andersons' leagues, either. Learn some humility."

Somehow, Seth's matter-of-fact tone infuriated Kenzie more than Iona's hateful one. He narrowed his eyes at Seth, summoning every ounce of his rage. In his mind, Kenzie saw the blond guy with his Aryan-blue eyes hurling racial slurs at him. Kenzie saw his white-haired preacher explaining to his congregation why women were inherently inferior creations in God's eyes.

Kenzie felt his energy ignite. Within two seconds, a green glow poured out of his body like a corona. He visualized the tree roots blasted into splinters. Unleashing the energy with a yell, Kenzie pushed out in all directions. The coils buckled. The limbs snapped. Splinters of wood flew, and the sweet smell of sap filled the air. But too many of the branches trapping Kenzie remained. He only managed to free one arm.

Seth flinched, but then smirked. He pressed a finger against one limb still holding Kenzie. Then the branch glowed green, and Kenzie felt his energy draining away. "You can draw energy from a tree, or you can use a tree to draw energy out of someone else. Everyone knows that. Don't be so elementary."

Kenzie's fury doubled. Seth was so smug. Iona and her friends on the bleachers laughed. *Fine. I can play your way.* He visualized the pathways for water and energy inside the tree, visualized the flow of energy currently draining from him and into Seth, and yanked. He pulled with all of his will, imagining that he could use the branches like a giant straw and suck Seth's energy into himself.

"*What?*" Seth fell to one knee, his tan face turning ashen. He pressed one hand to his heart.

Kenzie stoked his rage at the magic-hating protesters and at the police in the URA, who regularly threatened to arrest women for having hair above their waists. Or for dress hems that were an inch too short. Or for wearing colored lip balm. Then he shot that searing heat outward.

The branches holding Kenzie exploded. Smoldering shards of wood arced through the air and littered the sparring room.

The buzzer sounded, ending the match.

Seth pushed to his feet, trembling. He had two scrapes on his cheek from the flying wood.

"You ran the clock down on purpose so I wouldn't have time to counterattack!" He touched the scratches with his fingertips, then jerked his fingers away. "With that little trick, you might not get a zero for today's sparring match. But you'll still get an *F* for the course." He strolled toward the door.

Shaking with fury, Kenzie bit back a reply and followed him.

Seth stopped and looked up at the wall screen so suddenly, Kenzie almost bumped into his back.

Kenzie stepped around him and glanced up as well.

The scoreboard read: Seth 4 – Kenzie 5

Kenzie stared in shock. *I won? I won!* Now that his adrenaline faded, he was conscious of being cold and wet. Muddy water dripped from his hair and squished out of his shoes with every step. He glanced at Seth.

The scratches on Seth's face welled up with blood.

"First aid station," Dr. Grayson told Seth, tone brisk. She gestured to the side of the gym. There was a small kiosk there that Kenzie hadn't noticed before. No one had needed first aid during the first day.

"I can heal it," Seth said.

Dr. Grayson stared him down, her frown deepening her wrinkles. "Don't waste magic on things that aren't important. Wash your face and put on a Band-Aid. You'll heal on your own."

Seth stalked over to the first aid station.

Shaking her head, Dr. Grayson turned to Kenzie. "Sit down on the bleachers. A little water won't hurt them. You'll drip-dry."

Kenzie gave Dr. Grayson a half-smile and trudged to the bleachers. His wet briefs clung to him weirdly, making it more uncomfortable than usual to walk, and the wet fabric of his chest binder chafed. *God, I can't wait for top surgery.*

As he climbed the bleachers and sat down in the row below Logan, he finally noticed that the gym was silent.

Iona wouldn't look at him. She stared at Seth as he cleaned his face at the first aid station.

Logan caught Kenzie's gaze, grinned, and offered a fist bump.

Kenzie bumped his fist against Logan's and grinned in return, warm again despite the wet clothes.

⚡

KENZIE HADN'T BEEN OUT OF STRATEGIC MAGIC FOR TWO minutes when his phone beeped. He unlocked it and found a text message summoning him to the vice president's office. *Dr. Kitamori reported me! I forgot.* His sense of victory at having beaten Seth ebbed away.

Using the office number he'd been given, Kenzie entered the Torres Administration Building and headed to room 104. The door had a golden plate that read "Vice President of Academic Affairs." Kenzie stepped inside.

The secretary was a middle-aged White man with blond hair and blue eyes. "May I help you?"

"I'm here to see Dr. Dawson." Sweat built underneath Kenzie's arms. He took several deep breaths. He was still damp from Seth's spell, but he didn't want to take the time to change. It would just give him longer to stress out.

"Do you have an appointment?"

"I was summoned."

"Okay. Name?"

"Kenzie Okuda."

The secretary turned to his computer and clicked an on-screen button. After a quick video exchange with Dr. Dawson, he gestured to the door behind him. "You may go in."

Kenzie inhaled deeply again and strode forward, opening the door and entering without hesitation. A middle-aged blonde woman with blue eyes sat behind an expansive mahogany desk. *Oh, great. It's Aryan Delight around here.*

"Hello, Kenzie. I'm Dr. Dawson. Please have a seat." She looked Kenzie over. "Gracious! Are you all right?"

"Water spell. Strategic Magic class." Kenzie dumped his backpack on the floor and sat in one of the faux leather chairs across from Dr. Dawson's desk.

"Ah." Dr. Dawson smiled. "Well, it happens, and you

didn't have to rush here. Would you like to dry off first? Change clothes?"

Kenzie shook his head. "It's fine, really." *Don't delay the torture.*

"Very well." Dr. Dawson swiped through a few screens on her computer monitor and then read one.

While she did, Kenzie peered around the office, trying to get a sense of Dr. Dawson's personality. Two mahogany bookcases stood behind Dr. Dawson, and old books with cracked leather spines and gold lettering filled the shelves. Kenzie hadn't seen books like these outside of a museum.

The beige walls were covered in award plaques and holoframes displaying Dr. Dawson's three college degrees: B.S., M.S., and Ph.D. It all seemed official and scholarly.

"I want to talk to you about your confrontations with the entity everyone is now calling Top Hat," Dr. Dawson said. "Both Dr. Taksande and Dr. Kitamori messaged me to report you ran out of class to fight Top Hat. Why do you think that concerns them?"

"They don't want me to miss class time, and they don't want me to get hurt."

"Correct." Dr. Dawson checked her screen again. "I see you ranked in the top 20 of our incoming freshmen, and you have the unusual talent of mind magic—telekinesis and pyrokinesis."

"Yes." Kenzie was glad his record could somewhat stick up for him.

Dr. Dawson's brow furrowed. "We certainly don't want you to get hurt. We don't want *any* student to get hurt—or worse, killed. But keep in mind that mind mages are rare. The global community would experience a special loss if you died fighting Top Hat."

Kenzie decided he preferred Dr. Dawson's approach over Dr. Kitamori's. He wasn't getting chewed out, and she seemed sincerely concerned. "I understand."

"Good. Of course, we don't want you to miss class, either, or disrupt other students while they're trying to learn. But the bigger issue is your safety."

"Okay. But what if Top Hat attacks me? Or attacks someone near me?" Kenzie straightened his shoulders. "The first time I fought him, he had stabbed a protester right in front of me. I didn't have time to call campus security and wait for their arrival. Top Hat was already aiming for a second victim."

"That would be self-defense or defense of a bystander. That's different. You were already not in class, and the emergency unfolded around you. In a case like that, just use your common sense and don't overextend yourself."

Kenzie relaxed, pleased to have an opening to take action if he needed to. "Okay."

Dr. Dawson studied Kenzie for a moment. Her blonde hair was tucked in a tidy French braid, and her eyes were porcelain blue. In the URA, she would be praised as a beauty. "There's one more thing. Your hair color is a violation of university policy. Please see the JCU Student Handbook for more details. You need to dye it another color—perhaps red? —as soon as possible. No later than Friday."

"Yes, ma'am." Kenzie had a flashback to sixth grade when he'd been sent to the principal's office because his cherry lip balm had turned his lips too pink. Since the Bible said women shouldn't wear makeup, Kenzie was in danger of being expelled for breaking the law.

When he pulled out the lip balm as evidence, the principal threw it away and sent him back to class with the admonishment that he was to never wear cherry lip balm again. *Flavored lip balm is for boys,* he'd said. Kenzie had gotten the message: *You aren't important enough.* He felt no different now.

Dr. Dawson smiled.

"As a new ivy league university, Jefferson-Crowley has an

image to both uphold and build upon. I know you're trying to declare independence, and your hair is a statement about that. I did the same thing when I was in college, I promise. I'm from the URA myself. I lived in what used to be southern Kentucky before it was annexed by Tennessee, in a city called Bowling Green." She chuckled. "I cut my hair the same day I moved into the dorm here, and I threw away all my dresses." She pointed to one holo frame. "I'm an alumnus. Or, technically, an alumnae."

Kenzie read the degree certificate and discovered Dr. Dawson had a bachelor's degree in Elemental Magic. "Then you understand."

"Yes. Stay safe, Kenzie. Between Top Hat and this Jesus impersonator, our campus is in an uproar. The administration's working hard to increase student safety."

"Thank you." Kenzie stood. "The easiest way to make students safer is to ban John Paul Smith, Jr. from campus."

Dr. Dawson sighed. "I empathize with your point of view, and personally, I am no fan of his teachings or rhetoric. However, Dr. Russell, our university president, does not wish Jefferson-Crowley to come across as anti-Christian. The U.S. is different. They value tolerance and diversity here. That extends to allowing a person with an opposing viewpoint to speak their mind."

"But since you're from the URA, you already know that what The Apostles' Way teaches is not Christianity by U.S. standards. And how is it okay to give a person preaching the opposite of tolerance and diversity a platform?"

"I know it doesn't make sense to you. The URA doesn't have freedom of speech laws. And in some ways, that's simpler. Part of me wishes that the U.S. would declare people like Smith guilty of hate speech and silence them."

Me, too. "It *is* hate speech. And if Dr. Russell gives Smith room to talk, Smith will do everything he can to shut JCU down."

And since Dr. Dawson couldn't argue that point, Kenzie wished her a good day and left.

143

TWELVE

WHEN KENZIE RETURNED TO HIS DORM SUITE AFTER MEETING with Dr. Dawson, Zoe, Rachel, Logan, and Makari were waiting for him.

"What's up? And where are Shinrou and Moriah?"

"Shinrou's in Calculus II," Makari said. "As a magic science research major, he has to take all sorts of advanced math classes. Better him than me."

Rachel bowed her head. "I talked to Moriah about skipping classes, but her argument is that she is spending every moment she can with Jesus." She straightened, her hands folded in her lap. As usual, she wore the black women's skirt uniform. Her entire wardrobe was black, as far as Kenzie could tell. "However, I believe her absence is for the best, considering."

"You mean, considering we'll get another speech about being devil worshippers and how Jesus is the answer for everything?" Zoe asked. "Yeah. I think we'll be okay without another dose of Vitamin J."

Kenzie dropped his backpack by the couch. "First I have to go change clothes."

After retreating to his room, he grabbed underwear, a

chest binder, a red t-shirt, and a pair of jeans shorts. Then he transferred to the bathroom, where he peeled off his damp, disgusting clothes. He grabbed a biodegradable plastic laundry bag from the dispenser on the left side of the sink cabinets, applied one of the barcode stickers keyed to his school account, and stuffed his clothes in.

Once he sealed the bag with the built in adhesive strip, he dumped it into the laundry chute that took all the clothing in their dorm building to an automated laundry center. A scanner would identify his clothes and not lose them. He'd receive a package of the clean clothes by tomorrow morning, delivered to the dorm by a drone. That done, he set the computerized shower display at 104 degrees for five minutes and bathed. Drying off with the shower's heat vents and changing into clean clothes made him feel human again.

Dressed in his sanity-saving men's clothes, Kenzie rejoined the others and plopped onto the couch, sitting by Logan, who'd traded his uniform for jeans and a black t-shirt with a red anarchy symbol on the front. Kenzie glanced at Zoe, who now wore a polka-dotted mini skirt and a hot pink tank top. He figured Zoe was trying to look cute for Makari.

Meanwhile, Rachel sat at the kitchen table, staring into an empty fruit cup. Black tights and black Mary Janes had rendered her black uniform even more solemn, and her black hair fell forward, hiding most of her face. Kenzie looked back to Zoe.

"What did you find out from your spirit summoning?"

Zoe perked up. "I didn't do my summoning this morning. I got distracted when I heard Top Hat showed up to fight Jesus H. Christ and attack Smith!" She slapped her knee. "Man, that's hilarious. I want a video of that on permanent loop, especially since he called Shinrou a racist slur."

Kenzie grinned, his sense of camaraderie with Zoe expanding in his chest. *We need to stick together. There are too few People of Color on this campus.* "You and me both."

Now that it was over and Moriah was safe, having watched Smith run away from Top Hat was retroactively entertaining. *Is that the faith in God you keep preaching? Isn't God supposed to protect his holy Apostle?*

"I'm doing my summoning now, though," Zoe said. "You in?"

"Sure."

"Great! I'll go get my bag." Zoe ran off to her room.

Logan shifted on the couch and faced Kenzie. "You okay? I mean, Kitamori went off on all of us, but she really plowed into you. Did Dr. Dawson finish hacking you into pieces?"

Without thinking, Kenzie reached up and ran his fingers through his short hair. *Now I need more dye.*

"Nah. I'm okay. Pissed off and in need of hair dye. But okay." He crossed his legs on the couch by resting an ankle on one knee. "Dr. Dawson wasn't that bad. And Dr. Kitamori didn't say anything I didn't already know. I got the idea already from hearing Iona introduce her friends to Makari."

Makari groaned. "For some of the nobles around Logan and me, it's turned into a family tree contest: 'Well, before my family became magicians, we were witches, and we can trace our family back to England during the Burning Times' or 'One of my ancestors worked magic with Aleister Crowley' or 'My great-great-great-great-grandfather was in the Hermetic Order of the Golden Dawn' or whatever."

Logan snorted with laughter. "What bullshit! They're making all that up to sound good. With the number of personal records lost in WWIII when the global cloud storage facilities got flattened, nobody knows anymore who their ancestors that far back were. The huge genealogy craze of the early 2000s was for nothing. Here's a real story: My family converted from Catholicism to Wicca in the 1970s. We became Nordic Neo-Wiccans, specifically, in 1990-something. Some of us fought as science-based magicians in World War III, and we did a good enough job that we got ourselves added to the then-Noble Four in 2049. But so what? You don't have to be in the Noble Seven to be a powerful magician."

"I'm glad to hear you say that." Kenzie relaxed and smiled. "Well, my mom didn't even know she had magic abilities until she was pregnant with me. My dad could only do one type of spell: telekinesis. He hid it from everyone except Mom and me, including his own parents. The end."

Zoe returned with a duffle bag and frowned. "He shouldn't have to hide what he could do from his family. His parents should've accepted him."

"I never knew the entire story. He wouldn't talk about it much. He only shared his abilities with me because I inherited them. He felt responsible for teaching me what he knew. Also, I kept accidentally breaking dishes."

"Well, my mom's half-Chinese and half-Swedish, and she passed both parts of her heritage down to me. But my stepdad doesn't want to talk about the Swedish part. As far as he's concerned, Mom's a hundred percent Chinese like him, and so am I. But the truth is, I'm a real mixed bag." Zoe knelt on the floor, set down the duffle bag, and unzipped it. "This literal bag is equally mixed, but here we go."

Logan leaned forward and watched her with interest. "Wow. I never would've known. Your presentation in the National Division finals was super Chinese."

"My stepdad's idea," Zoe grumbled. She pulled out items Kenzie recognized from earlier: four wooden bowls, a box of incense, a bag of sand, a bag of salt, and several velvet bags.

"You're going to make the same kind of sacred circle Logan did," Kenzie said.

"Yep." Zoe pulled out a box of colored sidewalk chalk and went into the kitchen, drawing a huge orange circle on the floor. "I'll do it in here. You can make a circle out of anything, but for a spirit summoning, I prefer to use chalk."

Rachel seemed to pull herself out of her trance. She watched Zoe carry over the bowls and set them in place. After turning her chair around, Rachel stared with rapt attention as Zoe put sea shells in one, coal in another, and sand and incense in another.

Zoe grinned at her as she poured four small rocks into the final bowl. "Ooooh, scary, right? It looks all Wiccany and stuff. You think you'll go to hell for watching this?"

Rachel scoffed. "If there even is a hell, I'll go there no matter what I do, so it hardly matters. Besides, there has to be science to this."

"Fair enough." Zoe grabbed the bag of salt. "And this is for purification." She stepped into the circle and sprinkled the salt around. Then she sat and drew a smaller circle. "This one's for the spirit."

Logan stood and crossed over to the kitchen table, watching without sitting down. Kenzie and Makari followed and took chairs at the table. Kenzie propped both elbows on the tabletop and rested his chin on his clasped hands.

"Which spirit?" Kenzie asked.

Zoe grinned up at Logan. "Loki!"

"*Loki?*" Logan looked at Zoe like her hair was on fire. "Since when? You summon Chang'e."

"Who?" Kenzie asked.

Zoe's lip curled. "I don't want to talk to *her*. She was my stepdad's idea. There's no way I'm summoning her ever again. She's no fun at all. Just like those stupid clothes Dad made me wear in front of everyone. I hate traditional Chinese clothes. They're uncomfortable." Her sneer melted into a blissful smile. "Loki is way more fun. I would've gone insane without him."

"Will someone please tell me who Loki is?" Kenzie asked.

Logan plopped into the final kitchen chair. "Loki is a Norse deity, like Thor." He glanced at Rachel. "Wait. Do you know who Thor is?"

"No," Rachel murmured.

Kenzie shook his head. "And I don't know who Odin is,

either, and you mentioned him earlier. Schools in the URA aren't allowed to teach anything about 'Heathen' deities or other religions unless they're teaching you how to convert people of those religions to Christianity. My mom told me a little about the Greek gods, and before he died, my dad told me a little about the Japanese gods. That's it."

"That's insane," Makari said. "Since The Apostles' Way thinks their God is the only real god, why should they care if you learn about 'fake' Pagan gods?"

Kenzie shrugged. "Anything 'of the world' is considered 'tempting' and 'unclean.'"

"Tempting and unclean?" Zoe snorted. "Wow, so they wear crazy pants every day."

"Well, Odin, Thor, and Loki are all Norse deities," Logan said. "Odin is the 'All Father' or head god, like Zeus is for the Greeks. Odin's wife is Frigg, but we don't know much about her because ancient Nordic culture was oral. They didn't leave behind written records. Basically, all we have is some thirteenth century literature."

"It was the same in Ireland," Makari said. "Ancient Irish culture was oral. When the Christians came and made everyone become Christian, a few monks tried to write down the Irish myths, but they Christianized most of them. Our real knowledge of Irish deities is limited. The story of Noah's Ark even got all mixed up in Ireland's national founding myth."

"Got some Irish blood in with that Italian?" Logan asked.

Makari pointed to his red hair. "Oh, yeah. My mom's family is. My maternal grandfather came to the U.S. from Ireland after World War III."

"Cool." Logan turned back to Kenzie. "Anyway, Thor is the god of thunder and lightning, and he's Odin's son."

"My turn," Zoe said. "Loki is a badly understood god. Scholars have been arguing about him for centuries. The most famous theory is that Loki is a trickster god, but not everyone agrees with that interpretation. In the thirteenth century literature, Loki is shown both helping and fighting the other gods. He has a wife, but he also gives birth to an eight-legged horse by shape-shifting into a mare. There's some cross-dressing and gender-bending in the old Norse myths." She grinned. "That's part of why I like Loki so much!"

"I've never seen anyone summon Loki," Logan said. "I have no idea what we're getting into here."

"Fun." Zoe grabbed her wand, which was a finger-wide tree branch about eight inches long with a raw amethyst tied on the end with gold wire. It looked homemade.

Kenzie braced himself for another world-upheaval. He still had no idea what to make of seeing the supposed Thor, and now a second alleged deity was going to appear. Plus now his new friends were dropping entire pantheons into his lap.

"Is summoning a deity so easy?" he murmured to Logan.

He shook his head. "Very difficult. That's why Zoe and I ranked so high at Nationals. All the adults were blown away when I summoned Thor."

Suddenly, a see-through man wearing a green shoulder cloak appeared in the room. Kenzie had expected a Viking type similar to Thor. Instead, while Loki was tall, he was slender. He sported long black hair and a small goatee instead of a full beard. His only similarity to Thor was having fair skin. The garments under the cloak looked like Renaissance nobility, with a green and gold doublet, gold pants, and tan boots.

"Ah, my dear Zoe," Loki said, smiling at her. "We meet again."

Logan gawked. "He can talk out loud?"

"Loki!" Zoe hopped up, although she stayed inside her circle without crossing into his. "I have some friends this time: Makari, Kenzie, Rachel, and Logan, who's been talking to Thor." She gestured to each person she named.

Loki grinned at Logan. "Thor, eh? Is he being a bore? Or is he up to something fun?"

Logan held up both hands, wide-eyed. "Neither. I just asked him some questions."

"*Sure,*" Loki sing-songed. "Well, I hope he did something fun." He turned back to Zoe. "So how can I help my devoted priestess?"

Zoe clapped her hands together. "See how much smokier Loki is than Chang'e? Okay, Loki, here's the flash: We have a potential spirit invasion on our hands. First, a weird guy in a top hat showed up, and he's got a devil's tail on him. He even dresses in red. Some people think he might be Satan. Then Jesus H. Christ showed up! Or someone who looks like classic paintings of Jesus, anyway. Thor said they're not what they seem. Is he right? Are they not for real?"

"Ha!" Loki grinned. "By Odin's throne—not that losing it would cost me anything—no, they're not real. For once, Thor shows keen insight. They're both hoaxes, deceivers summoned by deceivers. The one you call Top Hat doesn't seem to even know what he is or should be."

Zoe tilted her head and tapped her forefinger against her chin. "Well, that's true. He's looked different every time."

"That's my priestess. You're too smart to fall for such obvious deceptions as these."

Zoe dropped her hand and gave a little hop. "Thank you, Loki! You're totally the only god for me."

"That's because you have good taste." Loki stepped out of the circle. "Let's go have a look at Jesus H. Christ and Top Hat, shall we? I want in on this action."

Logan gasped.

Zoe stared, her lips parted, but no sound emerged.

"That's not supposed to happen, right?" Kenzie couldn't bring himself to believe that Thor and Loki were actual deities, no matter how much Logan and Zoe wanted them to be, and the circle going wrong seemed to prove his skepticism was well-founded.

Rachel jumped out of her chair as though she'd flee, but then she hesitated.

Pausing, Loki returned Zoe's stare.

With a sharp inhale, Zoe nodded exaggeratedly. "O-Okay. Let's, uh, let's go see Jesus H. Christ and Top Hat."

Loki grinned. "That's my girl!" He marched toward the door, although his feet made no sound.

Zoe trailed after him, her hands clasped under her chin. "This is amazing."

"Now we have Loki on the loose?" Makari hissed at Logan.

"Don't ask me how this is possible," Logan said. "We just blew right past anything I know or have ever experienced." He stood and raced after Zoe.

Kenzie looked to Makari.

"We treat Loki as an ally," Makari whispered. "For now." His expression was grim, his green eyes darkened and his eyebrows scrunched.

They both stood and followed Logan, heading out the door, down the stairs, and to the sidewalk. After a minute, Rachel joined them.

Zoe and Loki walked side-by-side at the head of the procession.

"Now where would our little Jesus be?" Loki glanced around as he strolled. "Somewhere preaching, I assume."

"You don't just know automatically?" Kenzie asked, catching up to Logan.

Loki snickered. "What? Like piercing the buildings with X-ray vision or something? Or seeing the whole world at once? I've only got two eyes. And why would I want to see the entire world? Midgard can be incredibly boring, and there're just so many humans these days."

"God...I mean Jehovah...is said to be omniscient,

omnipotent, and omnipresent," Kenzie said. "I thought maybe you might just *know*. Or see, yes."

Loki halted and peered back at Kenzie. "All knowing, all powerful, and present everywhere at once? Not even Odin would make such a claim."

Rachel stepped up beside Makari. "That's why the Bible says that Jehovah is the best of all the gods and, according to Psalms 82, sits at the head of the divine council of the gods. He's their ruler."

"In order to claim you're the best, you must have other gods to compete with," Loki said. "You can't be the greatest god in a total vacuum."

He resumed walking, or he appeared to be walking, anyway. Kenzie wasn't sure about the physical dynamics.

"But maybe what makes one a great deity isn't knowing everything or being everywhere at once."

"Having a great sense of humor!" Zoe tossed out. "A god should have that."

"Preachers claim Jehovah has that," Rachel said.

"Compassion," Makari said.

"Jehovah claims that," Rachel said.

"Vengeful," Logan said.

"Jehovah also claims that."

"He also claims to be jealous," Kenzie added, thinking of the verse, *For I am a jealous God.*

"All-powerful, vengeful, and jealous?" Loki asked. "There's a terrifying combination."

"The compassion and love are supposed to mitigate that if you're among the 'saved,'" Rachel said. "Of course, if you're not, you'll burn in a fiery pit for the entire life of this universe, its death, the entire life of the next universe, its death, and then the entire life of the next universe, its death—"

"And on and on and on for all time, because for Jehovah, there is no end," Kenzie said.

Logan shuddered. "Really? Endless eons? For some

mistake you made during a mere 70 or 80 years of life on this little rock of a planet?"

"*The* mistake," Rachel said. "You didn't choose to worship Jehovah, and only Jehovah, in the form of Jesus."

Loki glanced over his shoulder again, held out his hand in a thumbs-up sign, and grinned. "Great show of compassion and mercy. I want to meet Jehovah!"

"Well, you can meet his son," Kenzie said. "Or someone's weird facsimile."

"Mythical!" Loki sped up, and with his long-legged stride, everyone but Makari had to scramble to keep up. "Where's the best spot? A big space, right, for all the faithful followers to gather?"

'*Mythical?*' Kenzie mouthed at Logan.

Logan rubbed the bridge of his nose as if he had a headache. "I guess Zoe's been teaching him slang," he whispered.

"Jesus H. Christ was at the library earlier," Makari said, "but just go for the quad in general. He could use the steps of the library, the Torres Admin Building, Griffen Hall, or Anderson Hall."

Loki zipped down a side path, seeming not to need a map or directions to know where the quad was. They passed the automated laundry center on one side and the greenhouse on the other.

"He vanished earlier after stopping Top Hat," Rachel said. "We don't know if he's back or not."

"Sure we do." Logan pulled his phone out of his pocket. "Let's check Directpic or Minuclick." He tapped the screen twice and then snickered. "Okay. Anderson Hall it is."

Makari groaned. "Mori, I mean Shinrou, must be furious. He probably can't even hear his professor over all the noise."

"But I don't hear them from here," Zoe said.

Only 20 feet in front of them on the sidewalk, Top Hat appeared.

Logan jumped back half a foot and snapped up both his fists. "Shit!"

Top Hat was still dressed in his red leotard and matching coat with tails. His face had Caucasian features once more, with normal-sized eyes instead of swirly cartoon eyes, and was painted white with the drawn-on red smile up to his ears. He lifted his hat, revealing slicked-back hair, although it was blond now instead of black. He gave them a genuine smile and bowed.

Kenzie didn't know what to do. *If he attacks, we attack back and hope we survive. If he doesn't make the first move, is attacking him a mistake?*

Zoe looked from Top Hat to Loki with the confidence of someone walking beside their god. "Top Hat! Looks like you get to meet the fake Satan first."

Kenzie stepped up to Loki's left side, although his heart was racing, and Logan joined him. Makari joined Zoe on Loki's right side. After a pause, Rachel stepped up beside Logan.

"So polite," Loki mused.

"Right until he attacks." Kenzie pulled out his phone and texted campus security. *At least I can do this much.*

Top Hat straightened, and his devil's tail appeared, curled like a candy cane just above his head. He held out his hand, but instead of summoning a pitchfork, he summoned a white cane.

"Sixpence for your hate?"

Makari was pale and silent, and Rachel's face was frozen in a wide-eyed grimace of fascination and horror.

Kenzie tucked his phone back into his pocket, his heart thumping against his ribcage like a blasting bass subwoofer. *What if we can communicate with this thing? Will it make a difference?*

"Sixpence is old currency, right? You're trying to buy our hatred?" Cold prickles flashed across his arms.

Loki gazed into the distance and fingered his goatee. "But I have so many creatures I hate. Do you have enough sixpence to cover that?"

Logan glared at Loki. "What are you doing? Don't encourage him!"

"Don't tell Loki what to do," Zoe snapped. "Have some respect."

Top Hat broke into a tap dance routine, twirling his cane as he did. He wore men's lace-up dress shoes or, rather, tap dancing shoes that clicked in a furious staccato. He struck a pose at the end, arms held wide. "Sixpence for your hate?"

Zoe applauded.

Rachel's eyebrows rose until they disappeared under her bangs.

Loki nodded. "Sure. I hate anyone who can deceive people better than I can, so I hate Jesus H. Christ." He grinned. "Does that work?"

"What are you doing?" Logan hissed.

Zoe flapped a hand at Logan irritably. "Relax."

Kenzie fidgeted, covered in cold sweat at this point. *Where is campus security? Damn it, stop rubbernecking at Jesus H. Christ and do your jobs.*

Top Hat jerked his cane to his lips, holding it like a microphone.

"'In the beauty of the lilies, Christ was born across the sea.'" He sang in a melodic baritone. "'He died to make men holy; let us die to make them free! He is trampling out the vintage where the grapes of wrath are stored; he has loosed the fateful lightning of his terrible, swift sword.'"

"That almost makes a certain kind of sense," Loki murmured.

"Almost," Kenzie said. "It's pieces of 'The Battle Hymn of the Republic.'" The URA was quite fond of the old song.

Top Hat snapped his wrist, and the cane vanished,

replaced by a red pitchfork. "Sixpence show, Loki!" He took off running with unnatural speed, headed toward the quad.

"God damn it, look what you did!" Logan shouted at Loki and Zoe as he gave chase, trying in vain to grab Top Hat with energy strings.

"No!" Makari flicked his hand toward his own chest, and blue energy erupted from his fingertips. Then he raced after Top Hat.

"If Top Hat's going after Jesus H. Christ, then that means Moriah's in danger!" Kenzie cast his own speed spell and flew after Makari, whistling past the campus' many oak trees.

The crowd of hundreds was straight ahead, people seated on blankets or lawn chairs on the grass. Yellow police tape sectioned off the area, and dozens of police officers bracketed the quad. Two news crews filmed from in front of the Torres Administration Building. Jesus sat on the top stair of Anderson Hall, Moriah once again perched at his feet.

The police turned toward the approaching Top Hat. One lifted a blue steel baton; two others aimed blue steel pistols. The U.S. had chosen blue steel for its police officers' magic-based weapons.

"Woot!" Top Hat howled. "Hate, hate!"

The officers with pistols shot off spells.

Top Hat vanished, putting Makari in the direct line of fire.

The police officers shouted in shock.

Makari flicked out his hand, and a magic barrier popped up around him, spherical in shape. The officers' spells slammed into it, one with red sparks and the other with gold.

The police fanned out and attempted to herd the crowd. "Clear the area! Clear the area!"

Idiots. Makari could have been killed. Kenzie zipped up behind Makari and skidded to a stop. "You okay?"

"Yeah. Barely."

A male campus security guard speed-spell sprinted up to

Makari, apparently having been dispatched to deal with the Top Hat sighting. "Mr. Idoni! Are you injured?"

Makari ran one hand back into his red hair. "No, I'm fine. We need to find Top Hat. Now."

"Yes, sir."

Top Hat reappeared behind Jesus H. Christ and slammed his pitchfork downward to spear Jesus H. Christ's skull. Screaming erupted from both Moriah and the crowd, but the pitchfork bounced off of Jesus H. Christ's head as though he were made out of thick rubber.

The campus security guard bolted toward the disturbance. "Shit! What is going on here?"

Jesus stood and whirled to face Top Hat. "I rebuke you! Get behind me, Satan!"

Camera flashes erupted like a supernova from the crowd. There were so many clicks that the phones sounded as though they'd made a collective gasp.

Top Hat cackled and broke into another tap dance routine. Even as he danced in a semi-circle around Jesus, he repeatedly stabbed him with his pitchfork. Each time it bounced off.

Kenzie stared, disturbed and confused. *This can't be anybody's plan.*

Logan caught up to Kenzie. "Rubber Jesus."

Zoe raced up next. "Top Hat should punch him. Maybe Jesus' head would bounce around like one of those little punching bags."

Rachel arrived last and gawked, her black hair blown back from her face.

Jesus held out his hand. A leather whip appeared. "You are like the money changers who defiled my father's house!" He swung back his arm and snapped the whip at Top Hat's chest.

Moriah shrieked and scrambled away.

"Moriah!" Rachel ran toward the stairs, pushing through the crowd.

Kenzie couldn't move. *I promised not to throw myself in harm's way or use my magic unless someone's in danger. Top Hat's not attacking Moriah. Rachel is going to her. Moriah will be okay.*

The instant the whip made contact with Top Hat, rose petal-shaped leather pieces flew outward, the whip having been transmuted. Jesus H. Christ was left holding the handle.

"What's that all about?" Makari asked.

Loki appeared on the steps just below 'Jesus' and 'Satan.' He extended his arms.

"People of Earth, see how your gods fight? How they wage war, even on a cosmic scale, using Earth as their primary battleground? Why do you worship them?" As he spoke, a brown mist surrounded him. When it disappeared a moment later, he was solid.

Zoe dropped to her knees, gasping, sweat springing to her face. "He manifested!"

Moriah paused in her scrambling and gaped at Loki with wide eyes. Behind her, Jesus H. Christ and Top Hat vanished.

Loki raised one hand. "Above you in the heavens, you have Jehovah and his Christ, who are omniscient, omnipresent, and omnipotent. With all their power, their meager gifts to you are guardian angels who don't actually save you from car wrecks or drowning or cancer or infanticide. In fact, they allow this ugly, black-and-white war of good and evil to rage around you when they could end it all with the snap of their collective fingers."

"That's not true!" Moriah cried out into the sudden silence of the crowd.

"I have a bad feeling about this." Kenzie's lungs grew tight with stress, driving his breathing shallow.

Zoe stood, giggling, and threw her hand over her lips. "I don't," she said through her fingers.

Kenzie grabbed her arm. "Do something! I'm serious."

"No way. This is too mythical."

Logan clenched his hands into fists. "Zoe! You're Loki's link to Midgard. Sever it. That's an order."

Zoe's jaw dropped. "Did you just pull rank on me?"

"You're damn right I did. Now do it."

Loki raised his other hand. "On the opposite side, you have Satan, who is also omnipresent, although apparently not omnipotent, or so Jehovah claims. Just like your God, your Satan follows you around all day, every day, reading your thoughts and whispering into your mind."

Kenzie glanced from Loki to Zoe. Zoe muttered something under her breath, eyes squeezed shut, and drew a circle in the air, using her forefinger as a wand.

Meanwhile, Loki continued, "Satan, like your God, watches everything you do, takes note of your every desire, and then does his best to encourage you to act upon them all, reaching into your heart to fan the flames of greed, hate, jealousy, and power lust."

"Zoe," Kenzie whispered.

Zoe brought her hand down in a slashing motion. "The circle is broken; our communion is done. When next we meet, there shall be more fun."

Loki didn't seem to notice. "With his near-omniscience, Satan telepathically barrages you with evil thoughts, just as Jehovah telepathically barrages your conscience with guilt. And, with their omnipresence, they do this to every human on Earth, all day and all night, across all continents and all time. Your very bodies and minds are their battlefield."

Zoe opened her eyes and tilted her head, watching Loki with a furrowed brow.

"Are you shitting me?" Logan demanded.

Zoe backed up a step, and then another, staring at Loki. "That's my formal dismissal."

Loki clasped his hands and grinned at the crowd. "Spare yourselves the pain, dear people of Earth, and follow me:

Loki. You needn't live in the Nordic countries nor have Vikings as your ancestors. Midgard belongs to the humans, and it is for the humans that I fought. I will fight for you again at Ragnarök. Or, if you like, call it Armageddon or the end of the world." He continued to smile. "I will spare you the endless cacophony of competing voices in your heads and hearts. I will not make your minds or bodies a battlefield. I will not burden you with harsh judgments or weigh your every deed night and day. I just want you to be brave. Be strong! And be brave and strong in the way that suits you as an individual person."

With that, Loki bowed and vanished.

Zoe cringed under the weight of Logan's glare. "I guess he just wanted to finish his speech."

Kenzie groaned and dropped his face into his hands. A stunned silence followed, and then a male voice roared, "This is only one God: Christ Jesus!"

With this yell, many others broke the silence, murmuring amongst themselves.

Moriah stood, her face a mask of determination. "False gods have come to challenge Christ, but the Lord will prevail!"

Kenzie took a step forward, but Logan grabbed his shoulder and said, "I don't think we should try talking to Moriah right now. She seems pissed." He turned on Zoe. "And you. Stop summoning Loki. He almost got people killed."

Zoe scoffed. "The real problem is Top Hat, and you know it. Now stop pulling rank on me."

Kenzie turned to Zoe. "Why did Loki manifest after all this time? Why now?"

"I don't know," Zoe said. "Because he felt like it?"

Kenzie's stomach transformed itself into a lima bean-shaped ice chunk. *This has to be related to Top Hat and Jesus H. Christ. But how? As soon as Loki learned about them, he left the magic circle Zoe made.* Despite the heat, he grew chilled. *Who or what is Loki? Has he been playing along with what Zoe wants all this time in order to wait for his opportunity to do something else?* "Zoe, it sounded like Loki wanted to take over the world."

"What? No," Zoe scoffed. "He's just trying to be helpful. He wants to see people reach their full potential. Which they won't, if they listen to people like Jesus."

"Don't let Moriah hear you," Kenzie said. "Christians claim Jesus helps people find and follow their calling. You won't win that argument."

Makari's shoulders slumped. "We need to talk to Shinrou. He's the research specialist. We need to tell him about Loki. This is a new piece of the puzzle."

"What puzzle?" Zoe asked.

Everyone looked at her.

Zoe propped her hands on her hips in outrage. "What? No! Loki manifesting is not related to Top Hat and Jesus H. Christ appearing." She pointed to Logan. "You're not accusing Thor of being connected to this mess. So don't accuse Loki."

"No one is accusing anyone," Makari said.

"You better not be."

Kenzie glanced at the stairs, where Rachel had reached Moriah and was leading her away.

Loki's speech to the cameras just changed everything for the worse. I'm sure of it. Whether Zoe could or couldn't control Loki — and how could she if he's a god? — this has exploded the situation.

THIRTEEN

LATER THAT AFTERNOON, KENZIE AND HIS FRIENDS CONVERGED upon Makari and Shinrou's dorm suite. Since his classroom had been on the opposite side of Anderson Hall, Shinrou hadn't witnessed the events. Shinrou held his phone and watched Loki's speech, which played on almost every news and social media site in the world.

Meanwhile, Kenzie and the others remained quiet and ate pizza. They'd ordered four pizzas delivered rather than risk crossing campus to the Idoni Student Building. Clustered around Domino's boxes, Kenzie, Logan, Rachel, Moriah, and Zoe filled up all the seating in the living room-kitchen combo.

Zoe sat sideways on one drab, brown living room chair, legs dangling over the chair arm as she tore through her veggie-laden slice. Moriah had huddled in on herself across the kitchen table from Kenzie, and Rachel and Logan sat with them, each of them with pizza on their plates. The smell of hot cheese, pepperoni, and grease filled the air.

Kenzie wondered what Shinrou was thinking as he watched the speech. Lines furrowed Shinrou's brow with obvious concern, and a frown pinched his lips. When the video finished, Shinrou lowered his phone.

"There are three million shares and over 50,000 comments just on Minuclick alone, and the post hasn't even been up six hours yet." He sighed and dropped his phone on the couch.

"Well?" Makari prompted. They shared the worn brown couch, two Domino's boxes on the coffee table between Zoe and them.

"Loki was see-through until he appeared before the cameras and crowd," Shinrou said.

"Loki loves a good audience." Zoe glanced at Logan. "By the way, Loki totally wants a public contest between him and Thor."

"No," Logan said through a bite of pizza.

Shinrou looked at her. "You claim to have done nothing to cause Loki to break the circle and then manifest?"

"I don't just 'claim' it," Zoe groused. "It's the truth."

"I think Mori means that as a turn of phrase," Makari said.

Shinrou nodded. "I'm just gathering data." He glanced at his best friend. "Makari, didn't you text some of the other Noble 10 students here on campus?"

"Sure," Makari said. "Why?"

"We need to talk to them *today*, if possible," Shinrou said. "While there's no reason to assume that only Noble 10 members could summon Top Hat and Jesus H. Christ, they're more likely to have the power to do it."

"So now we're going with the theory that someone summoned Top Hat and Jesus H. Christ?" Logan asked.

Kenzie, who sat by Logan at the table, stretched his arms high above his head, popping his back as he did. His body had become so tight with stress that he felt restless and bounced his knee.

"What ability is even tied to this? I mean, what system of magic?"

"Energy working." Shinrou picked up his plate of pizza from the coffee table. "If these so-called spirits or gods remained see-through, we could be dealing with mind magic. Perhaps a mass hallucination. But all three of them have physically manifested." He bit off the tip of his veggie and cheese slice.

"But how?" Rachel asked. Her folded hands rested on her lap, and her ankles were crossed—classic "proper woman" body language in the URA. "Wouldn't physical manifestation require transmutation?"

Shinrou grimaced. "I wish the English word for this was 'transformation.' 'Transmutation' implies alchemy, in which they literally tried to turn other metals into gold. This is science. You can turn sand into glass. You can turn coal into diamonds. You can't turn nickel into gold." He reached up and rubbed the arch of his nose. "At any rate, there may be transmutation involved, yes. Someone with superior energy working and transmutation abilities would be our best bet."

"Plus a little illusion magic." Makari sat with his legs splayed wide and his arms over his chest, radiating irritation and impatience. He'd abandoned his last piece of pepperoni pizza on a napkin. "They made it look like Jesus H. Christ was holding a whip, and then they made it look like flower petals."

"I have no idea who that would be." Logan grabbed his Coke can and washed down his final bite of pizza.

"If you ask the juniors and seniors, I'll ask the freshmen and sophomores," Makari said.

"Sure." The Coke can popped in Logan's hand. "Or we can ask them to call an official Noble 10 meeting ASAP. They're supposed to arrange one soon, anyway."

"Either way, that sounds good." Shinrou peered at Moriah. "I can tell you genuinely want Jesus H. Christ to be the real Jesus."

At the kitchen table, Moriah stared at the half-eaten pizza slice in her hand. "I'm here because Rachel asked me to be. Not because I agree with you that Jesus is a fake. The Bible says I can't let the sun go down on my anger, but as long as the sun is still up, I don't forgive you. Okay?"

Kenzie grimaced and ran his hand through his hair. "Okay. That's fair."

Actually, I think it's crazy that all our lives people have been making us try to stop being angry before nightfall every day, but I'm not starting that argument now. You wouldn't hear a word I'm saying.

Rachel, who sat between Moriah and Kenzie, squeezed Moriah's arm. "You know in your heart Jesus Christ is the real and true Living God. That's not the same as this manifestation being him."

"And, more to the point, Jesus H. Christ can't be," Shinrou said. "Unlike Top Hat-Satan, Jesus H. Christ's appearance hasn't shifted any, but he still speaks in disjointed Bible verses or other quotes."

"And Loki and Thor are real, because they'll actually talk to us," Zoe said.

Rachel clung to Moriah's arm and glared at Zoe.

"We don't know that, either," Shinrou said. "Passing a Turing Test doesn't mean the thing talking is truly alive."

Zoe kicked her heel against the chair leg. "Sorry. If Jesus H. Christ did more than just quote the Bible, I might be asking some serious questions about his validity. But he doesn't. I know I set out to summon the real Loki, and the spirit that showed up can speak for himself."

"I'm an atheist, but I'm not here to upend your religious beliefs," Shinrou said. "Let's just set up an experiment. Let's follow Zoe's advice."

"My advice?" Zoe leaned forward and grabbed another slice of veggie pizza.

"Really? Someone's going to take my advice on something other than fashion?" She paused. "Wait. Which advice?"

"Do you want Logan to summon Thor? If he does, and lets Thor leave the sacred circle, we can see how he is or isn't different from the other three. We need more data. The easiest way to get more data is to make a phenomenon for us to observe."

Logan pointed toward the windows with the Coke can still in his hand. "Hey, we already have a big problem out there. The police and campus security can't maintain the campus parameter now because so many people want to see fake Jesus. Kentucky's governor has called for the National Guard to help. That little crowd of 300 people is just a grain of sand compared to the people piling up in Louisville."

"Reports say all the southbound bridges from Indiana to Kentucky are jammed bumper to bumper." Makari held up his phone, showing the post about it. "And I-65 North is nothing but one long line of traffic. The U.S./URA customs point in Elizabethtown is overwhelmed."

"It doesn't matter what they think about Jesus H. Christ," Kenzie said. "Some are coming because they think he's the real Jesus. Some are coming just to get proof that he's not."

"And asking Thor to perform for a crowd will only make that worse," Logan said.

Shinrou sighed. "But...no offense, Logan...few people worship Thor. Thor and Loki are only as popular as they are because Marvel's been making movies about them off and on for nearly 90 years now. It's not a matter of Pagan worship as much as it's a matter of movie fandom."

Zoe pressed one hand to her cheek and smiled. "The first Loki and the third Loki are still my favorites. The actor for the second Loki got it all wrong."

"Exactly." Shinrou gestured to her. "The Loki you summoned looks like a fusion of the first, third, and fourth actors who played the part. I'm sorry, Zoe, but you didn't summon the god Loki. He would likely be broad-shouldered, have a bushy beard, and be wearing armor from head to foot."

Zoe narrowed her eyes. "Maybe the deity only manifests

in a way the human summoner can recognize." She gestured at Logan with her half-eaten pizza slice. "Did you imagine Thor with red hair, like in the old literature?"

"Yeah, I did," Logan said, "but he came out blond anyway."

"Like in the Marvel movies," Makari murmured. "They've cast a blond four times in a row now. The Thor you summoned looks like none of them, but he's still a blond instead of a ginger."

"That's got nothing to do with it," Logan said.

Shinrou held up his hands. "We got off topic. I apologize. My point is that the addition of Loki and Thor could cause some Marvel fans to be fascinated, but it isn't going to cause a religious pilgrimage."

"That's depressing," Logan sighed. "But you're right. I'll wait until tomorrow morning to summon Thor, though. We need time for the National Guard to move in and secure the campus parameter. Everyone from devout Catholics to cult freaks will show up to see 'Jesus.'"

Moriah frowned and set down her piece of pizza. "You act like it's unnatural to want to see the human manifestation of God."

"They just don't understand," Rachel whispered. "Patience."

Moriah took a deep breath, let it out, and glanced at Rachel, tears in her eyes.

Beside Shinrou, Makari gazed out the window. The sun hung low enough in the sky that its orange light filtered through the oak trees, dappling both Makari's face and the room. "Somehow, this is not how I imagined my first week at college would go."

Shinrou glanced at him, his brow furrowed with open concern. "I'll help you figure it out and stop it. Don't worry." He leaned forward, grabbing a second slice of vegetarian pizza from the box on the coffee table. Zoe and he had both turned out to be vegetarian, so they'd shared a pizza.

Turning to him, Makari smiled. "I know. I trust you."

Kenzie watched this interplay. As sure as he was that Shinrou loved Makari, he wasn't convinced Makari loved Shinrou in return. But if Makari loved Shinrou, Kenzie wondered whether clan politics would get in the way of their love or not. *Both in the U.S. and the URA, "free" people aren't really free.*

His mind turned to what he'd learned today: Whether Zoe liked it or not, someone had summoned Top Hat using a magic circle. And once that person had let Top Hat loose, they hadn't kept control of him any more than Zoe had dismissed Loki. That meant that someone had also summoned Jesus H. Christ using a magic circle. Or, if they hadn't, they were either a Merlin-class magician or close to it, which meant they were terrifyingly powerful.

And what was worse, with the exception of Zoe's case, Kenzie and the others had no idea what the summoners' true intentions were.

⚡

THAT NIGHT, RACHEL DEPARTED FROM HER DORM AT 9:00 P.M., unafraid to walk in the dark across campus to the practice rooms, thanks to her level of magical protection. The black, starless night fit her mood. Rachel believed her life was black: a black uniform, a black curtain of hair, and a black heart. She felt blackened: dirty and charred, burnt beyond recognition.

If I could manifest my inner self on the outside, my corpse wouldn't look human. I am everything my family hates most: female, part Jewish, lesbian, and worst of all, a magician. She wished her dad were still alive. He had been her proof that not all people were cruel or useless. His death had left her to face her uncle's censure, and now her hatred and pain ate her from the inside-out.

Upon reaching the three-story, red brick Griffen Hall, Rachel presented her wrist ID to the scanner on the side door and entered. The dark wooden floor amplified her footsteps, the clicking of her Mary Janes echoing in the empty hallway. She entered the first of four practice rooms, finding it unoccupied. The overhead sensor snapped on the cool white florescent lights, which hummed in the otherwise still silence. Three stainless steel casting machines lined the back wall. *Finally. Peace and quiet.* Rachel had until 11:00 p.m. to practice, and then security would shut the building for the night.

Choosing the elemental machine, Rachel scanned her wrist ID to activate the computer. A louder hum punctured the room, and the screen flashed green as the scoring program popped up. Rachel stared at the machine, hating it for its built-in judgmental software. The machine was ten feet long, five feet wide, and five feet tall, granting her space to cast her spell. The multitude of sensors in the walls and floor waited to criticize her performance.

She held up her hands, imagining the muddy, polluted waters of the Ohio River. *Here we go.* She pulled on quantum particles, imagining yanking the string on a carryall bag, compressing the energy and folding space-time. Then she pictured jerking the bag open and the dirty water pouring out.

A blast of brown water burst out of the air two feet in front of her, slamming into the far wall and then crashing to the floor with a spray of wild droplets. A water bottle bounced twice before being swept toward the floor drain. The sensors flashed blue as they measured her success. She lowered her hands. *I summoned more water and faster this time. Perhaps I'm gaining skill in this area.* As an energy work major, her strong suit wasn't elemental magic.

Beside her, the computer screen flashed its assessment: 97%.

"Well done," said a voice from the doorway.

With an icy flash of terror, Rachel snapped around, raising her arms as if expecting to be hit.

"God, sorry," Kenzie said. "I didn't mean to scare you."

Rachel scanned her suitemate: men's cargo jeans shorts, a black tank top with a skull on it, and men's faux leather sandals. The message rang clear in Rachel's mind: *You're a transman.* She wouldn't ask, though, and risk being wrong. "I thought I was alone." *Go away. I don't want friends.*

Friends are an expression of God's love for you, Moriah's sweet voice replied in her mind.

Rachel sighed, dropping her arms. Ever since she'd met Moriah, her world had been complicated by the presence of someone who might be as gentle as her father had been, and she resented the intrusion even as she felt herself drawn to Moriah's shining light. *Humans are more evil than good, destroying both people and the planet itself, and they don't warrant continued existence. Flies and cockroaches serve a far more beneficial purpose, and more consistently, too.*

"I'll go to a different practice room, then," Kenzie said. "I don't want to blow your concentration."

Defeated by Kenzie's polite consideration, Rachel's shoulders slumped. "Well...that's not really necessary." *Don't be nice, Kenzie. I was comfortable feeling the whole world was hell. It's easier that way.*

Kenzie's eyebrows bunched together with concern. He was passably handsome: tan-skinned with almond-shaped brown eyes. He'd dyed his hair a shocking shade of bright red, but more surprising was his being of Japanese descent. Given how few Asian Americans lived in the URA, Kenzie's existence shocked Rachel just on principle.

However, despite Kenzie's polite treatment of her, Rachel

could never be attracted to him. *Transman still means man. So, no thank you.*

"Are you okay?" Kenzie asked.

Never. "Just frustrated with my elemental magic scores in class." Rachel gestured to the computer screen. "Here, alone, I did just fine. In class, I'm freezing up."

"I feel ya." Kenzie turned to leave, then paused. "I have a question." He pivoted back and stepped inside, letting the door slide shut behind him. "I have a theory I want to run past you. Do you think Iona Anderson could be the one summoning Top Hat?"

The mere name of Top Hat jarred Rachel, and she tensed. "Why would you think that?"

"She's cruel." Kenzie leaned his shoulder against the wall. "And she hates both the protestors and some of her fellow students. What if her hatred has manifested as Top Hat? And, being unable to fully control what she summoned, he just rampages everywhere."

"Well, I can't argue with the fact she's cruel," Rachel drawled. She gave Kenzie a hooded-eye stare. "Even the bullies in my high school weren't as bitchy as that."

Kenzie grinned. "Hey, you cussed a little."

"I no longer believe in God, Satan, heaven, or hell," Rachel said. *And I better be right.* "So what's a few cuss words?"

"Nothing." Kenzie's grin faded. "So you got bullied, too, huh?"

Rachel nodded. "My dad's parents were first-generation immigrants from Israel. I'm not White enough to suit the URA."

"Same," Kenzie groaned. "You're like Moriah, then. Her dad's parents were first-generation immigrants from Israel."

"Who wants to live next door to a nuclear wasteland?" Rachel shrugged. Most of the Middle East hadn't survived WWIII. "Still, they should have immigrated to the U.S. instead. The URA is a cesspool."

"Agreed." Kenzie pushed off the wall. "Anyway, watch Iona, would you? And tell me if you see anything suspicious. I'll turn her into Logan and Makari."

Rachel inclined her head. "Sure."

"Thanks." Kenzie slipped out, leaving Rachel to her peace and quiet.

Rachel faced the testing station. *There better not be a hell. But to hear my family tell it, I'm here practicing magic so I can burn in hell harder.* She held up her hands and again focused on the image of the Ohio River.

Her pain quietly ate the lining of her stomach, and she hoped the afterlife offered her simple nothingness. It would be the greatest reprieve:

Nothing at all.

FOURTEEN

The following morning, Kenzie, Zoe, and Rachel—to Kenzie's surprise—converged upon Logan's dorm suite at 8:00. Kenzie hadn't thought Rachel would want to see another supposed deity get summoned.

Makari and Shinrou were already present and settled on the standard-issue brown couch, Shinrou wearing the black uniform today, like Logan, Kenzie, and Rachel. Makari seemed to prefer the white one, and along with his pale complexion and red hair, it set him up as the visual opposite of the black-haired Shinrou with his naturally tan skin.

Logan had set up his sacred circle; however, he stood in the kitchen corner, leaning against the wall and staring out the window.

"Trouble?" Zoe asked, plopping onto a brown chair, her white uniform skirt flaring wide. As usual, she dangled her bare legs over the chair arm.

"He doesn't want to do it," Makari said.

With a pulse of concern, Kenzie crossed to Logan and gazed up at him. He was roughly two inches taller than Kenzie, perhaps five foot seven. "What's wrong?"

Logan gave him half a smile, only to lose it and stare at the floor. "I've been summoning Thor for three years now. When I say that, it sounds like I'm controlling Thor, that I have some kind of power over a god. But that's not it at all. Thor doesn't have to come when I call to him, but he chooses to. It's an honor for me. I'm Pagan. He's my *god*. I don't slave away for him the way you had to for the God of The Apostles' Way. I don't call myself things like 'a slave in the service of Thor,' like some Christians call themselves 'a slave in the service of Christ Jesus.' But, dammit, it seems too insulting to run an experiment using Thor! Why would I want to dis him that way?"

For a moment, Kenzie remained silent as he continued to watch Logan. He wasn't cute or handsome in the Hollywood way, although he had a unique charm. However, more than Logan's physical appearance was this depth to his heart. Kenzie's infatuation with Logan clicked into place.

"I see what you mean." He had to mentally shift backward five years to do it, but he called upon his empathy. "When I was 13, I was still solidly Christian. The only two things I wanted in life were to escape the URA and to get closer to Jesus. I read my Bible almost every day. I prayed every day. I went to a youth Bible study group at my middle school, and I also did most of the youth activities at my church. I actually paid attention in school during our daily prayer and Bible reading and lesson. If you'd asked that version of me to summon Jesus and run an experiment on him, I would've been so offended I would've screamed at you."

Logan looked up and lifted one arm. After a second, Kenzie realized he was being offered a half-hug. A thump vibrated his chest from the excitement—his first hug from a guy—and he stepped closer. Logan slipped his arm around Kenzie's shoulders and gave him a quick squeeze before releasing him. Heat collected in Kenzie's cheeks.

"I get that." Zoe hopped out of her chair and walked over

to Logan as well. "My relationship with Loki is pretty laidback. Loki loves adventure, so he's not going to get offended. If anything, he'll have a blast."

"Well, that's true," Logan said. "He has *too* much fun."

"I wish I could summon Aphrodite." Zoe gazed off at the corner of the room with a smile. "Then I could watch all the men make fools of themselves. It would be hilarious." She paused. "I wonder if Jesus H. Christ would chase Aphrodite."

Kenzie wondered who Aphrodite was.

Logan glanced at Kenzie. "Greek goddess of sexual love."

Oh, she has to do with sex. No wonder she wasn't mentioned to me. Kenzie chuckled. "Okay, Jesus chasing Aphrodite would be pretty funny."

Shinrou spoke up from the couch. "Try thinking of it this way: It's Thor's decision. You can summon him and ask him how he feels about it."

Logan's shoulders relaxed, and he straightened, pushing away from the wall. "Well, okay. You've got a point. I'll just ask him pointblank and see if he agrees to do this or not." He walked over and sat inside the sacred circle.

From her position at the end of the entrance hallway, Rachel stirred. "What will happen if you anger him? Will he throw a lightning bolt at us?"

Kenzie turned toward Rachel, having forgotten she was even present. Rachel had been so quiet she barely qualified as attending. "A lightning bolt?" He tensed, his stomach clenching. *It's bad enough to face the fact there might be Pagan gods, but now they're violent, too?*

"Nah." Logan lit the red votive candle and the sandalwood incense. "He's not that oversensitive. If I tell him there's a potential fight with Top Hat-Satan, then he'll be intrigued. If I tell him Loki's been here and made a bid to rule all of Midgard, he might even insist on participating."

Makari chuckled. "I'm sure that's true."

"How sure are you that Thor won't do something violent?" Kenzie asked.

"Thor protects humans. Legends tell of him fighting trolls and giants for our sake, and he was invoked at weddings."

Kenzie's stomach unclenched. *Well, if you say so. I guess.*

Logan closed his eyes and held out his hands. "Here goes nothin'."

Zoe returned to her chair, sliding back into it as everyone watched Logan. Over a minute passed before a shape formed inside the circle. The figure drew into focus, as though someone was adjusting a camera lens, until Thor appeared, wielding his war hammer. Just like before, he wore a helmet with goat horns and a mix of leather armor and chainmail. His blond hair hung to his waist.

"Why have you asked to speak with me?" Thor's voice was gruff but quiet, as though someone had turned down the volume on his vocal cords.

Logan jerked. "You're speaking!"

Shinrou jumped into that opening. "Great Thor, Loki has come here to the city of Louisville and asked all the people of Midgard to worship him. As a result, we'd like your help in an experiment."

"He *what?*" Thor lifted his hammer and rested it on his shoulder. "What is Loki up to now? How did he escape captivity? Who freed him?"

Logan cringed. "We have no idea."

Kenzie was surprised. *Logan must have forgiven Zoe. He just covered for her, even though his god asked him a direct question.*

"But it's not just Loki," Logan said. "There are two others here: a spirit who claims to be Jesus, the son of a god called Jehovah, and a malevolent spirit who may be Satan, although we're calling him Top Hat."

"Never heard of them." Thor glanced around. "Where's Loki? Surely if he's here—"

Loki appeared, grinning. "Ah, Thor! Good to see you again after such a long time. And good to see you didn't lose your hammer again while sleeping." Being likewise unchanged, he had black hair and a goatee. He still wore a green and gold doublet, gold pants, and tan boots, along with a green shoulder cape.

Rachel covered her mouth with her hand.

"But I didn't even perform a summoning!" Zoe scrambled out of her chair.

Kenzie froze. *I knew it! Loki's like Top Hat and Jesus H. Christ!*

Both Loki and Thor ignored Zoe's outburst. Thor glowered at Loki and pointed at him with the hammer. "What kind of mischief are you up to now?"

"Why, dear Thor, none at all!" Loki glided over. "All the gods seem to have abandoned Midgard, leaving behind only someone called Jesus H. Christ and his arch nemesis, Top Hat or Satan." He spread his arms. "With such a paltry selection to choose from, why shouldn't they choose to follow me instead?"

Thor marched right out of the circle.

Logan gasped.

Rachel clenched her fist over her lips. "Oh, no. This is bad. *Bad.*"

Shinrou pulled his smart phone out of his blazer pocket and started recording. His brown eyes were wide and filled with excitement.

"Oh, no, you don't." Thor leaned into Loki's face. With each word, his voice grew louder until it was a normal volume. "Midgard belongs to the All Father. He alone is the one who hung himself from Yggdrasil for nine nights, having speared himself in the side, sacrificing himself to himself. By doing so, he gained truth and wisdom." He pointed to Loki. "You have little truth and no wisdom. You cannot lead Midgard."

"That's not true," Zoe said.

"Yes, yes, Yggdrasil, world tree." Loki reached up and poked his finger through Thor's eye. Since Thor was incorporeal, he didn't flinch. "Right now you can do little, dear Thor. You're a spirit, nothing but essence. My power has coalesced into this physical body."

Thor raised his hammer. "I can still summon my lightning, dear Loki."

"Not inside!" Makari shouted.

Simultaneously, Rachel yelled, "Not indoors! You'll burn down the building."

"Idiot," Loki said. "If we're going to fight, let's at least go outside." He headed for the door.

Thor marched after him.

Logan and Zoe traded looks. Zoe trotted after Loki.

"We have to alert campus security." Kenzie whipped out his cellphone and texted them about the new sighting.

"Well, you have your experiment," Makari murmured to Shinrou.

"Yes." Shinrou shot off the couch and hurried to keep up with Loki and Thor, still recording on his phone. "Logan, lightning isn't one of your elemental strengths. If I'm right, Thor will have difficulty."

"Wait, you want Thor to strike Loki with lightning?" Kenzie asked.

"It's a reasonable experiment," Shinrou said.

Logan snuffed out the candle and raced after Thor, and Kenzie and Makari followed, Zoe and Rachel bringing up the rear.

"Odin's never manifested like this for my dad," Logan grumbled as they exited the suite and headed down the stairs. "What's my dad going to say?"

Once they reached the sidewalk, Kenzie stayed a dozen feet behind Loki and Thor as they headed away from the dorms and toward the greenhouse, and the others paced him.

"Can't you dismiss Thor now? Campus security, the police, and the National Guard are already dealing with enough. Shinrou, you have enough data to say Thor and Loki are now acting like Top Hat and Jesus H. Christ."

"Whether Thor can use lightning will tell us something important," Shinrou said.

"I tried dismissing Thor before I snuffed out the candle," Logan said.

Kenzie raked a hand through his short hair. "This is insane."

"They're gods," Zoe said. "What can you expect? We can't tell them what to do."

Top Hat appeared a six feet in front of Loki and Thor. Everyone halted. Rachel clutched one fist to her chest over her heart.

"This is Top Hat," Loki said, gesturing. "I like him."

"Then you are a traitor," Thor retorted.

Loki waved that away. "Oh, please."

Top Hat had retained his red leotard, long-tailed coat, and signature hat. He lifted the hat, revealing two small, pointed devil horns and platinum blond hair, and bowed. Today he had a realistic goat's tail that flicked behind him. His face was painted white still, with its oversized red smile, but today instead of tap-dancing shoes he had cloven feet.

"I have no idea why he keeps changing," Rachel murmured.

Top Hat straightened and popped his hat back on. "Good morning, gentlegods."

Kenzie and Rachel both gaped.

"He said something normal!" Logan exclaimed.

Thor folded his arms over his chest, keeping his hammer in hand in a threatening manner. "Hmph. By what right do you say 'good morning?'"

Shinrou kept his phone trained on the manifestations. "We're watching this spirit form. Transform. Evolve."

"Mori, don't get too close," Makari whispered.

Loki offered Top Hat a return bow. "Good morning, gentlegod. Since we don't know you, may we ask what you are the god of?"

Top Hat summoned his white cane into one hand and twirled it. "By all means, my new friends. I am the god of suffering and pain. I am the god of hate. I am the god of Judas and Cain, and I am the god who lays bait."

"I think he just laid claim to being Satan," Kenzie said.

Thor shook his war hammer at Top Hat. "We have no use for a god of hate. Begone."

Top Hat whirled in a circle, arms spread wide. "Sa—tan's Day," he sang. "Sa—tan's Day. When nighttime comes, I leave my home."

"Then you will leave?" Thor asked.

Kenzie suspected he'd missed another pop culture reference. "You must be making a spoof of some recent American pop song."

Top Hat stopped and pointed his cane at him. "Right you are, my handsome redhead."

Kenzie flinched. He didn't want a compliment from a pitchfork-wielding psycho. It was also a sore reminder that he'd had to dye his hair again the evening before.

"You answer me with a song?" Thor clenched his jaw, muscles rippling.

Top Hat tap-danced his way over to Thor, his hooves making sharp clicking sounds on the concrete sidewalk. "And who are you, my brawny friend?"

"Thor, Odin's son. And I am no friend of yours."

"I'll give you a sixpence for your hate," Top Hat said in a near-purr.

"What's a sixpence?" Thor asked Loki.

"Some country's coinage, it would seem," Loki said.

Top Hat tap-danced a quick routine and then held up his

cane like a microphone to Thor's lips. "Sixpence for your hate, my friend. Name it."

Thor batted the end of the cane away with his hammer.

"Don't!" Kenzie blurted. "He's dangerous."

"What is your obsession with hate?" Thor demanded.

"Fear leads to anger, anger leads to hate, and hate leads to suffering," Zoe said. "It's basic *Star Wars* psychology, but I think it's pretty accurate."

Loki smiled and laid a hand on Thor's shoulder. "My dear companion hates Jörmungandr, the world serpent. He's fated to die after killing Jörmungandr during Ragnarök."

Kenzie tensed, expecting Top Hat to summon his pitchfork and descend into violence."The world serpent." Top Hat stepped back and grinned. "I'm said to have originally been a serpent. A serpent with legs."

"Doesn't that make you a lizard?" Shinrou asked.

Top Hat twirled his cane. "Better yet, the Hebrew text of Genesis never said the serpent was Satan, and the Christian character of Satan was created out of angelic characters called satans who were, in fact, not evil. They levied accusations, and 'satan' means 'accuser.' But they were simply angels who reported upon the deeds of men. Men like Job, for instance."

Rachel pressed her hand against her mouth as if holding in her reply.

"Characters," Shinrou echoed, his tone thoughtful.

"That is an intriguingly confusing answer," Loki said.

"I don't like it," Thor said.

"You're incredibly well-spoken today," Kenzie said, letting his guard down despite himself at Top Hat's acknowledgement that Satan wasn't real. "What happened to the nonsense words?"

Top Hat swept off his hat and bowed to him. "Dear redheaded gentleman, the people of Earth feed me their hate. They feed me their fear. They even feed me their hopes and their love."

Kenzie experienced a weird moment of having a supposedly evil spirit affirm his true gender identity. "What do you mean, feed?"

"All this attention is making Top Hat more powerful," Shinrou said, still recording footage with his phone. "Just like Loki solidified the moment all eyes and cameras were on him."

Top Hat popped his hat back on. "Japanese man, I daresay you understand this. Keep their eyes upon me." He held up his cane, acting as though it were a microphone again. "Come one, come all! See the mighty Satan. Call upon him to destroy your enemies, those you blindly hate. Feed him the fear you feel for all who are unlike you. Are they brown-skinned? Beg me to kill them. Are they gay? Beg me to kill them. Do they not share your god? Beg me to kill them. Did they steal your wife? Your girlfriend, boyfriend, husband, sex partner, love toy? Bring them to me to die!"

Rachel bowed her head, her black curtain of hair falling forward.

Top Hat whirled in a circle again. "I will eat all your hate and fear. Kill them all! 'Faster Pussycat, Kill, Kill!'" He stopped and his pointed his cane at Thor. "What do you think, god of thunder?"

"You lost me at the pussycat," Thor said.

"Don't actually kill Jörmungandr." Loki crossed his arms. "Whatever else I can say, which is quite a lot, Jörmungandr is my son."

Top Hat grinned. "Ah-ha! So you two hate each other?"

"Depends on the day," Thor said.

"We have excellent mad heists," Loki said. "And we always make up in the end, even though you repeatedly threaten to smash off my head with Mjölnir."

"That's not how I remember things," Thor said.

Loki flicked a hand in dismissal. "Figures."

"You disagree because you have different summoners,"

Shinrou said, a smile lighting his face. "This makes sense! The realities formed inside the minds of each person are different."

"It's not all in our heads," Zoe snapped.

"I don't believe in anything I can't prove," Shinrou replied.

Top Hat crept away like a cartoon villain sneaking, his movements inhuman and jerky. He grinned the whole way. "Then I'll leave you to your own mischief. I must be off. I have a date with the son of the god who supposedly threw me down from heaven except that the being who shone like the morning star and then fell from heaven was actually Nebuchadnezzar."

"Does this mean you're through attacking humans?" Kenzie asked.

"I don't kiss and tell," Top Hat called over his shoulder.

Makari frowned. "Just so you know, Top Hat, Satan isn't known for killing anyone directly. He only provides temptations for humans to hurt each other."

"I wish it were that easy," Rachel murmured.

Makari started after Top Hat, halted, and then looked at the others. "What do we do?"

Logan clutched Kenzie's shoulder and pressed his hand to his forehead. "Oh, God. I'm so dizzy."

Kenzie grabbed his elbow, but Logan sank to the ground.

"No, it's vertigo. Oh, God!" Logan lay on the grass. "I'm gonna hurl."

Thor disappeared.

"You lost him," Loki said. "Ah, well. He'll be back." He trailed after Top Hat.

Shinrou stopped recording and put his phone away. "I have all the data I need, Logan. I'm sorry you overdid it. I wasn't thinking about that."

"I'm too hot," Logan gasped.

Makari held out both hands, summoning wind strong

enough to feather back Logan's spiky brown hair. "Sorry, that's all I can do. I've got to go after Top Hat."

"I get it, man. Go."

With a blue flash, Makari cast a speed spell and sprinted past Loki.

Kenzie knelt beside Logan. "Is there anything I can do?"

Shinrou glanced at Kenzie. "Loki put it succinctly. Logan 'lost' the summoning. He used up so much energy keeping Thor here that he got dizzy."

Zoe looked between them. "I've kept Loki anchored here no problem. Although yesterday afternoon, I was super tired. I had to take a nap." She jogged after Loki. "Wait for me!"

Rachel lifted her head. "So keeping them here can exhaust you."

Shinrou nodded. "More than that, they're characters. Satan and Jesus are characters from Christian folklore and the Bible. Loki and Thor are characters from Norse mythology and some thirteenth century literature recorded about it."

"But people don't think like that," Rachel said. "They believe. It's the belief that feeds these creations. That's why they're out of control."

Kenzie stared at them. "You're saying it doesn't matter whether Jesus H. Christ is real or not." The idea hadn't occurred to him.

A gleam sparkled in Shinrou's eyes. "The next step is obvious: We *all* need to try summoning a character."

"You're insane!" Logan gasped. "You can't just summon characters from movies or books like they're gods."

"That's what I intend to find out." Shinrou pushed his phone into his pocket. "My prediction is that the emotional investment matters more than the story."

Rachel stared at him, then turned away without speaking and walked off in the direction that Top Hat had gone.

"You're seriously going to pit magic against faith?" Logan asked.

"I don't like having the ivy league magic university that I traveled half the world to attend be torn up by other people's gods," Shinrou said. "It's already a battle between science and faith."

"I didn't travel half the world to come here, but I feel the same way," Kenzie said. "I may as well have come from half a world away. No, more than that. The URA may as well be a different planet. I came from an entire planet away to attend the magic university of my dreams and get a chance at freedom and a real life. And I'm not going to let it be torn up by anybody's gods."

Logan fell silent. His internal battle played out on his face in scrunched eyebrows and a grimace. Finally, he gripped Kenzie's wrist gently. "Fine. Even if it means questioning my faith, I have to get to the bottom of this. People are getting hurt and nearly dying. They're having their dreams for a better life taken away from them. That's not right."

"Thanks." Kenzie met Logan's gaze. *If only you were bi or gay. If only you could look past my exterior. Top Hat did, and he's just somebody's character.* He suddenly wished he knew who Top Hat's caster was, because they had given Top Hat so many good things in with the bad. The more Top Hat formed, the more he reflected who the caster was and how they thought, and no longer what purpose Top Hat had likely been created for.

Kenzie looked up at Shinrou. "But our tactics need to be different. We shouldn't try to fight Top Hat or Jesus H. Christ once we bring our characters to life. Instead, we need to go after the people summoning Top Hat and Jesus H. Christ. We don't have the energy to spare for anything else. We all saw what happened to Logan. The summoners have limits."

"Then we need to find their summoners and confront them before their creations finish attaining alternate sources of energy," Shinrou said. "That's what Top Hat meant when he ordered us to keep all eyes on him and feed him. He's trying to break free of his summoner."

Logan sat up and flopped halfway down again, catching himself on one elbow. "Shit. We've got to stop him."

Horror swept through Kenzie, burning his veins. "We have to stop all of them."

FIFTEEN

After lunch, Kenzie and Logan rested on a stone bench near the top of the staircase leading down to the grassy quad. On one side of the stairs stood the three-story, red brick Torres Administration building and on the other the three-story Anderson Hall. A towering oak tree provided them shade, but hot wind buffeted them.

Cicadas vibrated the air with their calls. Below them sat the crowd listening to Jesus H. Christ, lined up on lawn chairs and blankets. Some had erected beach tents to combat the August heat. Once again, Moriah sat by Jesus H. Christ's feet on the library stairs. Kenzie could pick her out at a distance because of her distinctive long, curly pigtails. "Even if no one else is feeding energy to Jesus H. Christ, Moriah sure is."

"Yeah," Logan drawled. "I don't think JCU's new measures will work."

Shinrou had spoken with Dr. Dawson before lunch and showed her the phone recording of Top Hat's claims that attention could feed him. As a result, the university administration had issued a 200-person visitor limit on campus, and all visitors had to wear badges. Likewise, only two camera crews were permitted on campus at a time. The students, faculty, and staff had to keep their university ID bracelets openly displayed.

The buildup of waiting visitors now extended for a dozen blocks in all directions. The mere thought gave Kenzie the creeps. *Despite everything Shinrou said, they won't shut down the campus. These people are waiting to give Jesus H. Christ their energy, and we can't stop it.*

"Do you think they would line up this way to see the Buddha?" Logan asked.

"No." Kenzie took Logan's point about how specifically Christian this all was. Then again, after the population devastation caused by World War III, Christianity had emerged as the world's largest religion, with no real competitors.

"As a Pagan, I don't really get it," Logan grumbled.

Another news helicopter flew overhead, rendering hearing impossible for several seconds. The noise pollution from the helicopters also disrupted their classes.

Makari climbed the stairs toward them, resplendent in the white uniform, which glowed in the late summer sun. Kenzie and Logan scooted down to make room on the bench. Makari settled by Kenzie.

A group of women had followed Makari, but seeing him sit by Kenzie caused them to stop by the stairs and whisper among themselves.

"Your loyal fanbase?" Kenzie asked.

Makari groaned. "I'm not trying to do that on purpose, but it's been happening to me since sixth grade. I know I'm an extrovert, so I'm always talking to someone. And I try to be nice to them, but what I get is..."

Logan grinned. "A fan club of groupies who are all willing to sleep with you?"

Makari hung his head, his shoulders slumped.

Logan reached behind Kenzie and thumped Makari on the shoulder. "I can tell you're not working the crowd."

"Speaking of working a crowd." Kenzie pointed to a middle-aged woman in a long dress pushing a middle-aged man in a wheelchair. She made her way toward Jesus H. Christ. "Here we have it, folks: The first person to ask Jesus H. Christ for a miracle. That's probably her husband."

"Well, this oughta pop everyone's bubble," Logan said. "No way can that spirit heal someone."

A security guard stopped the woman. She gestured wildly, pointing to the man in the wheelchair.

Moriah waved the woman closer.

Kenzie groaned. "And here we go. I knew it. Moriah is ushering the man over for Jesus to heal."

"Moriah's blind persistence is confusing," Makari said.

"It all seems somehow inevitable," Kenzie said. "She's going to have to see Jesus H. Christ fail before she'll come back to reality."

Makari lifted his head and straightened. "It's unlikely, but if the summoner is good at healing spells, it might end up looking like Jesus H. Christ healed that man."

"Oh please God, no." A wave of icy panic rushed through Kenzie's stomach and up his throat, as if a glacier shot toward his mouth. "If it looks like he performs a miracle, this university will explode. Right now, we have a crowd. A healing will bring a stampede of desperate people." He saw the pattern of what was about to happen. *Lame Man Walks! Oh, God, no. Followed by Blind Man Sees and Leper Is Cleansed. It's just like what's in the Bible. And Moriah is playing right into the hands of the person behind this charade.*

Logan stood. "We've got to do something."

"If we interfere now, we'll look like the bad guys." Kenzie grabbed his arm. "Moriah already promised these people Jesus' healing."

Makari jumped to his feet as well. "Then Moriah's in incredible danger. An angry mob will hold her responsible."

Kenzie released Logan and scrambled up as well. "Shit! I didn't think of that."

The woman wheeled the man up the access ramp for the library. Jesus stood and joined Moriah, meeting the man and woman at the top of the ramp.

"No, no, no, no, no!" *Moriah will get ripped limb from limb!*

Moriah reached out and took the man's hand. The woman took his other hand. Jesus H. Christ leaned over and touched the man's legs. Gold light poured from his hands. Then he straightened and stepped back.

The man slowly stood, his knees wobbling and his wife and Moriah still holding his hands. But he did stand.

The crowd erupted into screams, shrieks, and cheers.

Kenzie fell back onto the stone bench. "Moriah's safe, but we're doomed."

"I can't believe it," Logan hissed.

"I wonder if it's too late to withdraw this semester," Makari said. "Maybe I can try again in the spring. Or even next fall."

Resignation crested in Kenzie's chest like a black wave. "I can't do that. Somehow, I have to keep studying and attending class and doing well on my lab work and sparring, or I'll lose my scholarship." *And go back to hell.*

"Brace yourself for another huge speech from John Paul Smith, Jr.," Logan said.

Makari rubbed his temples. "Mori's going to be furious. If Top Hat was truthful, Jesus H. Christ is going to break free of his summoner because of this."

Half the crowd surged up the library stairs, and the campus security guards who lined the staircase and library doors rushed forward, struggling to hold them back. The healed man released Moriah's and his wife's hands and made a V for victory with his arms. He yelled something, likely praises to Jesus, his voice drowned by the crowd.

Kenzie stood and walked away. "I can't bear to see this

anymore. The whole reason I came here is gone." Tears burned his eyes.

Logan and Makari fell into step with him a few moments later.

"Why do you say that?" Logan asked.

Kenzie sighed. "How can I explain what I lived through? When my mom was born, the women in the URA could still wear pants and jewelry and could still cut their hair. Secular movies still played in theaters, and you could access any streaming service you wanted for music, TV shows, and movies. By the time I was born, all we could watch was really old stuff like *I Love Lucy, Father Knows Best,* or *Gone with the Wind.* And we could only listen to classic rock like early Elvis. Anything after 1960 was declared defiled. There was too much of a youth and sexual revolution in the 1960s, and according to John Paul Smith, Jr., the United States was handed over to Satan in 1963 when the Supreme Court ruled against mandatory prayer and Bible reading in public schools."

Logan and Makari both stared at him.

"But that was forcing everyone to pray to the Christian God," Logan said. "Separation of church and state—"

Kenzie held up one hand. "Don't bother. In Smith's world, freedom of religion means freedom to choose which denomination of Christianity to be. And, by the way, he doesn't count Catholics as Christians, much less people like the Jehovah's Witnesses."

A sharp snort escaped Makari. "But the U.S. was founded based on religious freedom, among other things."

"And so the Southern states ceded from the Union," Kenzie said. "The Second Civil War succeeded where the first one failed. But their primary goal was done in stages."

Makari's brow furrowed, and his shoulders tensed upwards. "What do you mean?"

"They got rid of our rights in stages," Kenzie said. "They

chipped away at them. They didn't wake up on the first morning of the URA's existence and say, 'Let's ban almost all secular music, movies, and TV shows; deny everyone access to the real internet; make all women wear dresses and do away with their jewelry and makeup; and revoke Black people's voting rights.' No. If they'd done that, the citizens would have rebelled. They did it over the course of *decades*. It took them over 60 years total."

Behind them, another chorus of screams and cheers erupted.

"And there's another healing, I bet," Kenzie said.

"Are you saying that Jesus H. Christ could start a similar cultural revolution here?" Makari asked.

Kenzie nodded. "It won't happen overnight like a Communist takeover. There will be a repealed law here or there. A new law here or there. Both your Congress and your Supreme Court will see if anyone steps up to stop them. When they get away with it, then they'll add on more. Then you'll get the URA. There, a woman can be arrested on suspicion of aborting her baby. No matter how much she insists she had a miscarriage, no one will believe her. They'll convict her. In Mississippi, Alabama, Georgia, and Louisiana, her punishment will be the death penalty."

Makari stopped in his tracks. "Please tell me that's not true."

Kenzie halted and faced him. "It is true. My aunt served eight years in prison for taking one *half* of a weak Valium while pregnant with my nephew. She was convicted of 'chemical endangerment of an unborn child.'" *And don't get me started on what happens to trans people like me.*

Logan paused and looked between them. "She's not exaggerating. I'm from Arizona. With Texas so close, we hear plenty of URA news." He gestured to Kenzie's pants. "Women caught wearing pants in public are fined 40,000 dollars on the first offense. It's a three strikes and you're out law. You go to prison for a minimum of 10 years on the third strike."

"Because the Bible says women can't wear men's clothing," Kenzie said.

Makari pointed to his own pants. "But we have both men's and *women's* pants."

"You don't have to tell me it's illogical." Kenzie resumed walking toward the dorms and smirked at the irony of the fact that he was, indeed, wearing the men's uniform. "At the time the Apostle Paul was writing, dresses and pants hadn't even been invented yet. Still, in the URA, that Bible verse is interpreted to mean women can't wear pants. There's other stuff like that. Lots of it."

Makari crossed his arms over his stomach. "God! Terrifying. I'd heard life is bad in the URA. I didn't know it was that bad. Do you really think Smith can invade the U.S.? I mean, he's obviously a murk."

"Sure he can," Logan said. "According to what I looked up, The Apostles' Way now makes up 22% of U.S. Christians, especially in states like Kentucky, Indiana, Ohio, Missouri, and Arizona. That's up 14% in just five years. It's a growing movement here."

A third roar from the crowd erupted behind them.

"With every miracle Jesus H. Christ does, he's building a bigger platform for John Paul Smith, Jr.," Kenzie said. "He's made his objective clear to those of us in the URA. You see, his father's life goal was to Christianize the entire URA and make everyone members of The Apostles' Way, specifically." He flung his arms wide. "Smith Jr.'s life goal is to Christianize the entire U.S. The Apostles' Way is headed your way, starting right here in Louisville. And why not? Louisville is only about 50 minutes from the URA border, and Louisville has Jefferson-Crowley University, which to Smith is the Mecca of evil."

"Wait." Makari halted again.

Logan and Kenzie stopped as well. "What's up?" Logan asked.

Makari pointed at Kenzie. "That's it! What you said. Smith intends to launch his cultural invasion of the U.S. through Louisville and JCU. Top Hat-Satan shows up, and Smith also shows up, claiming Top Hat is the real Satan. But there's no proof of that. And Smith's stayed here in Louisville. Posts on Minuclick said he spoke at some local church last night."

"So Smith might be Top Hat's summoner," Logan said, "or Smith knows Top Hat's summoner. It's got to be one of the two."

Smith! Chills flashed through Kenzie, icing his heart and lungs. *Well, it won't be Smith himself. He thinks magic is a sin. But I guess he could have a patsy. It would be strange, though, if Smith let a magician work for him. At the same time, I can't argue that Smith seems to be benefiting from what's happening here. Still, it seems more believable that Iona is the culprit.*

"And something has gone wrong with Smith's plans from the start," Makari said. "Think of how Top Hat attacked him and how scared and surprised he was."

Logan growled. "So that murk unleashed an uncontrollable weapon of religious warfare on our campus?"

Well, if you're right, we're stuck having to prove it, Kenzie thought, but he fell silent, as if he were still playing the role of a woman in the URA next to these noblemen. *I should speak up like a man, but I can't prove Iona's the summoner. Until I can, I don't think I can argue anything with two princes.*

THAT EVENING, RACHEL OPENED HER DORM SUITE DOOR AND admitted Shinrou Kitamori. Kenzie and she had been awaiting him, Kenzie sprawled on the drab brown couch in their living room and wearing jeans and a black t-shirt with a rainbow flag on it. Given Kenzie's choice of attire and haircut,

Rachel was still sure he was a transman, but until Kenzie verified that, Rachel would maintain her silence.

Thanks to the supposed miracle healings, Shinrou had decided it was now imperative that they "summon" their own characters so they could prove Jesus H. Christ was just a character, too. Rachel had been asked to help Shinrou, Makari, and Kenzie create characters because her major was energy work.

"Thank you for having me," Shinrou said, unfailingly polite. Unlike Rachel, he had changed out of his uniform, and he now wore tan khakis and a navy-blue polo shirt. His sleek black hair hung stylishly in a straight curtain to his jaw in the front, but was shorter in the back. Although he seemed at ease, he radiated a crisp, professional air.

Rachel wondered if the politeness was a Japanese cultural thing or if it was just Shinrou's personality. She knew next to nothing about Japan. "No problem." Since Shinrou was shorter than the average man and roughly her same height— perhaps five foot five—she found she wasn't terrified to share space with him. Most men petrified her, and they had since her father had died and her uncle had taken over her life. "Let's work in the living room."

"Sure." Shinrou swept into the seating area and dropped onto the dull brown chair by the widow bank. "Thanks for agreeing to tutor Kenzie and me in energy work."

Sitting up, Kenzie glanced toward the door. "Where's Makari?"

"The Noble 10 Student Committee finally called a meeting." Shinrou stared out the window at an oak tree, his brown eyes narrowing. "I can't believe they waited three days to meet. I think most of them are relying on their parents too much. The crisis is on *our* campus, and we're adults now. We need to be working to solve the problem."

"You are." Rachel perched on the edge of the other dingy chair, careful not to lean back and aggravate the lash wounds on her back. She hated how bland the dorm suites and classrooms were: an endless barrage of whites, tans, and browns interrupted only by stainless steel machines. *So industrial. The dreariness depresses me. More.* "But I'm not sure that I can teach you how to summon a character. Just because I'm majoring in energy work doesn't mean I can assist you."

"I think you can," Shinrou said. "My theory is that it's energy workers who are essentially bringing mythical characters to life. Among the top scholars of Japan, North America, and Europe, there is no belief that the spirits summoned by magicians are actual supernatural entities."

Kenzie crossed his arms. "So how are these mythical characters being made?"

"There may be energy workers or spirit summoners powerful enough to manifest the being they want to see," Shinrou said. "This entity is called a 'thought form' in scholarly circles. We have anecdotal evidence prior to World War III that humans were headed in this direction. Some authors talked about their characters 'coming alive' while they wrote, so much so that the novel's plot changed course. Some actors talked about playing characters that consumed their entire personalities for the length of the filming. Now our breakthroughs in quantum physics and brain science have allowed us access to what was always considered fantasy magic. The next logical step would be the ability of an energy worker to access the quantum realm through the persona of a character, thereby manifesting it."

"Our experience here has jumped far past that," Rachel said. "Somehow, these thought forms have objectively real bodies."

Shinrou bowed his head. "I'm working on a theory to account for that as well. Possibly there are two systems of magic being used at once." He stared at his knees for a moment, apparently lost in thought. Then he lifted his head and gazed at Rachel. "So how do we start?"

Rachel pondered the question for a moment. "Well, Top Hat seems satanic because he is the convergence of humans' attempts to rip out their own humanity. This is because basic human desires have been declared 'unseemly' or a 'sin' in our world." She smoothed an imaginary wrinkle in her skirt. *Why is everything always about sin and punishment?* "The harder people both reject themselves and believe Top Hat is Satan, the more satanic he looks and acts. They aim their self-hate at him, and he then says he wants people to 'feed' him their hate. So I think the first step is emotional. The magician who wants to craft a character has to feel powerfully about the character and what the character represents."

"Feel powerfully," Shinrou echoed. He blushed and looked out the window again.

Interesting response, Rachel thought. *What came to mind for you?*

"I'm not sure I feel powerfully about any characters," Kenzie said. "In the URA, we were stuck with old movies and Christian novels so preachy and saccharine that they made me nauseated. I can't connect with a character that just sounds like my ex-preacher harassing me at home."

"You may have to watch something from the U.S. that's more recent, then," Shinrou said, pulling his gaze from the window. He seemed to have recovered. "I think I'll try Tiger Man. He was a cartoon character I idolized as a kid."

Rachel folded her hands on her lap and crossed her ankles, shifting into a schoolteacher-like demeanor. "Then the next stage of any energy working is visualization. Probably you've been taught that already: You can't form energy into what you need if you can't visualize it."

"Sure. That's basic enough," Shinrou said.

Kenzie leaned forward and propped his elbows on his knees. "Okay. Do you think a sacred circle would help? Logan and Zoe rely on the old traditions."

"It might." Despite Rachel's complete atheism, her fear

kicked her in the ribs like an angry horse. *But that style of magic is witchcraft!* She closed her eyes and dismissed the panic. *There's no God, no heaven, and no hell. I hope. Because if there is a hell, I'm going to it.*

"Whatever helps you focus," Shinrou said.

Rachel pushed away her dark thought, opened her eyes, and nodded. "Shinrou's right. Do whatever helps."

"I'll start without it, then, and see what happens." Kenzie sat cross-legged on the couch and shifted around, clearly getting comfortable. "What about you?" he asked Rachel. "Do you need any tools or items?"

"I'm too exhausted to try making a character tonight." Rachel's unending fatigue was so extreme she wanted to sleep for the next year, and she worried about falling asleep in class. *I never imagined my first semester of college would turn out like this.* "I promise I'll work on it, though. Just let me coach the two of you."

"Sure," Shinrou said.

Relieved that she wouldn't be harassed into trying, Rachel sat with Shinrou and Kenzie as they meditated and worked on visualization exercises. They both persevered for thirty minutes, despite not achieving any results.

While Rachel was impressed by their work ethic, she was glad they failed. As she walked Shinrou do the door, a single thought haunted her: *This kind of energy work is dangerous, and if you succeeded, you'd only make this problem worse.*

SIXTEEN

At 8:54 Friday morning, Kenzie flew out of his dorm, running down the stairs, his black bookbag bouncing against his back. He had six minutes to cross campus and get to Magic Application II on time. He'd overslept and had nightmares about trying and failing to summon a character and being stabbed to death by Top Hat-Satan. His hair was still wet, and he'd grabbed an apple for breakfast.

Logan stood leaning against an old oak tree in the dorm yard, waiting for him. As usual, he wore the black uniform, apparently agreeing with Kenzie that the white one was a no-go.

"Hey." Kenzie gestured with his head, indicating Logan should walk with him. "How did the Noble 10 Student Committee meeting go last night?"

Logan fell into step beside him as they strode down the sidewalk at a brisk pace. "Not good. We just argued the whole time about what to do."

"Oh, that's just *great*," Kenzie drawled, his tone filled with sarcasm.

Logan flicked one hand in dismissal. "Well, forget that for

now. I would've just texted you, but I'm in the camp that thinks these things should be asked in person."

"What things?" Kenzie took a bite out of his apple. The distinct crunch was followed by the signature honey-and-tang taste of honeycrisps. The sweet apple scent clashed with the smell of freshly cut grass as the drone lawnmowers manicured the campus lawns.

"Dating things."

In his shock, Kenzie swallowed prematurely. The piece of apple scraped down his throat to his stomach. *As in boyfriend?*

Logan shoved his hands into his pockets, striking a casual pose undercut by the anxious energy wafting off him. "Wanna go out tonight?"

"Sure!" Kenzie took another bite of apple, so he didn't have to speak again yet. In middle school, students had been forbidden relationships, and even in high school, authorities discouraged dating. In addition, no boys had ever shown an interest in Kenzie, especially when it got out that he was a magician. And, on top of all of that, Kenzie was a transman.

"Cool." A blush stained Logan's cheeks.

Kenzie's lungs twisted with fear as if being wrung like a dishrag. "Um, there's one thing you should know first, though."

"Okay. What's up?"

For a moment, Kenzie fought with himself about coming out. He stared at the campus with its pristine red brick buildings with their white Ionic columns and the oak and maple trees with the green leaves fluttering in the wind. It all looked so normal compared to the war in Kenzie's mind. *I'm gonna blow this date before I can even have it. But this isn't the URA, and Logan is Pagan, not Christian. Still, he's probably straight, and he won't want a transman. But I can't pretend to be someone I'm not. That's a terrible way to start a relationship.* "I'm a transman."

Logan nodded slowly. "I noticed your men's haircut and

the men's uniform, but I didn't want to jump to conclusions. People have all sorts of reasons to dress and look the way they do." He shrugged. "I'm bi, so I don't care if you're male or female. I'm just interested in you, period."

With the way Kenzie's heart leapt, he wondered if he'd just fallen in love instantly. His sinuses burned, and his chest expanded until he felt his lungs would pop. "Thanks! That means a lot to me." *Oh my God, he really doesn't care! I'm safe.*

"So what do you wanna do?" Logan asked. "We've got lots of options. There's the whole dinner-and-a-movie thing, if you want to be classic. If you're into nature, we could go hiking in Waterfront or Cherokee Park or even drive down to Bernheim Forest in Bardstown. If you want to get your ears pierced and then go to cool shops that sell all sorts of awesome stuff the URA doesn't have, we could hit Bardstown Road."

Kenzie's spirit rose until the crown of his head tingled. Other than the day he'd discovered he'd been accepted to JCU, he wasn't sure he'd ever been this happy. "How about three dates so we can do all three?"

Logan's eyes widened a moment, and then he laughed, blushing again. "Hey, sure! Sounds great. Okay, which one do you want to do first?"

"Ears pierced. Dinner. Cool shops."

"Excellent." Logan grinned. "We need to start with the dinner, though. You want food on your stomach anytime you intend to get a piercing or tattoo. It can make your blood sugar suddenly drop, and then you get all dizzy and nauseated."

Kenzie returned the grin. "Okay. And unless you hate it, I want to eat Japanese food at a real Japanese restaurant."

"I love sushi," Logan said. "It's good by me. Have you ever had it before? I don't want to assume just because you're Asian American that, you know, you eat Asian food all the time."

Kenzie appreciated Logan's sincere attempt not to be racist. "My mom and dad cooked Japanese food when I was little, but after Dad died, eating Japanese made my mom too sad."

Logan's gaze fell to the sidewalk, all his animation draining. "Your dad died?"

"Yeah, when I was 10. Cancer."

Logan's lips pressed into a thin line, and for a moment, he remained silent. When he spoke again, his voice emerged strained. "My mom died three years ago. Car crash. Dead on impact. EMTs with healing magic can do a lot of things, but they can't bring back the dead. The AI collision avoidance system malfunctioned. Then three months later, the news about the recall of that model of the car flooded in. My family got a million dollars from the class action lawsuit that resulted, but what good does that do? It's like getting paid to lose my mom."

"Oh my God! That's horrible. You didn't even get a warning you were going to lose her. At least I knew my dad was going to die, and I had time to say goodbye." Kenzie squeezed Logan's arm.

Logan cringed. "I didn't mean to make this awkward."

"No! No, you didn't." Kenzie's chest burned behind his sternum.

Logan gave him a weak smile. "I promise our date is going to be a lot more fun than this conversation. I don't even know why I brought it up and barfed it all over you. I never talk about this."

"It's okay, really," Kenzie said. *I get why you summon Thor now. Thor is powerful. Thor can protect those he loves with his lightning and his war hammer. You're terrified of losing anyone else. And you think you want to be in the Black Ops because you're angry your mom died, and men often act out their grief as anger. The understanding about men came courtesy of Kenzie's mom. Damn. I guess I have to get man training now on how to talk and walk and act like a man. All URA women are trained to talk in indirect ways and to never state their needs directly. Or sometimes, at all.*

Logan looked at his watch, a top-of-the-line computer and activity tracker hybrid. "I'll look up the best sushi restaurants in Louisville." He reached out to hit the display, but then lowered his finger. "Uh, I'll do that later. Right now, we need to use a speed spell to get to class on time."

"Right. Let's do it." Kenzie cast his with little thought, zipping away. Running with the speed spell burnt up some of his excited energy about the upcoming date, and the cool wind whipping over him buffeted his face and hair. He zipped past buildings and grass as if he were driving.

After a second, Logan caught up with him, and they arrived on time.

In class, Kenzie had trouble focusing on Dr. Kitamori's lecture. He did his best to jot down notes—most students handwrote them on their tablets because studies showed handwriting was better than typing for learning—but he obsessed over his wardrobe. *I need more men's clothes.*

Dr. Kitamori droned on. "There are five indisputable magical systems: elemental magic, energy work, locomotion magic, gravity magic, and mind magic. Everyone agrees that the first four are straightforward interactions between the caster and quantum physics. We can see people cast water spells or healing spells. We can watch the direct effect of a speed spell or a gravity manipulation spell."

She tapped her computer screen, and the smart board changed pictures from someone casting a wood spell to someone using pyrokinesis. "Mind magic is less straightforward. Empirical studies have verified telepathy, empathy, remote viewing, telekinesis, pyrokinesis, and magically induced hallucinations and illusions. So these first five systems are taught in magic magnet high schools and universities all over the world."

Kenzie jotted down a few notes. *Can Zoe take me shopping before my date?* Being born in the U.S., Zoe would know all about style, even for guys. *That means coming out to her, but I think she can handle it.*

"Spirit magic and transmutation are begrudgingly acknowledged in scholarly circles," Dr. Kitamori continued. "The Japanese equivalents of magic magnet high schools don't spend time on these systems. However, many magicians summon spirits." She changed the picture to a man sitting in a sacred circle.

Kenzie stared. Up until this point in the lecture, Dr. Kitamori had rehashed things Kenzie already knew. However, no one in the URA had told him spirit summoning was common. *So any number of spirit summoners could be connected to John Paul Smith, Jr. And, if spirit summoning is so common, will that make it easier for me to figure out how to "summon" a character?* He felt discouraged after his failure the night before.

"The nature of summoning spirits is in debate. Many scholars theorize that spirit magic is a cross between energy work and mind magic, meaning it is not a separate system."

At the reminder, Kenzie glanced out the window. Two hundred visitors sat on the quad's lawn, but Jesus H. Christ wasn't present. There was no sign of Top Hat or Loki, either. Logan hadn't been able to re-summon Thor the day before and had indicated he needed to rest until Saturday. *If mind magic is involved, then I have a good shot. It's my top skill, after all. I definitely don't want to summon some god from folklore, though. I don't even want gods to be real.*

"Transmutation magic transforms a substance into one of its other forms. For example, transforming sand into glass. A strong caster could do this in a mere second." Dr. Kitamori changed the slide to a man reading tarot cards. "The final three systems are divination, manifestation, and dimensional magic, with the last one being hypothesized but unproven."

"But Top Hat can teleport," someone said. "That's dimensional magic, right?"

Dr. Kitamori paused. "He seems to, yes. If he's the result of a spirit summoning, especially one that comprises energy work and mind magic, it's not a true teleportation. The caster is making him appear and disappear. It's similar to how an elemental magician can summon water from the nearby river. You can manipulate quantum particles to fold space in order to move the water, but you can't inter-dimensionally open a door so that a complex living being—either a mouse or a human—can instantly step from one place to another."

A murmur ran through the room. Kenzie peered around. Makari and Shinrou were trading pointed looks. *So Dr. Kitamori has come to the same conclusion Shinrou has, or maybe they talked. They agree it's not true teleportation.*

Moriah raised her hand. Since Jesus H. Christ wasn't present, she was in class, but she looked haggard, her blonde pigtails frizzy.

Dr. Kitamori turned to her. "Yes?"

"The only one who can see the future is God. How does any scientist believe a mere human can look into the future using divination?"

The students grew silent and still. The room vibrated with tension, as though everyone held their breath.

Dr. Kitamori didn't even blink. "Movies and TV shows misrepresent it. Real diviners touch quantum particles and read their directionality. An excellent diviner will sense a minimum of two probable tracks, with most aiming for three. But quantum particles are in flux. There is no such thing as an unavoidable prophecy."

"Unless Jesus made the prophecy," Moriah said matter-of-factly.

Kenzie flinched and hoped no one made fun of Moriah. *I used to sound just like you. I used to think just like you. I don't want people bullying you when you're being totally sincere.*

Dr. Kitamori inclined her head. "I'll leave that assessment up to you, Moriah." She clicked to the next slide, which showed a woman meditating in a forest clearing. "The ninth system is manifestation. Modern humans first noticed it as the power of positive thinking. Medical studies showed that cancer patients who visualized their white blood cells attacking and killing their cancer fared better. Sports science studies discovered that athletes who visualized hitting the ball or basket performed better. Then, as studies continued, scientists discovered there was truth to the phrase 'mind over matter.' As a result—"

Kenzie stopped listening. He stared at Moriah, who had bags under her eyes and less pink in her lips than usual. *You're spending so much time with Jesus H. Christ that you're not sleeping? This has to stop.* He glanced at Rachel, who sat by Moriah and gazed at her with open concern as well, her brow furrowed. *I have to speak to Rachel. Alone.* No one except another member of The Apostles' Way could understand Moriah's devout dedication.

However, Dr. Kitamori's lecture ate up the entire class period, giving Kenzie no chance to talk to Rachel, and then everyone dispersed to their next classes, chatting in groups of two or three. As nice as it was to have a group of friends in college, having everyone around made squeezing in a private word to Rachel impossible. Even after Strategic Magic I, which was Kenzie's best shot, Rachel disappeared in the two minutes it took Kenzie to pack his tablet and grab his backpack from the bleacher.

"Where'd Rachel go?" Kenzie asked Zoe, trying to act casual. Around them, everyone else talked in clumps or raced down the bleachers.

Zoe shrugged. "I dunno. She got a call and said she was having lunch off campus."

"Was it a call like the other weird phone call?" Kenzie asked.

"I dunno. Maybe it's a date." Zoe grinned. "Speaking of dates, you said you wanted to go clothes shopping for your date with Logan."

"About that…" Kenzie paused and sized up Zoe. *You're all about fun and freedom. Surely you'll be as cool about this as Logan was.* He stepped forward and whispered in Zoe's ear, "I'm a transman. Do you still want to help me?"

Zoe hugged him. "Of course! I'll make you badass. Now let's go!"

Kenzie returned the hug, speechless. He was so glad he'd trusted Zoe. *Now two people know the secret I would've been killed for in the URA, and I'm not only still alive but also have a friend and a boyfriend.*

Heading out of the gym with Zoe, Kenzie allowed himself a sliver of hope. *Maybe I can actually get the life I want, even if I have to go one step at a time.*

SEVENTEEN

KENZIE HAD JUST RETURNED FROM CLOTHES SHOPPING WITH ZOE when Moriah burst into their suite, eyes wide and face pale. Kenzie and Zoe had settled at the kitchen table, snacking in the dim light. The afternoon had turned stormy, thick gray clouds crowding the sky. Thunder cracked overhead, vibrating the windows and floor. The sensation felt like a mini earthquake under Kenzie's feet.

"I need your help." Moriah rushed to Kenzie's side, her blonde pigtails tangled and her white blazer unbuttoned, revealing the sweat-dampened white Oxford shirt underneath. "John Paul Smith, Jr. is back on campus, and he's asked to meet me because I'm always with Jesus. The Reverend! *The* Reverend Smith! Wants to meet me!"

"I'd run away screaming." Zoe ran her spoon around the side of her yogurt cup. "Wait, rewind: You already met Smith. He's always there when you're fanning Jesus."

Moriah frowned at Zoe. "But this is different. He wants to *talk* to me. Alone. He was only beside me because we were both listening to Jesus' sermons." She turned to Kenzie. "Why does he want to talk to me? I'm nobody compared to him or Jesus."

Kenzie wasn't sure if Moriah felt excitement or fear and suspected it was both. "Well, you don't have to go if you're not comfortable." He popped a cracker in his mouth and crunched it, trying out Zoe's favorite veggie-flavored crackers. This one was green and spinach-infused, but all Kenzie tasted was rice and an earthy mystery herb.

Moriah tugged on her skirt hem as if she could magically extend her uniform skirt to her ankles. "I can't turn down Rev. Smith!"

"That's what everyone says," Kenzie drawled, "and that is precisely the problem."

"Kenzie!" Moriah implored.

Kenzie pushed aside the cracker bag. "How can I help?"

"Go with me." Moriah clenched her skirt hem so hard her hands trembled.

Kenzie's chest burned from equal parts curiosity and fear. Given Smith Sr.'s and Smith Jr.'s systematic reduction of women's rights and absolute annihilation of LGBTQIA rights —upheld by laws passed by both federal and state legislatures—Kenzie could never feel safe around the man.

But, then again, Kenzie had magic, and Smith didn't. Smith's condemnation and hatred of magicians made him an unlikely candidate. If he had a magician as a patsy, he had to be doing what so many Christian authorities had done throughout history: allying himself with someone willing to do the things that would send someone to hell so that he could still get his soul into heaven. *At least in his own mind.*

Kenzie thought of Shinrou's quest for data. *He'd never get invited to talk to Smith, and while I didn't either, I've got an in with Moriah. She's still trying to "save" me, and she still considers us friends. If I come along, I could learn something about Smith that might give us a clue who his summoner accomplice is—assuming Makari's theory is right.* "All right. But I'm not putting on a damn skirt." Kenzie pushed up from the table. "It's me in short hair and pants, or it's nothing. I'm just going to pretend to be from the U.S."

"Thank you so much! Just let me go change clothes." Moriah ran from the kitchen.

Kenzie used that time to text Logan about what he was doing and why. Moriah emerged from her bedroom in an ankle-length, blue, floral-print dress with a high collar and long sleeves. Then Moriah and Kenzie exited their dorm, Zoe trailing behind them. Two bodyguards dressed in black suits —tall, muscular, White men with identical buzz cuts—waited outside the dorm building. They wore black sunglasses despite the overcast sky.

What a stereotype these guys are, Kenzie mused. *Does Smith enjoy the effect the stereotype has on people?*

"Kenzie is coming with me," Moriah said. "Rev. Smith said I could bring a friend. Kenzie is my friend."

One bodyguard pulled out a cell phone, dialed a number with the press of a touchscreen button, and turned on his earpiece. "Plus one confirmed." He listened for a moment. Then he looked to Kenzie. "Full name?"

"Kenzie Okuda."

The security guard repeated that. Then he affirmed something and hung up. He tucked the cellphone in his inner coat pocket. "Let's go."

They crossed campus to the Idoni Student Building. Zoe trailed them by twenty feet, dressed in short shorts and a tank top and no doubt enjoying defying Smith's worldview. The bodyguards took Moriah and Kenzie to one of several study rooms on the Student Building's third floor. Zoe dropped into a chair in the hallway, not hiding her presence. Through the study room's glass door, Smith could be seen sitting at the head of a conference table.

As they entered, Smith smiled at them with perfect white teeth and stood. "Welcome!" He stepped around the table and extended his hand to Moriah. "We meet once again, Miss Goldstein."

Moriah blushed and bowed her head, but she shook his hand. "Y-yes, sir."

"It's a pleasure to speak to you, hon—the girl who sits at Jesus' feet like Mary did." Smith laid his other hand over their clasped hands and gave Moriah's hand an extra squeeze. "Your devotion to our Lord and Savior is awe-inspiring."

Moriah ducked her head farther. "There's nowhere I would rather be than at Jesus' feet."

"Now there's a true Christian girl!" Smith released Moriah and turned to Kenzie. "And you must be Kenzie Okuda."

Kenzie extended his hand and dropped his voice, hoping to sound like a man. "Yes." He met Smith's gaze without hesitation.

Smith shook his hand, bearing down with considerable strength. "Nice to meet you, hon."

Kenzie strengthened his grip, matching Smith's, and didn't look away. "Thank you, Rev. Smith."

There was a pause in which Smith continued to squeeze Kenzie's hand too tightly, and a fake smile flashed across his lips. Then Smith released him and headed to his chair.

Kenzie took a seat without being asked. He refused to stand. His hand throbbed from the handshake, but he didn't let on, relying on his stoic mask to appear unaffected.

"Have a snack, if you like." Smith gestured to the table, which held a fruit and cheese tray and bottled water.

"Thank you." Moriah sat by Kenzie, perched on the edge of the chair, and picked up a water bottle.

Kenzie grabbed a bottle, as well as serving himself some mustard yellow cheese cubes with toothpicks in them on a little white plastic plate. Unlike Moriah, he didn't intend to be dainty or too polite to eat, as was required by their culture. He pulled a cheese cube off the toothpick with his teeth.

"I wanted to talk to you about Jesus." Smith focused his

attention on Moriah. "The U.S. National Guard wouldn't let me on campus yesterday because I had already met Jesus. They're trying to cycle through a large crowd." He grinned again, and the corners of his eyes crinkled. "I'm honestly impressed with the sheer number of people who have decided to see Jesus in person."

"Me, too." Moriah tried to open her bottle of water and failed. Her hands shook. "I'm glad to see there are other devout people out there."

Kenzie took the bottle without comment, opened it, and passed it back. Moriah drank a sip of water, then set the water bottle down on the table in front of her, almost toppling it thanks to her trembling hand.

"Yes." Smith served himself a heaping plate of cheese cubes, apple slices, and red grapes. "As I said, you've been with Jesus every day so far. Tell me your impressions. You know I hope Jesus is the real article, but we must be careful. Not all the prophesies surrounding the Second Coming have been fulfilled yet."

Moriah glanced at Kenzie and then stared at the table. "Yes, I know. But Jesus is so kind. He's taught the Beatitudes and the Sermon on the Mount, and he's covered all the parables. When people asked for explanations of two parables yesterday, he explained." She finally looked up and met Smith's gaze. "And he healed three people!" An honest smile overtook her face.

Jesus H. Christ finally said something original? Kenzie supposed he should have tracked his social media feeds, but the comments and posts had been pouring in so fast that he'd given up. He wouldn't sacrifice doing homework, going to class, or sleeping for the spectacle.

"Yes," Smith murmured, still smiling at Moriah.

Kenzie didn't trust that constant smile. Something about Smith's vibes seemed off. In the URA, when a man smiled at a woman, it only meant one of three things: *I want to own* you, I am demeaning you, or I am only coincidentally smiling at you because I am actually smiling about something else while looking at you. Smith's gaze bored into Moriah with uncomfortable intensity. Kenzie didn't think he was staring through Moriah. *So it's either condescension because she believes Jesus H. Christ is real, or he wants to own her. Oh, shit. She would make a great PR shill for Jesus H. Christ on a bigger platform, and she's one of the Noble Three. Why didn't I put this together?*

"Tell me about those healings," Smith said. "You were there for all three, up close. And the three healings were medically substantiated either yesterday afternoon or this morning. To quote a phrase from history: 'The whole world is watching.'"

Moriah clapped her hands together. "It was amazing! Just like in the Bible. Jesus touched them and spoke to them, and then they were healed. The power radiating out of him was so extreme it made me lightheaded."

You were lightheaded because you did the healing, Kenzie realized, popping another cheese cube into his mouth. It was so obvious in retrospect that Kenzie felt disgusted at not thinking of it sooner. *That has to be it! You believe in Jesus H. Christ because you summoned him. This is exactly like Zoe arguing with Shinrou that her Loki is real.* A chill passed through him, goosebumps flashing over his skin. *Shit! What am I going to do with this information? I need to tell everyone, but at the same time, only Rachel and I will understand you and why you did it.*

A worse problem slammed into Kenzie's brain like two trains colliding: *If Smith figures that out, what will he do to you? Oh, God, I can't tell. I can't tell anyone. Not yet. I have to make sure Moriah is safe from Smith first.*

Smith leaned back in his chair and fingered his chin. "So you felt the divine power all around you?"

Moriah nodded.

"I ask because the Bible says that in the End Times, there

will be false prophets proclaiming to be the real Jesus," Smith said.

"But like you said, the healings were verified by doctors," Moriah said. "They're real. When the Pharisees said Jesus was Satan and casting out demons using Satan's power, Jesus replied Satan would not act against Satan: 'And if a house be divided against itself, that house cannot stand.' If the healings were real, then they had to come from God."

Smith smiled, and this time it seemed genuine. "You know your Bible. Good girl."

"Woman," Kenzie corrected, his voice calm and as low-pitched as possible. "Moriah is eighteen. She's no longer a girl."

Smith stared at Kenzie as though he'd just sprouted a buffalo head. "What difference does that make?"

"You would never call a grown man a boy," Kenzie said. "Men are referred to as 'man' and given adult status. Even white-haired women are still called 'girl' and are treated like they're kids. It's the psychology of linguistics: psycholinguistics. Research studies have shown that psycholinguistics has genuine power. How you talk to someone and how you talk about yourself make real, measurable impacts." Anger burned in his veins that Smith would never call his mom a woman, never give her the time of day, and his mom might have been too frightened in this situation to speak up. *Who does the speaking, then? When will someone draw the line?* Until the words "good girl" left Smith's mouth, Kenzie hadn't understood how much rage he had dammed up behind the stoicism he'd perfected to survive.

Moriah stared at Kenzie, her face sickly pale. "K-Kenzie..."

Kenzie met Smith's gaze without blinking.

"Ah, the scholarly *woman*," Smith mused.

It's still obvious I have a female body, even with the chest binder. Dammit! I want to pass. "By which you mean the most dangerous woman there is," Kenzie said. "Isn't that right? It's better if women don't think for themselves. Only men should do that."

"Kenzie!" Moriah grabbed his arm.

But Smith laughed. "What pep! You're a real spitfire, sweetheart. I like it. I hope you use that same zeal when you witness for Jesus."

Kenzie gave him a tight smile.

Smith waved his hand through the air as if batting away a gnat. "Very well." He turned to Moriah. "A good Christian *woman*, then, sweet pea. And I'm impressed by it."

Moriah released Kenzie's arm and blushed. "Thank you."

"Other than the healings, is there anything else you noticed that made Jesus seem like the genuine article to you?" Smith returned to his plate of food, popping a grape into his mouth.

Moriah gazed at the corner of the room, eyes narrowed in concentration. "Nothing specific. He's loving and kind and patient. Just being in his presence is so awe-inspiring that I get tired. And, well, he hasn't done anything Jesus *wouldn't* do."

Smith rolled a grape between his fingers. "What of the counterclaim that he's just a magician's creation?"

Moriah balled her hand into a fist and slammed it against the table. "Never! No mere human magician could ever wield such power! Not to mention, the magician would have to have entire passages of the Bible memorized, along with the correct interpretations of those passages. No. Jesus is the real Jesus. He's here, on Earth, with us."

Kenzie raised his eyebrows and drank his water, covering up his real reaction. *Smith's actual reason for interviewing you is that he knows Jesus H. Christ is a fake, and he's looking for the caster. He started at the most obvious place: the one person who won't leave Jesus alone. Moriah's in a shit ton of danger.*

"A-ah." Smith stared at Moriah a moment, clearly

surprised by her sudden show of strength and passion. "I see. Well. Good points, all. Thank you, Miss Goldstein. I appreciate your taking the time to share your impressions of Jesus with me."

Recognizing the dismissal, Kenzie stood, nabbing his last cube of cheese as he did.

"Of course, Rev. Smith." Moriah stood as well, smiling now. "I'm honored to meet you."

One of the unmoving, stoic bodyguards came to life and opened the door. Kenzie grabbed his water bottle and headed out with Moriah.

Both Zoe and Logan were in the hallway, sitting across from each other in brown, plush chairs that nearly blended into the dark hardwood floors.

Logan hopped to his feet. "I heard some raised voices. Is everything all right?"

Kenzie glanced back to make sure the door was closed. "Yeah. That was just Moriah standing up for Jesus H. Christ." *And now I have a piece of information I can't do anything with. I wasn't trying to figure out who summoned Jesus H. Christ. I was trying to figure out who summoned Top Hat-Satan!* He headed for the stairs, not wanting to take the elevator. Elevators made him feel claustrophobic, and he preferred the exercise.

Moriah sighed. "I shouldn't have raised my voice, but I expected him to have more faith that Jesus is Jesus. I see why he's worried about a false prophet, or perhaps even the Antichrist, but he's seen Jesus up close. A man of faith shouldn't be so skeptical."

Zoe fell into step with Moriah, Logan, and Kenzie, the four of them spanning the hallway as they walked. "Actually, yeah, that seems weird to me. I mean, the same thing is happening with Loki, though. Most people are posting that he's a fake. Just a guy in a medieval costume."

Moriah shot Zoe a look. "Even if Loki was an actual spirit and not a demon, Loki didn't save all of humankind. Jesus did. In fact, the Bible says not to believe in or worship anyone else. Eventually, Loki will trick you into doing evil, and if you don't repent and believe in Jesus instead, you'll go to hell. And I don't want that for you. I don't want that for *anyone*."

Moriah! Kenzie swallowed a groan as he pushed open the fire doors and entered the stairwell.

Zoe scoffed. "Loki's not evil. You refuse to ever be around him, so how would you know anything?"

"If you don't stop summoning Loki, something bad is going to happen to you," Moriah said. "Isaiah 13:9 says, 'Behold, the day of the Lord cometh, cruel both with wrath and fierce anger, to lay the land desolate: and he shall destroy the sinners thereof out of it.' And Isaiah 13:11 says: 'And I will punish the world for their evil, and the wicked for their iniquity; and I will cause the arrogancy of the proud to cease, and will lay low the haughtiness of the terrible.'" Her loafers rang on the white, tiled stairs as they descended, as if each step underscored the Biblical proclamation.

Logan remained silent, a faint frown tugging at his lips.

Zoe's eyebrows scrunched up. "You're warning me about Loki, but when you quoted the Bible, it says your deity is cruel and angry."

Moriah shook her head. "God is only punishes people who disobey him."

"That sounds scary and demonic to me." Zoe traced one finger down the steel railing as they reached the landing and started down the next flight of stairs. "Are you sure you're in the right camp? Loki would never terrorize humans. He fights his fellow gods sometimes, but never humans."

Listening to them argue, Kenzie grew tenser until his shoulders ached. *I used to sound like this. I used to force my religion on other people. I used to try to convince people to give up their beliefs and swallow mine instead.* He felt ill. *Why couldn't I just respect what they believed?* He gripped the water bottle in his hand so hard the thin plastic crinkled loudly in protest.

"But we're *sinners*," Moriah insisted. "We brought this on ourselves when Adam and Eve ate the fruit from the forbidden tree of the Knowledge of Good and Evil."

"That's just a creation myth," Zoe said. "In Norse mythology, the first man and woman came out of a tree. There's this thing about trees and humans, apparently."

"No, it's true," Moriah said. "Adam and Eve were the first two humans, and God created them. They didn't evolve. They were special, and they were 'specially made.' The Bible says so."

Kenzie saw Zoe's eyes narrow and knew this was about to get nasty. "Wait! Hold up. Let's stop here. Moriah loves Jesus, and Zoe loves Loki. Let's just leave it at that, okay?"

"At least I know humans evolved and didn't really come out of a tree!" Zoe snapped, halting as they reached the bottom of the staircase.

"Humans were intelligently designed by a loving God who wants the best for us! We didn't come from apes!" Tears sprang to Moriah's eyes, and her face flushed crimson.

Logan stepped between Zoe and Moriah. "Everyone pause. Just pause."

"*You* pause!" Moriah slammed open the door and marched out. The scorching August heat billowed inside like a dragon's breath and battled the air conditioning. Then the door closed and sealed them in the coolness.

"I have to go out there," Kenzie said to Zoe and Logan. He pushed through the door and into the sweltering heat. Moriah wasn't far. She'd only gone about eight steps. Her shoulders were hunched and her arms folded tightly over her chest.

Kenzie took a deep breath and approached. *I hate this. The only thing that's going to work is Christian rhetoric.* "I know this is a difficult situation in the dorm right now. There are three of us from the URA, and then there's Zoe. We're the minority here, like the Jews in the Roman Empire. Jesus says to turn the other cheek and to love our enemies."

Moriah sighed and dropped her arms. "Well, Zoe's not my enemy. She's just rude. But you're right. Jesus would want my good witness to help Zoe come to believe in him. Then she could get saved." Her lower lip trembled. "It's not like I want Zoe to go to hell. It's too *horrible*."

"You're really sweet," Kenzie said.

"Moriah!" Rachel ran toward them, her curtain of black hair streaming out behind her. "Moriah, are you okay?"

Moriah ran forward several steps, stopping as Rachel reached her. "I guess. I mean, I'm upset because Zoe was making fun of me. Why?"

Rachel bit her lip for a moment. "But you texted me you were meeting with Smith."

"It was a great honor for Rev. Smith to want to talk to me." Moriah grabbed one blonde pigtail and worried it, wrapping it around her finger repeatedly. "He was nicer than I imagined he would be. He forgave Kenzie for picking at the way he talked, and he didn't even seem angry when I yelled at him for not believing Jesus has come to save us. I wish I could go back and apologize to him, but I know he's busy. I'm amazed he made as much time for me as he did. I'm nobody."

"You are not nobody," Rachel said. "Besides, if you measure yourself against Jesus, even Rev. Smith is a nobody. And I'm glad Smith was in a good mood when he spoke to you and Kenzie."

Kenzie met Rachel's gaze. "That's right. Moriah shared that being in Jesus' presence makes her lightheaded, so she really needs to rest." *Please help me protect Moriah.*

"I see." Rachel reached out and squeezed Moriah's arm. "Yes, being in Jesus' presence and sitting so close to him would be overwhelming for anybody. This is why I keep saying you need to take breaks. The only people who could withstand that much holy power emanating from Jesus were the Apostles."

Moriah's shoulders sagged. "I guess you're right. I can't expect to do what an Apostle can. Rev. Smith stood next to Jesus, too, and he didn't seem affected at all."

Rachel averted her gaze.

"I don't think it's fair, but I agree with Rachel." Kenzie stuck with the Christian rhetoric. "Ordinary people like us need to rest from the experience of Jesus' immense holiness." *Maybe this tactic will buy us time until we can solve the problem. We have to slow one of these summoners down, and it won't be the summoner of Top Hat. We still have no clue who Smith's accomplice could be, and I didn't get any clues from meeting him. Unfortunately.*

EIGHTEEN

That evening, Kenzie stood in front of the full-length mirror installed on the back of his bedroom door. He wore camouflage cargo shorts that came down to his knees and a black tank top with a design in all caps that read PARENTAL ADVISORY: SUBVERSIVE THOUGHTS. A pair of beige men's sandals and a choker that looked like a bicycle chain finished the outfit.

Zoe stood beside Kenzie, grinning. "Logan'll love it. Man, you look badass. But do *you* like it?"

Kenzie matched Zoe's grin. "I *love* it." The chest binder flattened his chest well, so between it, his masculine haircut, and the outfit, he passed as a man. "I finally feel like an individual person and my real self instead of a wallpapered woman rolled over with granny-style floral dresses."

"Ugh." Zoe mimed vomiting. "I'll say it again: Don't go back."

"I'm not." *I just hope the U.S. doesn't end up exactly like the URA.* Kenzie ran his fingers through his straight, fine hair and wished he could have kept it magenta. *Blood red isn't bad, though.* Then he grabbed his men's wallet and phone off his desk. The wallet he connected with a chain to a belt loop, and the phone he stuck in his other back pocket.

Zoe assessed him and gave a thumbs up. "Good luck. Try to score a first kiss."

Kenzie blushed. "Oh, God. Okay, maybe." *Maybe if I focus on getting my first kiss, I won't be obsessing about Moriah being the summoner of Jesus H. Christ. I'm so stressed out I've got to get that out of my mind for a few hours. It's not like I know what to do about it yet, anyway.*

Zoe grinned wickedly. "Remember, we Asians are the smokiest people on the planet, and that's why everyone is jealous of us. As my grandma used to say, work that Asian rizz!"

"Thanks." Kenzie hugged her. After Moriah's somber declaration earlier that she was going to pray for his safety on his date with the 'demon worshipper,' he needed the pep talk. *I hope I also have some trans rizz, whatever that would be.* He wondered if there were any other transmen on campus, and if so, how he could find them. He hadn't even had time to look up the club offerings on campus thanks to the Top Hat-Jesus-Loki-Thor crisis. *Maybe there's an LGBTQIA+ club.*

Kenzie headed out the door and skipped two or three steps at a time down the stairs. Logan waited for him under the oak tree, leaning against it with his arms crossed. He met Kenzie's gaze and smiled. Logan wore denim cargo shorts and a black t-shirt with a red design reading *The Sex Pistols Live On*. Kenzie assumed it was some old movie, TV show, or rock band.

"You look awesome." Logan pushed away from the tree.

"You always look awesome," Kenzie shot back.

Logan threw a hand over his heart. "Ah! Slain in the compliment category within the first sixty seconds! I can see how this date will go."

Kenzie laughed. "I just say whatever pops into my mind.

It's probably a fault. Sometimes." He felt so giddy he wondered if it were like being tipsy.

"Nah." Logan strolled down the sidewalk with him. A light breeze caressed them, providing relief from the 100-degree heat index. The storm had passed, leaving the sky bright blue with a few thin, white clouds. "I forgot to ask about transportation. I've got my motorcycle here. And just so you know, I don't use the autopilot."

"I'm cool with trying your motorcycle with you controlling it."

Logan grinned. "I kinda thought you might say that. You seem like you'd want to try a motorcycle."

"I want to try a lot of things now that I'm free," Kenzie said. "Except not drugs. One of my uncles died of an overdose."

"Okay, yeah. That's scary." Logan pointed toward the eastern parking lot, and they veered that direction. Ahead, the perfectly manicured green lawns gave way to an ocean of fresh black asphalt. "So what's the URA like about dating? I mean, we're actually from two different countries here, so I really should ask." He cringed. "Plus my older sister—she graduated from here last year—said I shouldn't make any assumptions."

Kenzie found amusement in imagining an older sister giving her younger brother a talk. "Most of the adults discouraged us from dating. Before we were in high school, if the teachers found out two kids were together, they'd order them to break up. We were sneaking around them all the time, of course. But you would get suspended for a week if you were caught holding hands in the hallway. Kids who were caught doing more than holding hands faced expulsion from the school. Some adults call it Purity Culture, but the kids call it Purity Nazism."

"Yikes. Creepy." Logan wrinkled his nose. "So what about high school?"

"The adults still frowned on dating, and you still couldn't hold hands," Kenzie said, "but they knew we'd date no matter what, so the adults focused solely on the topic of sex."

Logan snorted. "Let me guess. Having premarital sex is a sin. Don't go past kissing. Abstinence is the only form of birth control."

"Yep." Kenzie gave him a tight smile. They stepped off the sidewalk onto the asphalt and ambled past a line of electric and solar-powered cars, far more than he would have seen in the URA, which still relied more on gas and oil. "Of course, they banned sex ed, and since not even condoms are sold, you can imagine the outcome. I knew seven girls in high school who were expelled for getting pregnant."

"That's ridiculous! In the U.S., studies show that good sex ed courses *reduce* the rate of pregnancy and STIs."

"But don't you know?" Kenzie gave Logan a mock-innocent look. "No one who is unmarried has any reason to know anything about sex, and the only acceptable way to learn is to fumble around in ignorance on your wedding night and hope you don't hurt each other."

Logan slapped his palm against his forehead. "Well, considering how many details you need to get right to make sex decent, you can be guaranteed to cause pain, if not injury, if you both just jump in and try to hump each other."

"*All* the girls who had sex in high school told me it hurts the first time, plus after that, if something goes wrong." Kenzie chuckled nervously. It wasn't until he said the sentence out loud that Kenzie realized he was terrified to have sex. *No, thanks. I'm a man, and I don't want anyone touching the female equipment that way. Much less injuring it.*

Logan flinched. "Idiots. And if they had access to the real internet, they could just go read up on what to do so, you know, it actually *feels good*. God, what a concept! Besides, you probably don't want to, um..."

"Nope, I don't. I'm a man." Feeling reassured by Logan's

apparent willingness to educate himself for his partner's sake, Kenzie relaxed a fraction. "Well, how people date in the URA is really beside the point. I've never had a boyfriend. This is my first date."

"I assumed that because the URA is so oppressive," Logan said, "but it sounds like I could've been totally wrong. You could have rebelled instead." They rounded the first line of cars and headed down a second one.

"Your turn. How do people date in the U.S.?"

"Lots of fun. Lots of seeing places and eating good food and watching movies," Logan said.

Kenzie's excitement returned. "Sounds good. In the URA, it's all about finding out if the other person is 'Christian enough.'"

"Uh, no. It's not like a weird job interview." Logan stopped by a shiny black motorcycle and opened one side compartment. He pulled out a helmet and offered it to Kenzie. "Here. Safety is important. If we weren't magicians, we'd need to wear leather gear in case of an accident in order to avoid getting road burn."

Once they both got their helmets on, Logan drove them to a sushi restaurant on Bardstown Road, one section of which was just as Logan had described: filled with novelty and retro shops, coffee shops, and restaurants. The sushi restaurant turned out to have a bar with a constantly moving conveyer belt, as well as the usual tables and booths. Kenzie had never seen anything like it. Instead of robots, two human sushi chefs worked in plain view in the center of the room and placed each item they made on a dish, refilling the conveyor belt as people ate. People thought "un-American" food was weird in the URA, so it was a shock for Kenzie to see that most of the customers were White.

"Wow, so vintage," Kenzie said. "Actual humans work here."

"Yep. And you still have a great experience." Logan

gestured to the belt, which was filled with little plates of sushi. "You don't have to wait, you can eat as much as you want, and the plates are color-priced so you can track your tab."

"Awesome." Kenzie glanced around for a spot at the circular bar where they would be more to themselves. Two stools were empty at the back. "Look. An opening."

Kenzie and Logan grabbed the seats. Kenzie took a plate of salmon maki going by. Logan snagged a dish of tuna maki with bright orange sauce drizzled over the top. Instead of eating, he glanced around and frowned.

After nabbing some chopsticks, Kenzie poured soy sauce into a tiny square cup and dipped a piece of his salmon maki in it. "What?"

"Sorry. It just hit me that John Paul Smith, Jr. would want to close all the Asian restaurants in the U.S. on the assumption that they're not Christian." Logan grabbed some chopsticks. "I know, I know. I'm not supposed to be thinking about anything except you."

Kenzie waved that away. "I think if anyone is Satan on Earth, Smith is. If I'm honest, he's always in the back of my mind." He shook his head and ate another piece of salmon maki. *In the name of God, Smith and his father used their power and influence to strip away almost all human rights. He forced all the Latin Americans out of the country. Asians have to pass a literacy test. They don't allow Black people to vote. I'm surprised we have any sushi restaurants even for non-Whites to visit.*

Logan laid one hand over his. "I've heard news stories, but I still don't understand what you've been through."

"Honestly? I don't want you to understand it. To understand it, you'd have to live it, and I don't want that for anyone. Besides, it'll be okay, at least for me and my mom." Kenzie said that with more confidence than he felt. "With the degree I'll get at JCU, I'll be able to get a work visa. My mom can do the same. Unlike the last time she applied, she's written and published her fifth book now, and it won an award. A sociology professor with publishing credits and an award is a lot more attractive in the U.S. than a professor with none." *Or at least that's what I've got to keep telling myself. Otherwise, I really gave up my mom in order to escape.*

"Your mom's a professor? Being super smart must run in the family."

Kenzie blushed. "Thanks."

"Score!" Logan made the victory sign with his fingers. "Now we're one for one on the compliments."

Kenzie laughed.

After supper, they headed to Logan's newly discovered tattoo and piercing shop. Kenzie opted to get not only a traditional ear piercing but also get his nose pierced. Although Logan claimed to be bad at healing spells, he cast one with enough strength to erase the redness, swollenness, and throbbing.

Kenzie left the shop feeling ridiculously cool. "I feel so badass I'm being such a faid right now."

"Faid?" Logan echoed.

Kenzie realized the term might be URA-only. "Dork? Nerd? Geek?"

Logan smiled. "Oh! Yeah, those work. A popular one in the U.S. right now is 'ratbag.' We stole it from Australia and kinda changed its meaning for our own use."

"Ratbag. I like it." Kenzie put his helmet back on.

"But you're not being a ratbag. You look good." Logan pulled on his black helmet, too. "There're a ton of other shops we can go to. But if you really want to be defiant, and you don't think you'd feel uncomfortable, I can take you to the adult gag shop."

Kenzie's brow furrowed. "Is it all porn or something?"

"Nah. They've got all sorts of stuff. Gag presents, body jewelry, sex toys, incense, hemp clothing, and beaded curtains." Logan hopped on his motorcycle. "Just about everything."

"I'm in." Kenzie climbed on behind him.

Ten minutes later, Kenzie walked into the weirdest store he'd ever seen. There weren't just bongs, there were fancy apparatuses for drinking alcohol. There weren't just beaded curtains, there were lava lamps that looked straight out of the 1960s. The nose rings and studs filled three displays. There was also a section of joke gift cards, including ones that said 'over the hill' and cake toppers that were shaped like tombstones for both ages 40 and 50.

And then he found the sex display: scented massage oils, furry handcuffs, "how to" books for better sex, and a glass case full of sex toys, the uses of which varied from obvious to inexplicable.

"If my sister finds out I brought you here on a first date, she's going to break my nose," Logan said.

Kenzie leaned over the glass, his brow furrowed. "John Paul Smith, Jr. would say I'm going to hell just for seeing this stuff still in its packaging."

A White woman stepped in behind the case. She had neon green streaks in her jet black hair and a half dozen facial piercings, including one in the middle of her cheek. "Hi. Can I help you with something?"

Kenzie took a chance. "I'm a transman, so I'm not sure."

"In that case, I have a suggestion." She pointed to the toy she recommended and gave Kenzie more sexual education in two minutes than he'd had since his mom's basic sex talk when he was nine.

Kenzie and Logan both walked away, blushing.

"Well, at least I know what my options are now." Kenzie felt a bit stunned.

"Yeah, and it's important to know what's open to you," Logan said.

Setting aside his shock, Kenzie bought a nose stud and a

birthday card with a tombstone on it for his aunt, whom he knew would be amused and not offended. The mere fact it was a *paper* card would be thrilling enough for her.

Four stores later, they returned to campus and walked to one of the many gazebos. The one behind Anderson Hall proved empty. The white wooden structure was roughly twenty feet across, with wooden benches built into its sides, so they sat and watched the last of the sunset. Red brick buildings and maple and oak trees blocked the horizon, but Kenzie enjoyed the patch of sky with a mix of orange and rose still visible over the city skyline. A waning crescent moon shone above the Torres Administration Building, with Venus sparkling to its side.

Logan offered his hand, and Kenzie took it, relishing its warmth. Little happy tingles danced through Kenzie's stomach at both finally having a boyfriend and getting to hold hands.

"Humans are sexual creatures, and sex is also how we get babies. So why do so many humans spend so much time trying to deny or control sex?" Kenzie murmured.

Logan squeezed his hand and stroked the back of it with his thumb. "I guess because it *is* important. People with power will always try to control or take away what's important."

"Well, I'm not in the URA, and their obsession with our private lives is totally perverted." Kenzie smirked. "So here, let me 'sin.' Kiss me."

"Glad to." Logan smiled and leaned in.

Kenzie met him halfway. His lips were warm and soft, and for several minutes, the URA was the last thing on Kenzie's mind. For the first time, he imagined what it would be like to have a husband. All the sermons about how evil the U.S. was for condoning gay marriage had ignited his longing for a husband when he was fourteen years old. Instead of being stuck with a Bible-thumping, physically and sexually abusive man, Kenzie wanted a kind man who enjoyed philosophical discussions and who accepted him for who he was.

When the kiss ended, they pulled back and gazed into each other's eyes. The soft light of affection in Logan's brown eyes filled Kenzie with wonder. Then, unbidden, his revelation that Moriah was the one who had made Jesus H. Christ flashed through his mind, and he glanced away.

"What is it?" Logan asked. "Did we move too fast, after all?"

Kenzie shook his head. "No." *I kissed you, but I won't trust you with the secret that Moriah's the one who is causing so much trouble that our university might shut down.* "Well, maybe." Guilt pressurized his chest. *I can't trust you not to blow up at her. And she's just confused. She didn't do it on purpose.* "I mean…" He struggled to take a deep breath as he searched for an excuse. The deep breath made the chest binder pinch him. He winced. *Okay, good enough.* "Actually, my chest binder may have overstayed its welcome."

Logan jumped up. "I wasn't thinking! I'm so sorry. I should've guessed you were wearing a binder, and we're sitting out in the heat after hours of you wearing that thing."

Both relieved and ashamed, Kenzie stood. "Yeah. Sorry. But remember, you owe me two more dates."

Logan took Kenzie's hand and squeezed it gently. "Looking forward to it already. Let me see you back to your dorm, okay? Not because of chivalry. Murky shit keeps happening around here."

"Right." Kenzie's split-second of horror and embarrassment was removed by Logan's explanation. "But who's seeing you back to your dorm?"

"I've been rotating through people," Logan said. "If you're not using a buddy system, you should be."

"I have been," Kenzie assured him. "Zoe and Moriah, mostly. Sometimes Rachel."

They set off for the women's dorm. Only now, Kenzie felt

the uncomfortable weight of being misgendered by his own housing arrangements. *I should have seen if there was a way to get accommodations. I didn't even ask. I lost my nerve and didn't speak up. But if I weren't here, I couldn't keep an eye on Moriah, so at least that's something.*

To his frustration, when he entered the dorm, he found a note from Rachel on the smart fridge touch screen notes app. She had said she wouldn't be back until late. *Not again! Rachel and I need to talk about Moriah. She's the only one I can trust with my realization.*

Kenzie headed to bed with equal parts joy and frustration, worried about what to do about Moriah.

NINETEEN

On Saturday morning, Kenzie, Logan, and Zoe sat on the expansive balcony of Anderson Hall, eating a late breakfast at a table. The morning wasn't too hot yet, despite the still air and glaring sun. Below them, a crowd of 200 visitors clustered around the library on the grassy quad, the white-robed Jesus H. Christ sitting at the top of the stairs as usual. Moriah had already eaten, donned a porcelain blue prairie dress, and joined Jesus at his feet, listening to his latest sermon.

It had been impossible to get Rachel alone this morning so that they could talk about Moriah. Kenzie didn't even know where Rachel was; she kept vanishing from campus. Kenzie felt like a super volcano building up to a stress eruption. He needed Rachel as his ally, and a terrible thought had occurred to him overnight: Moriah was abusing magic, and the Noble Seven of the U.S. thought it was their job to control how people used magic in their country. *For all I know, they can send Moriah to prison—and will, because they don't understand her.* He wanted to enjoy the company of both his boyfriend and his trans-affirming friend, who was of Asian descent like he was, but he couldn't.

Loki appeared beside Jesus H. Christ, not six feet from where Moriah sat. Moriah shot to her feet and hid behind Jesus. Jesus regarded Loki calmly.

"Zoe," Kenzie hissed, shooting his friend a look.

"What're you glaring at me for? I had no idea Loki was going to do this." Zoe lifted her bare legs and crossed them on the iron balcony railing. As usual, she had cutely dressed herself in a pink tank top with daisy-print and purple short shorts, as if she had no cares in the world.

"He's *your* god," Logan said.

Zoe held up her hands. "That doesn't mean he tells me everything!"

Loki turned and addressed the crowd. "Good morning, residents of Midgard! I challenge the great Jesus Christ to a debate of words and deeds. I would like to see his miracles for myself. Who knows? I might even convert." He grinned. His voice carried across the quad as if he wore a mic.

Zoe dropped her legs, stood, and pointed. "There's Thor."

Logan shot to his feet. "What?"

Kenzie's gaze followed the line of sight from Zoe's finger. Thor strode with purpose across the grass toward the crowd, Loki and Jesus H. Christ. He rested his war hammer on his shoulder.

"Loki!" Thor's voice also boomed across the quad without amplification. "Don't complicate my protection of Midgard by starting a fight with some other god."

"But I didn't do this." Logan looked from Kenzie to Zoe. "You've gotta believe me."

"Copy and paste. Now you know how I feel," Zoe said.

Logan groaned. "Yeah. Sorry." He leaned over the railing and stared at Thor. "But I don't understand it. I asked him not to do this and explained why, and he agreed. He knows this can only make the situation worse. Thor isn't stupid. And he's always protected me before."

That got Kenzie's attention. *Protected you from what?* He

knew men were sensitive about looking weak, so he didn't ask. But he did text Shinrou, Makari, and Rachel about Loki and Thor appearing again. Then he abandoned what was left of his breakfast and joined Logan and Zoe at the railing. "So Thor and Loki can now both appear without being summoned with a sacred circle?"

"Yes." Logan was tense. "And I have no idea how."

Below them, Loki turned and faced Thor. "My dear Thor! Excellent to see you again. Let the good times begin."

Thor pointed his hammer at Loki. "No tricks and no games. And will someone please tell me how you got free of your cave?"

Ignoring Thor, Loki turned to Jesus. "I just got an excellent idea. You're a god who can walk on water." He looked to Thor. "And you're a god who can summon lightning. This is an amazing combination. Let's find a lake. Even a pond will do."

"What are you up to?" Thor demanded.

"The cameras are doing their work." Logan raked his fingers through his spiky hair. "I could already feel Loki's energy from here, and now I can feel Thor's, too."

Kenzie rubbed his temples. "If Shinrou's right, the reason this is happening is because you want it to."

Logan pulled up straight and glanced at Kenzie. "What? No, I don't!"

"Yeah, I'm not doing anything," Zoe snapped. "I don't have to. But, um, read the FAQ. I *want* Loki to show people Jesus H. Christ is full of shit. Maybe Loki can make people stop feeding rubber Jesus. Then it might disintegrate or something."

Kenzie gestured toward Moriah, who stood behind Jesus. "Christianity doesn't work that way. *Humans* don't work that way. Christians will see this as a test of their faith and believe in Jesus H. Christ even more. They will think God is judging them and taking notes about their level of faith." He turned to Logan. "If Zoe's not willing to stop this, you've got to try."

"The sight of Loki drives Thor mad," Logan said. "I can't keep Thor from showing up if Loki is around. It's Thor's responsibility to protect Midgard. And Loki can't be trusted."

Zoe snarled. "Shut up! It's Thor who's always ruining Loki's fun."

Kenzie stared at them. *Your beliefs about your gods put you on a collision course with each other. Shinrou is right. This disaster is all about us. The students. Not the Noble 10 clan heads. We're the ones who have to stop it.*

Loki faced the crowd. "We need a pond, lake, or river. Want to see Jesus walk on water and prove once and for all that he's the real Jesus Christ? Point our way."

"This is a trick," Thor warned the crowd.

A student in a black uniform stood up from where he'd been sitting at the bottom of the stairs. He pointed to the side of campus.

"Dammit! I can't believe someone actually answered him." Kenzie jumped off the balcony, using gravity magic to slow and cushion his fall. The others weren't far behind him, and they ran toward the crowd.

"Wonderful!" Loki linked his arm with Jesus' arm. "Let's go, son of Jehovah. Or is that the son of Elohim?"

Moriah covered her mouth with both hands in apparent distress at Loki touching Jesus.

"Either will do," Jesus said, "but I needn't prove my godhood to you."

Thor stepped in front of Loki and Jesus and gestured with his hammer. "Yes, don't go with him. Loki is not to be trusted. He is a trickster by nature, and it is his son Fenrir who tore off Tyr's hand. It is his trickery that will bring about the end of the world."

"Lies," Loki scoffed. He turned to Jesus. "It's not for me. It's for them." He gestured to the crowd.

Jesus shook his head. "Belief is a matter of faith."

"Belief and faith are the same thing," Loki said. "That was a circular sentence. Besides, nearly three billion people will see this. That means you can convert the entire world in one day!"

"Leave Jesus be," Thor ordered.

"I performed many miracles during my human lifetime," Jesus said. "Plenty of people still didn't believe."

Loki strode down the side staircase, dragging Jesus with him by the arm.

Moriah jogged close behind, exclaiming, but without the unnaturally amplified voice of Jesus H. Christ, Thor, and Loki, she couldn't be heard.

Loki gestured grandly with his free hand. "Humor me. Or am I being cruel? 'Turn the other cheek.' Am I asking for something ridiculous? 'Walk the extra mile.' Are you getting angry at me? 'Don't let the sun go down on your anger.' Tempting you to sin? We all know you won't sin, anyway. Unlike actual humans, you're above sin."

"Loki!" Thor bellowed, and then with a sigh, he followed.

Zoe, smaller and faster, raced out in front of Kenzie. "Why won't Jesus H. Christ just yank out of Loki's grip?"

Kenzie sped up to match her. "The summoner sees Jesus as kind, patient, and loving. Unless Loki tried to desecrate a church, Jesus H. Christ won't lose his temper. Remember why he summoned the whip before."

"You don't have to lose your temper to pull away from someone," Zoe said.

"Jesus didn't resist arrest by the Romans," Kenzie said. "Trust me. The summoner thinks Jesus won't fight back. More than that, the viewers and crowd don't, either. Despite some harsh things Jesus said and did, a lot of Christians see him as uniformly sweet. Basically, some of them see Jesus as the loving one while God is the harsh punisher." He scanned the crowd. *I can't see how to catch up to Moriah. There are too many people in the way.*

Kenzie, Logan, and Zoe stuck together in the throng following Jesus H. Christ, Loki, and Thor. Two camera crews also rushed along with the mass, doing their best to film the excitement.

When the supposed gods reached the pond behind the greenhouse, the crowd surrounded the water. Logan and Zoe picked a spot one fourth of the way around the pond from the gods' position.

Kenzie squeezed between people, struggling to reach Moriah. "Moriah! Jesus doesn't have to prove anything!" *Moriah was already exhausted. If she tries to use more magic, she might die of magic-based fatigue.*

Loki grinned as he released Jesus H. Christ's arm. "By all means, the son of the one and only true God should go first." He gestured to the water.

Jesus H. Christ gazed at the water. "I assure you, no number of miracles will ever bring people to faith."

"I am not participating in this game," Thor said. "And neither will Jesus. Your machinations bode ill."

"Moriah!" Kenzie screamed, still stuck with about 20 people between him and his friend. "That's right! Jesus doesn't have to prove himself. People will believe what they want to believe."

Moriah still faced Jesus, her face pale and her pigtails frizzed. She didn't acknowledge hearing Kenzie.

Thor grabbed at Loki. "You are coming with me."

Loki shoved him away. "Don't you dare!"

As Thor lunged for Loki again, Loki used a speed spell to glide out of the way. He flitted across the ground as if he were ice skating. "Too slow," he sing-songed.

Thor whirled to face Jesus. "If you cooperate with Loki, you will accomplish nothing but evil. Tell these good people to go home."

Jesus inclined his head. "I take orders from no one. But you must understand the son of God has power and dominion over both the heavens and the earth." He stepped onto the water and walked to the center of the pond.

The crowd erupted into gasps, shouts, and shrieks.

Moriah fell to her knees.

Kenzie shoved people aside, making the gaps between them larger with his telekinesis, and rushed to Moriah's side. "Moriah! Moriah, no."

Tears streaked Moriah's cheeks, and she clasped her hands. "Look," she whispered. "It *is* Jesus." She was deathly pale now and had gray smudges under her eyes.

Despair lanced Kenzie's chest, stealing his breath and threatening to seize his lungs. The throng became a nightmarish blur around him. He remembered the preacher of his childhood church screaming in a fervor that all of them should be willing to die for Christ. He wrapped his arms around Moriah. She was clammy to the touch.

Loki clapped. "Well done! Bravo, bravo." He turned to Thor. "My dear Thor, if you would be ever so kind?"

"You both leave me no choice!" Thor shouted. "I will protect Midgard at all costs!"

Kenzie glanced over his shoulder and saw Logan had joined them to be closer to Thor. *Stop. Can't you see what you're doing?*

Thor lifted his hammer and looked to the sky. Anxious murmurs raced through the crowd. For a moment, the sky remained clear and blue, with only a few fluffy clouds in sight. Then the clouds shifted toward each other, darkening. The pale gray bruised into darker gray and then black. Thunder rumbled over the crowd. The contrasting blue sky surrounded the dark blotch, as though the blue ringed the black. Yellow flashes emanated within the clouds, and a streak of lightning shot down, connecting to Thor's hammer. Thor himself lit up in a blinding flash. A deafening clap of thunder followed. The throng shrieked and screamed.

Thor swung his hammer. Lightning leapt from his hammer and arced to Loki and Jesus H. Christ. Their bodies absorbed the lightning , leaving behind only a small scorch mark on their chests. For an instant, their appearances faded to a lighter color, but they just as quickly returned to normal, the scorch marks also disappearing.

"Is that the best you can do?" Loki asked.

Logan fainted, collapsing onto the grass beside Moriah.

This time, Thor didn't vanish. Instead, he turned toward Logan. "My faithful priest!" He ran to Logan and knelt by him, touching Logan's forehead. "I don't understand. Why did you take ill?"

Panic and rage warred inside Kenzie. *Because he used up his magic creating lightning for you, you idiot!* Behind the wall of adrenaline, he realized with horror that the thought forms weren't conscious of their connections to their creators. The core energy that made Thor had come from Logan, but Thor didn't know it. *That means Jesus H. Christ doesn't know he owes his existence to Moriah, and Top Hat, even if we could interrogate him, wouldn't be able to tell us who his summoner is.*

Moriah turned and reached out, holding her hand over Logan's chest.

"Stop!" Kenzie grabbed Moriah's wrist. "You can't heal him. You're out of energy."

"I forgive you for summoning that demon," Moriah whispered to Logan. A golden glow shone from her palm as she cast a healing spell. Then she, too, fainted, toppling over onto the grass.

"Damn it!" Kenzie felt Moriah's pulse and then pushed some of his energy into Moriah's chest, using the only healing spell he knew: a first aid technique for stabilizing someone who had had a heart attack or was struggling to breathe. "Zoe, help me!"

Zoe didn't seem to hear him over the screaming, yelling, and arguing of the crowd.

Jesus H. Christ crossed the pond and knelt by Moriah. "This woman needs rest. She's driven herself into exhaustion."

"Her name is Moriah Goldstein," Kenzie snapped at him.

"The weary should rest in the Lord."

"You owe her a lot more than you know." *She's not your Mary Magdalene, she's your Mother Mary! And in this case, it really is a virgin birth.*

"She is one of the faithful," Jesus said.

Kenzie narrowed his eyes. "She's more than that."

Logan stirred, and Thor helped him sit up.

Since Zoe hadn't reached them, Kenzie continued using both hands to pour healing energy into Moriah's chest. At the same time, he looked over at Logan. "Are you okay?"

"Woozy," Logan said. He peered up at Thor. "Damn, that was amazing."

Thor grinned, the smile giving him a boyish handsomeness. "Thanks, priest."

Ducking his head, Logan blushed.

Kenzie finished his spell. "Okay. Moriah's stable. She probably won't wake up for a few hours, though." *And we have to talk later. This was not "amazing."*

Thor helped Logan to his feet and pulled his arm over his shoulders. Then he wrapped his other arm around Logan's waist. "You need to rest somewhere." They headed away, Logan stumbling every few steps.

Jesus stood over the unconscious Moriah as Kenzie glared up at him.

"Well? You can't tell me you're less generous than Thor." Kenzie's face burned with rage.

"Intimate touch between an unmarried man and an unmarried woman is forbidden." Jesus H. Christ's voice lacked any intonation.

"Faker," Kenzie hissed. He lifted Moriah into a sitting position against him.

Rachel broke through the crowd, emerging near Jesus, and held up one hand. "I'm getting Moriah out of here."

Jesus glanced at Rachel. "A wise idea."

"Let me!" Makari emerged from the crowd behind Rachel and swept over to Moriah. He picked her up in a front carry.

"I found Makari on the way," Rachel explained to Kenzie. "We saw your text at about the same time." She faced the crowd clustered behind them. "Move. I'm rescuing Jesus' most loyal attendant." She marched forward as though she could part the Red Sea, and sure enough, people got out of her way. Makari followed, carrying Moriah with apparent ease.

Kenzie trailed in their wake and found Zoe. "Come on."

Zoe stared at Makari's back. "Lucky! I want to be swept up in Makari's arms."

Kenzie took her elbow. "Enough. Let's go. Moriah and Logan have both been hurt by this."

Zoe shook him off and turned back toward the main show. "I'm not missing what Loki's going to do next."

Loki transformed himself into a mirror image of Jesus H. Christ. "Maybe I'll look like you. Everyone wants to worship you. Well, actually, that's not true. But in the URA and other such places, people are forced to worship you, so looking like you could be a sweet deal."

"You're an obvious fraud," Jesus said.

"You're an obvious fraud," Loki repeated in the same voice.

Kenzie nudged Zoe's shoulder. "Let's get out of here before this turns into a riot."

Zoe looked around. Her face fell. "Okay, yeah, you're right." She headed out of the throng, Kenzie close behind her.

A helicopter roared overhead, no doubt with another news

crew. In his gut, Kenzie knew Loki's brief presentation had turned what had been a house fire into an entire forest fire.

TWENTY

Although Moriah had awakened briefly while Makari carried her, she'd passed out again, staying asleep for five hours. Zoe had gone back out. Meanwhile, Kenzie and Rachel had parked themselves in the kitchen of their dorm suite, granting him the opportunity he needed to speak with her. They sat across from each other at the oak table with an orange origami crane between them. Kenzie had practiced origami during his senior year, having used it as stress relief, and so he offered the crane as a practice prop for their homework. In short, the crane was a puck.

"Moriah is the one summoning Jesus H. Christ." Kenzie aimed one finger at the crane, summoning a tiny burst of wind. The crane rolled like tumbleweed across the table. "You've stayed pretty close to Moriah during all this. Did you figure that out?" It felt bizarre to be doing schoolwork after the clash of the thought forms, especially since Moriah had almost killed herself with magic fatigue. However, none of their professors had canceled class or moved deadlines. The university was still determined to act like this was all under control.

Rachel halted the crane with her hand and aimed her finger at it. A puff of air blew it back toward Kenzie. "Yes. I've known for three days now."

"So you've been protecting her. Me, too." With a sigh, Kenzie stopped the crane and took aim again. "We can't turn her over to the Noble Seven." He summoned a micro blast that blew the crane off the side of the table. "The person we need to find is the person who summoned Top Hat-Satan."

Rachel snatched the crane midair and set it back on the table. "How do you know that would solve anything? Top Hat is already independent."

Kenzie gauged Rachel's flat tone. *Exhaustion?* She showed signs of sleep loss: smudges under her eyes, irritable behavior. *You've been staying up all night because of whatever is going on with you, and you're probably trying to comfort Moriah. When do you sleep?* "But we need to know why Top Hat-Satan was made. And what we saw today proves that the moods and wishes of the people who made the thought forms still influence them. Loki and Thor fought because Zoe and Logan did. Jesus caved in to peer pressure to prove himself because Moriah couldn't stand the questioning of Zoe's Loki."

Rachel blew the crane across the table again. "I still don't understand how learning more about Top Hat could help."

Kenzie caught the crane. "Moriah only made Jesus H. Christ because of Top Hat."

"No, any stress added on top of Iona's bullying would've had the same result."

Kenzie held onto the paper crane. "I don't think so. I think it's opposing beliefs that fuel the thought forms. Think about it: nothing is more tightly held than our beliefs." He tapped the crane against the table as he realized he'd given himself a clue. "Whoever made Top Hat believes humans are beyond redemption. Moriah rejected that belief so strongly that she made Jesus H. Christ."

Rachel bowed her head. "She's sweet. She's sincere. She's...a white light. She truly believes Jesus can save anyone."

Kenzie re-creased folds in the paper crane. "And Top Hat's summoner doesn't believe anyone has ever been saved."

Rachel didn't look up. "What do you believe?"

Setting down the crane, Kenzie searched inside of himself. He thought of everything his mom had taught him about civil rights movements. The closed circuit of the URA's internet circulated viral videos, showing parents lifting cars or collapsed walls off of their children, all claiming them as evidence of miracles. He thought about Moriah stepping in between him and his bullies and rebuking them. "I think people save people."

Rachel lifted her head and stared at him.

"While the Noble 10 Student Committee is arguing about what to do, Smith suspects Moriah of summoning Jesus." Kenzie resumed tapping the crane against the table as a surge of panic spiked his chest. "He wants to use her as a pawn in his schemes to expand the URA and the influence of The Apostles' Way. For all we know, the Noble 10 Student Committee will want to arrest Jesus' summoner and hand them over to the clan chiefs. We can't let either group have her. Help me save her."

Rachel's gaze fell to the tabletop. "I'm already doing all I can."

Kenzie blew the paper crane back across the table. "I appreciate what you've done for Moriah. We've got to work together to convince Moriah to send Jesus back to the side of God the Father. We don't know who made Top Hat. Even if we did, I don't think this person would help us. I think they're part of a conspiracy Smith cooked up to take over the U.S."

Rachel grabbed the paper crane and pressed it flat

between her palms. "Weren't you the one teasing me about being a conspiracy theorist?"

"I changed my mind. You were right."

Rachel pulled on the shape of the paper crane, making it 3-D once again. She shot the crane across the table with enough force that air fanned Kenzie's face, neck, and chest. The crane zipped off the table. "No. I was wrong. Whoever created Top Hat…their ideas are too confused. I don't think they know what they're doing. And when Top Hat became independent, he said things that imply his creator is an atheist."

"Or Top Hat's creator has Religious Trauma Syndrome." Kenzie rescued the crane from the tile floor and set it on the table.

Rachel scoffed. "That's a good one."

Kenzie looked at Rachel until she met his gaze. "Oh, I wish I were kidding, but I'm not. It's a real diagnosis in the U.S., Canada, and the UK. At first, people were being diagnosed with Complex PTSD, but the symptoms were so specific that RTS was created as a diagnosis. My mom told me about it, so I looked it up when I got here. Psychologists believe most of the behaviors of people in the URA come from the symptoms of Religious Trauma Syndrome. Other nations think basically our whole nation has RTS."

Rachel looked away. "I don't think there is any diagnosis severe enough to describe how I feel. The world is full of hate, and all that hate piled on top of me until all I can do is hate them back. But I hate myself, too, for being that way. I hate us all for being *human*."

"Is it really humanity that's the problem? Or is it inhumanity?" Kenzie murmured.

She folded her arms over her stomach. "How can I feel anything but disdain for humans? They waste the only life they have hoping they'll be good enough to live in heaven forever once they're dead—a heaven they can't prove even exists."

At least now you're talking to me for real. Kenzie nodded along with what Rachel said. "I wish people would focus more on this life, on what's right in front of them. People are so worried about getting into heaven that they're willing to send everyone else to hell for it."

"Except maybe Moriah. She is light, and I am all too aware that I am darkness. My skin is 'too dark,' my eyes are dark, my hair is black. I wear nothing but the color black. I've been told my father's Jewish blood is a black mark upon me in the Kingdom of God. They say I'm the descendent of the 'evil' Jews who 'killed' Jesus. And worst of all, I'm a woman: the blackest mark of all. I am a descendent of Eve, the mythical woman who supposedly dared to gain the knowledge of good and evil and, therefore, the maturity of adulthood."

Kenzie gazed at Rachel, empathy warming his chest. "I've felt that way, too. Sometimes I think the ugly mass of scars inside me would scare off anyone who really knows me."

Rachel glanced at Kenzie, her lips parted. No sound emerged. She looked away and frowned. "Well, I wasn't going to say anything, but...you're really a man. You don't have to carry the burden of Eve's sins."

Shocked, Kenzie stared at Rachel Abrams, reassessing her. "Wait. You figured out I'm trans?" *And you accept that as valid?*

"Moriah might be naïve, but I'm not."

Uneasiness coiled in Kenzie's guts like an icy snake. "How many other people noticed?"

Rachel shrugged one shoulder. "I have no idea. You aren't being subtle. But some people probably assumed you were a lesbian until you started dating Logan. Now more people might start guessing the truth."

Kenzie's stomach clenched. "I wish that didn't scare me so much."

Slowly, Rachel turned her head and looked at him. "But I

understand why it does. Some people won't see you as human anymore."

As much as that hurt, Kenzie couldn't deny that Rachel had bulls-eyed his fear. "Like Moriah?"

Rachel's brow furrowed. "Her devotion to Jesus and the canonical teachings is genuine. She's working to be the most loving and helpful person she can be. She sincerely cares for others and their welfare. Christianity isn't a political move, a community status symbol, or a chore to her. She's a True Believer. Moriah would never see anyone as less than human. What worries me is that her determination to love everyone doesn't extend to herself."

Moriah stepped around the wall that separated the living room/kitchen combo from the hall of bedrooms. Her white uniform was wrinkled, and her long, blonde pigtails were frizzy. She still had gray circles under her eyes, but she smiled at them. "Don't worry about me. And thank you, Rachel. That's a really wonderful compliment."

Rachel blushed. "It's—well, it's just true."

Moriah stumbled to the cabinet of chocolate and pulled out a candy bar.

"Oh, no you don't." Kenzie abandoned the crane. "You need to eat some actual food. We're going to the ISB." He noticed the conversation with Rachel was over, and he'd failed to convince her that there was anything they could do except keep sitting on the information that Moriah had created Jesus H. Christ. *This isn't going to stay a secret if we can't get Jesus to go away. The crowd of Christians is masking Moriah for now, but Jesus H. Christ still acts out Moriah's deepest wishes, and Logan, Makari, and Shinrou are going to notice that sooner rather than later.*

"Only the fast-food joints are open right now," Rachel said.

Kenzie snorted. "Okay, fine. Pseudo-real food. Something more than sugar."

"All right." Moriah took a bite of her chocolate bar. "But I'm eating this first."

Kenzie caved into the inevitable.

"Then after fast food, you need to try summoning a character again," Rachel told Kenzie. "Shinrou wants someone to succeed by Monday morning."

With a groan, Kenzie laid his head on the table. "Okay, okay." *I guess being in college means you don't really get weekends. Where did Zoe get the idea any of us could party?*

BY SUNDAY EVENING, KENZIE WAS EXHAUSTED. RACHEL HAD given him guidance the previous night and that morning. Also, Kenzie had practiced all afternoon. His problem was he didn't feel strongly enough about any character to focus his energy.

Logan arrived at Kenzie's dorm after supper, and Kenzie admitted him. Logan wore camouflage cargo shorts and a white t-shirt with an unfamiliar cartoon character on it.

"I didn't have any luck," Kenzie announced, shutting the door harder than necessary. "Maybe I just need way too much training for this. Or maybe I'm just not a strong enough magician to do it." He had dressed in jean shorts and a black tank top for the evening.

"Nah, that's bullshit." Logan squeezed Kenzie's shoulder. "I think you need inspiration. Were you allowed to read anything other than the Bible? Or watch anything not Bible-related? Didn't you mention watching old movies and TV shows from before 1960?"

"Yeah, but everything was either too old for my taste or Bible-flavored. Even things that weren't directly Biblical were still...Well, like my favorite episode of *Jesus and Friends* in which Mickey stowed away on a spaceship headed for the moon."

"*Jesus and Friends*?" Logan echoed.

"It was the most popular cartoon when I was a kid. When I was in middle school and high school, the big high school drama series was *The Apostles' Twelve Thrones.* It was vaguely sci-fi in the 'set 50 years from now' kind of way."

Logan grimaced. "Oh, God. I don't even want to know. Also, don't go back. You don't even get quality TV."

Kenzie laughed. Then he composed himself. "Okay, back to concentrating on the problem. Anything from the 1950s or earlier was considered okay as long as it would be rated G on a modern movie scale today. We could also read some Shakespeare plays, like *Hamlet.* You know, the stuff that was considered classic already a century ago—or longer. But all of that is boring."

Logan plopped onto the worn brown couch. "Did you *ever* like any of the things you read or watched?"

Sitting by Logan, Kenzie took his hand, a sharp thrill shooting through him at actually being able to do so. "When I was in middle school, I was obsessed with Sherlock Holmes. All the old short stories and books were allowed. But as soon as I realized that a real life Sherlock Holmes wouldn't even talk to me except to accuse me of murdering a White person, I got too depressed to keep being a fan."

Logan pulled Kenzie into a gentle hug. "That's like if I thought Thor would reprimand me if we ever met. He protects humans but also confronts human wrongdoing in the old stories."

With a groan, Kenzie rested against Logan's side. "My Religious Trauma Syndrome is showing. I never thought of that. I loved Sherlock Holmes and wanted him to love me, so my trauma fired off. I thought he'd accuse me of being evil, just like God. Dammit, that's so clear now."

"Sherlock Holmes can be whoever you want him to be." Logan pressed a kiss to Kenzie's lips. "What if people were wrong about him? He's so intelligent, and he doesn't pay attention to things that don't matter. Isn't he the most observant person in the world? If he existed, he'd see who I see: someone brave, intelligent, and honorable."

"I want to believe that."

"Then let's watch a more modern Sherlock Holmes movie and see if you can reconnect with the character."

"Sure." Kenzie was excited at the thought of seeing a modern U.S. or UK production of his old favorite character.

For the next two hours, Kenzie and Logan snuggled on the couch, watching a Sherlock Holmes movie from 2091 on Kenzie's laptop. Kenzie almost forgot the outside world existed while seeing his favorite character brought to life masterfully with an excellent plot and a sterling actor. Plus, best of all, this Sherlock Holmes called out someone for racism and proved that a French-African immigrant doctor wasn't the killer. *Now this Sherlock Holmes I can fall in love with, guilt-free.*

As the credits rolled, Kenzie turned to Logan. "I'm inspired. But I'm still no energy worker."

"I really think mind mages have a good shot at this." Logan caressed Kenzie's hand with one thumb. "You're still in the top 20 at the U.S.'s only ivy league magic university. Seriously, man. You've got this."

Kenzie shook his head. "If I had a month, then sure. I could believe that. But we need this to happen *right now.* So how about helping me create Sherlock Holmes? Do you think we could team up?"

"That's a great idea! Let's try." Logan stood. "Let's use your room so your roommates won't walk in and interrupt us."

Kenzie showed Logan his bedroom, thrilled about trying the combination. "I hope this works. We can't waste any more time, and you said it took you *years* to summon Thor in such a way that you could see him." He had borrowed candles from Zoe to make his first sacred circle. They were small jar candles in green, blue, white, and red to represent the four elements.

"Well, I was also twelve when I started," Logan said. "You've been practicing magic longer than I had been when I began."

"If that even helps." Kenzie sat inside the circle, which he'd drawn on the brown burlap carpet with Zoe's sidewalk chalk.

Logan sat inside the circle facing him. "Well, I have to have hope it helps." He held out his hands. "Let's try to funnel our energy into the center of the circle."

"Okay." Kenzie took Logan's hands and watched as Logan closed his eyes. For a moment, Kenzie couldn't think about casting a spell of any kind. The sight before him was too beautiful. Logan held his hands, and dim candlelight surrounded them in the dark bedroom. It was the most romantic thing he could think of.

Forcing himself to concentrate, Kenzie closed his eyes. Logan's energy filled the circle, and he added his own. He moved through visualizations, imagining how Holmes would look, how he would act, what he would say. The energy between Logan and him felt increasingly heavier, and he peeked. Logan's blue energy and his own green energy bled together, creating a brilliant aqua glow. Encouraged, he closed his eyes and resumed the visualizations. He imagined molding the aqua energy into Holmes' shape. Then he reminded himself of what the renowned magician Aleister Crowley had said: Magic took willpower. Kenzie had to assert his will upon the universe to manifest his goal. *My will is done*, he told himself, pouring all his conviction into the sentiment.

I believe he has it, a voice whispered inside of Kenzie's mind. Kenzie opened his eyes and gasped at the faint, see-through image of Sherlock Holmes standing between Logan and him. "Logan!"

Logan opened his eyes as well. "We did it!"

Holmes smiled and glanced over his shoulder at Logan. He looked like the newest movie actor and was dressed in the same Victorian clothing: a rich, deep brown sack coat with a matching waistcoat and trousers. A brown derby hat adorned his head. He had black, wavy hair and a moustache, and he held a pipe in one hand. His lips moved, but no sound emerged: *I seem to be in the strangest predicament. And, if I may ask, where is Dr. Watson?*

Kenzie and Logan traded looks. Kenzie continued to hold Logan's hands tightly. "We haven't summoned Dr. Watson yet. Sorry. But we need your help to solve a mystery."

Holmes stared at his feet. *Egads! My feet are inside your crossed legs. How did this happen? I don't seem altogether solid.* He looked up and met Kenzie's gaze. *Wait. Mystery, did you say?*

"Yes. Someone is parading around our university campus claiming to be Jesus Christ," Logan said. "He even seemed like he healed three people. But it can't be Jesus."

"What's worse, someone who claims to be Satan keeps showing up and trying to murder the students." Kenzie felt like the best chance of pouring energy into Holmes and materializing the thought form was to treat it as though it were a real person.

Good heavens! Sherlock shook his head. *Well, that most certainly will not do. Perhaps we can stop this scoundrel before he murders someone.*

"That would be great," Kenzie said. "Can we call upon you tomorrow to begin the case?"

You certainly may, Holmes replied.

"Thank you," Logan said.

Holmes faded away.

Kenzie and Logan stared at each another. Kenzie had the nearly tangible sense that a third person had been present; it was almost as though he could smell a whiff of the pipe's smoke. In fact, he experienced the internal resonance he associated with meeting someone charismatic and powerful. It was a sense of *presence*.

"I could feel him," Logan whispered.

"Me, too." Kenzie squeezed Logan's hands. "I think I understand now why you and Zoe say Thor and Loki are real. It isn't just your spiritual devotion. You both must feel whatever it is I'm feeling now."

Logan returned the squeeze. "Yes. There's a specific feeling to it. Just now, I could hear Holmes talking inside my head, and it didn't feel forced like when I'm writing a paper. You know what I mean, right? When you write a paper, you hear your own internal voice. Or I do, anyway. And it comes out slowly. It's usually hard. But Holmes' dialogue just seemed to gush out like I wasn't controlling it at all."

"I wasn't controlling it," Kenzie said. "You're right. It was just pouring right out of us. We watched the movie together, Holmes showed up looking like the actor, and he reacted like we expected."

Logan smiled. "I knew you could do this!"

Kenzie became hyperaware of their hands still touching. *Man, I've got it bad for him.* "Well, we can do it. Together. We can summon Holmes and show everyone how it's done."

Logan gave Kenzie's hands a final squeeze and then released them. "Yeah. I mean, we'll need permission from both the Noble 10 Student Committee and Dr. Dawson to add even more characters to this shit show. But if they agree to our plan, we can show it live every day, if necessary, until Holmes becomes as solid as Jesus H. Christ, Top Hat, Loki, and Thor."

"Zoe won't be happy about that part," Kenzie groused. "Will it upset you, too?"

"I'm not fragile about it," Logan said. "I've done a lot of soul-searching about this, and I know Thor is a real god that I worship. I'm not worried about whether or not the materialized Thor is the same one I usually summon. I think he is, but if he's not, it doesn't make the real Thor less real."

He shrugged. "I think Zoe's tough. She can handle it, too. But if she can't, we can't spare her."

"No, we can't." Kenzie paused. "Thank you. Because we did it together, it worked."

Logan grinned again. "Hey, we make great partners."

Partners. Kenzie blushed and returned the smile. "Yeah. The perfect partners."

TWENTY-ONE

On Monday morning, Rachel shook Kenzie's shoulder until he snapped awake. "What? What is it?" He scrambled upright in bed.

"Two magical researchers and the Archbishop of Kentucky for The Apostles' Way sent text messages to me, Moriah, and Shinrou. They want to interview us about Jesus H. Christ." Rachel backed up as Kenzie swung his legs out of bed. "And there are strict instructions that no one else is allowed to listen in."

"If you refuse, it will look suspicious," Kenzie said.

"I know." Rachel turned away. "I woke you because the interview is going to take place in twenty minutes, and I didn't want Moriah and myself to disappear on you with no explanation." She glanced over her shoulder at Kenzie, her black curtain of hair cascading down her back. "Also, if we don't come back, I want you to know who's taken us hostage."

Kenzie's heart jumped and then raced. "They can't legally detain you."

"That's why, if we're not back in time for class, you need

to raise the alarm. The Apostles' Way doesn't care about the law."

"Oh, trust me. I *will*." Kenzie stood, his fear blooming into the burn of rage. "Take care of Moriah. I know Shinrou won't go down without a fight, and I trust him to call for backup from Makari. He's got strong enough gravity magic that he was never in danger from Top Hat-Satan. I know he can take people in a fight. But what I don't trust is that Shinrou knows how to protect Moriah."

"I understand. I'll protect her."

Kenzie watched Rachel's back as she swept from the room, an image of solid black: black skirt uniform, black tights, and black Mary Janes. His gut twisted and raised the red flag, his intuition catching fire. *You're always so grim, and you're always leaving to go somewhere off campus. What are you not telling me?*

IN THE THIRD-FLOOR HALLWAY OF THE IDONI STUDENT BUILDING, Rachel sat with Moriah. There were two plush brown chairs with a small table between them, so they were comfortable as they waited to see the investigation team. Shinrou paced back and forth in the hallway, not hiding his nervousness.

"You really think it's not safe for me to meet with them alone?" Moriah mumbled. She tugged on the hem of her white skirt, wrinkling it as usual. She had pulled her long hair into its signature curled pigtails that hung past her elbows. The effect was a child-like stylishness that Rachel found herself attracted to.

"Definitely not." Rachel turned her stare upon her black tights, studying the ribbed pattern in the thick material. "They think you summoned Jesus H. Christ."

Moriah bounced her foot, her black patent loafer gleaming

in the light. *"What?"* Her sharp voice filled the hallway. "But that's ridiculous! I can just tell them I didn't. They should understand that's impossible."

"They don't think he's real. They're in Shinrou's camp. They think he's a thought form."

Shinrou paused and faced them. His black uniform made him seem somber today. "I'm not your enemy. I'm only putting forth the most logical hypothesis."

Moriah crossed her legs and resumed bouncing her foot. "Well, asking me to control Jesus is a waste of time. Never mind that it's *Jesus*. Even if they were right, and they're not, I haven't done anything to control Jesus. I haven't cast any spells outside of class other than healing spells. Shinrou, you don't understand that saying I made Jesus isn't logical. But I get it. I forgive you." Her brow furrowed. "What I can't understand is why anyone who believes in the Lord would think this."

Rachel pondered the nature of human denial.

Shinrou opened his mouth, paused, closed it, and resumed pacing.

The door opened, and Dr. Taksande emerged. She smiled, greeting all three of them as she passed.

A man stepped into the doorway. He wore navy pants and a white Oxford shirt, both of which seemed to hug his frame. His lack of a suit jacket underscored his gaunt body. It made him look unwell. "Moriah Goldstein, Rachel Abrams, Shinrou Kitamori. I'm Dr. Thompson. Please step inside."

Moriah and Rachel both stood, and the three of them followed Thompson into the conference room. Moriah walked with her shoulders curled inward and her head bowed. Shinrou had gone blank-faced and ramrod straight. Rachel entered after them, her chin up and her posture rigid. *I won't let you take advantage of Moriah. She's not your pawn.*

Dr. Thompson sat alongside two other men, and once

Moriah, Rachel, and Shinrou were seated, Thompson spoke. "We called you three here because you've all had close dealings with Jesus since his appearance on this campus. I'm a magic scientist, and so is Dr. Bradley here." He gestured to the man on his left.

Dr. Bradley, who wore a short sleeve button-up shirt, glanced up from his tablet and nodded. He was Thompson's opposite: short and round with black hair not showing any gray.

Rachel had done research for her own protection, and she sized up the men, knowing they were here at Rev. John Paul Smith, Jr.'s behest. Dr. Thompson had been chosen because he was a member of The Apostles' Way. Rachel suspected Dr. Bradley, who was unaffiliated with the church, had been chosen to waylay skeptics' arguments that Thompson was too biased.

"And Archbishop Ramsey is the leader of The Apostles' Way in Kentucky." Thompson gestured to the thin, gray-haired man with sagging jowls. He wore a black suit with the baby blue insignia of The Apostles' Way on the breast pocket: a shield that pictured three crosses with a sword horizontally behind them.

You were chosen to force The Apostles' Way theology down everyone's throats, Rachel thought, bristling.

Archbishop Ramsey took one look at Rachel and Shinrou, frowned, and focused on Moriah instead.

Rachel's lungs tightened as if crushed by titanium bands. *Not good.*

"Mr. Kitamori," Thompson said, "you shook Jesus' hand. Miss Abrams and Miss Goldstein, you stood near him, watched him, and listened to him preach. Miss Abrams and Miss Goldstein, have either of you also touched Jesus?"

Moriah flushed. "No, I wouldn't dare. I'm not even worthy to wash the dust from his feet."

"I have not touched Jesus, nor has Jesus touched me," Rachel said.

Dr. Bradley looked to Shinrou. "It seems we will need to rely on your testimony, Mr. Kitamori. What did you notice?"

"Jesus' hand felt like silicone," Shinrou said.

"Because he has a new body." Moriah glanced at Shinrou, her brow furrowed.

Shinrou folded his hands in his lap. "I did a simple long-range content analysis spell. Jesus' body is made of silica clay mud with impurities consistent with the Ohio River Valley."

"That's because Jesus made himself manifest right here," Moriah said. "Just like the Bible says, God made a body of mud and breathed life into it."

"We also did a content analysis spell and discovered the same results," Thompson said.

"What do you think about the theory that this Jesus is a golem created by a priest or pastor?" Archbishop Ramsey asked.

"No Christian would make a golem of the Lord," Moriah said. "That's no different from creating a false Christ, like the Bible warns about. No believer would introduce such confusion and chaos."

"Let's set that aside," Thompson said. "Miss Goldstein, you are the person on campus who has spent the most time with Jesus. Isn't that right?"

"Of course I am. Where else would a Christian wish to be?"

Archbishop Ramsey smiled. "Every Christian should aim to have your devotion."

"Thank you." Moriah stared at her lap.

Stop flattering her. Rachel narrowed her eyes at the man. *You're just trying to use her.*

"We'd like to talk to Jesus ourselves," Thompson said. "Our job here is to verify whether or not he's actually Jesus

Christ. However, he comes and goes randomly, seeming to teleport, and either the crowd or campus security is in the way."

"He is the real Jesus Christ, and he isn't teleporting. He's coming and going the way he does because he is a spirit in a new body," Moriah said. "If you had seen the way he confronted the demons impersonating the Pagan gods Thor and Loki, you would know that Jesus has come. And he fought Top Hat-Satan."

"Yes, we saw footage of those confrontations, and it's very promising," Archbishop Ramsey said.

"Miss Goldstein, could you help us speak with Jesus?" Ramsey asked.

Moriah tilted her head. "Me?" Then she smiled. "Oh, because I'll be one of the first people to notice when Jesus has arrived again. Would you like me to text you when Jesus arrives so that you can meet him?"

Thompson and Bradley exchanged glances. "Actually, we were hoping you could ask Jesus to appear," Thompson said.

"How would I do that?" Moriah asked.

You're wasting your time, Rachel thought, the tightness in her lungs spreading to her stomach and abdomen. *And if you press on Moriah too hard, I don't know what will happen to her.*

"He would hear your prayers, wouldn't he?" Thompson asked.

Moriah's brow furrowed. "Well, I guess he would. The Holy Spirit is with him, and he is God incarnate. But Jesus also has a plan. If it isn't in his plan to appear at a certain time, then it won't happen."

"And what is Jesus' plan?" Bradley asked.

Moriah stared at him. "Why would you think that I could have any insight into Jesus Christ's plan other than what the Bible says and what he has preached?"

Shinrou rubbed his forehead with his fingers.

"Let's cut to the chase." Rachel gestured to Thompson and

Ramsey. "The truth is that you think Moriah summoned Jesus H. Christ as a thought form, and you think she can control him."

Moriah gave Rachel a wide-eyed look. "But I *said* that's—"

Rachel stared down the three men. "I don't know what you want, Dr. Bradley, but I know, Archbishop Ramsey and Dr. Thompson, that you want her to police Jesus' words for you so he won't say anything counter to The Apostles' Way's teachings. You're both here to protect the interests of the URA."

Bradley laughed. "Oh, that's priceless." He sneered at his companions. "You've been caught out, and by a student no less. You really have been obvious."

Moriah gaped at Thompson and Ramsey. "You think—you want—That's ridiculous!" She shot to her feet. "I will not be used to control Jesus! Not that it's possible." She pointed to Archbishop Ramsey. "You're a shame to your profession. You should believe in Jesus, and you should know no one can control or summon the son of God. And also, you shouldn't be trying to censor what Jesus says." She glared at him. "Instead of warping God into your image of what he should be, you should be listening obediently to Jesus even if he says something you don't like. Otherwise, you're just like the Pharisees." She pushed her chair away and stormed out of the room.

Shinrou sat still and silent, gazing at his hands.

As soon as the door closed, Rachel snorted with laughter. "See? She's not an utterly spineless pushover. You can't just turn her into a puppet. She's a True Believer."

Archbishop Ramsey gaped at Rachel speechlessly.

Thompson's face flushed dark red. "You'll regret sabotaging this interview."

Rachel stood. "Oh, I'll regret everything for reasons that have nothing to do with you, but I knew that from the beginning."

Shinrou shot to his feet as well. "I'm sorry, Dr. Thompson and Dr. Bradley." He gave them a short bow. "I understand about blind studies and not alerting human participants to the nature of the test. But technically Moriah didn't consent to be experimented on, and you should have asked her to sign a release form. Without paperwork in hand, your results wouldn't be publishable anyway." He glanced at the Archbishop. "I don't have anything to say to you, sir, because I'm not Christian. I am a conscientious religious objector." He looked back at the scientists. "And I'm afraid I'll have to report you, doctors, for trying to experiment on a student without a release form. Moriah and the university could both sue you. Please excuse me." He marched out of the room.

Rachel headed to the door, but paused when she reached it. She glanced over her shoulder. "I will protect Moriah. No matter what it takes. Be careful, Dr. Thompson. Top Hat isn't the real Satan, but I know someone who is. If I play my cards right, I can unleash him on you." She pushed open the door. "Leave Moriah alone." She whisked out of the room.

Shinrou was already out of sight, probably on his way to talk to the university president or vice president.

Rachel found Moriah sitting on the first staircase landing and leaning against the wall, her arms crossed over her stomach.

"What they want to do is evil." Moriah stared at her feet.

"Incredibly cruel, yes."

Moriah peered up at her. "You want to protect me, don't you?"

"Yes." *Although it would probably horrify you to know it, I'm falling in love with you and your relentless shining light. You have the most pure soul I've ever seen, even more so than my father.*

A small smile lifted the corners of Moriah's lips. "You're very kind."

"Only to you. You're the truly kind one, and I don't want

you to lose that over jerks like Ramsey and Thompson and religious fakers like the Archbishop."

Moriah stood and headed down the steps. "You're being too hard on yourself. But thank you. Coming here with no close friends and only knowing Kenzie was really scary for me. I'm glad I met you."

A rare swirl of warmth rose in Rachel's chest and made it twinge. "Getting you as a roommate was an extraordinary stroke of luck for me."

Moriah looked back at Rachel with a smile. "I feel blessed to meet you and have you as my roommate, too. I think this is all part of God's plan."

"God works in mysterious ways," Rachel murmured. *If you knew who I really was, you wouldn't want to be my friend. But because you're who you are, you would forgive me, too. You feel you have to forgive the entire world.*

THAT AFTERNOON, KENZIE REPORTED TO THE GAZEBO BESIDE THE greenhouse, having been summoned by Logan, who waited for him on the steps. Inside of the gazebo sat Rikki Griffen, the president of the Noble 10 Student Committee, her dark hair slicked back like the first time Kenzie had seen her. She wore the black skirt uniform and exuded vibes so serious as to be grim.

"Here we go," Logan said as Kenzie settled beside him. "Rikki got permission from Dr. Dawson for us to summon Sherlock Holmes again, and this time for the cameras."

Kenzie inhaled sharply. *Already? Really?* "God, I hope this works." *I didn't think I'd have to do it again this soon!* He stared out at the oak trees, their green leaves whipping in the wind and showing their silver undersides as a storm blew in. A few yellow leaves were mixed in. Dark clouds encroached upon the horizon.

"It will." Logan patted his arm. "Shinrou and Makari will join us once they finish their Energy Work lab. They both want to watch. And everyone has insisted that Moriah be here, too, so we can convince her Jesus H. Christ isn't the real deal."

Great, an in-person audience. Kenzie fought off the sting of performance anxiety. "Okay." *This is important. This is the big turn we've needed in the case.*

When Makari and Shinkuro arrived, both of them looked as nervous as Kenzie felt. Makari's smile was tight, and Shinrou picked at his sleeve. Moriah arrived a minute later, stared at the ground, and tugged on the hem of her white skirt.

"Shinrou and I still haven't had any luck summoning characters, so it's up to you," Makari said. "At least you have mind magic. Neither Mori nor I specialize in mind magic or energy shaping magic."

Gee, thanks. A hive of panicking bees swarmed in Kenzie's stomach.

"I'm getting closer to a dismissal spell, though," Shinrou told Rikki.

Moriah looked away. "I don't want to even hear you say that. But I feel like I have to be here in case this works."

No one spoke for a beat.

"Excellent," Rikki said to Shinrou. She stood from the gazebo bench. "Please keep working on that spell. And I'm glad Kenzie could get results so fast. I'm not going to convene an official committee meeting today, but I think I can say on behalf of everyone: Thank you all for your hard work."

Shinrou flinched. "Don't thank us yet. I don't know if I can get the dismissal spell to work."

"And I've only done this once," Kenzie said. "We have to do it while you're recording us."

"Hey, I'm glad you did it at all," Makari said.

Kenzie and Logan entered the gazebo and sat in the

middle, the floorboards the same white as the columns and railings. Everyone but Moriah pulled out their phones to shoot a video of the session. Rikki explained she would send it to Dr. Dawson, who had agreed to upload it to the university's website. Shinrou would upload it to his own social media accounts.

"Explain what you're doing." Rikki angled her phone for the best shot.

Logan faced Rikki's phone and gave a brief explanation of thought forms. Then he proceeded to the main event. "Today we're going to show you stage one of summoning a new thought form. Makari Idoni, Zoe Wang, and I all witnessed Loki and Thor during this stage."

Kenzie realized Logan wanted to mention anyone whose name would ring bells in the magical community.

"All thought forms, including the ones being called Satan and Jesus, go through this stage: see-through and either silent or barely speaking," Shinrou said, stepping up beside Logan. Then he gestured to Kenzie. "Everyone watch carefully."

Kenzie gave Shinrou a nod and then held out his hands to Logan.

Logan took Kenzie's hands, and they closed their eyes, retreating into meditation. *Imagine the new movie. Imagine those old novels and stories. See Sherlock Holmes as real.*

Once Kenzie felt the drain of energy, he opened his eyes. A see-through thought form of Sherlock Holmes appeared between Logan and him. Holmes was dressed in the brown Victorian suit and derby hat Kenzie had pictured. He once again sported black, wavy hair and a moustache, and he held a pipe in one hand. Holmes peered around at the group, frowning, his brow furrowed.

"Thank you for joining us again today," Logan said.

Holmes focused on him. "I daresay people wear the strangest clothing. Is this normal in your country? For surely

I'm no longer in merry old England." His voice was faint but understandable, and he had a British accent.

"They do," Kenzie said. "We're wearing our university's uniforms, actually."

Holmes tapped his pipe against his chin. "I see. Well, tell me more about this mystery you said you need solved."

"The one who calls himself Jesus Christ is over in the quad, preaching from the library steps," Kenzie said. "Millions of people have been duped by his excellent performance."

"What a wretched state of affairs," Holmes sighed. "Very well. I shall begin by observing him, and then I'll speak with him personally."

"Of course." Kenzie peered at Rikki's phone's camera. "We'll discover if he has enough energy to walk across the campus with us."

Holmes looked from Kenzie to Rikki and back. "Why would I lack energy? I assure you I am a healthy, vital man."

Logan smiled. "No offense intended." He released Kenzie's hands and stood.

Kenzie stood as well, his gaze pinned on Holmes. The thought form rippled, but didn't vanish. "This way, please." He headed for the gazebo stairs. *Maybe now Moriah can come to terms with what is really happening here. But that's a big maybe.*

Logan fell into step by Kenzie as they reached the walkway. "Stay focused," he murmured. Kenzie nodded and glanced over his shoulder. Shinoru, Makari, and Rikki followed them, all recording the incident on their phones. Moriah trailed ten feet behind them. *Please let this be our big breakthrough.*

Holmes walked behind Kenzie, his feet not touching the ground. Logan shifted position behind Holmes, which kept the thought form between Kenzie and him.

Rikki sped up and paced them from several feet to the side, staying in the grass. "Where are you from, Mr. Holmes?"

"London. 'Tis strange, though. I don't remember crossing the Pond. How could I forget an entire sea voyage? I'm most perplexed."

"It's a mystery to solve once you've discovered the truth behind the hoax of Jesus," Makari said.

"Perhaps it is a case of amnesia, some head trauma shortly before embarking or disembarking," Holmes mused.

"Of all the cases you've worked on, which was the easiest to solve?" Rikki asked.

"Why, the case concerning the missing fiancé of one Miss Mary Sutherland," Holmes said. "Given the details of the case, it was easy to conclude that her fiancé, Mr. Hosmer Angel, was in reality her step-father, Mr. James Windibank. The typewritten letters made the issue all too obvious."

Kenzie nodded. "That's how I always felt about the story 'A Case of Identity.' You see, I've read Dr. Watson's accounts of your exploits. I always believed that case was too easily resolved and wasn't enough of a challenge for you." He saw what had happened: *My opinion of the story transferred to my thought form of Holmes.*

"That sounds creepy," Rikki said. "Her own step-father tried to marry her? How did he think that would ever work?"

"Perhaps he was a very dull-witted man," Holmes drawled.

The group made their way past the campus laundry mat and approached Griffen Hall. The grassy quad came into view. As they walked, Holmes smoked his pipe. A specter of the smoke even appeared as he seemed to exhale.

When they reached the edge of the quad, they stopped. Thanks to a campus-wide near lockdown, only 50 students surrounded Jesus H. Christ today. The administration had banned all but a dozen visitors thanks to the social media and crowd explosion caused by Jesus H. Christ seeming to walk on water.

The thought form in question sat on the stairs, talking with the students.

"I want to ask about the Parable of Talents," one student said. "In the parable, you said that the servant who buried his one talent had it taken away from him when his master returned home, while the other two servants who invested their talents and made more money were rewarded. And we know a talent was a type of money in your time."

"True," Jesus said. "What would you like to ask?"

"I want to ask what would happen to the servant who buried his talent based on what we know about psychology today. Preachers say that the 'talents' don't have to be money. They can be talents in the sense we mean it now: abilities. So what if the servant buried his talent because he had PTSD or something like that? What if he wasn't lazy? What if he was traumatized?"

Holmes turned to Kenzie. "Whatever is PTSD?"

"Post Traumatic Stress Disorder," Kenzie whispered. "We first noticed it in war veterans."

"But I did specifically say the servant was lazy," Jesus said. "And sloth is a sin. That is why the man was cast into the outer darkness."

"The man went to hell for being lazy," the student said. "Isn't that extreme?"

"The servant didn't understand his master, which means he wasn't truly a servant. He didn't recognize his God. Besides, my father gives people talents so that they might serve him and his kingdom. This servant wasted his talent and did nothing to expand my father's kingdom."

Holmes gazed at Jesus H. Christ. "He looks the part."

"Only if you go by Renaissance paintings of Jesus," Kenzie said. "He's too pale to be the real Jesus. He looks White, not Jewish. Also, his hair should be short and black, and his beard should be longer. He doesn't look like a first century Jew." *At least according to my internet research.*

Holmes raised both eyebrows. "I daresay that's spot on. Good observation, young man. I stand corrected. And so we have our first clue: This man doesn't look like a first century Jew. Any Christian could say what this man is saying about the Parable of Talents. That tells us nothing."

Kenzie began feeling shaky, and his stomach audibly rumbled with hunger. Worry pulsed in his gut. *Even with Logan's help, I'm losing energy fast.* He looked back at Logan. He was pallid.

"I shall go speak with him." Holmes strode forward.

Kenzie stayed at his side, but his legs trembled now.

"I apologize for my interruption," Holmes said as he reached the group. His voice was a normal volume, and while he was still see-through, the image was more opaque. "But I wish to speak with you, given you claim to be the son of God."

Jesus folded his hands in his lap. "Indeed, I do. And 'I AM.'"

Holmes smiled. "Ah, an opportune quote." He took a heavy drag from his pipe. "Let's start with some simple theology." The smoke escaped with his words. "What is the fate of those souls who live in lands that have never heard of Christ Jesus?"

The group of students had focused on Holmes.

"I'm sorry, but who are you?" one asked.

"My apologies." Holmes took off his hat and offered a sketch of a bow. "I'm Sherlock Holmes." He popped his hat back on.

Whispering ensued. "He looks just like the 2091 movie!" one guy said.

"Even those who live in unreached lands have the witness and testimony of nature," Jesus said. "Who can look upon the world which my father has created and not see his hand at work? The existence of my father is obvious, so everyone is responsible for accepting or rejecting me."

Kenzie toppled onto the grass, dizzy.

"Kenzie!" Logan shot forward, only to drop to his knees beside him. "Oh, God. Too much of an energy drain." He lay on the grass by Kenzie.

Sherlock Holmes vanished.

Rikki turned her phone camera toward herself. "And there we have it, everyone. Proof that a thought form of just about anyone can be created by a magician. It just takes a lot of energy." She turned off her camera. "Time to upload this for the world to see."

"We need to get them sodas," Makari said. He ran toward the nearest building.

Kenzie barely registered the words before fainting from energy loss.

When Kenzie awakened on the grass with a pounding headache, Rachel stood over him, blocking out the afternoon sun as it peeked through the storm clouds. She leaned in with a can of Sprite in one hand. She frowned and lowered her voice. "Now that you've proven anyone with sufficient concentration and energy can make a thought form, we can no longer put off a conversation about Moriah with the taskforce."

"We can't?" Kenzie sat up and accepted the soda. It was still chilled from the vending machine and had a mist of condensation on it that turned to water against his hand. He glanced around to make sure Rachel wasn't being overheard. However, Logan was talking with Rikki, and Makari and Shinrou were speaking with Moriah.

"Dr. Ramsey, Dr. Thompson, and the Archbishop suspect Moriah," Rachel continued. "We're out of time. We have to report what we know. But we have to make sure Moriah isn't in attendance. If she thinks we all turned on her, she's going to shatter. She still sees you and me as her friends."

Kenzie popped the tab and drank, hoping his headache would recede. "Okay. Tonight, then. We'll meet in Logan's dorm suite and tell them. I'll round everyone up. I just hope they don't attack her or arrest her."

"Better them than Rev. Smith and Archbishop Ramsey," Rachel said.

Kenzie couldn't argue that and had to concede the point, but he was still terrified about the fate of their friend.

TWENTY-TWO

At 7:00, after supper, Kenzie, Rachel, Makari, and Shinrou converged upon Logan's dorm suite. They waited until Logan's roommates headed off to the campus practice rooms and then held their summit.

As usual, Makari and Shinrou settled together on the worn brown couch. For once, both were out of uniform. Shinrou wore khaki pants and a red polo shirt, and Makari wore jeans with a t-shirt and matching baseball cap.

Logan wore cargo shorts and a Black Night Hail t-shirt, leaving Kenzie to assume it was a U.S. rock band of some kind. Logan grabbed a kitchen chair, carried it over by the couch, turned it around backwards, and straddled it, draping his arms over the back. Kenzie, who was dressed similarly in a t-shirt and jeans shorts, dropped onto one living room chair.

The person who stood out was Rachel, who wore a black Victorian Rococo dress with a white rose on the chest and white roses around the hem of its flared bell skirt. It was the best of the URA's 2094 fall line. Shinrou stared at her with open shock, and Makari gazed out the window.

"We need to talk about Moriah," Kenzie said, hoping to waylay the million questions likely popping up in Shinrou's mind about Rachel's attire. "And some context about Moriah and the URA might help."

"I'll say we need to talk about her," Shinrou grumbled.

Arranging the massive skirt of her dress, Rachel perched on the remaining living room chair. "I've only known her for a little over a week, but since we both moved in before Zoe and Kenzie arrived, we talked a lot. We discovered we have several things in common: the URA, The Apostles' Way, an energy work major, and even living in Georgia. So despite the short amount of time, all the talking means I got a good read on Moriah. She doesn't actually want to be in the Noble Three. She doesn't want to stand out, and more than anything, she wants life to be simpler."

"You're right," Kenzie said. "I knew her in high school. Moriah is terrified of the status and responsibility. She doesn't know what to do."

Shinrou remained silent for a moment before speaking. "So basically she's not ready to leave childhood behind. And I don't mean that to be judgmental. I'm just stating the facts of the case."

"She doesn't feel supported enough or ready enough for that," Rachel said. "She only came to JCU because it was her ticket to escape her parents."

Kenzie hadn't known that. *She really opened up to Rachel.* "She told me she was here to please her parents, and they wouldn't let her go back home."

Rachel sighed. "The full story is that she was ashamed of her initial rebellion in coming here instead of the college they picked out in the URA, which isn't a magic-based university but has an energy work major among its programs. Once Iona bullied her, Moriah folded and wanted to go home, but because she chose JCU and not her parents, they punished her by telling her she had to stand by her original decision."

"That is completely unfair, unfeeling, and cold," Shinrou said.

"She must feel really alone," Makari said.

"And this is why she's clinging to Jesus H. Christ?" Logan asked.

Rachel gazed at Makari, Shinrou, and Logan, her stare piercing. "In the URA, we're taught that if we feel alone and scared, we are supposed to tell it all to Jesus and ask him to help us."

"And Moriah took second place on the entrance exam." Kenzie's heart pounded. *Please don't arrest her after I say this.* "She's right behind the two of you." He pointed between Makari and Logan, who had tied for first place.

Shinrou gasped and then pressed his hand to his forehead. "It's so obvious! You're telling us that Moriah's magic is so powerful that her stress and fear caused her to create Jesus H. Christ. Incredible!"

"Yes," Rachel said. "Moriah is much more talented than I am. She doesn't even understand she did it. It's not like she used a sacred circle or a summoning spell. Moriah just *did* it with the power of her mind alone." She slumped. "If only Moriah could see how powerful she really is."

Silence filled the little living room for a beat.

"Oh, shiiiiiit," Logan groaned. "We are *never* going to convince her she's the summoner."

"You're right," Shinrou said. "She's convinced it's blasphemy."

"And, damn, what talent!" Logan rubbed his face with both hands. "I could have *never* created a thought form just by intention alone."

Kenzie focused on Makari, his heart still racing. "If the Noble 10 arrest Moriah, she's going to shatter. She's already under too much stress, she doesn't understand she's done it, she's going to college in another country, she's—"

Makari held up both hands. "Whoa! No one's going to arrest her. We need to stop her, not throw her in jail. Also, she hasn't broken any U.S. laws. Jesus H. Christ hasn't harmed anyone. Sure, it's a real spectacle, and it's straining our campus. But that's not illegal. It's just inconvenient."

"Top Hat-Satan is the one who's broken laws and hurt people," Shinrou said.

"And Top Hat-Satan is the one we have to stop first," Logan said. "Precisely for that reason." He shook his head. "I'm not telling my dad yet that Moriah is summoning Jesus H. Christ. Besides, if we can stop Top Hat-Satan, then Moriah might *stop* summoning it on her own." He rested his chin on his arm where it was draped over the chair back.

Rachel folded her hands on her lap and stared at them. "That's possible."

"I won't tell my parents yet, either," Makari said. "I think our focus should remain on proving that Jesus H. Christ and Top Hat-Satan are thought forms."

Shinrou lifted one finger. "Yes, we need to return this campus to normal as soon as possible. And I'm working on a way to dismiss the thought forms."

Makari turned to Logan. "If you and Kenzie would funnel more energy into Sherlock Holmes, you two could show that people who know their thought form is just a character can also cause the thought form to develop the same way that Top Hat-Satan and Jesus H. Christ did."

"Good idea," Logan said. "We just have to build up enough energy to do it first. Summoning Thor is way easier than this is."

"Plus Makari and I have a serious piece of information to share, too," Shinrou said.

Makari pulled off his cap and squeezed it between his hands. "Yeah. We did some research on John Paul Smith, Jr. and found out his mother was a member of the Anderson clan."

Rachel's eyes widened unnaturally. "*What?*"

"You're kidding me!" Kenzie shot straight in his chair, his back muscles twinging in protest. "He and his father *hate* all magicians, but his mother came from a magician family? I bet she didn't practice magic anymore after she married Smith, Sr.!"

"Couldn't have," Rachel whispered.

Kenzie was reminded of his theory that Iona was summoning Top Hat. "Do you think Smith could be using a member of the Anderson clan as a patsy and having them summon a Satanic thought form for him?"

"You mean like Iona?" Makari asked. "No way. She hates Smith and everything he stands for."

"But maybe he could use his mother's family connections to find himself a patsy," Shinrou said.

"Maybe he hired someone that way," Logan said. "But what magician would be insane enough to help Smith invade the U.S. with his Apostles' Way bullshit? You could never pay me enough money to do something like that. Smith wants to *destroy* magicians."

Kenzie fell back against his chair again. "I have no idea. To me, that just makes the mystery *worse*, not better."

Everyone agreed with that, and with their plan in place, Kenzie and Rachel returned to their dorm, Kenzie preoccupied with whether Iona could be bought by Smith.

His only consolation was that Makari and Logan didn't want to arrest Moriah.

⚡

THE NEXT MORNING, RACHEL LEFT HER DORM SUITE AT 8:30 SO she could watch Jesus H. Christ. This situation merited surveillance, and Kenzie would be busy with Logan trying to make Sherlock Holmes stronger. That left staying on top of the problem with Jesus H. Christ and Moriah to her.

She strolled to the quad with its thick carpet of grass and towering oak trees. As calm as the campus was this morning, she knew it couldn't last. An estimated 10,000 people clogged the Louisville sidewalks in all directions around the campus, and that didn't count the people camping in parks or filling up the motels. Social media and the news reported that among the sidewalk crowd were dozens of people on crutches, in wheelchairs, and even on cots. The people claimed the university had no right to withhold Jesus' healing power or miracles. The newest protesters' signs now read LET US IN OR LET HIM OUT, JESUS IS FOR EVERYONE, and YOU WITCHES CAN'T KEEP JESUS HOSTAGE.

Three men sat in lawn chairs under an oak tree at the edge of the quad: Dr. Thompson and Dr. Bradley, the magic scientists, and Archbishop Ramsey. Rachel glared at them. *I have to know they are up to, especially since it might harm Moriah.* She approached the oak tree from the opposite side and cast a simple "don't look this way" spell as she climbed. Climbing a tree in such a short skirt proved easy. Once she was in place, she cast it again. She would have to recast it several times in order to stay hidden, but for her, the spell was easy.

Below her on the quad was a collection of perhaps 50 students, faculty, and staff. Two news crews were still allowed access, and with the smaller crowd, they set up much closer. The three investigators watched the scene.

As usual, Jesus H. Christ sat on the library stairs and preached. Moriah sat at Jesus' feet, so close that her shoulder almost touched his knee. "The poor, the widows, and the orphans are still among you. Do your hearts go out to them? Do you work to feed and clothe them? Or are your hearts hard? Do you resent their poverty and blame them for their condition? I assure you that the poor, the widows, and the orphans will see the Kingdom of Heaven. But will you? Surely I say to you that your hard hearts put you in danger of the fires of hell."

Archbishop Ramsey, distinct from the others thanks to his sagging jowls, glanced over at the two scientists. "So far, he sounds like Jesus."

"Just let someone ask him about LGBTQIA rights or abortion," Thompson said. His steel gray hair shone in the sunlight. "That ought to put his identity to the question."

"When I came in the flesh, I spoke with the most hated and feared people in my society," Jesus H. Christ continued. "Those included lepers, tax collectors, and prostitutes. How do you treat the most hated and feared members of your society? Do you break bread with them? Do you minister to them? Do you make them feel loved?"

Rachel leaned against the tree trunk and stretched her legs out on the thick branch, her black skirt hanging off each side. *I'm impressed. The audience pouring life into Jesus H. Christ is currently sticking to the merciful and compassionate version. This is probably Moriah's influence. It's not going to last, though.*

"I once told the Parable of the Prodigal Son," Jesus said. "The Christians among you seem to understand that the young son who sinned was easily forgiven by his father, who is my father. You tell each other, 'God will forgive any sin.' And yet you miss the second part of the parable: the older son. He believes that since he never left home nor lived riotously, since he'd remained faithful, he had the right to judge his younger brother. He complains to his father, angry that his brother was forgiven and reinstated as a child of God. So I will say it one more time: Judge not lest ye be judged."

Ramsey glanced at the scientists again. "I have to admit that Jesus would say that."

Dr. Bradley mopped his forehead with a handkerchief. "And yet you don't believe he's Jesus."

"The Bible is very clear about The Second Coming of Jesus." Ramsey's jowls quivered as he spoke. "Also, Jesus H. Christ isn't doing what he's supposed to do. Jesus will come to Earth to collect all the faithful believers, who will spend all of eternity on New Earth with Jesus, forever free from all suffering. The unfaithful and the unbelievers will spend eternity in hell as a punishment for their sins."

Bradley sighed and mopped his forehead again. "Makes me glad I'm atheist. I can't imagine what my life would be like if I had to walk around believing that rubbish."

"You wouldn't worry about it," Dr. Thompson said, "because you would be convinced you're one of the saved who will go to heaven."

"What conceited nonsense," Bradley groaned. He stood and walked away. "I know what my report is going to say. I leave you two gentlemen to this mess, whatever that means about the PR statement you'll need to make to protect your cult. Oh, and Thompson—don't call. I wouldn't publish a paper with you if my life depended upon it. I would be a laughingstock in the scientific community."

Dr. Thompson turned to Archbishop Ramsey. "I agree that this is a straightforward case of fraud. The Bible is far too clear on this count." He appeared to dismiss Bradley as easily as Bradley had dismissed him.

"And yet we need a way to control Jesus H. Christ," Ramsey said. "This false prophet will dupe many people, both believers and unbelievers. We need him to endorse the truth. If he starts preaching things that are out of alignment with Rev. Smith, we'll have a mutiny on our hands."

"Well, that's easy," Thompson said. "Despite her protests, my money's on Moriah Goldstein. She's supporting this false prophet with all her blessed little heart. During her interview, she staunchly defended him. All the other students and faculty talked science. Only Miss Goldstein spoke religiously. I think she summoned him."

Ramsey rubbed his jowls. "You're probably right. And if that's the case, whoever controls Moriah Goldstein controls Jesus H. Christ."

"We better move fast, then," Thompson said. "You know the abomination that is the Roman Catholic Church will figure this out, and then the pope will try to control Miss Goldstein himself."

Rachel's rage and fear spiked until her heart thudded. *This is just as bad as I feared!*

Top Hat popped in at the edge of the crowd, facing the two men. He wore his red leotard and red coat with tails, and he still had cloven feet. He grinned, sweeping off his red hat and bowing.

"The Satan figure?" Archbishop Ramsey jumped to his feet. "Here's a simple test: By the name of Jesus Christ and the blood of Jesus Christ, I bind you!"

"Oooooh," Top Hat said. "Scary." He summoned his pitchfork and rammed it through Ramsey's gut.

Ramsey collapsed with a wail. Screaming, Thompson vaulted from his chair and ran.

Top Hat lifted his hand. "Wait. Wait! I was going to offer you a sixpence for your hate."

Thompson kept running, not even glancing back.

Top Hat shrugged. "Oh, well." He threw the pitchfork like a javelin, lancing Thompson's back.

Thompson hit the ground and flopped a couple of times like a fish startled to find itself suffocating on the deck of a fisherman's boat.

Top Hat turned and headed for the students. Some ran away, but a few stomped toward Top Hat, clearly ready to take him on. "Nice! Competition. Well, I'm supposed to kill some magicians now. I've gotta look like I'm doing Satan's business or something like that. I dunno. Doesn't actually make sense to me." He summoned another pitchfork into his hand.

Rachel hopped out of the tree. "Don't kill anyone!"

Top Hat took off, not responding.

Snatching her cellphone out of her skirt pocket, Rachel called 911, reported the incident, and walked over to the bleeding Ramsey. She tucked her cellphone away, knelt by the archbishop, and met his terrified gaze. "Be sure to tell your congregation that a magician saved your life. Unless, of course, you want me to let you die here."

Archbishop Ramsey shook his head vigorously.

Rachel extended her hand, holding it over his wounds. "So you give consent for a healing spell?"

Ramsey nodded.

Rachel's hand lit up in a purple glow as she poured her energy into the wounds. Healing spells weren't her specialty. In fact, she was so poor at them she could only heal minor injuries of her own. However, she visualized the process at hand: the puncture wounds in Ramsey's intestines fading as the organ knitted itself back together.

Around her, shouts and screams pierced the air, but she didn't look up. She couldn't afford to divide her concentration, and she wasn't afraid. "I once believed in your Jesus. There are many reasons my faith died, but among them is the fact your people hate my people. 'Jesus hates magicians; magicians will go to hell.' I was born a magician through no action of my own, and your God has ordered my eternal damnation for it. Why would I follow a God like that?"

"I don't hate you," Ramsey gasped.

"Don't you?" Rachel smirked. "Well, John Paul Smith, Jr. wants every magician in the world to die because the Bible says 'Do not suffer a witch to live.' And the Christian church's list of atrocities spans two thousand years, including murdering Jews, murdering 'heretics' and 'infidels,' force-converting entire nations, and raping children and nuns."

"I'm not—" Ramsey gasped.

"Like them?" Rachel shrugged one shoulder. "Perhaps not. And yet what have you done to stop the rapists among The Apostles' Way? Anything? If your Jesus was real, he'd cast you all into hell. Lucky for you, he's not." She finished her spell and stood. "Of course, Christianity really isn't anything except Zoroastrianism, which was regurgitated with a Jesus sticker slapped on top." She walked away. "That's the best healing spell I can do, but the ambulances should be here soon."

Ramsey didn't thank her, and Rachel didn't want him to. She headed to Thompson. *I'll do what I can to keep him alive until EMTs or mage healers arrive. It's a matter of principle. I have ethics even if people like him don't.*

The student taskforce arrived, Makari and Logan leading them, and fought Top Hat as Rachel reached Thompson. Evidently they distracted Top Hat, because the pitchfork in Thompson's back vanished. After he granted her permission to heal him, she worked on stabilizing him, this time allowing herself to glance at the battle every few minutes. Jesus had corralled Moriah and other bystanders out of the way and led them in prayer. Meanwhile, Thor had shown up. He batted Top Hat's pitchforks out of the way with his hammer. Then, as usual, Shinrou showed up to gravity slam Top Hat, and Top Hat only suffered being pinned down for a moment before disappearing.

Rachel sighed. *And none of this will stop unless Shinrou figures out how to dematerialize the thought forms. What a nightmare!*

But Rachel Abrams wasn't sure how she felt about destroying the thought forms.

TWENTY-THREE

That evening, Kenzie and Rachel accompanied Moriah across campus as her unspoken bodyguards, joining the students heading toward the Idoni Student Building for supper. Several guys zipped past them on hoverboards, the high-pitched whine of the engines hurting Kenzie's ears until they were farther way. The campus squirrels that darted between the oak and maple trees proved how tame they were by ignoring the noise and commotion.

The ISB was roughly a 10-minute walk from their dorm suite, but to Kenzie, it felt longer in the heat. The temperature had soared to 101 degrees with a heat index of 104. Thanks to the topography of the Ohio River Valley and the level of pollution, Louisville's air quality was also poor. To Kenzie, it was like inhaling air that was liquefying. *To call this a free smog sauna would still be too kind.*

As they neared the red brick ISB, the crowd grew dense, with roughly forty visitors mixing with the uniformed students coming and going, seeking both air conditioning and food. Groups clustered on the grassy areas and around benches, their voices raised.

"The energy's bad," Rachel whispered.

Moriah clutched Rachel's arm. "Maybe this isn't a good idea."

Irritation seared Kenzie's lungs. "What? We're supposed to go without food all day?" He didn't want pizza again. "This is our campus, not theirs. We're the students. We should get to eat."

"I understand that," Rachel said. "But the energy is *too* bad."

Kenzie sighed and turned around, but they didn't make it five steps before the nearest cluster swarmed around them.

"You're the girl who's always by Jesus," one White man said. He towered over Moriah, six feet tall, bald, and red-faced. "What makes you so special?"

Kenzie's heart mule-kicked his ribs. *Shit! If they've noticed and started talking to each other, then it's all over. The other noble clans will arrest Moriah for being Jesus' summoner, even if the Idonis and Steensens argue not to, and there's nothing I can do about it. These people might not know what their accusation really means, but the magicians will.*

Moriah pressed herself against Rachel's side, still clinging to her arm. "I just *want* to be at Jesus' feet. He's kind enough to let me."

"Honey, we all want to be at Jesus' feet," a woman in the crowd called out.

"Leave her alone," Rachel growled. "If Jesus doesn't have a problem with it, you shouldn't either."

The man sneered at her. "Don't you mean 'Hay-Soose?' Stay out of it, Mexi-rat. I'm not listening to some immigrant tell me how to think about my Jesus, especially one who's *Catholic.* You're only here because your mama squatted down and pushed you out as soon as she snuck across the border."

Rage burned through Kenzie so hot that his magic ignited. It was all he could do not to slam the man with a spell. He pulled out his cellphone and texted campus security. Then he swiped over to the camera function, hit record, and held his phone up. "If you're so proud of yourself, say that again."

The man smacked Kenzie's hand to one side and leaned into Kenzie's face. "Can it, Chini-dog. As much as I don't want to hear some Mexican Catholic lecture me about Jesus, I want even less to hear self-righteous prattle from a Chinese terrorist."

A cold burn iced Kenzie's veins. *Shit. I'm a half-Japanese transman with two women of Jewish descent surrounded by a crowd of White supremacists.* He kept a grip on his phone and recorded the audio even if he didn't dare aim the camera at the man again.

The blonde woman standing by the tall, bald man thumped him on the arm. "Mike, stop it." She narrowed her eyes at Moriah. "All we really want to know is why Moriah Goldstein is so *special.*"

Moriah had halfway wrapped herself around Rachel by this point. "I'm not special! I just want to be with Jesus."

"Stop sayin' that!" the blonde woman shrieked at Moriah. "We all wanna be with Jesus! But you're actin' like you're Mary Magdalene!"

"Goldstein?" echoed an unseen man farther back in the cluster. "Goldstein? You're a *Jew*?"

Tears rolled down Moriah's cheeks, and she sniffled with each breath. "I don't understand why you hate me. I love Jesus, too. We're the *same.*"

"My wife is not like a filthy Jew!" Mike shouted.

The strange itching sensation Kenzie associated with a magic surge erupted through his entire body. If he couldn't get his magic under better control, he was going to either break out in hives or inadvertently discharge telekinetic energy in every direction. He shoved his phone into his pocket before he accidentally broke it.

"What a wonderful Christian you are," Rachel drawled.

"Moriah the Jew is a thousand times more Christian than you can ever dream of being."

Mike lunged at Rachel, fist raised, and Moriah screamed.

Kenzie's telekinesis erupted in a bubble around him as he dashed between Mike and Rachel. The shockwave of energy shoved away Mike, his wife, and five other people standing too close. Moriah and Rachel got shoved in the opposite direction, behind him.

The blonde woman shrieked and charged at Kenzie. "You fuckin' witch!"

Kenzie wasn't sure if he was going to be slapped, punched, or clawed, but it didn't matter. He held up his hands and released his backed up energy, but with more finesse this time, keeping Moriah and Rachel on the inside of his bubble and pushing the crowd back like an invisible bulldozer. "I have the right to protect myself and my friends! You came to our campus. Don't you dare be surprised that we're using magic."

Top Hat popped into the crowd, towering over even Mike by a foot. Today, he wore a three-piece business suit, plus his top hat, all crimson. He wore no white face paint or painted-on smile. Instead, he was a White man with cloven feet and black eyes. Whipping off his hat, he bowed to Kenzie, Rachel, and Moriah, revealing center-parted platinum blond hair and little devil horns. Then he straightened, set his hat upon his head with gentlemanly flair, turned, and faced the crowd, revealing that he had a goat's tail poking out the back of his pants. "Whoo! Feel that hate! Yes, feed me. Pour your hate into me. Make me even more powerful." He spun in a circle, arms wide. "I am the convergence of the human need to blame the supernatural for their own misdeeds." He lifted one cloven foot. "I am the original scapegoat."

The crowd was so silent that when someone dropped their cup of soda, the thud of plastic and half-melted ice against the ground seemed deafening.

Top Hat lowered his hoof. "I must thank you. I had no mind of my own until yesterday. The world was little to me except flashes of color and screaming faces."

Someone in the crowd coughed—or maybe sobbed.

"I eat hate," Top Hat purred. "I drink fear. And humans feed me freely." He paced a few steps to the left, and then to the right, surveying the crowd.

No one moved, but the tension rose until the air crackled.

Kenzie glanced around. *Where is campus security?* He slipped his phone out of his pocket and group-texted Logan, Makari, and Shinrou. Then he tucked his phone away again. He needed his hands free. Top Hat was working himself up to another attack.

"Christian men believe they would have lived in a paradise forever, would have remained in the womb forever, if only that evil woman Eve hadn't given them the forbidden fruit to eat." Top Hat's baritone voice was pleasant, melodic, filled with charisma like a well-trained preacher. "To eat the fruit is to be born into the knowledge of good and evil. To eat the fruit is to leave the safety of the womb and know life, which is suffering. And humans believe suffering is evil."

Despite himself, Kenzie became nearly entranced by the speech.

Top Hat barked out a laugh. "So they're really saying, 'How dare my mommy give birth to me!'" He gestured theatrically. "So, yes, hate women. Hate them all! Hate yourselves for being born." He summoned his pitchfork into his hand. "I'll give *all* of you a sixpence."

The crowd erupted into screams and ran in all directions.

Top Hat skewered Mike and hurled him to the ground. "Don't flee! I love your hate. I covet your hate. Give it to me. Make me the greatest god of all." He raced after Mike's wife and hurled his pitchfork at her back.

Kenzie telekinetically grabbed it, stopping it only inches

from the woman's spine. "Don't kill them! You're just making it worse."

Top Hat turned toward him. "But I was born a killer. My cosmic role is killer." He summoned another pitchfork. "And what's more, humans *want* me to be a killer." He raced after Mike's wife.

Kenzie flung out his arms, igniting his energy so hard his body glowed green. He snatched Top Hat up and held him 10 feet off the ground. Clenching both fists, Kenzie imagined two huge hands wrapped around Top Hat's body, holding him still. "You aren't Satan. You're someone's thought form. Someone's personal creation. You don't have to be what humanity asks you to be. And now that you're gaining strength, you don't even have to be what your creator intended. You can *choose* who you want to be."

Top Hat stared at Kenzie, his black eyes wide. "Me?"

He vanished.

Only then did Kenzie realize Top Hat's appearance could mean his summoner was nearby. He looked in all directions, but no students hovered nearby to watch the spectacle.

Moriah ran to Mike and sank beside him, crying. "It's awful. It's all too awful." She held her hands over Mike's bleeding chest, pouring golden energy into the wounds. "Why so much violence? Why so much hate?"

Rachel knelt by Moriah. "I'm sorry. I'm so sorry."

"It's not your fault." Moriah's lips trembled. Tears streaked down her face as she continued to pour healing energy into Mike. "It's all of humanity's fault for insisting their group has to be better than some other group. It's every culture and every century." Another sob escaped her. "But why? *Why?* Jesus came to save everyone!"

Rachel hung her head, the black curtain of her hair hiding her face.

Mike stirred, and he stared up at Moriah. "What are you

doing?" He slapped her hands away. "Get away from me, witch!"

Moriah recoiled.

"She was healing you," Kenzie said.

"I don't want to be healed by a Satanic agent." Mike pushed himself to his hands and knees and crawled away. "Where's my wife? Julie? Julie! Oh, God! Someone call 911."

"I wasn't done." Fresh tears streaking down Moriah's cheeks. "He's still in terrible shape."

"Oh, darn," Kenzie drawled. He pulled out his phone and dialed 911. "Rachel, get Moriah inside and fed, please. I'll stay with the bigot until the ambulance arrives."

"Okay." Rachel helped Moriah to her feet and wrapped an arm around her, steering her toward the Idoni Student Building doors.

As Kenzie talked to the dispatcher, he used telekinesis to stop Mike's crawling before he accidentally killed himself from moving too much. Once he hung up, he stared at the doors of the ISB, the image of the weeping Moriah healing Mike stuck in his mind. He knew the memory would haunt him for years.

The blonde woman, Julie, came running toward Kenzie. "Let go of him! You're tryin' to kill him!"

Startled, Kenzie released Mike from his telekinesis. "I am not! I was trying to keep him from hurting himself."

The campus police chose this moment to come rushing in, wands drawn.

Julie pointed at Kenzie. "Arrest her!" she shrieked.

"For what?" Kenzie yelled back.

He found himself explaining the entire story to campus security and then the city police. The police made him repeat his story several times, took notes, and asked where Moriah and Rachel were. They collected Moriah and Rachel from the Idoni Student Building, interviewed the two of them, and then gathered statements from as many witnesses as they could find, ordering Kenzie, Moriah, and Rachel to stay in the ISB with campus security.

In the end, the Louisville police officers returned to the ISB and placed Kenzie and Moriah under arrest for unlawful use of magic and magical assault.

⚡

THROUGH THE TINY WINDOW AT THE TOP OF THE HOLDING CELL, Kenzie watched the sky first turn gray and then pink. He hadn't slept. The thin mattress on the bunk bed had nothing to do with his insomnia, however. He'd been too angry to rest. He'd stared at the white cinderblock walls, the wire mesh sealed into the window glass, and the chipped, dirty, off-white paint of the cell bars. Before the sky could reach blue, the florescent lights flickered on, their hum filling the silent cell.

When they'd been brought in the previous evening, Moriah had suffered a panic attack. The police had no sympathy or patience for this, shoveling her through the booking process with gruff orders. One female officer had yelled at Moriah for crying and made it worse.

By the time they stowed Kenzie in the holding cell, he had developed a raging hate for the precinct's officers as well as Mike and Julie. The instant the words "magical assault" had been spoken, everyone eyed Kenzie like a hardened felon. He might have received better treatment if he'd been arrested back in Georgia for attempting an abortion.

However, anger did not sustain Moriah. Kenzie had held her and rocked her for 20 minutes before her first panic attack abated. Then Moriah had slept with her head on a pillow on his lap. Moriah had been too terrified to let him climb onto the top bunk and be out of sight. A rotation of sleep, panic, and more sleep had followed until three in the morning. Then Kenzie and Moriah had talked in low voices about the problem of finding legal counsel in a foreign country, and Moriah had fallen asleep again. Kenzie's head ached from the sleep loss. By 7:00 a.m., he was hungry but too tired to be angry anymore. Moriah was still asleep on his lap.

But not sleeping had also given him time to think. *Everyone lied. The Second Civil War never ended. Life is a never-ending war. Whether or not I like it, I live in a warzone. Me against them. Magicians versus non-mags. People of Color versus Whites.* Most people in the world weren't magicians. Kenzie had always known that, but he'd never fully considered what it meant. *The police side with the non-mags. The law sides with non-mags. The police employ magicians, but they protect non-mags.* And with John Paul Smith, Jr. feeding the hate, Kenzie knew he would be forced to repeatedly break the law to protect himself and the people he cared about. *This arrest is going to turn into the first of many.*

The pieces of the problems he and the others had experienced up to this point fell into place. *It's the same people stopping us from doing something every time: the administration, the campus police, and even the Noble Seven. The administration wants us to ignore it. Campus security wants us to turn over control to them. The Noble Seven wants us to fight Top Hat head on. None of that will work.* If he wanted to solve this and prevent Smith from winning, he was going to have to defy all of them.

After a buzz, the door in the hallway opened, and Kenzie hoped it was someone arriving to feed them breakfast. He hadn't had anything to eat for 13 hours.

A young male officer walked in, his navy blue uniform neatly ironed into perfection and his access card in hand. "Okuda and Goldstein, you've been released." He swiped his card through the reader on their cell and then put his thumb on the scanner.

Moriah awakened and raised her head from Kenzie's lap. "Released?"

The officer smiled. "Yeah, hon. Your bails have been paid. Let's go."

Hon? Kenzie hated the particular behavior of calling complete strangers *hon, baby,* or *sweetheart,* but he held it in. The officer seemed nice, and he didn't want to get his face ripped off on the way out.

With locked knees, Moriah stood and stumbled toward the door. Kenzie followed. Kenzie and Moriah were given back their possessions and then led to the front of the station. Makari and Logan stood by the front counter, both of them dressed in plain jeans and t-shirts. Kenzie had expected to see his mom, but as confusing as his mom's absence was, he was still glad to see Logan. He rushed over to him, and Logan took his hand.

"Let's get outta here," Logan murmured, his face impassive and unreadable.

Kenzie nodded, clinging hard to his hand so he didn't explode. He figured if he emotionally reacted in any way at all, he'd be thrown back into the cell.

Makari corralled Moriah out the door, and Kenzie and Logan followed. Makari led them to a red car parked in the mostly empty lot, and Kenzie and Logan climbed into the backseat together. Moriah sank into the passenger seat and curled into a ball.

"How did you get us out?" Kenzie asked, wondering what the difference might be between the U.S. and the URA concerning bail.

Makari glanced over his shoulder at him. "You didn't need to be at the special bail hearing at 6:00 a.m. because my parents and Logan's dad arranged for you both to have attorneys. The Steensen lawyers will represent you, and the Idoni lawyers will represent Moriah."

"They will?" Kenzie was too stunned to fully grasp what Makari was saying. *You did that for us? Really? Wait. How am I supposed to pay your lawyers? Mom and I aren't rich.*

"Since you aren't a flight risk," Makari continued, "you're allowed to go back to campus. Our attorneys will try to settle it outside of court so there's not even a trial."

Logan patted Kenzie's knee. "It'll be okay. I promise."

"Then, food, please," Kenzie said. His hunger headache won over every other concern. *I guess the Idonis and Steensens are so powerful and rich they can do pretty much whatever they want. Non-mags might hate magicians, but the noble magicians are still celebrities in the U.S. Clearly.* "God, I'm starving."

"Sure." Makari started his car and, to Kenzie's surprise, manually backed up and drove toward the street instead of using autopilot. "Do you like pancake joints?"

"Yes. Pancakes are awesome." Kenzie took Logan's hand again, steadying his nerves at the warmth of Logan's hand against his half-frozen fingers. The jail's A/C and his stress had proven to be a poor combination. His nose and cheeks still ached with cold. "Why are you guys picking us up? I mean, I'm glad. Thank you. But where's my mom?"

Logan shook his head. "Stuck at the border. I asked Dr. Dawson to give your mom my number when she called her about your arrest. I've talked with your mom about six times now. So many people from the URA are trying to enter the U.S. to see Jesus H. Christ, the Kentucky border's still clogged."

"It's the same for your parents," Makari said to Moriah. "Your parents are famous enough that I already knew their names, so I looked up their number and called them. They tried to fly up here, but all the flights to Louisville, and all other nearby airports, are sold out."

"Okay." Moriah's voice was tiny.

Logan squeezed Kenzie's hand. "Just so you two know, Makari and I went into overdrive. I mean, you're my boyfriend, so of course I would."

Kenzie flinched. *Shit! You're so Pagan you don't realize you can't say that in front of Moriah.* He stared out the window, watching a mix of steel skyscrapers and historical stone or red brick buildings flash by the window. Storm clouds encroached upon the horizon, eating the sun and dousing the city with gray bleakness. *I wonder if she'll condemn me now. She still thought I'm a woman.*

Moriah remained silent.

"And Moriah's a member of the URA's Noble Three," Logan said. "Even though the U.S.'s Noble Seven is a separate system, we feel like it shouldn't be. We should be the Noble 10."

"Not all the families in the Noble Seven feel that way." Makari glanced at Moriah. "But the Idoni and the Steensen do, and that's what counts in this situation."

"All of that is to say, our families will be providing you our lawyers for free," Logan said.

Kenzie jerked his gaze to him. "Seriously?"

"Yeah," Logan said. "You're from another country, for God's sake, and you need the top lawyers this country can provide you."

Moriah uncurled and peered over her shoulder. "Really?"

"Yes," Makari said. "And my family is 'Old Money.' Trust me, we can carry the cost."

Kenzie's stomach growled as his relief fueled his appetite. "Oh, God. Now I'm twice as hungry." He leaned in and kissed Logan's cheek. "Thank you. And tell your dad thank you."

Logan blushed. "Hey, no problem. What's the use of being noble if you don't help people with all that power?"

I'm falling in love with the right guy, Kenzie thought. *You have a noble heart, not just a noble status.*

"Yes, thank you, Makari." Moriah slumped into her seat. "And thank you to your parents, too. God's been very merciful to me today."

"No problem," Makari said, pulling into the parking lot of

the restaurant. "Logan's right. I'm in the position to help. I should be using it."

Moriah sat up straighter. "I want the chocolate pancakes with chocolate chips and chocolate syrup with whipped cream on top."

Kenzie hoped this meant Moriah would recover her equilibrium.

$$\lightning$$

AFTER BREAKFAST AND A LONG, HOT SHOWER, KENZIE SPENT TWO hours on his cellphone holo-video chatting with his mom. Once Kenzie had vented as much anger as he could, and his mom was convinced he was safe enough, Kenzie expressed his fears about the U.S. turning into the URA and his escape plan being blown.

"Don't assume that Smith will get his way with the U.S.," Alexandria said. "Smith hasn't won yet. You just stay in college and be the real you, okay?"

"Okay." There wasn't much he could say to that. His mom could encourage him, but she couldn't understand what it was like to be him. *Be the real me, even if everyone hates me.* Kenzie fell silent. *Hate. Somehow, this is all about hate. Whoever made Top Hat is convinced everyone hates him. Or her. The most hateful and insecure person I've met so far is Iona Anderson, and she has refused to do anything to stop Top Hat this entire time. She even said she hoped Top Hat would kill Smith, and then Top Hat started trying to kill Smith. And, on top of that, Smith's mom was an Anderson, like Iona.*

He hit the mental wall he associated with studying too much. "I love you, Mom. I'm going to get some sleep."

"I love you, too."

With profound and overwhelming relief to be back in his dorm, Kenzie crashed onto his twin bed and slept for five hours.

TWENTY-FOUR

Kenzie awakened in bed and stared at the white cinderblock walls of his dorm room. The tiny space, which was crowded with a bed, nightstand, desk, and chest of drawers, was filled with his magical energy. Right now, it was also quiet.

Flashes of memory filled his mind: Iona making fun of Moriah's hair and calling Kenzie and Moriah murks; Iona's disgust that John Paul Smith, Jr. had arrived on campus and her hope that Top Hat would kill Smith; Iona, not caring Moriah was also in danger; and Iona screaming that she wanted a rematch in Battle Magic class. *I think everyone missed the obvious here.* He grabbed his phone from the nightstand. Logan had texted and asked him out for supper. He agreed, and eight minutes later he stumbled out of the dorm in denim shorts, a red tank top with a skull on it, and sneakers. His hair remained tousled, defying his efforts to fix it. *Take me as I am,* he thought grumpily.

Logan was leaning against what Kenzie now thought of as "his" oak tree, and he smiled when Kenzie made eye contact. He wore camouflage cargo shorts and a white t-shirt with a Celtic tree design. "You look ready to commit murder."

"If I end up with another bigot screaming at me, I just might." Kenzie took Logan's hand, and they headed toward the parking lot. The dorm yard was browning from lack of rain, and a few yellow oak leaves lay curled on the sidewalk. *September is not too far away.* "Also, I have a theory: I think Iona is the one summoning Top Hat."

Logan glanced at him, raising one eyebrow. "Really? She hasn't been nearby every single time he's shown up. Don't get me wrong. I think she has the talent and the bad attitude. But like we said before, why would she want to help Smith?"

"Maybe that's not the point. Maybe that's an accidental side effect. Iona said to me on the first day of class she'd heard that people from the URA were enrolled this year, and then she started her bullying campaign. She shares most of our classes, and Top Hat kept bowing toward our classroom window. She's refused to fight Top Hat, even though watching me fight Top Hat is making her murky, and she's against the taskforce being a thing. And, because she has mind magic, she doesn't need to be anywhere near Top Hat to communicate with him."

"Okay, that last point definitely has my attention," Logan said. "All the other stuff is good circumstantial evidence, but that last part explains why no one anywhere around Top Hat seems to be responsible."

"All the bowing Top Hat does toward us is fake aristocratic superiority," Kenzie said grimly. "Exactly Iona's style. And let's not forget the Asian incident and how Iona treats me and Shinrou."

"It's definitely possible. And John Paul Smith, Jr.'s mother was an Anderson. Even though I can't imagine Iona helping Smith on purpose, we should tell Shinrou and Makari your theory."

"And then what?" Kenzie scanned the other dorm yards for danger, but no one was in sight. The row of red brick buildings sat silent in the heat. Not even the tree leaves moved, the air still.

"If Shinrou and Makari think this is as logical as I do, Makari and I will confront her. We're in the Noble Seven." Logan headed diagonally across the parking lot. "We can get away with it."

"I don't think she'll care who she hears it from, especially if she's guilty."

"If she doesn't like hearing it, then maybe she'll stop doing it," Logan said. "We've got to take at least one spirit out of the equation. Zoe and I don't have control over our gods, and Moriah's in denial about summoning Jesus H. Christ."

Kenzie frowned and halted on the hot asphalt. "Iona might also say she doesn't have control. But you're right that we have to tell Shinrou and Makari." He texted Makari his theory. Makari texted back that they needed Shinrou, who was doing evening lab hours and couldn't be interrupted. Kenzie set up a time after Shinrou's lab work would be over, agreeing to 9:00 p.m. "Looks like we still get our date. Shinrou's tied up in the chemistry lab."

They headed out for Tex Mex. Logan took him to a buffet, so there was no wait for food. Thanks to the food and rest, Kenzie had enough energy to be enraged again. They checked the time, and since it would be almost another hour, Logan took him to the walking trail in a local park. He parked his motorcycle at the edge of the parking lot, and they climbed off and stowed their helmets. Picnic tables filled the half dead grass that stretched to the tree line, and the area was blessedly human-free. Kenzie relaxed at the energy washing over him in waves from the earth and trees, and chirping robins and cardinals dotted the lawn. A squirrel raced past them as they walked toward the trailhead, and it climbed onto a metal picnic table, sniffing someone's abandoned fast food bag.

Once they reached the trail, oaks, maples, and pines shaded them from the sun, and the cicadas' loud calls vibrated the air. Kenzie stared at the well-worn dirt path under his feet as he recounted what happened at the police station from start to finish. "So, yeah. Seriously, everything that happened was dumb as hell."

Logan fiddled with the chain that connected his wallet to his belt loop. "You're right. It's stupid. But let's talk procedure here: Tomorrow morning, you need to press charges against that woman—I found out her name is Julie Young—for attacking you. She charged you, so you charge her. If the Youngs decide to sue, then you counter-sue. You don't have to just stand there and be a victim of their hate and hysteria."

"Good." Kenzie clenched his fists. "I'm tired of being a victim."

"You'll never be a victim ever again," Logan said. "You've got too much spirit for that. If someone hurts you, you'll fight back. At least here in the U.S., you've got rights."

Kenzie faced the facts again: His bid for freedom, rights, and a good life rested on his succeeding in the U.S. and never going home, and he couldn't let Julie Young steal that from him.

⚡

When Kenzie and Logan returned from their date, Logan sat on the stairs outside the Kenzie's dorm suite and waited for Makari and Shinrou. Kenzie walked in on Zoe, Moriah, and Rachel clustered in the living room, standing and talking. Zoe wore her usual PJs, men's boxers and a men's white undershirt, and Moriah and Rachel still wore their school uniforms. It made for an interesting contrast. Moriah was flushed and Zoe smiling. "What's up?" Kenzie asked.

"Moriah was telling us about Makari," Zoe said.

"There's nothing to tell." Moriah grabbed her skirt hem, twisting it in a brutal grip.

"Makari went dashing off to rescue her this morning after

already carrying her halfway across campus the other day. And then she spent two hours in Makari's dorm suite talking to him. Alone." Zoe waggled her eyebrows. "That sounds like something to me."

Moriah's knuckles turned white. "I wasn't totally alone! Shinrou was there. Besides, nothing happened. Makari just explained why I need to get someone's permission before I heal them, and then he reassured me that the Idoni would protect me from the Youngs."

Zoe snorted. "For *two hours*? You talked about way more than that." She propped one hand on her hip. "Did he ask you out?"

A brutal blush stained Moriah's cheeks. "No! I'm telling you, it's not like that."

Kenzie still thought Shinrou and Makari might be dating, but he'd never say that. Zoe would explode, and Moriah might delve into a homophobic rant of censure. "Makari didn't flirt with Moriah in the car this morning. Or over breakfast, either."

"But Makari went out of his way to help her," Zoe said. "And—and—a *two-hour* talk!" She spread her hands. "Tell me you see my point! Makari's sending all the signals. He's brushed off all the other women on campus, but he's pulling her into his arms and saving her from the horrible anti-mag police. It has to mean something."

Kenzie walked to the refrigerator and pulled out a water bottle. He twisted off the cap with a distinct *snap*, then turned to Moriah. "Are you interested in Makari?"

Rachel flinched as if the question hurt her and turned toward the window. Outside, the campus lights flickered on as night fell, casting her face in a yellow glow.

"No!" Moriah wailed.

Kenzie shrugged. "Then that's all that matters." He gestured at Zoe. "You like him. You go after him."

"But he likes Moriah," Zoe said.

"So? By the way, he and Shinrou are coming over here to talk about taskforce stuff and our latest theory about Top Hat. You have a chance in ten minutes or less."

Zoe smiled slyly at Moriah. "Fine. If you're not going to pounce, I am." She bounced off down the hall.

"I don't understand her," Moriah whispered. "I'm scared of men. Our preacher says men only want sex. And don't let a man do more than hold your hand. Anything more signals you're ready to have sex, and he'll pressure you into it."

"Sounds about right," Rachel groused. "Your preacher's spot on."

Kenzie took another swig of water and considered the litany. "I think the sermon translated into 'All men are rapists, so just don't date.'"

Moriah stalked into the kitchen to her cabinet of chocolate, opened it, and fished out a candy bar. "My parents said they'd arrange a marriage for me if I want them to. But how will they know he's a good man? He could act all pious around them and still drive me off into the countryside and—and—" She tore open the wrapper. "You know. And then I wouldn't be a virgin anymore." She bit a huge chunk off.

"It doesn't count if you were violated." Kenzie flared with rage at the inherent chauvinism. "But look at the bigger picture here: Our *preacher* is a *man*. Is he admitting to date-raping all his previous girlfriends and his wife? How are any of us supposed to date or get married if all men are rapists and dates are just hunting games?"

Loki popped into the room, resplendent with his sleek black goatee, his green and gold doublet, and his gold pants. "Good questions! As a male myself, I would like to protest. And I'm a good one to protest. I gave birth by transforming into a mare. I'm the only male to ever exist who actually understands pregnancy and labor pains."

Moriah stared at Loki, a bit of chocolate decorating her lower lip.

Kenzie waved off Loki. "Stay out of this. You're not real."

"I'm real." Loki pointed at his pants. "Do you wish to see the proof?"

"No!" Rachel shouted. "Don't you dare!"

Loki held up both hands. "Just offering the evidence so you don't think I'm lying." He swept over to Moriah, his short cape fluttering behind him. "If you're scared of men, date me. I have a unique perspective on women's issues."

Moriah backed up a step, her hip hitting the edge of the kitchen counter. "That's okay. I don't need to date or think about marriage until I graduate from college. Besides, I can't marry you. You're not human."

Rachel stepped in between Moriah and Loki and crossed her arms again. "She's not interested. Back off."

"Oh! Spicy." Loki grinned. "I like you. I like spunky people."

"Well, I don't like you," Rachel said. "Leave Moriah alone."

"I still think I have something unique to offer." Loki folded his hands. "It's quite simple. I get you used to men, and you can go off and marry the prince of your dreams."

Zoe zipped into the room, her toothbrush sticking out of her mouth. She still wore her PJs. "What's going on?" The toothbrush muffled her words. "Loki?"

Loki grinned at her. "Just helping your friend." He clapped his hands once and gasped, "Oh, my! You look so adorable this way. These clothes look cute on you, and I like you better without makeup."

Zoe blushed. "Um, thanks." She raced back out of the room.

"Go away, Loki," Kenzie said, setting his water bottle on the kitchen table.

"I say pump it up," Loki said. "If you really want to make it hot, invite Thor. Lots of women get crushes on him. But if you want to make it kinky, invite Top Hat instead. I bet that would get really interesting." He waggled his eyebrows.

Rachel gaped.

Kenzie narrowed his eyes. "Zoe likes to think you're fun-loving, not an asshole. Prove her right. Stop tormenting Moriah."

"I'm not tormenting Moriah," Loki said.

"Yes, you are. And there's no reason to harass Moriah, anyway. Moriah already said she's not interested in Makari, not interested in men, and not interested in dating." Kenzie poked his chest. "Being insensitive to Moriah's pain makes you exactly like the men Moriah fears."

Loki's eyes widened. After a moment, he bowed. "I'm sorry." He vanished.

Kenzie was surprised, but only for a moment. *Top Hat listened to me, and now Loki has, too. It's true. They've gained minds of their own. If I can just get close to Jesus H. Christ, maybe I can reason with him as well. Is it too much to hope for that he might agree to rise into the sky in front of a crowd of witnesses and disappear?*

The door opened, admitting Logan, Makari, and Shinrou into the dorm suite. Makari wore jeans and a white t-shirt advertising a Catholic high school, probably the one he'd graduated from, and Shinrou wore his black uniform.

"Look at us rule breakers, meeting after co-ed visiting hours are over," Logan said with a grin.

Moriah whimpered with distress and finished her candy bar.

Everyone got settled. Zoe emerged, now dressed in a cute pink- and orange-striped sundress, and sat on the couch by Makari. When Makari asked her to scoot down so Shinrou could sit on the couch, too, she smiled when she and Makari ended up thigh to thigh. Meanwhile, Moriah took the kitchen chair the farthest away from Zoe. Rachel sat beside Moriah at the table. Kenzie relaxed in one brown living room chair and Logan in the other.

Shinrou took his phone from his pocket. "I'm going to be taking notes as we talk. Now tell me about your hypothesis."

Kenzie took a deep breath. "Okay. I think Iona's the one who made Top Hat and then lost control of him." He outlined his case and how all the pieces of evidence fit. When he finished, Shinrou continued tapping out notes on his phone, and Makari was pale. Rachel and Moriah stared, and Zoe's eyebrows were raised.

"Wow," Zoe said. "I feel like we should've suspected her all along. She's done nothing but hate on us. I guess I just thought the summoner is a man."

Rachel made a choking noise.

"Yeah, yeah, I get the sexism," Zoe said in response.

Shinrou looked up from his phone and gazed at Kenzie. "I'm trying to poke holes in your theory, and I can't. This means we have to give it serious consideration. Would you consent to an experiment?"

"Possibly," Kenzie said.

"The last time you had a direct conflict with Iona was the first day of classes. Since then, you've been trying to avoid her." Shinrou tucked his phone into his pocket. "This is reasonable, but if your theory is correct, she's been striking out at you ever since you stopped her creation from attacking the anti-magician demonstrators and then stalemated her in your sparring match. She's willing to attack students— apparently any student she feels has insulted her—and all thought forms respond to their creators' deepest desires. I want you to try starting a verbal altercation with Iona on purpose during a situation in which no one else is tense. If Top Hat shows up and attacks you, which he hasn't been doing because the religious fervor has been distracting Iona, at least according to your theory, then we'll have enough circumstantial evidence for the Noble Seven to detain her on suspicion of being the summoner."

"As long as you all are nearby to give me backup in case Top Hat attacks me, I'm willing." Kenzie's entire body burned with a mixture of fear and determination until even his fingertips tingled.

"Sure," Makari said.

Together as a group they strategized the details of how to handle the confrontation.

TWENTY-FIVE

In the morning, at exactly 8:00, Kenzie marched into the police station, Logan at his side, to press charges against Julie Young. The entire process was ridiculous. Julie Young hadn't landed her blow, and Kenzie had restrained her and not hit her. However, bigotry easily turned nonissues into convictions, so Kenzie followed Logan's advice, which had come from the Steensen family's lawyers.

They made it back to campus in time for Magic Application. The glares Iona, Heather, and Natalie aimed Kenzie's way said nastiness was in store. *Good. Now I have to shape this to my advantage. I need to delay Iona until we're outside of class and everyone can provide backup.* He stayed with Logan for the entire class, not giving them a good chance to approach him. Makari and Shinrou stuck with Moriah and Rachel.

After lunch, Zoe and Logan rushed to meet Makari and Shinrou at Griffen Hall. They would track Iona and conceal themselves nearby in case they needed to fight Top Hat.

Kenzie walked with Moriah and Rachel, heading to Strategic Magic with no Noble Seven protection. *Come on, here we are: the three "murks" from the URA. You know you want to bully us.*

Clearly taking the bait, Iona stood on the sidewalk in front of the red brick Griffen Hall with its white Ionic columns. Seth Torres had positioned himself beside her, and Natalie and Heather behind her. As Kenzie, Moriah, and Rachel approached, the group spread out over the sidewalk and grass and blocked them. Iona tossed her head, flicking her long platinum ponytail over her shoulder. Like Moriah, she wore the white skirt uniform, while Seth wore the black uniform. Heather wore the white skirt uniform and Natalie the black skirt uniform, like Rachel. Thanks to the color divide, Kenzie imagined everyone as the black and white pieces in the old Othello board game.

"You can't keep avoiding us." Iona crossed her arms and lifted her chin.

Kenzie stopped and braced himself, igniting his magic with a storm of tingles through his veins. He held his magic in check, not allowing a telltale green glow to rise from his skin. Rachel and Moriah stood behind him. "You're awfully self-centered. I'm not avoiding you. I don't have anything to say to you. Why would I?"

Iona flushed. "*I* have something to say to *you!*"

"I don't care," Kenzie drawled, his expression flat.

Other students slipped around the group as they headed into Griffen Hall, walking over the grass to avoid them and staring at them as they passed.

Seth stepped forward. "Enough." His facial muscles were tight, a mask of anger-tinged stoicism. He glared at Kenzie. "What do you think you're doing? We are here to become the next generation of magic-capable soldiers. You let yourself become distracted by petty religious arguments and the infantile pranks of energy workers who have figured out how to model 3D forms. The Noble 10 Student Committee has coordinated with the campus police on the *real* investigation into what's been going on around here. *You* don't need to do anything except shut up, attend classes, and study."

"Those demons might be summoned by people who think it's funny to play around with evil spirits, but Jesus Christ is not a prank," Moriah said.

Iona snorted. "This has gotten ridiculous. You got yourself arrested for meddling with nonmags. Then the Steensen clan went running to your rescue, making themselves look naff. I mean, more naff than they already are. The Idoni clan and their white knighting are equally naff."

Kenzie's shoulders tensed at the insult to Logan. *Don't insult my boyfriend, loser.*

"You weren't present at the situation," Rachel said. "You didn't see what happened. You weren't the ones in danger, and you don't have any business passing judgment."

Seth stalked forward, nearly toe to toe with her. "Iona and I are from the Noble Seven. How people use their magic, or abuse it, is very much our business. It's our responsibility to make judgments and keep people in line."

Iona pointed at Kenzie. "And you're completely out of line. You think you're hot shit because Logan asked you out, but you're still an NPC in our game. And as long as you're in the U.S., you're answerable to the Noble Seven for how you use your magic."

"So let's make this clear," Seth said. "Stop your unauthorized investigation into the occurrences on campus and stop using magic outside of class assignments, or I'll petition the administration to expel all of you."

Iona leaned forward. "And it won't just be Seth. I'll sign that petition, and so will several of the other Noble Seven here. The rest of the nobles haven't gone naff over you woobs."

"There's a hierarchy here," Seth said, "and it's time you learned your place."

The tension of unreleased magic expanded around Iona,

Seth, and Kenzie. Displaced air molecules shifted, generating subtle steam-like patterns around their bodies.

Kenzie's magic burned through his veins so hotly it made his skin throb and itch. *Perfect. Iona is on edge, and Seth and she have stayed away from religious bashing for the most part, meaning Moriah won't feel compelled to prove herself. If I push Iona one more time and Top Hat appears, it'll be because Top Hat is Iona's creation and not because Top Hat was attracted by Jesus H. Christ showing up.* "Sorry, but the administration won't care about a few whiny babies from rich families throwing a tantrum about having scholarship students on their campus."

Iona gaped at him, her shiny pink lips parted and her blue eyes blazing.

Kenzie smirked. "Until your families get tired of playing by the rules and decide to buy JCU so it can be a playground for their little princes and princesses, relieving you of any responsibility to grow up, including making sure you just happen to all get perfect grades and graduate as an entire elite class of valedictorians, all with degrees that you never needed to earn because you could have all used private tutors to get the same education that you get here, this is a real university. And at real universities, the administration doesn't give one solitary shit whether you like any of your classmates. You're responsible for pretending to care about other people, not just yourselves."

Iona's magic bristled in heat mirage waves around her body. "You only think you're better than us because you got lucky in Dr. Grayson's class!"

"You're all classists, and you're all racists," Rachel said. "Students from the URA can detect that better than anyone. You want to enslave all the non-nobles and bring feudalism back. Have us scrub your kitchen floors for you. Cook your meals, do your laundry, and for the People of Color like Kenzie, Moriah, and me, maybe pick your cotton."

Iona clenched her fists. "I'm not going to listen to this! I'm going to mute you once and for all!"

Top Hat appeared between Iona and Kenzie, a white cane in his hand. He wore a scarlet leotard, a scarlet coat with tails, and a matching scarlet top hat. His grin stretched his mouth unnaturally wide. "Did someone call for me?"

Moriah screamed and jumped behind Kenzie, clutching the back of Kenzie's uniform jacket. All the blood drained from Iona's face. Seth and she sank into battle stances, but Kenzie stood firm.

Top Hat's goat hooves clicked on the sidewalk as he did a little tap dance routine, whistling a melody and twirling his cane. He still appeared Caucasian, and his eyes were black. His goat tail was curled like a candy cane, making him look like a happy cat.

Everyone watched Top Hat in silence, waiting. Seth raised a blue magical shield in front of his friends and himself.

When Top Hat finished his routine, he tossed his cane into the air and caught it, then took off his hat and bowed, first to Kenzie's side and then to Iona's. Two little horns protruded from his center-parted platinum hair. "My, my. Such fierce hate here." He straightened and set his hat upon his head. "I'll give you each a sixpence for it."

Iona's mouth opened and closed a few times. "It's you," she said at last, staring at Kenzie. "You're the one who's been doing this."

Kenzie exploded. "Typical! A typical reversal attack. You denied, attacked, and reversed the victim and offender. You're the one summoning Top Hat-Satan, Iona. You always were!"

Iona took a step back. "*Me?*"

"You're the one attacking and denying," Seth said to him.

"It's been you all along!" Moriah shouted from behind Kenzie. "You're the one making fun of Christians the most. You're the one with the most hate. You're the one who won't stop attacking us!"

Logan, Makari, Shinrou, and Zoe burst out of Griffen Hall and spread out around Iona, Seth, Natalie, and Heather. "Surrender," Makari commanded.

"I don't have anything to surrender *for!*" Iona yelled.

"What do you say to my offer?" Top Hat asked, looking around with an expression of amusement.

"Yes, what will it be, Iona?" Kenzie pointed at her. "Now that you know you're the reason Top Hat-Satan exists, what will you do? Use him to strike us down? Or surrender? What you want guides what Top Hat-Satan does, not what you think you want. Your deepest desires. What's on the inside of you? An endless well of hate? Or something else?"

Iona looked from Kenzie to Seth, and from Seth to Makari. Slowly, she lowered her arms. "You all *really* think I'm doing this?"

Top Hat stopped smiling. He looked at them with an expression of saddened surprise. "Oh. The fun's over, it seems. No sixpence show today, folks." He vanished.

Makari and Logan were solemn and stern as they approached Iona.

Seth stared at her as if he had never seen her before. "It was you?"

Iona wrapped her arms around herself, curling inward. "*No.* I've never summoned a spirit in my life."

"We're not saying you did it on purpose," Makari said quietly. "But now you've got to come with us and report this to Vice President Dawson."

Iona's pale complexion flushed crimson, and she started crying. "I can't *believe* you people. I'll prove I'm innocent." Wiping away tears, she let herself be escorted away by Makari, Logan, Seth, and Shinrou. Natalie and Heather trailed behind them, whispering to each other.

Moriah let go of the back of Kenzie's uniform jacket. Kenzie turned to face Moriah and Rachel just in time to see

Moriah hug Rachel. Rachel's head was bowed so that her hair was a straight black curtain hiding her face.

"Do you really think there's something under the hate?" Rachel whispered, releasing Moriah.

"There's always something under the hate," Kenzie said. "It's never hate all the way down. Hatred, as terrible as it is, is just an ego defense." He realized he was quoting his mom, something she had told him over and over until he grasped it, so that racist attacks he experienced didn't crush him. No one else was likely to know what he was talking about. "An ego defense is something you use when you feel threatened by other people. So, yes, there's something underneath hatred, even for someone as shallow as Iona."

Rachel raised her head and looked at Kenzie for a long moment. Finally, she said, "What's underneath Rev. John Paul Smith, Jr.?"

"I wish I knew," Kenzie said.

Rachel tilted her head. "Do you really? Surely you don't."

"Yes, I do," Kenzie said. "I mean it. If I understood what was going on, I might be able to form a response that isn't idiotic. I want to understand. I want to know. More knowledge can't be a bad thing. Not if it's true knowledge."

"The truth can hurt sometimes," Rachel said.

Kenzie shook his head. "The truth can never hurt. It can piss you off, but it can't hurt you more than living a lie. Real truth, the whole truth, is what we need in this world."

Moriah grinned. "God is love. That is the only truth we need."

Rachel sighed, then smiled at Moriah. "That's very idealistic, but I can't deny that your hopefulness is appealing."

"Oh, shit, we're gonna be late for class," Zoe said.

They glanced at each other and ran for the doors of Griffen Hall. Kenzie relegated the problem of Iona and Top Hat to Dr. Dawson, at least for now.

⚡

AFTER STRATEGIC MAGIC I, KENZIE HEADED TO THE VICE president's office. That morning, Dr. Dawson had requested to meet with him between his classes, but he'd pushed it out of his mind because they'd needed to deal with Iona first. When Kenzie stood in the outer office facing the look of censure on the secretary's face, the full impact of his arrest hit. *I could get expelled. Dr. Dawson can kick my ass back into the URA.* And as a gay transman, he'd be dead within a week.

Icicles clogged Kenzie's veins as the secretary waved for him to enter the vice president's office. *I'll have to buy a wig.* If he got caught with short, bright red hair in the URA, he'd be arrested by what everyone had nicknamed The Morality Police. They called themselves The Daughters of the Republic and patrolled the streets for violations of the dress code laws. However, Kenzie's appearance would be the least of his concerns. *At least if I end up in jail because of my hair, that will protect me against the men who would take it on themselves to rape me to "teach" me a "lesson" and then kill me. But what about prison guards? They would rape me. Oh, God.*

Dr. Dawson glanced up from her computer screen. Today her blonde hair was French braided, showing gray hairs mixed in. "Please have a seat."

Kenzie sat. His palms sweated, and as soon as he tried to sit still, his knee bounced. The warm beige walls and rich mahogany furniture did nothing to relax him.

"I've reviewed the security footage of the Top Hat attack and your subsequent arrest from four different angles," Dr. Dawson said. "I've watched it in both normal speed and slow motion, and so has our university president, Dr. Russell. But you tell me what happened."

Kenzie took a deep breath. "It was a verbal assault first. Mike Young was saying nasty racist things to us. Then he lunged at Rachel Abrams. I cast a spell to stop the attack. This made Julie Young strike out at me, so I cast a spell to stop that as well."

"Dr. Russell and I agree with your claim. To us, the security footage seems clear: It was defense and then self-defense."

"Does this mean you won't expel me?" Kenzie couldn't stop bouncing his knee.

"We won't expel you." Dr. Dawson swiveled her chair to face Kenzie directly.

Kenzie took a deep breath. It felt like he was breathing through a straw.

"However, I think you should be made aware of the consequences." Dr. Dawson's eyebrows pinched together. "The university has a PR nightmare on its hands. The media reported that a student magician attacked two ordinary citizens."

Kenzie bristled, his shoulders clenching. "That's not true! And they left out the part where Mike Young started the whole thing by storming up to Moriah and then saying a bunch of racist stuff. I even recorded the audio on my phone."

"We have already combated the claim with our own press releases," Dr. Dawson said. "But we can release a statement to the press to that effect. I'll need to you message me your audio file. The faster you can get it to me, the better." Her brow furrowed. "Why was Moriah verbally attacked?"

"She's got Jewish heritage, so even though she's Christian, that's all that counts to people like Mike Young," Kenzie gave Dr. Dawson a hooded stare. "And she's with Jesus H. Christ a lot. That made the visitors jealous. Mike Young also assumed Rachel was Latina and said cruel stuff to her, and he got in my face and hit me first. He smacked my wrist."

Dr. Dawson folded her hands on her mahogany desk. "I hope you have recorded everything that was said in the audio file. We've already released the security footage to the press, but the audio's not very good. You were too far away from the cameras. Still, two news outlets have walked back their stories and corrected them. We need more proof it was self-defense. We have to defend the university's name."

"Yes, ma'am." Several seconds of silence followed. Kenzie realized how long a second could be.

"Don't stop to speak with any visitors or protesters," Dr. Dawson said. "They want to offend you. They want you to get angry. They want you to yell back. They're seeking an escalation. It's possible that Mike and Julie Young approached you in hopes you would magically attack them and started this fight on purpose."

"Why?" Kenzie's lungs tightened. "Just because they hate People of Color?"

Dr. Dawson shook her head. "No, so they can sue the university in addition to suing you personally. Since Jefferson-Crowley is an ivy league university, people assume that we're incredibly wealthy. I won't be surprised if the Youngs ended up suing us for billions of dollars."

Although Kenzie had heard of stunts like that, he'd never imagined being in the middle of one. "And *I'm* supposed to be the evil one?"

Dr. Dawson snorted with laughter. "Seems backwards, doesn't it?" She paused. "Normally I wouldn't talk about these things with students, but I believe part of my job is teaching students to think critically. I'm telling you this because I'm trying to help you see the wider context of what can go wrong. You got arrested and charged with assault. You also might get sued. The university will probably be sued, and if we lose the case, the financial burden would impact many people and programs. While I'm not blaming you for this incident—and I truly am not—it was still something that could have been avoided if you'd ignored the Youngs and walked away."

Kenzie sat with those thoughts for several more silent seconds. *What I need to do right now is play dead.* "You're right.

None of those things occurred to me. I'll calculate in the consequences in the future." *You might be right about the Youngs, but at the same time, the administration hasn't really handled this crisis. I hope you'll get it under control now that you've been handed Iona, but excuse me if I feel cynical.*

"Thank you, Kenzie," Dr. Dawson said. "That's all. You can go now."

"I'll send you my audio file right away." Kenzie stood and marched out.

As Kenzie left the building, Rachel appeared from behind an Ionic column, startling him. She fell into step with him. "Was it bad?"

"No. Dr. Dawson was nice. Firm, but nice."

"Good." Rachel stared at the sidewalk as they walked. "I don't want to get anyone in trouble. You're innocent. Moriah, too. And I've been thinking about what you said about Iona. About there always being something underneath."

Kenzie was confused. "Look, even if you hadn't talked back to Mike and Julie Young, the whole thing would have happened anyway. They were determined to start a fight. Dr. Dawson pointed that out. No one blames you." He studied Rachel's profile, or what little of it he could see. Once again, the black curtain of Rachel's hair covered most of her face. "And what about Iona?" He offered her a small smile. "Did I manage to change your mind about us irredeemable humans even a little bit? Because that might be a miracle as big as Jesus healing the lame. I know how much it hurts to go through everything we've gone through the URA. The URA doesn't produce Moriahs. It produces Rachels."

Rachel shot him a doubtful look, her brow furrowed. "Do you really think I'm so common?"

"Utterly predictable," Kenzie said. "I'm like you, not Moriah. And you're no more evil than the rest of us." He glanced around at the campus with its lavender fall-blooming crocuses lining the sidewalks around the Torres

Administration Building and the maple trees now dotted with yellow and orange leaves. Everything looked peaceful for the moment. *Can it stay that way now that Iona's been forced to face what she did?*

Rachel straightened, squaring her shoulders and lifting her chin. "We need to meet tonight. All the members of the taskforce."

"Why?" Kenzie asked.

She strode out ahead of him, her black hair flying behind her in the wind. "I know something about the situation that I didn't know before. And I'm not talking until everyone is gathered in one place."

Kenzie turned down the sidewalk that would take them to their dorm. "Okay. Well, then everyone from our little group is going to meet tonight. I'm sure they'll agree."

TWENTY-SIX

THAT EVENING, AFTER EVERYONE HAD FINISHED WITH CLASSES and labs for the day, Makari and Logan called the meeting at Rachel's request. Shinrou suggested the women's dorm suite again, and Rachel, Kenzie, Moriah, and Zoe agreed. Moriah seemed less nervous about it since the first meeting in their dorm suite hadn't turned into anything sexual, and Makari had apparently been a gentleman during her talk with him. Everyone piled into the little living room. They carried over the chairs from the kitchen table so they could cluster together. Kenzie and Zoe sat on the plush living room chairs, and Logan, Moriah, and Rachel on the kitchen chairs.

"Just so everybody is clear," Makari said, taking the middle cushion on the sofa, "this meeting was requested by Rachel."

Zoe sat next to Makari again, taking the opposite side from Shinrou. She looked at Rachel, who was as solemn as usual. "Yep. And she's been on mute about it. Premiere already. What's going on?"

Rachel stood from her chair, which was stationed by Moriah's. Instead of changing outfits for the day, she still wore her black skirt uniform with black tights and Mary

Janes. "I'm prepared to talk now that we're all here. I've decided I can't go through with Iona facing the consequences of being Top Hat's summoner."

"I don't think you get to decide that," Logan said with a bewildered half smile. He'd changed into cargo shorts and a t-shirt.

Rachel acted as though he hadn't interrupted. "I have a confession to make."

Pressure swept through Kenzie, and his stomach dropped. He stared at Rachel. *No. You can't be serious.*

"A confession about what?" Moriah asked. She now wore her floral-print prairie dress.

Rachel stared straight ahead at the bank of windows. The open blinds admitted the crimson glow of the sunset. "I know the truth about Top Hat."

"What truth?" Shinrou asked.

Rachel didn't directly acknowledge him. "I thought it didn't matter. I thought it didn't matter who did what, because if there's a God—and I'm not convinced there is—then we're all going to hell anyway. The biggest lie in the Bible is that anyone is saved. Everyone hates everyone. The world is nothing but destruction. I knew that once I learned about World War III in school. Once I learned America bombed countries such as Iran, Iraq, and Afghanistan out of existence and turned the Middle East into a nuclear wasteland, I knew. That was the day I figured out Earth *is* hell."

Kenzie's eyes burned with unshed tears. *Rachel... Oh, God. I understand. I do.*

Rachel's lower lip trembled. "But I didn't lose my faith until my father died. What my uncle did to my mother and me once my father died confirmed it: surely God isn't real. And then it was *inside* me. I thought I myself was hatred all the way down to the black lump that is what's left of my soul. I thought everyone's souls were made of hatred. So I carried out my uncle's orders. I thought it wouldn't matter anyway. Then I met Moriah and knew I'd made a mistake. But I still tried to deny that my actions mattered. People got hurt. And I still thought, 'What good would it do? Hatred is the most powerful force on Earth.' I knew people would die, and I still told myself that dead or alive, it doesn't matter. Nothing matters. But Moriah…kept showing up." She turned to face Moriah. "You believe so hard and so much. And then Kenzie told me the truth today: hatred is a lie. Hatred itself is a lie. It's all a lie to cover up the real emotions underneath it."

Holding his breath, Kenzie lifted his hand and pressed it against his lips, forcing himself not to cry. *You're who I would be if my mom died, too. I almost lost hope when my dad died, but my mom was there for me.*

Rachel wrapped her arms around herself, bowing her head. "And what's underneath is… pain. I hurt. That's all. I fashioned Top Hat out of pure pain and the desire for vengeance. I'm Top Hat's summoner. It's me."

"But you didn't *make* Top Hat," Moriah whispered. "Humans can't make demons. Demons are fallen angels. And it's not your fault. Your uncle ordered you to summon the demon. You were in his power. Once your father died, you and your mom were required to be obedient to him."

"The Bible says I should have died rather than sin."

Moriah frowned. "The Bible also says that all you have to do is repent, and you will be forgiven! You can't take part of the Bible out of context."

Top Hat appeared, holding a white cane. A wave of gasps shot through the room. He now wore black: his signature top hat, an old-fashioned suit with coattails, and tap-dancing shoes that apparently covered human feet and not hooves. He appeared to be a White man, and his face was unpainted. His eyes were dark brown, almost black. He bowed to Rachel, sweeping off his hat, revealing center-parted brunette hair and no horns. "I praise my Dark Lady for the gift of life."

Rachel confesses, and now Top Hat looks normal? Kenzie gripped the chair arms with both hands, tense and ready to defend himself. *Confessing untwisted Rachel's magic, but will Top Hat also act normal?*

Rachel covered her face with her hands. "No. This was a mistake. If I hadn't been so weak, this never would have happened."

Top Hat straightened and popped his hat upon his head. "Ah, but you didn't create me alone. Of the three billion humans now left on this planet, a huge number of them believe in Satan or, in the case of religions like Islam, something similar enough."

"You aren't Satan," Shinrou said. "And there's no hell."

Top Hat turned and faced the couch. He regarded Shinrou with an expression of curiosity. "I *am* Satan, and Jesus Christ walks the earth, and yet there is no hell?"

Moriah stood and lifted her chin. "Excuse me, Mr. Top Hat, but you're not Satan."

Top Hat spun toward her. He rested the bottom of his cane on the floor and leaned on it, striking a gentlemanly pose. "No?"

Moriah shook her head, making her long blonde pigtails bounce. "No." She made eye contact with him, staring. "You should know this. When you disappear, you go back to hell where the real Satan is."

Top Hat lifted his cane and rested it on his shoulder. He paced in casual, measured steps around the drab brown and white living room and the plain white kitchen with its oak cabinets. "I don't rightly know where I go when I disappear. I remember where I was before I was here." He whirled to face them, smiling. "A stage. Yes, a grand, lit stage, with a red carpet and stairs leading up to it."

Moriah's brow furrowed. "That doesn't sound like hell."

At Top Hat's contemplative mood, Kenzie grew bold

enough to speak. "You keep tap dancing and singing. Do you enjoy performing?"

Top Hat did a little tap dance routine on the spot, his shoes clicking on the white tile kitchen floor. "I love it! I love a good show."

Rachel raised her head and uncovered her face. She gazed at Top Hat.

Logan looked from Top Hat to Rachel with an odd expression. His forehead wrinkled. "I get it. You repurposed him, didn't you?"

Rachel flinched. "I'm not like Moriah. I'm not nobility. I spent years secretly making myself a friend so that I could survive the loneliness after Father died. Mother was too depressed to do anything, and my uncle isolated me. When my uncle found out about my friend this year and ordered me to summon him a demon to do his bidding through me, I only had one choice. I had to use my friend as a base."

Logan shook his head. "But I already know from projects in high school that if you mix forms like that, the base always comes through the form on top of it."

"You dressed a tap dancer in a Satan suit, but it all went haywire before you even arrived here," Kenzie said. *No wonder the magic felt so twisted.*

Rachel's hands curled into fists. "I tried to tell my uncle it wasn't working, but he wouldn't listen!"

Suddenly, Kenzie understood. "No one's died because you don't want to kill anyone, and the thought forms can't do something their summoners don't want to do. Deep down inside, whatever *you* want most is what they do. Our surface desires don't matter. We'll get what we really want, whether we think we want it or not. You've wanted to hurt people. You've wanted to be the powerful one for once. But what you haven't wanted is for anyone to die. If you did, then Top Hat would have struck fatal blows on the first try, such as stabbing people through the heart."

"The sixpence shows are for John Paul Smith, Jr.," Top Hat gasped, as if the thought had only now occurred to him. "The hate you have, milady, came from him. He gave it to you, and you to me, and now…" He twirled his cane. "I've become tainted with that man's hate."

Shock slammed into Kenzie as if someone had smashed him through a wall of solid ice. "Wait. John Paul Smith, Jr. is your *uncle*?"

"Yes." Rachel stared at the brown carpet.

Moriah gaped and plopped back into her chair. Everyone else stared.

Wrapping her arms around herself, Rachel faced Top Hat. "I'm so sorry. All you wanted to do was dance and make me smile."

"But that man, he prevents the entire world from smiling." Top Hat looked thoughtful. Then, slowly, he frowned. "I think…I think I hate him. For real."

An icy feeling trickled into Kenzie's stomach like a half-frozen stream. "Let's talk about this. Because you're a real person, that means you have the ability to negotiate with us."

"Negotiate?" Top Hat grinned. "You want to make a deal with the devil? Does this mean you hate someone?"

"What if we deal with John Paul Smith, Jr. ourselves?" Kenzie asked. "We could reveal what he forced Rachel to do. We could have him arrested."

"I'm afraid John Paul Smith, Jr. is far too powerful for you," Top Hat said. "You would be forced to fight him, and even with help from your friends and my lovely Dark Mistress, I doubt you could win against a Merlin class magician with no moral inhibitions. I must fulfill my 'satanic' purpose to kill. I'll kill Smith." He bowed and vanished.

"*What?*" Kenzie howled, stunned.

Almost everyone in the room yelled alongside him.

Rachel bowed her head again.

Zoe shot to her feet. "Smith is a magician? That fucking

hypocritical asshole!" She raised both fists. "Here he is saying how evil we all are, and he's one of us."

"Well, we learned his mother was an Anderson," Shinrou said. "So it makes sense."

Makari pulled out his cell phone. "I'm calling my dad. Capturing rogue magicians is part of the Noble Seven's job."

Logan raked a hand through his spiky hair and pulled out his own cell phone. "Dad on speed dial. Here we go."

They both left the room to make their calls.

Kenzie turned to Shinrou. "You've been working on a spell to destroy the thought forms' bodies, but will destroying their bodies be enough? Or will they just rematerialize within a day or less?"

Shinrou closed his eyes for a moment and pinched the bridge of his nose. "Based on what I've worked out so far, I don't think so. The level of the thought form's power is tied to whether they are materialized or not, and that is tied somehow to the amount of belief and energy that's been poured into them. Dematerializing them will reduce their power considerably. After that, we'll have to launch a plan to keep their spirits off camera. Maybe Moriah and Rachel will regain the ability to summon them and dismiss them. If so, it will be as simple as not summoning them."

"But I *don't* summon Jesus," Moriah groaned.

"In other words," Kenzie said, ignoring that, "we just need to dematerialize them and then problem shoot from there."

Shinrou lowered his hand to his lap. "Exactly."

Makari and Logan ran back into the room.

"Problem," Makari said.

"Our dads can't fly in until tomorrow," Logan said. "They have private jets, but the air traffic is still too extreme. Louisville International Airport is swamped."

"But our dads are scrambling the rest of the clan chiefs," Makari said. "They're going to descend on Louisville and take care of John Paul Smith, Jr. themselves. We just need to hope they get here in time to stop Top Hat from killing Smith."

Logan walked to Rachel's side. "Top Hat stopped earlier because you lost the will to fight Iona. This is all about your will. Magic is will. That's a basic tenet."

"How do you control your deepest desires? Do any of you do any better?" Rachel asked in a harsh whisper. "You're asking me the impossible."

"At least Smith can defend himself with magic," Shinrou said. "He's not helpless."

A cellphone rang, and by the ringtone, Kenzie knew it wasn't his.

Logan, Makari, and Shinrou checked theirs, paused, and tucked them away. The cellphone kept ringing. All eyes turned to Rachel. She pulled her phone out of her skirt pocket with shaking fingers and answered it. "Yes." With everyone watching her, no one making a noise, she stared back with panicked eyes. "Yes. I understand." She pressed the touch screen, ending the call, and slowly lowered her phone.

"You can't be serious." Kenzie understood who kept calling Rachel and making her leave campus. "You can't meet your uncle *now*."

Rachel turned away, wooden. "I don't have a choice. If he finds out I told you everything, there isn't a force on Earth that could save any of us. And our only hope for buying Shinrou enough time to learn how to dissolve the golems' bodies and for the leaders of the Noble Seven to get here is for me to play along. Also, if I'm with my uncle, I might be able to stop Top Hat from killing him—at least in your estimation."

She trudged out of the room. Logan stepped forward as if to stop her, but he halted and stared after her instead.

"God," Kenzie whispered. "I hope he doesn't flog her for disobedience."

Moriah burst into tears.

$\mathcal{Z}$

Twenty minutes later, two silent bodyguards dressed in black suits escorted Rachel down a hotel hallway. This had been the routine for over a week: Rachel's uncle demanded her presence, and two bodyguards picked Rachel up from campus and drove her to Louisville's nicest hotel, the Prince Albert Inn. The padded carpet muted Rachel's every footfall, underscoring the quiet, and she stared at the upcoming door, her heart thudding. Her palms sweated. *Has Top Hat already tried to attack him? Will my uncle kill me now?*

One bodyguard unlocked the door and gestured for her to enter first. She walked into the suite, which contained a sitting area and fully stocked kitchenette in one room and in another, a bedroom and bathroom. Sitting in a leather chair by the window was the man Rachel hated more than any creature in the universe: John Paul Smith, Jr.

Smith glanced up at her and smiled, calculating and cold. Although he was 52 years old, he was tanned and muscular. His gray hair was dyed a platinum blond that brought out the blue of his eyes. As always, he wore a light-colored, three-piece suit; today, it was pale beige. His features were strong: a blocky jaw, hawkish nose, and thick, pale eyebrows. He drank seltzer water from a bourbon glass.

A full two minutes passed before Smith spoke. In conversation terms, it felt like an hour. Rachel clasped her hands behind her back and straightened her shoulders, taking the position of parade rest.

Finally, Smith spoke. "Despite several attacks on your campus, Top Hat *still* has no fatalities. It's infuriating! As much as I want him to kill the filthy magic-using students, I *need* him to kill protesters. If he doesn't, then the tide of hate against magicians can't rise high enough. And right now, he's killed no one. Why is that?"

"Healing spells. Not only can magicians fight back, they can heal the damage. Students and professors have healed the protesters and visitors, too."

"'But also,'" Smith snapped. "The phrase 'not only' is always followed by 'but also.'"

"Not only can magicians fight back, but also they can heal the wounds."

Smith nodded. "Very well. I should have foreseen that outcome. It just surprises me that none of Top Hat's attacks resulted in instant kills." He thunked down his glass on the end table beside his chair. "On top of that, one of our archbishops even got attacked."

Rachel's stomach clenched. Ramsey shouldn't have been able to identify her, given Smith had never publically laid claim to her, but if Ramsey had learned of their connection, Rachel would be tortured.

Smith pushed to his feet and headed for the waiting platters of cheese and fruit. "As per your surprising request the last time we met, I spoke with Mike and Julie Young. They agreed to drop the charges against Miss Goldstein and that filthy Okuda creature."

"Thank you." Rachel's stomach partially unknotted when her uncle didn't mention Ramsey again.

"Well, you are my niece after all." Smith grabbed a small plate and began creating his usual pile of cheese cubes. "Family should be there for each other." He turned to face Rachel. "And I think it's time to make Moriah Goldstein part of our family." He picked up a cheese cube by a toothpick and swirled it in a small circle. "Do you think she would be interested in becoming a children's minister?"

Cold shot down Rachel's arms and legs like ice spikes, her heart skipping a beat in horror. "S-she might." *You're going to bribe her into a position where you can control her!* A female children's minister was allowed in their religion, although rare, and for Smith to offer such an elevated position to Moriah meant he was aggressively pursuing her.

"Ask Miss Goldstein to meet with me. You can reveal to her, and only her, that you're my niece. If she accepts the offer to go into the ministry, she'll have to move back home and attend a Bible college, but I'll entice her by making the offer ironclad in the form of a contract." He leaned against the edge of the countertop and ate a cheese cube. "I'll have the contract written up that she'll begin her job in the summer of 2099. Earlier if she can graduate faster." He grinned. "I know! I'll offer to have the church pay her tuition. That should be motivating."

Rachel could barely breathe. She had often witnessed her uncle give birth to his smaller plots, but none had ever impacted her personally except the one to create Top Hat. *You can't have Moriah. I won't let you. I love her. I'll do whatever it takes.*

Top Hat popped into the room right at Rachel's side. He smiled and looked Smith up and down. "My, my. I'll give you a full schilling for your hate."

The bodyguard in the corner pulled out his blue steel pistol and pointed it at Top Hat.

Smith stared first at Top Hat and then at Rachel. "What's the meaning of this?"

Top Hat shot forward, far faster than the bodyguard could fire his spell. He summoned a pitchfork, aiming it at Smith's heart.

Smith flicked up one hand, and red energy flashed from his hand, forming a barrier. Top Hat's pitchfork slammed into it. "By all that is holy! You just made me sin. Wretched creature."

The bodyguard fired a spell with a flash of blue energy, but Top Hat didn't even look in his direction when it hit him.

Instead, he engaged in a staring match with Smith, the bodyguard's spell having no effect.

"Rachel, I asked you a question," Smith hissed. He didn't break eye contact with Top Hat. "What is the meaning of this?"

Rachel knew that either Top Hat would succeed, or she would die. *But I promised to buy time for Shinrou and the Noble Seven. Do I want that enough?* "I can no longer control him. I can neither summon nor dismiss him. He comes and goes as he pleases. The worldwide audience believes him to be Satan, which means your plan worked. However, the audience has fed him so much belief he's now an independent entity. They believed him into being real, like the toys in the book *The Velveteen Rabbit*."

Smith's eyes widened. "You're sentient?"

Top Hat grinned. "Don't be so surprised, dear Reverend. According to your religion's creation myth, your God spoke the world into existence. The myth continues by saying that your God made humans in his image. It can't be his physical image; Jehovah has no flesh and blood body. So what image is this? Why the image of the Creator, of course—and the destroyer! Whether by flood or by fire and brimstone, your God destroys as easily as he creates." He leaned as close to Smith as he could get with the crimson barrier in place. "To follow your religion's logic, humans are creators, and humans are destroyers. In my case, they created a destroyer."

With a trembling hand, Smith set down his plate of cheese on the countertop without looking. "A second Satan literally walks the Earth in the flesh." He narrowed his eyes. "And because I am God's greatest servant, you came to kill me."

"Ha!" Top Hat's sharp laugh cut through the air. "What priceless arrogance!"

Red energy outlined Smith's body for a moment as he glared at Top Hat. "So why kill me?"

"You hate with the depth and breadth and height of your

soul. You hate with the all the breaths, smiles, and tears of your life. Your hatred is so grand, so soaring, so towering that it's like an Elizabeth Barrett Browning love poem to the darkness in humans' hearts." He smirked. "Your heart is pumped by hate instead of blood."

"Oh?" Smith drawled. "Is that so?"

"You gave your hate to Rachel, and she gave it to me. Now I am here to give it back to you: I hate you, John Paul Smith, Jr."

Smith shrugged. "Humans are filled with darkness and sin. In all his inexplicable wisdom and justice, God has chosen to love us despite our evil natures. That will have to do. As for me, I'm in the same camp as the Apostle Paul, who had an affliction God wouldn't deliver him from. God told him, 'My grace is sufficient for you.' The same must be true for me."

"Ha!" Top Hat's voice cracked through the air again. "So your sin of unending hate is forgivable, but magicians' 'sin' of magic is not? Your hypocrisy is priceless."

Smith waved one hand in the air dismissively. "That's between God and me. It's none of your business."

"But everyone else's sins are your business?" Top Hat asked.

"You're boring me," Smith said.

Top Hat snorted. "Am I? You are the reason for my present form, are you not? You wished for me to kill for you, and the world believes me to be Satan. That means I should be killing Christians. I'll start with your family." He took off his hat, revealing a mirror copy of Smith's platinum blond hair, and bowed. "Shall I be off? Do you love your family? Any of your family? Let's find out." He vanished.

Rachel gasped.

Smith surged forward, his palm glowing with red energy, but Top Hat was already gone. His barrier collapsed. "My family?" He turned to Rachel with wide eyes. "Summon him back!"

Is this what I want? Is this what is in my heart? She'd blamed everyone in her family for not stopping Uncle John Paul from abusing her and her mother. Longing for vengeance poured through her like a flash flood through a desert, her soul a cracked and barren landscape. She wanted them all to pay. "I can't," she whispered.

"You're too stoic!" Smith screamed. "Too calm!" He lunged forward and slapped her face. "This is your family, too. How can you not care?"

Rachel stumbled sideways, falling to the floor. Her ear rang so loudly that she barely heard her uncle's words. An instant headache lanced her skull, and her jaw had been knocked out of alignment. Her cheek stung with sharp, radiating pain. "You beat it out of me."

Smith reared back his foot and kicked her in the hip with all his strength. She was thrown onto her stomach. "You're disgusting! Win over Moriah Goldstein for me, or I'll have you stoned to death!"

Rachel pushed to her hands and knees and crawled toward the door. She wondered if her hip bone had been cracked. The pain made her nauseated. She tripped on her skirt.

"Not so fast," Smith snarled. "You'll call her from here."

The bodyguard walked over, picked Rachel up, and laid her on the sofa. She stared at the ceiling and sent all her hate and pain to Top Hat, silently begging him to return and kill her uncle, if not for her, then to save Moriah. The bodyguard took the phone from her pocket and put it in her hand. Through her haze of pain, she unlocked her phone, pressed the phone icon, and then icon labeled MG. *It's too late to stop Top Hat, and it's too late for me. But I have to save Moriah! Somehow, someway, I have to save her.*

TWENTY-SEVEN

Shinrou had returned to his dorm to pull an all-nighter, something Makari said Shinrou did way too often, so he could finish his dematerialization spell. The rest of them stayed in the women's dorm suite and talked.

"Rachel isn't back until late when this happens," Kenzie said.

"She's been meeting Smith behind our backs the entire time?" Logan asked.

Moriah shot to her feet, tears in her eyes. "Don't blame her! Rachel is our friend!" She glared at each of them. "She clearly never had full control over what Mr. Top Hat did after her uncle forced her to change him. She was confused. Hurting. Alone." Her tears spilled over, racing down her cheeks. "The exact kind of person who Jesus comes to and saves." Tears dripped off her jaw.

Logan groaned and rested his head in his hands. "We have to tell the vice president in the morning that the summoner isn't Iona. We need to be there at 8:00 a.m. sharp when Dr. Dawson gets to her office."

"And we need to get Rachel a good lawyer," Makari murmured.

"The person you need to tell on is Rev. Smith!" Moriah shouted.

From somewhere else in the dorm suite, the ringtone of Moriah's cellphone played a clip of the song "When the Saints Come Marching Home." Moriah ran to her bedroom. The ringtone stopped. She rushed back to the living room with the cellphone pressed to her ear, wide-eyed. "No." She paused in the middle of the living room. "Yes, I'm listening." Her gaze traveled over everyone. "Are you hurt?" Her brow furrowed. "Oh. Okay."

"Is that Rachel?" Zoe hissed.

Moriah nodded.

A pressure wave swept through Kenzie, his fingers and toes throbbing. *What now?*

Moriah tilted her head to one side. "Rev. Smith wants to offer me a job?"

A job? What kind of ploy is this? Kenzie's arms itched at the sudden surge of magic in his veins, and he rubbed them.

Moriah glanced away from everyone. "But—No, no, I would never do that. I'll be there. But how will I get there?" She tugged on her left pigtail with the hand not holding the phone. "I will. Wait. You've got to tell me—" She lowered her phone and looked to Kenzie. "She hung up."

"You can't meet Smith. It's a trap," Logan said.

Moriah frowned at him. "I know. And Rachel knows, too. That's why she asked me if anyone else was listening to our phone call before she even told me why she was calling. She said I couldn't have an audience, but I came out here anyway. Rev. Smith ordered her to call me and tell me he wants to meet me. Tonight. I'm supposed to go to his hotel's restaurant."

Kenzie shot to his feet. "We can't wait for the Noble Seven leaders to do something. They won't get here in time. We can't tell Dr. Dawson. She's not in her office, and she's not the police. She can't arrest Smith. But we also can't tell the police.

If the police cared about stopping Smith, they would have by now, and they're anti-mag. And now he's got Rachel, and I'm sure he's holding her hostage."

"I have to meet with him, or he'll hurt Rachel," Moriah said. "We *have* to save Rachel. I know Rachel would save me if the situation were reversed."

Kenzie looked from Logan to Makari. "You're from two of the most powerful clans in the U.S. You're the ones with the power to do something in this situation."

"Of course," Makari said. "I'll just have to act in my parents' places. As an heir, it's my duty."

Logan stood. "Hell, yeah. Now we're talking. Let's finish this. I know my dad'll stand behind me. He'll support whatever decision I make."

"We'll follow you to the place you're supposed to go," Kenzie said to Moriah. "No one's going to help us save Rachel, so we've got to do it ourselves."

"Rev. Smith is sending a limousine," Moriah said. "Just trail it."

MORIAH MET THE BLACK LIMOUSINE IN THE PARKING LOT NEAREST the women's dorm row. A bodyguard got out and helped Moriah in. Then he climbed back into the limousine, and it glided out of the parking lot onto the street. Kenzie and the others followed using deflection spells over their motorcycles or cars, aiming the *"Don't Notice Me"* spells at the limousine specifically, but not deflecting other drivers.

Once the limousine stopped in front of the Prince Albert Inn, the taskforce slipped into the hotel using a side entrance to avoid being detected by the bodyguards. Since the hotel had locks on the side doors, they used magic to bypass them.

The only place a hotel didn't have security cameras with picture feeds was the lobby restrooms; by law, they could only record audio. Kenzie and Zoe slipped to the women's restroom and Logan and Makari into the men's. Zoe used her energy working skills to form false images on top of Kenzie and her, changing their appearances through the manipulation of superimposed illusions and light refraction. Logan would do the same for Makari and himself.

When Zoe finished, the bathroom mirrors reflected two people that hotel employees and other guests would expect to see at a five-star hotel restaurant like this one: middle-aged, White, and well-dressed. Zoe was now a blonde in a tasteful green cocktail dress and Kenzie was a six-foot-fall brunette in a tuxedo. "A tuxedo?" Kenzie hissed. "Tone it down."

"Fine," Zoe whispered. She flicked her fingers.

Kenzie's clothing changed to a slate gray three-piece suit and a blue tie. "Better."

They left the bathroom and found two middle-aged White businessmen in black suits waiting in the richly decorated hallway with its maroon and beige Oriental runner. One of them was tanned and muscular, as if he played outdoor sports, and had salt-and-pepper hair cropped in a buzz cut. The other was shorter and thinner and had trendy, pomaded black hair with layers.

The trendy one grinned at Kenzie. "Nice," he said in Logan's voice.

"Yeah, but Zoe can't do anything with sound," Kenzie murmured. "I'll have to whisper to disguise my voice not being deep enough to pass."

"Let's go," the muscular man said in Makari's voice.

They paired off, Zoe with Makari and Kenzie with Logan, and walked down the hall into the hotel restaurant. The tranquil décor of pastel blues, a water fountain, and a view of the indoor pool jarred Kenzie, the offered relaxation contrasting with his stress. The hostess podium had a touch screen display showing which tables were empty. Inside each table icon was a number that represented how many people each table could seat. Makari tapped a table icon for four and received on-screen directions about where the table was. This late at night, the restaurant was mostly empty and would close in less than an hour. Considering a magical battle might break out, Kenzie counted that as lucky.

As the taskforce walked to their table, two bodyguards escorted Moriah to Smith's table. Smith and Rachel occupied chairs on opposite sides. He sipped sparkling grape juice. Rachel sat stiffly upright, her hands in her lap.

For a moment, Kenzie caught Rachel's gaze and raised his eyebrows. Then he looked away, not wanting to tip off Smith that Rachel now had backup.

⚡

RACHEL WATCHED WITH DREAD AS THE BODYGUARDS BROUGHT Moriah. *Did you understand what I was trying to tell you? Did you bring anyone? Or at least tell the others?* A male patron entering after Moriah caught Rachel's gaze for a moment and raised his eyebrows before looking away. *Wait. Did that mean something?* She didn't dare hope.

Part of Rachel wished Moriah hadn't come, even though that would have meant her death at her uncle's hands. Even yesterday, she wouldn't have cared. However, her friends' reaction to her confession—not one of disgust, anger, or blame, but to solve the catastrophe she had helped Smith create—had given her, at the worst possible time, the will to live. *Either way, I have to protect Moriah, even if no one else does.*

Smith stood and smiled. He had changed into a cream three-piece suit with a pale green shirt.

"Welcome, Miss Goldstein. Do please have a seat." He gestured to one cherry wood chair with a blue padded seat.

"Good evening, Rev. Smith." Moriah still wore her white and red floral prairie dress, but she'd released her hair from her pigtails, so it cascaded down her back in pale blonde

338

waves. She took a seat at the four-person table and scanned the menu on the table's built-in tablet.

"You look lovely tonight," Smith said, taking his seat. "It's a relief to see you in something other than that hideous school uniform. I still think it's ridiculous that universities adopted uniforms. This is not high school or the military."

The two bodyguards took a table, joining four other bodyguards.

Moriah flicked through the menu screens. "There are so many choices, and they're all so expensive. What should I get?"

"Anything you want, hon."

Moriah glanced at him. "That's very generous, Reverend."

"And I'm prepared to be even more generous," Smith replied. "Now, please, order whatever you like. It's not proper to discuss business without good food."

They ordered using the foldable touch screen installed in the center of the table. When not in use, it could be closed and turned into part of the tabletop. The tablet informed them the wait time for food was currently 20 minutes at their place in the queue. A live human brought them water, sparkling grape juice, and a basket of fresh Parker House rolls with a dish of butter on the side.

Smith chatted while they awaited their food, asking about their first two weeks of college and how their classes had been. For several minutes, he seemed like an ordinary man.

Rachel bore sitting up straight in the hard restaurant chair with stoicism. Smith's personal physician, whom he brought with him everywhere he traveled, hadn't been allowed to do anything for her except pop her dislocated jaw into alignment and use a small healing spell to ensure her face didn't turn black and blue. Then her uncle had flogged her again. He had promised healing if she played her part and delivered Moriah into his hands. She'd ordered bisque. Pureed soup was the only thing she thought she might be able to eat. She needed something she didn't have to chew.

Once their food arrived, Smith came to the point. "Well, Miss Goldstein. I know Rachel has told you about my offer. What do you say? Would you like to be a children's minister?"

Moriah stared at her cornmeal crusted catfish fillet as she cut off a bite. "I'm sorry, Rev. Smith. God granted me the ability to heal people, so I'm going to be a mage doctor. Anything else would be a waste of God's gift to me."

Rachel took a sip of lobster bisque from her spoon in order to hide her reaction. Moriah well knew how to crouch her arguments in solid Christian rhetoric.

Although Smith's smile didn't waver, it seemed strained. "A logical choice, of course." He took a bite of his steak and eyed Moriah. "Very well. Then you should work at The Apostles' Mercy Hospital in our nation's capital. And, if you're concerned about visiting family, Montgomery, Alabama isn't so far away from Athens, Georgia. Perhaps a four-hour drive. Two if you go by bullet train."

Rachel fought to keep a stoic expression. *Only Whites may ride your new bullet trains. Are you going to give Moriah a pass, then?*

Taking another bite of catfish, Moriah chewed slowly and peered up at Smith. Only after swallowing and taking a drink of water did she reply. "I suppose that's an offer of assistance."

"Yes, of course." Smith continued to smile.

"Why?" Moriah asked.

Rachel's heart almost stopped. However, in the same moment, she realized Moriah was too confident to have come here alone. *You understood. You brought them. The taskforce is somewhere close, out of sight.*

Smith tilted his head. "Because I'd like to adopt you into the Smith fold. Should I not be impressed with someone whom God has granted the gift of healing? Someone that Jesus himself has allowed to sit at his feet?"

Moriah cut herself another square of catfish, holding her knife and fork continuously in the European style. "The Archbishop of Kentucky told me he believes Jesus Christ is not our Lord and Savior, but is a magical creation that I made. It makes more sense to me you want me because of that." She met Smith's gaze. "Because you believe that, too."

Startled by Moriah's tactic, Rachel stared at her uncle. She had no idea how he would handle this confrontation.

Smith set down his fork and dabbed his lips with his napkin. Then he resumed smiling at Moriah. "All right, you're a big girl. Let's talk like adults. Miss Goldstein, your abilities are worthy of your family's new status as a noble clan. God granted you the ability to heal, and on top of that, you can create a likeness of our Lord and Savior. In addition, you created a likeness that talks and acts in alignment with the Scriptures and has been teaching the world the Christian way. How could I not be impressed? Why would I not want to help you secure a good future?"

Moriah calmly cut off another square of catfish. "I'm honored, Reverend. But why should I believe that I have this kind of power? Who am I to make a likeness of Jesus that is true to him? I'm no one special. How could God allow this to happen?"

Taking a sip of her water, Rachel considered Moriah's tactic. *You're fighting, even though you don't have Jesus H. Christ at your side. Why?*

"It's God's will that you should proselytize the world and use your talents in the service of God," Smith said.

"If I were a man, I could understand this," Moriah said, finally setting down her knife and fork. She picked up her glass of water with both hands and sipped it. "We live in an age that badly needs new prophets. But I'm only a woman." She glanced at Smith. "You want to control Jesus Christ, our

Lord and Savior. You aren't any different from Archbishop Ramsey. I'm not Jesus' summoner. That is blasphemy. I'm sorry, Reverend. But I can't help you take over the world. And Jesus wouldn't, either."

Smith's smile morphed into a sickening fake copy of itself that showed his teeth. "Well, I have to give you credit. You're smarter than I thought, and you have determination. So let me be clear: When John Paul Smith, Jr. offers you a position in his church or hospital, your only response is 'Yes, sir.' You will use your talents in whatever way I say you will. Your cute little act that you don't believe that walking, talking doll of Jesus came from you is over now, you hear? The Bible says a woman answers to her father until she's married and then to her husband thereafter. You're right: You're only a woman. Your role in life is to be obedient to men. At what point did you think the decision was yours to make?"

Moriah stared at Smith and set down her glass. "What are you saying?"

"I'm saying, Miss Goldstein, that you are going to help me win the world for Christ, whether you want to or not. Do what I say, when I say, and you won't get hurt. Otherwise, I'm going to have to discipline you."

Anger rose in Moriah's cheeks like a cherry red rash. "Jesus showed up because Satan did first. How can you say that I did that? Jesus was responding to the threat of Satan."

Rachel pursed her lips. *In her fear, has Moriah reverted to believing Top Hat is Satan? Or is she fighting having to believe she summoned Jesus H. Christ?*

Smith burst out laughing. "Oh, honey. That creature isn't Satan. He's a silly doll my niece created and has since lost control of, because she's nowhere near as powerful as you are. Bless your little heart. Did that little old thing scare you?" He glanced at Rachel coldly, his amusement seeming to drop out of him. "If Top Hat hurts our family, I am going to punish you severely, girl." Then a smirk twisted his face. "However, I will take into consideration that it was Top Hat who persuaded Miss Goldstein to make Jesus. At least by sheer accident you did something useful for me."

Moriah trembled. "No, the real Jesus showed up because Top Hat put everyone in danger and he…" She trailed off.

Rachel watched the moment play out over Moriah's face as Moriah's story to herself about Jesus fell apart. Moriah flushed, and tears filled her eyes.

"That's enough," Smith chided. "Surely you can see you're being foolish now." He scanned her and then laughed again. "You really believed it. You *really* believed Jesus would come down from heaven just to protect you from scary ol' Top Hat."

Moriah lifted her hands and cried into them, muffling herself.

Rachel narrowed her eyes, her entire body throbbing with rage. "Stop it."

Smith kept chuckling.

Rachel stood. "I said, stop it!" She could barely stay on her feet. Her hip was swollen, her body so out of alignment that one leg was higher than the other, and the fresh lash wounds pulled and seared. But none of that mattered. "You are cruelty personified." Deep vibrations of magic thrummed inside of her. The purple glow of escaping energy rose out of her pores like a hot mist. "If anyone is Satan on Earth, *you are.*"

Other people in the restaurant looked their way. The tables were spaced far enough apart and their conversation had been quiet enough that no one had paid them any attention—until now.

"No." Smith stood and faced her. "I am God's chosen one. And I will not suffer to be talked to that way by you, you little witch." He held out his hands, red energy glowing around his fingers.

People around them screamed.

Top Hat appeared at Rachel's side, knocked aside the

dining table, and threw up a barrier of purple energy between them. Red lightning arced from Smith's hands and sizzled and sparked against the barrier.

"How naughty of you to start a sixpence show without me," Top Hat drawled. He wore a red leotard and tuxedo jacket along with his signature hat, his form having reverted. An ear to ear grin stood out on his pale face in bright red stage makeup.

Filled with awe, Rachel gazed up at her friend. *You came.*

Several diners fled as the six bodyguards in black suits jumped up from their seats and surrounded Rachel, Moriah, and Top Hat. They drew blue steel pistols, pointing them at Top Hat.

Smith erected a crimson energy barrier and sneered at Top Hat. "You aren't Satan. You're some low-level demon with a doll body."

"You're right. I'm not Satan. Let me correct that oversight." Top Hat gestured at his own body, and his outfit morphed, turning into a white suit with a red shirt and white dress shoes. He pulled off his hat, revealing his platinum blond hair, which was cut like Smith's, and his horns. Then he gestured at his face, and it reshaped itself to mirror Smith's. When he spoke, even his voice was Smith's. "Now I am."

"I shouldn't be surprised that you would mock God's prophet," Smith said through clenched teeth.

Rachel held out her hand, imagining demons, each one eight feet tall, adorned with bullhorns, and crimson-skinned. Her energy exploded outward in a purple glow, and then four demons surrounded the bodyguards, slashing at them with razor claws. The bodyguards screamed and wildly fired spells with their guns. Rachel hadn't been able to materialize the demons, so they couldn't inflict damage. The bodyguards would realize that shortly. In the meantime, she turned toward her uncle and summoned a volleyball-sized energy ball, then threw it, aiming it at her uncle's head.

Smith's barrier deflected the attack, and the energy clash disintegrated it. "I'll have you stoned for that. I never thought you would be so disobedient."

The burn of magic erupted in Rachel's veins. In rapid flashes, she saw herself at age seven being beaten for using a pair of crafting scissors to cut her hair and at age twelve dancing in her room with Top Hat. She saw herself at age fourteen bringing her father's philosophy books out of their hiding place and reading them under the covers of her bed with a spark of light magic to see by. She saw herself two weeks ago confiding in Moriah about the reason for the lash marks on her back when Moriah had walked in on her changing clothes, and three days ago when she threatened Archbishop Ramsey to stay away from Moriah. "I disobeyed you every minute of every day," she hissed. "You *never* had my soul."

At her words, four diners at a corner table burst to their feet and ran toward Smith. Moriah shot to her feet and raised a golden energy shield around Rachel and herself.

Then the world seemed to explode with magic.

TWENTY-EIGHT

As Rachel had taken her stand, Makari had whipped out his phone and dialed 911. He had supplied their location, and Kenzie bolted from the table, Logan, Zoe, and Makari following. The illusions disguising them broke apart into multicolored sparkles and faded as they surrounded Smith and his bodyguards.

Rachel's illusionary demons flickered and vanished. Not losing a second, Logan snapped his hands out. Thin blue beams of energy shot from his fingertips and attached to the bodyguards' blue steel pistols. He yanked, and three of the bodyguards lost their grip on their pistols, while the others struggled against the energy strings. Zoe fired a sheet of crimson energy at the floor and knocked two of the bodyguards off their feet. Kenzie lashed out with telekinesis. One of the bodyguards who was still armed flew sideways and slammed into the wall, his pistol ripped from his grasp. Logan's blue energy string snapped the pistol in the opposite direction. The first three bodyguards braced themselves against Kenzie's attacks with gravity magic, making themselves too heavy to be moved.

Top Hat extended his hand, his hat vanishing and a sword

appearing in its place. He pointed the sword at Smith. "'Mine eyes have seen the glory of the coming of the Lord; He is trampling out the vintage where the grapes of wrath are stored; He hath loosed the fateful lightning of His terrible swift sword.'"

"Surrender!" Makari shouted. "I've called the police, and we have the authority of the Noble Seven to make a citizen magicians' arrest."

An ugly purple tide crashed over Smith's face. "You've not only willfully sinned against me, but also you've willfully sinned against the Lord."

"It's over," Makari snapped. "Give it up. Do you really want to be responsible for even more magic violations by the time the leaders of the Noble Seven get here?"

Logan held out his hands, pressing his thumbs and forefingers together to create a circle. Blue energy ropes appeared around Smith, tightening like a boa constrictor. He struggled against Logan's binding spell, his red energy billowing out around his body in a nearly blinding glow. The blue energy ropes dimmed under the onslaught. Logan tightened his right hand into a fist. The ropes constricted tighter, the blue energy flaring so brightly it was nearly white. "You're not going anywhere except to prison."

For an instant, Kenzie thought it was all over. The presence of multiple witnesses and the hotel security cameras meant Smith couldn't talk his way out of this. The Noble Seven, the most powerful magicians in the country, the people who had control over all magicians in the United States, wouldn't care how important Smith was or wasn't in the URA. This was U.S. soil. Smith had to know that the Noble Seven would seek revenge if Smith did anything to their children. Logan and Makari were nobility.

Smith's pupils dilated with rage. Crimson light exploded out of him and disintegrated Logan's energy ropes. Logan,

Kenzie, and Makari recoiled, throwing up their hands to shield their eyes. Black and red spots dotted Kenzie's vision.

Taking advantage of their pause, Smith pulled back his arms and then snapped his hands forward, hurling two red energy blasts the size of beach balls. One smashed into the golden barrier protecting Rachel and Moriah and the other into Top Hat.

Top Hat charged, unfazed, sword tip leading. Purple energy shot from the tip, but Smith raised a new crimson barrier, defeating it.

The security guards recovered and leapt into action. Half of them shot pellet-sized balls of purple or green energy bare-handed, laying down fire, while the other half recovered their pistols and joined in barraging the taskforce.

Kenzie, Logan, Makari, and Zoe erected their own individual glowing energy shields, a mix of blue, green, and crimson. Each pellet that hit their shields made the thin sheet of energy crackle and fizz.

Smith flung two more crimson blasts at Top Hat, but they dispersed over him without effect.

At the bodyguards' willful decision to side with Smith, to disregard all warnings that the law was not on their side and the consequences would be severe, something in Kenzie internally snapped. Smith's arrogance he wasn't shocked by. However, the bodyguards choosing corruption over justice burned Kenzie in a way he hadn't thought possible.

Kenzie imagined the bodyguards as toys, mere action figures, and telekinetically lashed out, slamming into their arms. The bodyguards' spells went wild. One shot another through the eye with his energy pellet, and another man got hit in the knee. One energy pellet flew wide and smashed the window by the pool, and another blew a hole in the floor. White flakes of ceiling plaster rained down as the remaining energy pellets hit the ceiling.

Logan charged, and this time, Zoe joined him. They both

fired energy ropes and wrapped the four bodyguards in cocoons.

The remaining two bodyguards acted in the same moment, dashing in opposite directions. One fired a mud cannonball at Logan.

Makari pulled water from the indoor swimming pool and crashed it into the mud ball. It exploded, splattering the tables and floor. Then he hurled a blue energy ball at the man, slamming him into the far wall and knocking him unconscious.

The final bodyguard aimed at the floor, his barrel flashing with blue energy. Kenzie and everyone on his side of the battle, including Moriah and Rachel, lifted off the floor as if buoyed by a pressure wave under their feet. Kenzie recognized the sensation: gravity magic. *Great, my weakness! Damn it!*

Moriah flicked out her hand. "Dismiss! Dismiss!" Golden light flared from her fingers.

Even as Moriah cast her spell, the bodyguard fired again, and gravity amplified. In the second before it fully took hold, Kenzie grabbed the kinetic energy the spell generated and snapped it back at the bodyguard. Instead of everyone being crushed against the floor, six people's worth of kinetic energy slammed into the bodyguard. He flew back and hit the wall with so much force that his head made a sickening crack.

Everyone except Moriah and Rachel caught their balance as they fell. Moriah stumbled and tripped over her long dress. Rachel's legs buckled as she landed, and she fell to her hands and knees.

Smith lunged for them.

Moriah pointed her finger at Smith. A geyser of pale blue water erupted from her fingertip. Gallons upon gallons of water from the indoor pool slammed against Smith's red energy shield. The stench of chlorine filled the air as water sprayed in all directions.

Spared the onslaught, Smith shot out his hand. He grabbed Moriah by the throat.

Everything and everyone stopped.

Kenzie stared at Smith's meaty hand wrapped around Moriah's slender neck, afraid to even breathe. *Shit! He'll break her neck before any of our spells can stop him.*

"Keep blaspheming against me and she dies," Smith snarled. Red energy crackled down his arm and stabbed into Moriah. She screamed.

Rachel forced herself to her feet, but she fell to her knees again. "Let her go!"

With his free hand, Smith slapped Rachel's face so hard her neck audibly popped three times. She was hurled onto the floor. "You don't tell me what to do!"

Top Hat disappeared.

Kenzie, Zoe, Logan, and Makari all jerked. Kenzie's fear pounded through his blood like poison.

Smith held Moriah aloft by the neck. "Just relax, dear girl."

Moriah clutched at his hand around her throat and wheezed.

Smith faced everyone. "I'm going to tell you how it all began, and then you will understand this—this affliction I've been suffering from. The Anderson clan is spread over New York and New Jersey, with the main family in New York. My father, having been born in 2005, grew up in the still-unified U.S. He lived in Alabama, but he attended college in New York City. He barely graduated before the U.S. split apart, but when he returned to Alabama, he didn't return alone. He returned with a wife: Lily Anderson."

Mind magic crested over Kenzie in waves, and he erected mental shields. *Hypnosis! He's telling this story so he can use magic to induce a hypnotic state.* He glanced around him. Disheartened, he saw everyone was already trapped in Smith's spell. They hadn't seen his intention coming in time, and none of them were mind mages. His gaze snapped back to Smith. He didn't dare reveal that he was holding out. *Hopefully, he's so distracted by everyone else that he doesn't notice I'm still free. I just have to utilize the best opening I can find.*

Smith pulled Moriah close to him. "Please understand that my father had always been a devout and God-fearing Christian and, of course, had no magical inclinations. However, the Andersons had been practicing various forms of magic for centuries. My mother adored my father, and she gave up magic for him and converted to Christianity. That didn't save me. It didn't save any of their children." He began pacing, hauling Moriah with him, his crimson energy now outlining her entire body.

"While my father worked hard to create a pure Christian denomination, having realized that even the Pentecostals and Baptists had gone to hell, my mother was busy giving birth to children carrying the curse of magic." Smith snapped around and looked at them all. "The sick irony of it! The disgusting horror. My father slaved for our great God, his life goal to emulate Christ Jesus—or, at the very least, John the Baptist. And yet he was presented with five children who had to be constantly disciplined for spewing out Satan's toxic powers."

Rachel glared at Smith with an expression of seething contempt. That gave Kenzie a flicker of hope that, as a branch member of the Anderson clan and someone familiar with Smith's tactics, Rachel had also shielded herself.

"My mother spent her life repenting for having infused her children with evil, but what can I say? Eve also passed on evil to her children, having been responsible for the fall of all Mankind. Perhaps my mother found forgiveness and peace when she died and faced her Lord and Savior." Smith sneered. "Or maybe she got cast into hell. It would be no more than she deserved."

Moriah whimpered, but she clearly didn't have the breath

to speak. Without Smith's holding magic at work, he would have already suffocated her to death from his grip.

Smith paced, Moriah's feet dragging the floor as he did. "I have struggled all my life to never use magic. But on those occasions when my human frailty makes itself known and I fall from grace, I at least try to use my magic to serve our Lord. I suppose that makes my life a bizarre paradox, using Satan's powers to further God's goals, but I take comfort in knowing that must infuriate Satan."

Despite having lived outside the URA for only a few weeks, Kenzie now understood how insane Smith would sound to people like Logan, Zoe, and Makari. However, to the residents of the URA, Smith's "confession" was normal and an excellent cover for a hypnosis spell.

Smith smirked at them. "My point is this: I'm going to use my cursed abilities to fix your bad attitudes." He dropped Moriah.

Falling to her knees, Moriah clutched her throat and squeaked, her breaths whistling.

Smith spread his hands. Crimson, mist-like energy emanated from his hands and formed a dense fog that wound around Moriah's head. Then it trickled out, snake-like, toward Rachel, Kenzie, and the others. "You're all going to find Jesus."

Moriah whispered something.

"What's that, sweetheart?" Smith asked.

Moriah breathed deeply, her chest expanding. "I. Forgive. You."

Jesus H. Christ appeared in front of Smith. He glowed with golden light. His face was impassive as he looked upon Smith.

Smith froze. The red mist dissipated. He stared at Jesus H. Christ with a look of incomprehension.

This is my only chance. With Smith's guard completely down at the surprise appearance of Jesus, Kenzie had about two seconds before Smith's mental shields would be back up. And with his own shields failing under the pressure of Smith's Merlin Class mind magic, in a few seconds he wasn't going to be able to think clearly enough to use his telekinesis.

Kenzie visualized John Paul Smith Jr.'s brain inside his skull, a mass of gray folds suspended in cerebral fluid. With the most precise telekinetic control he could muster, he shoved Smith's brain against the inner wall of his skull and set off a series of collisions as Smith's brain bounced and rebounded.

Smith collapsed to the floor, unconscious.

Released from the magical hypnosis, Logan, Makari, and Zoe all stumbled forward a step and rubbed their temples.

Top Hat reappeared, pitchfork in hand. "Show's over!" He lunged for Smith.

Jesus H. Christ stepped in the way and grabbed Top Hat's pitchfork. It transformed into red rose petals and rained down on their feet and the unconscious Smith.

"Vengeance is mine!" Top Hat shouted.

Jesus H. Christ took Top Hat by the upper arms. "No, my brother. Amen, amen, I say unto you, vengeance is the Lord's." He pulled Top Hat into a hug.

Top Hat struggled against Jesus H. Christ's embrace.

Kenzie darted in between them and Smith and flung out his hands. "More to the point, if we let you kill him, Rachel will go to jail for murder, and we'll all be accessories. They'll convict her. The jury will be non-mags, and they'll never believe Rachel lost control. And you know Rachel won't lie. She'll admit she wanted you to kill her uncle. The only way to keep that from happening is for the police to interrogate Smith and find out the truth. They can't do that if he's dead. We've made a lot of advancements in magical science, but talking to the dead isn't one of them. It likely never will be. Smith will have to convict himself with his own words while compelled by a truth spell." He pointed to the security cameras in the corners of the restaurant. "Also, we have security footage showing Smith is guilty."

"I understand." Top Hat slumped in Jesus H. Christ's arms.

"Moriah!" Rachel crawled to her side. "Talk to me. Are you still you?" Tears escaped her eyes, streaking down her face.

Moriah flinched and groaned. She reached up and bathed her throat in golden healing energy. Then she took a deep breath. "I don't know. I felt Rev. Smith in my mind." She embraced Rachel, resting her head on Rachel's shoulder. "But I forgive you for making Top Hat-Satan."

Rachel hugged her in return and cried.

"Don't panic," Makari said gently. "My dad is friends with people in the Anderson clan, and one of them, Iona's mom, is already on her way here. They'll do all they can to undo or reverse whatever Smith has done to us."

Rachel took a deep breath, held it, and then exhaled slowly. "Okay. Just swear to me you won't give up until Moriah is Moriah again."

"We've come this far. We're not giving up on Moriah now," Kenzie said. "We're all going to graduate from JCU with honors. You'll see. We'll show the world what women from the URA are really made of. Well, and honestly, a transman." He didn't feel like holding in his identity a second longer.

"What happened to me?" Moriah asked.

"Smith tried to telepathically rearrange your brain," Kenzie said. "All our brains. Promise me you'll let mage doctors heal you, okay? You need to be you."

Moriah frowned, her eyes narrowing. "Of course I must be me. Being me is all I really have in life."

Kenzie reached out and squeezed her shoulder. "Just hang onto that."

The police and ambulance arrived a few minutes later.

TWENTY-NINE

The next day, a little before 1:00 p.m., Kenzie, Moriah, and Zoe joined Makari and Logan in Makari's dorm suite. None of them wore their uniforms, and with the exception of Moriah, they all wore jeans and t-shirts for the sake of comfort. Both hungry and exhausted, they ordered pizzas and then brewed coffee. All of them had missed their morning classes, having met with Dr. Dawson, cleared Iona's name, and also explained Smith's attack on Moriah and Rachel. After that, they'd met with Iona's mom, a psychologist who specialized in treating victims of telepathic assault, and received treatment.

When the pizzas arrived, Kenzie and Moriah dropped onto the worn brown couch and set a box between them. Moriah slumped from fatigue and psychic injury, her blue prairie dress wrinkled. Makari and Logan sat at the kitchen table with Zoe. As they ate, Makari explained that Shinrou had stayed up all night completing the spell to dematerialize the thought forms. He'd told Makari about his breakthrough at 8:00 a.m. before passing out.

"Good," Kenzie muttered around a mouthful of pepperoni pizza, "this nightmare can be over." Even a cup of coffee and the spicy pepperoni couldn't fully resurrect him from his exhaustion.

About 15 minutes later, Shinrou stumbled into the kitchen, wearing stylish black plastic glasses. Kenzie realized he probably wore contacts. *What? No laser surgery? That's unusual these days.*

"Up already?" Makari's brow furrowed. "You didn't sleep very long." He pushed a pizza box across the table toward Shinrou. "This one's half-vegetarian."

"Thank you." Shinrou fell into the chair and pulled a slice out of the box. "I need more sleep, but I'm just too tense, maybe even excited, about the new spell."

Kenzie grinned. "Hey, you look cute in glasses. Well, it helps that they're cool glasses."

"Yeah, he does," Logan chimed in, but he was looking at Makari instead. "Right, man?"

Makari glanced at Logan, blushed, and didn't answer.

Shinrou blushed, too. "I—ah, thanks." He took a big bite of his pizza.

At this exchange, Kenzie smiled at his boyfriend. *You think they're a couple, too, don't you? Or, at least, you think they should be.*

"We can go dematerialize Jesus whenever you're ready," Makari said. "We might as well start with him. He's already out preaching today."

Logan snorted. "There's a sentence for you: 'We can go dematerialize Jesus.' Without context, that sounds pretty wild."

"You're right." Zoe took a swig of coffee from her mug. "Sounds like a religious horror movie."

Shinrou glanced at Moriah and lowered his pizza slice. "Is she okay?"

"Worn out," Kenzie said. "Iona's mom said Moriah's case is more advanced because Smith channeled energy into her directly, but Dr. Anderson seems confident she can heal her."

"Mn," Moriah said in a vague sound of agreement. She had closed her eyes and looked ready to fall asleep.

Shinrou set down his pizza. "Oh. I see. What about Rachel? Is she okay?"

"She's at the police station answering questions," Zoe said. "When I saw her last, she was just pissed off."

"Dad arrived and is with Rachel at the police station," Makari said. "Dad's already gotten Rachel a lawyer." He sighed. "Top Hat injured demonstrators and students, so the police are asking a lot of questions. Dad's explaining thought forms and materialization to the precinct's magic consulting officer. The official story is that Smith created Top Hat and then forced Rachel to let him loose on campus. We need to all stick to that so that the right person gets blamed. Non-mags aren't going to understand the fine details here."

Shinrou nodded and resumed eating his pizza.

"My dad arrived and went to the hospital where Smith is," Logan said. "Smith isn't awake to answer questions, so that's all we know since we're not family."

Shinrou cringed. "I'm surprised the police aren't still questioning you, Kenzie."

"They would be if it hadn't been for Iona's mom," Kenzie said. "How's that for a sentence? That sounds as wild to me as saying, 'Let's dematerialize Jesus.' Iona spent every moment we're stuck in the same class together attacking me, and her mom defends me to the police and tells them the only way to stop someone from ripping out our brains would be to knock them out, which I did. She said I didn't use excessive force, and they can't contradict her, because they're not magic users and Smith isn't dead."

"Now I hope you see what people in the Noble Seven are supposed to be like," Makari murmured. "We're supposed to be helping, not giving people a hard time."

Logan turned to Shinrou. "So how does the dematerialization spell work?"

Shinrou groaned. "It took me a while to figure this out, but the system of magic Rachel and Moriah used can't be transmutation. The actual system of magic we're witnessing must be something larger, with transmutation being merely one example." He paused and squared his shoulders. "I propose Matter Magic. In other words, the ability to manipulate matter to create something, recreate something, or pull something apart."

"You mean creation and destruction magic," Makari said.

"Like a god," Zoe whispered.

Moriah shuddered.

"It makes sense," Shinrou said. "If you can transmute sand into glass, then why can't you take a chair and reform it into a small table? The wood already exists. You're simply manipulating the matter." He slumped. "The thing is that thousands or even millions of people unconsciously combined their energy to make bodies for Jesus H. Christ, Top Hat, Loki, and Thor. No single magician did that, and I can't imagine a single magician having the *power* to do that."

"True." Makari rested his head in his hand. "So how are you supposed to cast your spell?"

Shinrou stood and headed to the coffeemaker. "Destruction is always easier than creation. But it will take more than one magician." He pulled a mug out of the cabinet. "You and Logan will have to help me."

"No problem," Logan said.

"We just have to make sure Dr. Dawson and the president of JCU know what we're doing," Makari said.

"As soon as we have their permission, we need to unmake Jesus H. Christ and Top Hat-Satan." Shinrou poured himself a cup of coffee. "However, it would be better if we could dematerialize all the thought forms."

Zoe clenched her fists. "Wait. *What?* You're going to kill Loki?" She twisted in her chair to face Shinrou and glared at him. "Oh *hell* no!"

Shinrou grimaced. "I'm not going to kill anyone." He carried his mug to the table and sat down. "Loki's thought form can't be unmade. As an idea, a concept, or a spirit, Loki can't be destroyed. I'm just talking about unraveling the matter. Without bodies, they won't be able to command such worship and fascination. It'll reduce the size of the mess we have here."

"If you do this and Loki vanishes entirely so that I can't summon him anymore, I'll fucking kill you." Zoe's face turned crimson, and she looked ready to angry-cry. "My life was hell before Loki came along and saved me! I never had any fun. Everything was always work, work, work. Even playing was work! I had to play with the right toys and have the right hobbies so that my parents could show me off— show me off to other parents, to teachers, to judges. First it was singing. Then it was ballet. Then my magic talent popped, and they made me practice summoning my ancestors all day. When they figured out that was too 'easy' for me, they started making me summon deities. Loki's the first spirit I ever wanted to talk to, and he's the first one who loves me!"

"Zoe, don't worry about it," Kenzie said, pitching his voice to be soothing. "Loki's a god, right? How could anyone dismiss him so thoroughly that you couldn't summon him in private?" Although Kenzie didn't believe in deities, he wasn't above trying to calm Zoe with her own logic.

"Okay. True. All right." Zoe didn't sound thrilled, but she leaned back in her chair, her flush fading.

Shinrou gazed at her for a moment. "Zoe brings up a good point. We can undercut the public's obsession with both Jesus H. Christ and Top Hat by dematerializing their bodies, but now we have an ethical question on our hands: Do we have the right? Are these thought forms officially alive? How do we define 'alive?'"

"And on top of that, will they just materialize bodies again in a short amount of time?" Makari asked.

Logan reached up and rubbed his forehead. "Shit."

"Loki is a *god*. Of course he's alive." Zoe crossed her arms and stared out the window.

"I think Top Hat is alive," Kenzie said. "He can hold conversations, and he's capable of making his own decisions without input from others. Jesus H. Christ is probably alive, too, now."

Moriah stared at her lap, picking at a loose thread on her sleeve.

"The surest test of being alive would be fear of death," Shinrou said. He glanced around the room. "Is anyone willing to summon their thought form and quiz them about death?"

Zoe sighed. "Loki! I'm not having fun. Show up and save me!"

Loki popped into the room. "Not fun? Not fun is not good." As usual, he was dressed in medieval gold and green clothes and a cloak, a black goatee gracing his face. He grinned at everyone. "Are you boring my poor Zoe? Shame on you!"

"Are you afraid of death?" Shinrou asked pointblank.

Loki's brow furrowed, and he raised one eyebrow. "Afraid of death?"

"Yes." Shinrou shrugged. "If a magician created a spell that could destroy your body, would you be afraid of dying?"

Loki snorted. "No. I'd just reform myself again. I'm a god. It's no big deal."

Zoe peered at Loki with an expression of vague hope.

"And there's the potential problem," Makari grumbled.

"Then would you let me run an experiment this weekend and dematerialize your body?" Shinrou asked. "Your spirit can't be destroyed. We respect that. We're not your enemies."

Loki shrugged. "Sure! Sounds like a fun game."

"Thank you." Shinrou picked up a second veggie pizza

slice. "We can ask Thor, Top Hat, and Jesus H. Christ the same question, although Top Hat might not get a choice, considering he attacked people. Either way, I doubt any of them will care, so as soon as I finish eating, we can go dematerialize Jesus."

"Then I'll call Dr. Dawson and get permission," Makari said, pulling out his phone.

THIRTY MINUTES LATER, AFTER EVERYONE HAD CHANGED INTO their university uniforms, Kenzie headed to the grassy expanse of the quad with his friends to dematerialize Jesus H. Christ, nervousness fluttering in his stomach like moth wings. Dr. Dawson had given Shinrou permission both to cast the spell and to perform it publically. Mr. Idoni, Mr. Steensen, and Dr. Anderson had all voted in favor of this tactic as well.

Jesus H. Christ sat on the library steps, teaching. Roughly 50 visitors had gathered below him, along with a news crew, all of them braving the heat. That was as many people as the administration would allow to be present. Kenzie, Zoe, and Moriah stopped at the edge of the crowd. Shinrou, Makari, and Logan headed up the stairs to Jesus.

"Should you be up walking around?" Zoe asked Moriah.

Moriah frowned and gazed at Jesus H. Christ. "I need to be here. This is my responsibility."

"I understand how you feel," Kenzie said.

"The real Jesus can't be destroyed," Moriah said. "And nothing can destroy my devotion to him." She dropped her voice. "Besides, worshipping false idols is a sin. Even if it looks like Jesus, it isn't. And I worshipped him." Tears welled up in her eyes. "I have to sacrifice my false idol to the real Jesus to prove my devotion."

Kenzie glanced away. *And now I don't understand.* The disconnect between them remained huge. For Moriah, everything that had happened still had to do with faith. It seemed irrelevant to Moriah that the first two weeks of their freshman year had been torn apart. She seemed unconcerned that they had to work extra hard to keep their grades up for the rest of the semester. Kenzie didn't think Moriah could see that John Paul Smith, Jr.'s plan to use Rachel and Top Hat to kill protestors and start an anti-magician movement could have destroyed religious liberty in the United States as everyone was forced to convert to The Apostles' Way. In Kenzie's mind, Smith's plan had been a deliberate attempt to rob Moriah, Rachel, and him of their futures, and not just them but everyone like them.

Zoe squeezed Moriah's arm and grimaced. "I'm glad you're getting therapy from Dr. Anderson."

Kenzie took a breath. *That's right. I need to have patience. Moriah isn't thinking clearly right now. Iona's mom easily healed Logan, Makari, and Zoe. Surely she can heal Moriah, too.* "Brace yourself. This is going to be extra tough to handle."

"I know." Moriah watched Jesus H. Christ. As usual, he was dressed in a white robe with a crimson sash draped over one shoulder. "And I'm praying everyone will be understanding toward Rachel. Nothing that happened is really her fault. Empty Christians who only gave God lip service are at fault."

"And it's not your fault, either," Kenzie said.

Moriah fell silent.

"We'll work on that," Zoe said.

Dr. Dawson sat in a chair several feet behind Jesus H. Christ, covered by the shade of the library's awning. Sitting in a chair beside her was Shinrou's aunt. Shinrou, Makari, and Logan joined them.

"Dr. Kitamori is here?" Kenzie muttered. "Oh, great."

Shinrou and Dr. Dawson spoke for a moment, and then Shinrou returned down the stairs to Moriah. "Dr. Dawson thinks you may need to explain to Jesus H. Christ what we're doing. Since you created him, he might react better to you."

"Well, it *is* my responsibility." Moriah squared her shoulders.

Kenzie shook his head. "Moriah shouldn't stick out. The URA will see this footage."

Moriah bit her lip and tugged on one of her pigtails. "Oh. Right. But won't it be strange if I don't go up there? Everyone already knows I love Jesus."

Shinrou looked to Kenzie. "She's right."

"Are you sure this spell will work?" Zoe asked. "It'll be bad if it doesn't. Everyone's watching. The entire world will see the footage."

"Yes, I'm sure." Shinrou inhaled deeply. "I dematerialized an aluminum can early this morning. Dematerializing a 'person' will make this a Merlin-level spell. That's why Makari and Logan have to help me. But it'll work, all right." He turned to Moriah. "I'd still like to have you up there in case Jesus H. Christ panics, and Dr. Dawson wants you, too."

"Okay." Moriah started up the stairs. "Also, I have one last protest to make."

Kenzie sprinted after her. "Not without me!"

They climbed the side stairs to the library's porch and walked over to Dr. Dawson, Zoe following.

Moriah stopped by Dr. Dawson and bowed her head. "Please, Dr. Dawson, let me apologize to Jesus for what my friends are going to do. Everyone explained to me that Jesus H. Christ is a thought form I created, but I can't just let Shinrou throw a spell at him without apologizing first."

Dr. Dawson looked at Moriah, apparent sympathy in her blue eyes. "All right. But once Shinrou starts his spell, you need to get out of the way and let Jesus handle this. The real Jesus wouldn't want you to put a stop to this test of faith. This spell doesn't come from an evil place in our hearts, and if this Jesus is a thought form, then the real Jesus won't be harmed."

"Okay."

Kenzie was glad Dr. Dawson was from the URA and could understand Moriah's position.

Dr. Dawson nodded and stood. "All right. Let's bite the bullet, then." She walked over to Jesus H. Christ's position and addressed the crowd, holding a finger to her throat and casting an amplification spell. A pea-sized golden orb appeared next to her Adam's apple. "Thank you, everyone, for visiting our campus and taking such an interest in Jesus." She paused. "However, it would be inappropriate of the university to allow anyone to be misled about the man teaching here. We've devised a magical test that we hope will make matters clearer. The students who have devised the test are ready to begin their experiment, so please stand by and remain calm."

On cue, Moriah ran up to where Jesus H. Christ sat on the steps and threw herself at his feet. "Jesus, please forgive them!"

When the crowd stirred, Dr. Dawson held up her free hand. "Don't be alarmed. Those of you who are Christian know the real son of God couldn't be harmed by a mere mortal magician."

The grumbling died down, and the crowd just shifted around and whispered.

Jesus touched Moriah's shoulder. "Rise, child."

Wiping tears from her face, Moriah stood and brushed off her white skirt. "Lord Jesus, I love you."

"My father is Love, and my father and I are one," Jesus replied. "Love cannot be destroyed by any number of trials." He seemed serene.

Kenzie sighed. *That's as close as he can get to saying it back, isn't it? And it's still less than Moriah deserves. Her thought form should be able to say "I love you, too." And what does it mean about Moriah's inner fears that he can't?*

Dr. Dawson gestured Shinrou forward. Shinrou walked up

to Jesus H. Christ, who stood to meet him. Makari and Logan joined them.

"It's nothing personal," Shinrou said. "We just have to prove that you either are or aren't the real Jesus."

"If you are Jesus, then you understand why," Makari said. "False prophets need to be shut down. And quickly."

Jesus H. Christ inclined his head. "It's true that false prophets should not be tolerated, although they are inevitable. I'm unconcerned about your test. You may proceed."

"Thank you. You're polite and kind, even if you aren't divine," Shinrou said.

Dr. Dawson rested her hand on Moriah's shoulder. "All right, we have an agreement. You were allowed to speak. Now come with me."

Moriah allowed Dr. Dawson to lead her out of the spell's zone and to the sidelines, where she joined Kenzie and Zoe.

Shinrou turned to his friends and held out his hands. "It'll work best if we're touching. We're going to create an energy ball together, but instead of firing it as an attack, I'm going to direct it with the new spell."

"Okay." Logan took Shinrou's right hand and then held out his other hand to Makari. Makari took Shinrou's left hand and closed the circle by holding Logan's hand.

"Focus and begin," Shinrou said. Then he closed his eyes. After almost a minute, he opened them, and golden energy flowed from his hands.

Blue energy surrounded Makari's and Logan's hands. Their energy arched off their hands and joined Shinrou's, creating an energy ball the size of a soccer ball. The sphere turned aqua blue and swelled, expanding to beach ball-sized. After a pause, it grew again, first doubling, then tripling. An aqua ring sprouted out of it, then several more, making the sphere look like a blue Saturn. Lightning strikes erupted inside the orb, sizzling.

The crowd fell silent except for a few gasps. Kenzie glanced at Jesus H. Christ. He watched with impassive attentiveness.

"I understand what is going to happen," Moriah murmured, surprising Kenzie. "What Jesus seems to be will fade away, and then whatever I made him out of will fly apart." Tears slipped down her cheeks. "It won't be any different from the smaller things I made explode apart because I couldn't keep my spell steady."

"You were making things on purpose?" Kenzie whispered.

"My parents gave me clay to practice energy work on." Moriah bowed her head. "For hours at a time, I had to practice in my room by myself after I finished with my personal trainer. It was lonely. I imagined my clay sculptures were my friends."

Kenzie hugged her. "Well, now you have real friends."

Moriah clung to him and wept.

As Shinrou shaped the spell, the aqua blue energy darkened, shifting to true blue, then navy, then black. The energy sphere bulged, and the rings exploded away from it, flashing through Jesus H. Christ.

Jesus H. Christ glanced at his body, still appearing unconcerned. "What a peculiar sensation. Rather hot and full of static shock."

Moriah burst into sobs and clung to Kenzie harder. Kenzie patted her back.

The energy sphere elongated into an oval and arched over Makari's head toward Jesus H. Christ. Once the oval encompassed Jesus H. Christ's chest, it sucked the rest of itself into his body, briefly turning into a ball again before vanishing.

The crowd burst into shrieks and gasps.

A black glow outlined Jesus H. Christ's body. His facial features and clothing faded, leaving behind only a humanoid, dark form. He didn't thrash or scream. In fact, he merely raised his hands, glancing at them as the fingers faded. Then the black glow sank into the figure, and it lost its human shape. A dark cloud formed where Jesus H. Christ had stood.

Shinrou released the spell. The cloud condensed. Mud splattered down the stairs, easily over 100 pounds' worth. A golden burst of energy flew out of the mud as it landed, splattering it farther. Then the energy vanished.

Moriah continued to sob. "No! I wanted it to be true!"

Kenzie rocked Moriah against him. "I know you did."

The crowd stared in stunned silence for several more moments, and then shouts and shrieks erupted.

Dr. Dawson stepped forward again, holding up her hands. It took a full minute, but the noise died down. She pointed her finger to her throat again, recasting her amplification spell. "We have our answer. The being who was here was not the son of God. It was a magical creation. It wasn't even human. Please, simply be glad the creation spoke to you about parables instead of directing you to do terrible things to yourselves, such as drink poison and commit suicide."

Whispering erupted at that, the crowd seeming grim or horrified.

"The university will discover how this being was created and ensure it doesn't happen again," Dr. Dawson said. "Please go home and spend the rest of your day with your family or doing something relaxing. It's almost Labor Day weekend. Let's make the most of that."

Kenzie was glad that Dr. Dawson was keeping Moriah's identity as the caster a secret.

The crowd grumbled and broke up, heading toward the flagged sidewalk that had been appointed for those entering and exiting.

Shinrou, Logan, and Makari rejoined Kenzie, Moriah, and Zoe. Kenzie still hugged Moriah, and Moriah hadn't stopped crying yet.

"This group was pretty mature about it," Logan said, watching them go. "Something tells me that Minuclick is lighting up like a supernova, though."

"You know it," Makari said. "Half of them will say 'I knew he wasn't real,' and the other half will say 'Magicians killed Jesus!'"

Shinrou groaned. "I'm sure you're right. I need more sleep before I deal with it. Makari, would you get a sample of that mud for me? I want to analyze it later and see if it's been permanently altered by the magic. Much later. After much sleep."

"Sure," Makari said.

They all headed toward the stairs. Kenzie kept his arm around Moriah's shoulders.

Shinrou's aunt stepped up to him, smiling, as he reached the top stair. "Well done. I'm proud of you. Be sure to write up your spell and findings in a paper. You can definitely get published in a journal. The scholarly community will want to know everything."

Shinrou returned the smile. "Thank you, *Oba-san*. I will."

"And come over for tea tomorrow," Dr. Kitamori said.

"I will. Thank you." Shinrou stumbled away, looking every bit as exhausted as he claimed.

Zoe pulled out her phone as they descended the stairs.

"What're you doing?" Moriah asked, letting go of Kenzie and wiping her eyes.

Zoe grinned. "Call it morbid curiosity." She unlocked her phone screen and went straight to Minuclick. "Whoo, yeah, there're already nine threads. Ooh, this looks like a good one." She chuckled like a comic book villain. "Look at all the people who're pissed off that Jesus got publicly executed again."

"Put that away," Kenzie sighed.

"I just want to know so I can be ahead of the curve when we get hate messages."

"*We* won't," Kenzie said. "Shinrou and Dr. Dawson will."

"Nope. You're wrong," Zoe sing-songed, holding up her phone. "Everyone who participated in Logan and Makari's taskforce is getting called out."

"That's got to be Iona's fault," Kenzie grumbled.

Zoe burst out laughing. "Badass! We should start a band."

"What?" Kenzie grabbed Zoe's wrist and looked at her phone screen. Someone had posted a candid shot from their phone of Logan, Makari, Shinrou, Zoe, Moriah, and Kenzie with the caption "The God Slayers," followed by a mini rant: *the woobs that think they're so snazz they made JCU look bad.* "Oh my God, that is definitely Iona or one of her friends. Creepers! What were they doing sneaking around and taking pictures of us?"

"That's so cruel," Moriah murmured. "Cyber bullying is serious, and that post already has 12 replies."

"I know Iona means it sarcastically, but I say we run with it," Zoe said. "Loki would be on drums. He's definitely sexy drummer material."

Kenzie massaged his temples and let it drop.

THIRTY

The rest of Thursday was a world-wide social media explosion that kept Kenzie's phone buzzing. The only news that spread as quickly as the dematerialization of Jesus H. Christ was the fact Smith was in a coma in ICU at Louisville's Norton Hospital and that he had been responsible for engineering the creation of Top Hat-Satan. By Sunday morning, people in 97 different countries were demanding Top Hat's dematerialization. Posts on Minuclick and a dozen other such platforms reached one billion and repeatedly tanked the servers. Some people raged about Smith's satanic creation and his betrayal of Christianity, and others reacted only to the fact a pastor had been caught on camera using magic to attack college students.

Thanks to the world-wide detonation of emotion, Kenzie and his roommates dressed in uniform and arrived on the quad at 9:00 AM Friday morning. Shinrou, Makari, and Logan also stood by, in uniform and waiting to be called forward to dematerialize Top Hat. Dr. Dawson had campus security deliver Top Hat to the library stairs, making a spectacle of the "evil" thought form of "Satan" being "punished." Kenzie was surprised Top Hat had agreed to this plan, but he had. In fact, Top Hat stayed calm as he faced the crowd of spectators and the cameras.

Kenzie glanced at Rachel. "Are you upset? Worried?"

Rachel shook her head. "I don't believe they can destroy Top Hat's essence, and this is the only way to appease the masses and get our lives back. Plus I want this body destroyed. It was flawed, and it made him into a monster. He isn't. He's my friend. I want him back the way he should be."

Moriah hugged her, and while Rachel didn't immediately respond, after a moment, she hugged Moriah back.

Dr. Dawson and Dr. Russell, their university president, stepped forward to address the crowd that stood on the grassy quad along with seven news crews. "Thank you for joining us here today," Dr. Russell said. He was a silver-haired White man in his fifties with a youthful face. Tall, slim, and dressed in a navy blue suit, he struck a handsome figure for the cameras. "We are aggrieved to hear that Rev. Smith is in critical condition, and we are giving our thoughts and prayers to him, his family, and his friends."

"It's smart to say they're praying," Rachel said. "It appeases the watching Christians." She turned to Shinrou. "I want to help dematerialize Top Hat."

Shinrou raised his eyebrows. "Are you sure?"

Rachel frowned. "If I don't help 'kill' Top Hat and then my uncle lives, he'll kill me for not 'avenging' him by destroying my creation. Of course, he might kill me regardless."

A pulse of rage and horror burned through Kenzie's chest, the injustice of it grating on his soul. "Then of course, we have to let you help!"

"As many of you know, Rev. Smith is responsible for the creation of a magical construct the world has come to know as Satan," Dr. Russell continued. "While we wait for crucial answers about why he created the construct, we cannot wait to take action. To reassure everyone the threat is over, we will now publically dematerialize this construct."

Top Hat glanced toward Rachel and grinned. The campus police had left him handcuffed, and they pulled him forward to the top step.

"He's going to put on a show," Rachel whispered to Kenzie. "I just know it."

"Yeah. Well, it wouldn't be like him to not be theatrical."

Dr. Dawson motioned Shinrou forward, and he and Makari headed up the steps, Rachel following.

Kenzie turned to Logan. "I'm going up there with Rachel to help cast the spell. She might need the emotional support."

"Sure. No problem." Logan gestured toward the stairs.

Kenzie jogged up the stairs after the others, and they created a circle by Top Hat and held hands. Shinrou nodded, and Kenzie focused on releasing his magic. Gold energy surrounded Shinrou's hands, blue around Makari's, green around Kenzie's, and purple around Rachel's. A massive energy ball bloomed into existence between them.

The energy waves washed through Kenzie's chest. Arcs of electricity flashed through the orb as it swelled and turned darker. The power of it pressed upon Kenzie's body until he was almost breathless. Then the orb turned black and arched over Kenzie's head, elongating itself into an oval. The black energy poured into Top Hat's torso.

"No, spare me!" Top Hat shrieked. "Spare me! It wasn't my fault! The people of Earth believed me into existence and filled me with their fear and hate. They called upon me to be their Satan!"

Kenzie suppressed a smile. The shriek was convincing enough, but he couldn't take it seriously with Zoe choking on laughter below them. He glanced at Rachel, but she remained stoic.

A black glow outlined Top Hat's body, and he stared down at himself as his appearance faded, turning him dark brown. "No! I'm supposed to be red. My beautiful crimson suit!"

Kenzie cringed. *Okay, that was real.*

Top Hat's humanoid shape rippled. "No! I'm melting! I'm melting!"

For once recognizing the classic movie reference, Kenzie snorted.

The spell lifted before reaching the molecular stage, and mud splattered the stairs. Purple energy flew upward, slinging mud in a four-foot radius as it did, and then vanished. Kenzie felt a sucking sensation, as though someone had energy-punched him in the chest. *That spell's a real ass-kicker, but I'm glad this is over.*

Only half the crowd clapped. Kenzie suspected the rights of thought forms would be a hot discussion for the entire next year: Sentient or non-sentient? Alive or not alive? Did this count as an execution? And who even had the right to decide?

Kenzie set aside his ponderings and headed down the steps, Rachel at his side. Shinrou stayed behind with Makari to answer questions about the spell and collect a sample of Top Hat's "body." Kenzie watched Rachel with worry. "You okay?"

"Just tired." Rachel kept her chin up. "Even though that spell was draining, I'll summon Top Hat later to see if he still exists. But I think he does. I think I would know it if he were truly gone."

Moriah ran up to Rachel and hugged her again. Rachel, smiling slightly, hugged Moriah in return with one arm and rested a hand on Moriah's back.

As soon as Kenzie reached Logan, he took his hand, and they headed toward the dorms. It didn't surprise Kenzie that he was exhausted. The pull of the creation-destruction magic on his insides was unlike anything he'd ever felt before. *We are made in God's image,* he thought unbidden. *Smith believed he'd been made in Satan's image, probably thanks to what his father said. What was John Paul Smith, Sr. like? Where did he get his beliefs? How many generations back does this go?* His head ached, and all he wanted to do was sleep.

But Logan's warm hand in his reminded him that there was more to the world than fear of magic and fear of people who were different. He squeezed Logan's hand. "Hey, after my nap, can we go on a date?"

Logan smiled at him and swung their joined hands. "Yes. I'd love to. Let's do it."

As they reached the women's dorm and Kenzie let go of Logan's hand, he decided he was walking into the wrong dorm for the last time. He pulled out his phone, unlocked the screen, and tapped the JCU student app. After flicking through a few screens, he found a form to request changing dorms. He filled it out, and in the *Reason* box, he typed: transgender accommodations.

"Whatcha doin'?" Logan asked. "Checking Minuclick?"

Kenzie looked up from his phone and met Logan's gaze with a sense of calmness he thought he'd never feel. "No. I put in a dorm change request." He exhaled a soft laugh. "I'm a man."

Logan hugged him. "Hell, yeah, you are!"

⚡

THAT NIGHT, ONCE RACHEL WAS SURE MORIAH WAS comfortably asleep, she charged Kenzie and Zoe with monitoring Moriah and headed to the gazebo behind the greenhouse. Moriah had healed her back, both of the old lash marks and the new ones, so she moved with ease and could enjoy her walk. Thanks to the fact it was Labor Day weekend, there were fewer people than normal on campus for a Friday night, and the gazebo was vacant.

Pleased, Rachel climbed the wooden steps and stood in the middle, her arms extended at her sides, palms up. She closed her eyes and imagined Top Hat the way he had been when they had secretly danced together in her bedroom before her uncle had discovered him. Before, he'd been nameless. As Rachel's private creation, he hadn't needed a name. Now that the students had named him Top Hat, she was happy with what they'd chosen.

Rachel's energy shifted, and tiredness washed through her. *It's done.* She opened her eyes. Top Hat stood in front of her. He was see-through again. Tall, slender, and dapper, dressed in crimson and white from head to foot, he wore his signature top hat and his suit with coattails, complete with crimson tap dancing shoes instead of goat hooves. When he took off his hat and bowed, he had no horns. He also didn't have Smith's platinum blond hair. Instead, his head was shaved. His facial features had reverted to looking vaguely like Fred Astaire.

Top Hat straightened and popped his hat back on. "My dearest Rachel. You called."

"You knew I would." Rachel smiled despite herself.

"Yes." Top Hat tilted his head and extended his arms in a grand gesture. "Shall we dance?"

Rachel sniffed out a chuckle. "Yes."

"Yay!" Top Hat spun in a circle, his hands clasped in glee. Then he burst into tap dancing, summoning his white cane as he did. He paused and held out his hand, inviting her.

Rachel wished she owned tap shoes. In the URA, women weren't allowed to participate in 'noisy' dances. Tap dancing had been ruled an activity appropriate for boys and men only. *But I'm in the U.S. now. I can go to a store or go online and buy whatever I want.* She pantomimed taking Top Hat's hand and whirling around him, miming tap dancing.

He pivoted and mirrored her, grinning.

They danced back and forth, answering each other. Rachel even jumped up on the bench inside the gazebo and danced on it, truly letting go for the first time in her life. She laughed as she jumped down, Top Hat pretending to spot her with one hand.

When they finished, Top Hat remarked, "I know you love Moriah." For an instant Rachel was worried, but he added, "I'm happy to see you letting someone hold you and care about you."

To her surprise, Rachel believed him. "Then, ironically, you're the best person I've ever known."

"I'm glad you consider me a person. And that brings me to my request: Might I have my body back someday?"

"After I graduate and leave here. I don't want to get expelled." Rachel's brow furrowed. "I know I can't materialize you alone, but I think Kenzie and Zoe would be happy to help. Maybe Logan, too. Perhaps Shinrou would just out of scientific curiosity. Surely four or five people will be enough, since we'll be doing it consciously."

"Yay!" Top Hat twirled and spun his cane like a baton.

Rachel snorted. "And to think I created you." *Maybe I'm not filled with darkness after all.*

⚡

ON TUESDAY MORNING, ONCE THE LONG WEEKEND WAS OVER, Kenzie walked into Dr. Dawson's office and sat, squaring his shoulders. Today, being summoned into the office with its mahogany desk and bookshelves didn't scare him.

"I received your dorm change request form," Dr. Dawson said. "If you're comfortable, could you explain a little more about what you mean by transgender accommodations?"

Kenzie lifted his chin. "I'm not a woman. I'm a man. I don't want to live in the women's dorm. I thought I would be more comfortable because I'm pre-transition, but I'm not. I want to live in a dorm with other men. Preferably other transmen, but I don't know if there are any on campus."

Dr. Dawson took all of this in without a look of disgust.

"As you know, there are students who have left due to what happened with the thought forms. This means the dorms have vacancies that free up space to change dorm assignments to accommodate student requests." She reached up and swiped through screens on her computer for a moment. "I'm documenting your request."

Kenzie waited, doing his best to pretend he was patient and not bounce his leg.

"I can confirm that you are not the only transman living on campus. However, I need to speak with the students in question and ask them if they wish to be connected with another trans student. There are privacy issues at stake."

"And if at least one of them says yes?" Kenzie asked.

Dr. Dawson smiled. "If one or more transgender students agree to room together with you, then we will ask their current roommates if they are comfortable being reassigned. I sincerely hope this works out for you. I always do my best to honor student housing requests."

Kenzie decided authorities weren't uniformly useless.

THREE DAYS LATER, AFTER HELPING DEMATERIALIZE BOTH LOKI and Thor, Kenzie raced around his old room, packing his belongings into his two suitcases.

Moriah poked her head around the door. "You're really leaving?"

Kenzie looked over his shoulder. "I'm a man."

Moriah's expression clouded over, her gaze falling to the floor.

"I'm leaving the women's dorm, not leaving campus," Kenzie said.

Moriah sighed and stepped into the room. "I know, but it's not going to be the same without you here." She tugged on one of her blonde pigtails. "Besides, what if we get a stranger assigned to us?"

"You probably will," Kenzie said. "But it'll be okay. Most people are nice. Not like Iona." He couldn't blame Iona for being angry at the accusation of creating Top Hat, but he didn't have any sympathy for her, either. She'd been nothing but hateful. "Meeting new people is part of college."

Moriah stepped back into the doorway. "Well, I *am* glad I met Rachel."

"And Rachel's not going anywhere," Kenzie said gently. He couldn't help but feel a little parental toward Moriah. She still exuded an innocence that seemed impossible for anyone to have.

Zoe, Rachel, and Moriah saw him off. Moriah hugged him. Kenzie hugged her back and said, "I'm still going to see you in classes and at lunch, and we can still eat together and visit during coed hours."

Moriah nodded and put on a smile, apparently resolving to be brave. Rachel laid one hand on Moriah's arm reassuringly.

Kenzie walked down the stairs, his rolling suitcases thunking on each step, and followed the directions on his phone to the new dorm. The men's dorm row he was familiar with, but the exact building he wasn't. He wanted the reassurance of the GPS map.

When he found 128A, he knocked on the suite door and called, "It's Kenzie Okuda, your new roommate."

A male voice that wasn't deep called back, "Come in."

Kenzie presented his ID to the door scanner, and it unlocked and opened. He rolled his suitcases into the dorm suite's combined living room/kitchen. It had the same brown carpet, brown couch and chairs, and oak kitchen table as his previous suite.

Two men sat at the table. One of them was a guy with honey-colored skin and a bleached blond Mohawk that was nearly white. Mismatched earrings adorned his earlobes. He wore the men's white school uniform. His short, broad nose was cute, and he had the most gorgeous dark brown eyes and dark eyelashes. The soft shape of his face and his smooth, hairless upper lip and chin suggested to Kenzie that he was pre-transition. He gave Kenzie a half wave and a shy smile. "Hi. I'm Shane."

The other man was a natural ginger with fair skin and a flaming shade of hair one step more auburn than carrot-red. He sported a mustache and goatee that were a little thinly grown in but still handsome and well-defined. His men's school uniform was black, like Kenzie's. He grinned, jumped up from his chair, and extended his hand. "Hi. I'm Taryl. We're glad to get another trans roomie. Make yourself at home."

Kenzie shook Taryl's hand. "Thanks." *I am truly home.*

FUTURE SLANG DICTIONARY

Bot: a follower, someone who doesn't think for themselves, a stereotype, a sheep
Deranged: badass, crazy-good
Fanning: like fanboy-ing or fangirl-ing
Feeder: a bottom feeder, a loser
Flex: bragging rights, claim to fame
Murk: an idiot or psycho
Mythical: awesome
Naff: bad, boring, psychotic
Snazz: an awesome/great/fantastic person
Stonking: badass, smoking awesome
White knighting: protecting someone or something in an overblown fashion
Woob: a noob, newbie, unskilled person, or someone not "with it"

The name Shinrou is pronounced Shinrō. The long "o" sound in Japanese can be indicated by transcribing the name Shinrou, Shinro, or Shinroh. I chose Shinrou because that transcription is listed first by Hiroki Tanaka, author of Japanese-names.info.

ACKNOWLEDGMENTS

I would like to acknowledge Keith J. Miller's efforts as both my life partner and freelance editor. He read seven drafts of this novel over the course of seven years and always offered helpful commentary. Likewise, he championed my revisions and queries to publishers. I'm forever grateful to his persistence in assisting me. Also, I'd like to thank Keith for providing the Romanized transcription of the Japanese conversation between Dr. Kitamori and Shinrou. Keith was lucky enough to take Japanese in high school.

I would also like to thank Marvel for inspiring me to research Thor, Loki, and the ancient Norse deities, whom I likely would have never learned about otherwise.

ABOUT THE AUTHOR

© *Patrick Bryce Wright*

Patrick Bryce Wright, an unconventional English professor adorned with tattoos and piercings, whose passion for supernatural horror, fantasy, and science fiction fuels his impactful storytelling. Patrick proudly embraces his neurodivergence, third-gender identity, and survivor status, all of which enrich the narratives within his books.

As a vocal LGBTQIA+ activist, Patrick focuses on portraying diverse characters in his novels, aiming for sensitive depictions of the queer, d/Deaf, and dissociative identity disorder communities. Armed with degrees in English and Psychology, Patrick weaves intricate tales that reflect his academic background.

www.patrickbrycewright.com

instagram.com/patrickbrycewright
tiktok.com/@patrick_bryce_wright
x.com/PBryceWright
youtube.com/PatrickBryceWright

www.ingramcontent.com/pod-product-compliance
Lightning Source LLC
Chambersburg PA
CBHW031159310726
48969CB00001B/142